Joan Johnston continues her acclaimed
Bitter Creek series with this page-turning
New York Times bestseller that goes deep into
the hearts of two extraordinary Texans

THE PRICE

Luke: Fiercely driven to succeed, the former high school bad boy rides a Harley in his down time from his high-pressure legal career. His ambitions have cost him everything—and everyone—close to him. Can he risk letting one special woman in and make it last for a lifetime?

Amy: Piecing her life together after her divorce has been a challenge for the now-single mother of a young daughter. Her heart has always guided her work as a legal advocate. Now it's leading her into a thrilling affair with Luke Creed—still the rebel she adored years ago. But will his love ask too great a price?

Critical Acclaim for *THE PRICE*

"[Johnston's] characters make THE PRICE worth the cost."

— Sun-Sentinel (Ft. Lauderdale, FL)

"A truly memorable read. . . . Compelling, masterful storytelling. . . . Cover to cover, nail biting, edge-of-the-seat reading! THE PRICE is Joan Johnston's best book to date. Filled with intrigue, sex, greed, and murder, THE PRICE is much more than standard romance fare. . . . THE PRICE will be on my list of the ten best books of 2003."

—AOL Romance Fiction Forum

"With a story that could have been ripped out of the headlines, Johnston expertly blends facts, romance, and suspense with poignancy."

—Romantic Times

"A particularly timely tale."

—Booklist

**THE PRICE is also available on
Simon & Schuster Audio**

JOAN JOHNSTON

THE PRICE

POCKET STAR BOOKS
New York London Toronto Sydney

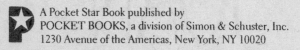 A Pocket Star Book published by
POCKET BOOKS, a division of Simon & Schuster, Inc.
1230 Avenue of the Americas, New York, NY 10020

This book is a work of fiction. Names, characters, places and incidents are products of the author's imagination or are used fictitiously. Any resemblance to actual events or locales or persons, living or dead, is entirely coincidental.

ISBN-13: 978-1-4165-4477-7
ISBN-10:   1-4165-4477-1

This Pocket Star Books paperback edition July 2007

10 9 8 7 6 5 4 3 2 1

POCKET STAR BOOKS and colophon are registered trademarks of Simon & Schuster, Inc.

Author photo © Jeff Stine

Manufactured in the United States of America

For information regarding special discounts for bulk purchases, please contact Simon & Schuster Special Sales at 1-800-456-6798 or business@simonandschuster.com.

For my readers
who have been there through the years
and those reading one of my books
for the first time.

1

"Blackthornes and Creeds are like oil and water," Luke Creed told his brother Sam. "They just don't mix."

"If that were true, Mom wouldn't have married a Blackthorne after Dad died, would she?" Sam replied as he stuffed his mouth full of blueberry pancakes.

"I take it back," Luke said, pouring blueberry syrup over the newest batch of pancakes his sister-in-law had dropped onto his plate. "Oil and water don't mix, but at least they can coexist in the same space."

"Big brother is always right," Sam said. "I—"

Luke waved his fork to cut off his older brother. "Blackthornes and Creeds are more like gasoline and matches. Put them together and you end up with one helluva blaze."

Too often in his youth, Luke had seen the deadly conflagration burn white hot, destroying without care or conscience. In the twelve years since his mother had married Jackson Blackthorne, Luke hadn't forgotten or forgiven the devastation his family had suffered at Blackthorne hands. His father murdered, his brother crippled, their cattle infected with brucellosis, priceless cutting horses disappearing into thin air, with every disaster leading straight back to some Blackthorne.

Which was why Luke dreaded having lunch with his mother and stepfather today. These days, Blackthornes and Creeds were supposed to be one happy family.

Luke hadn't bought into the fantasy.

He looked across the breakfast table at Sam, who would spend the rest of his life in a wheelchair thanks to an "accident" on the high school football field that involved a Blackthorne. "How can you stand working with that Blackthorne bastard day in and day out?"

"At least I'm working out-of-doors. How can you stand working in a law office in the big city every day?" Sam replied.

It wasn't easy for Luke, living in the city, but it beat the alternative—working for his stepfather—all to hell and back.

"We don't see nearly enough of you since you moved to Houston," Sam said. "Why don't you come back here and work with me on the ranch?"

"You mean work for Blackjack," Luke said bitterly. "He owns Three Oaks now."

The two modern-day South Texas ranching families, one rich and powerful, the other poor and struggling, had been mortal enemies since the Civil War, fighting over a piece of land owned by the Creeds along Bitter Creek, a trickle of water that never ran dry, even in the driest years.

Generations of Blackthornes had killed and crippled generations of Creeds in an attempt to force them off that precious piece of land. But the Creeds had hung on. And Three Oaks had remained lodged, like a chicken bone in the throat, smack dab in the middle of the Blackthorne ranching empire, an eight-hundred-square-mile ranch named for that same Bitter Creek.

When widower Jackson Blackthorne had married widow Ren Creed, their marriage had united the two families—and the two pieces of land. With nothing left to fight over, the feud should have been over.

As far as Luke was concerned, there was too much bad blood between them to end the fight. When Luke had been given the chance to work at Three Oaks, he'd thrown the offer back in Blackjack's face.

"No thanks," he'd snarled. "My father hated you and so do I. Just stay the hell out of my life!"

"What is it you plan to do with your life?" Blackjack had challenged. "Let me help you, boy."

At the time, Luke had been twenty years old, and the inconsequential *boy* had been an insult. He'd replied with a few choice words acquired over years spent working with cowhands who never used a longer word when a four-letter one would do.

His tirade had ended, "I don't want a goddamned thing from you. Ever."

Easy words to say, but they'd left Luke without a direction for his life. He'd spent every day up to that point on the back of a horse—or a Harley.

Blackjack had done his best to make amends. He'd shared his wealth with the Creed kids. Along with his two older sisters Callie and Bay, and his older brother Sam, Luke had been given a trust fund that had made him a millionaire. Unlike them, he had no intention of ever touching Blackjack's blood money.

"You have to stop fighting the inevitable," Sam said, interrupting Luke's rumination. "Mom loves him. He loves Mom."

"I'll never stop fighting those Blackthorne sonsof-bitches," Luke said through tight jaws.

"Have you looked at Mom lately?" Sam asked. "I mean, really looked at her?" Sam slipped an arm around his wife Emma's waist, as she dropped another stack of pancakes onto his plate.

"Hey, I want some of those!" The male voice cracked halfway through the sentence and slid down an octave, and the twelve-year-old boy sitting across the table turned red, as the three adults exchanged surreptitious glances and hid grins at his adolescent discomfort.

"I'm making another batch for you, Bronc," Emma said as she crossed and tousled her son's short, straight brown hair.

Luke noticed that Daniel Lucas Creed, better known as Bronc, had the same cowlick on his crown as Luke did. He tried not to notice that sort of thing, and if he did, he tried to ignore it. Bronc might be Luke's biological son, the result of a one-night stand with Emma, but when Emma and Sam had fallen in love during Emma's pregnancy and gotten married, the three of them had decided there was no reason to tell Bronc the truth.

Luke had been Uncle Luke to the boy from the day he'd first held the tiny wriggling baby in his large hands.

Luke had never regretted his decision. His brother was a great father, and because of complications from his accident, Sam couldn't have kids of his own. And Emma and Sam were deeply, happily in love.

Luke had no son of his own, but he had two daughters, ten-year-old Brynne and six-year-old Midge, who lived with his ex-wife and her new husband in Houston. His daughters had been away at camp all summer. They were returning the following weekend, and he could hardly wait to see them.

"Are you going to stick around for Sunday lunch?" Sam asked.

Luke made a face. If he wanted to see his mother—and he did—it meant seeing his stepfather, since the two were inseparable. "Yeah. I'm staying."

"Then how about riding the fence for me this morning? I can't account for some cattle. I think there might be a break in the wire."

In days gone by, the "break" in the three strands of barbed wire strung between cedar posts would have been made by wire cutters, and the cows and their unbranded calves would have strayed onto Blackthorne land—where the mavericks would have ended up with a Blackthorne brand on their sleek red hides.

Now that Bitter Creek and Three Oaks were all part of the same vast corporate entity, the Bitter Creek Cattle Company, that sort of high jinks didn't make much sense.

"Sure," Luke said. "Where do you want me to look?"

"The south pasture," Sam said. "We've made some changes you should know about."

The result of an endless infusion of Blackthorne money, Luke knew. He couldn't help resenting the fact that his family had struggled so long and hard to hold onto Three Oaks, hating Blackthornes body and soul, and in the end the ranch had been lost because his mother had fallen in love with the enemy.

"We've put in more bump gates, so you can drive from one pasture to another without getting out of your truck," Sam said.

Luke knew that was a big help to Sam, who could drive himself around, but would have had trouble getting in and out of his truck to open and close a lot of gates. Bump gates, which were nudged open by the grille of a truck and swung closed on a center pivot after the truck had gone through, were a good idea, a smart improvement when the foreman of the ranch was a paraplegic.

"I think I'd rather spend the morning on horseback," Luke said, "if it's all the same to you."

Sam shrugged. "I can tell you where the cattle have gone missing. You can trailer your horse there and take off."

Luke dropped his fork on his plate and said, "That was a great breakfast, Emma. If I eat one more flapjack I'm going to explode."

"I could eat a few more, Mom," Bronc said. "If it's no trouble," he said, catching his father's surprised look.

"He's a growing boy," Luke said. All skinny arms and long legs, the same as Luke had been at that age.

"It's no trouble at all," Emma said to her son.

Luke shoved his chair back from the table. "Excuse me, folks. I'll see you at the Homestead for lunch."

Sam lived in the foreman's house at Three Oaks, and Luke walked the short distance from Sam's house to the stable, liking the feel of the sun on his face. He enjoyed the dryness of the air and the endless flat, grassy prairie, both a sharp contrast to the ever-present humidity and burgeoning humanity that defined Houston.

Luke attached a horse trailer to his Chevy truck—a ridiculous, gas-guzzling vehicle to have in Houston, considering the distance between his two-bedroom condo downtown and his ex-wife's house in The Woodlands, a planned community north of the city.

But he couldn't give up the truck any more than he could turn his back completely on Three Oaks and walk away. He kept his Harley in an old barn at Three Oaks filled with antiquated farm machinery and rode it when he came home for a visit.

He'd carved out a new life for himself as a lawyer for the largest firm in Texas, DeWitt & Blackthorne. The irony hadn't escaped him that he was working for a firm that had been started by a Blackthorne and bore that hated name.

Slowly but surely over the past six years he'd spent at D&B, he'd earned a reputation as one of the best litigators in the state. In another year, he'd become a partner and have the financial security that he'd lived without all his life.

Luke had kept his promise to Blackjack. He'd never asked his stepfather for a thing. When he became a partner at D&B, his success would be complete, his independence assured. He could look Jackson Blackthorne in the eye and tell him, "Take your million-dollar trust fund and stick it where the sun don't shine."

—⁓—

Amy Hazeltine Nash urged the bay mare to a gallop and leaned forward, her face in the animal's mane, urging her mount to even greater speed. Amy needed to escape. She wanted to run away from her problems to someplace like Tahiti, but since she was too responsible to do such a thing, riding hell-bent-for-leather was the next best thing. The speed was thrilling, the danger exciting, the escape, unfortunately, temporary.

The horse's breathing was labored and foam flecked the animal's neck. "Run, Lady," she whispered in the mare's ear. "Run!"

The terrain was nearly flat, dotted with an occasional mesquite and the red Santa Gertrudis cattle raised by Jackson Blackthorne and his wife Ren.

She'd borrowed a horse from the stable at Three Oaks and gone riding early this morning at the invitation of Ren, whom she'd met in town on Friday.

"What are you doing here?" Ren had said when they bumped into each other shopping for groceries in the H.E.B. "I thought you were living in Virginia."

"I'm home to visit my mom and dad," Amy said. It was the truth, but by no means the entire story.

"I hope you'll come by and visit," Ren said. "We're expecting Luke this weekend."

"I . . ." Amy felt awkward. Ren's youngest son had been Amy's boyfriend all through high school, and Amy had spent more time in Ren's kitchen in those days than her own. But she'd dumped Luke when they were seniors and two years later married a much older man, an orthopedic surgeon, and moved to Virginia, where she'd spent the next eleven years. Last year, she'd moved back to Texas.

"How are your parents?" Ren asked.

"They're fine," Amy said. It was the answer she'd always given. Again, not the entire truth. Actually, not even close to the truth. Her mother was an agoraphobic. Amy hadn't know what that was, growing up, only that her mother stayed at home. But agoraphobics were afraid of the outside world, and Amy's mother never left the house.

Which meant that Amy had become responsible for a lot of chores that should have been her mother's. Her father was patient with her mother, but it was plain to Amy that he pitied her. As Amy got older, and her mother—and father—remained so dependent on her, she began to fear that she'd be tied to her parents forever.

Looking back, Amy could see how Luke Creed, a rebellious troublemaker who didn't follow anyone's rules, would have appealed to her. Luke had the freedom Amy craved.

"Just leave," Luke had told her when he'd found out her greatest fear.

"I can't do that. They need me."

"They're grown-ups. They can take care of themselves," he'd said.

It sounded right. It also sounded ruthless. Amy

yearned to be as carefree as Luke. She settled for being his girlfriend. For her, getting on the back of his Harley without a helmet and riding around town, her long blond hair flying behind her, was about as much freedom as she was willing to allow herself.

That and letting Luke touch her.

She'd never realized how meek she was until she'd met Luke, who was brash beyond words. He'd flashed a grin at her, and she'd been excited and intrigued by having such a "bad boy" interested in her. Being with Luke, who was afraid of nothing, was thrilling after growing up with a mother who was afraid of everything.

In hindsight, Amy realized that Luke had been as scared as she was of the love budding between them. He'd just been better at hiding it behind laughing brown eyes and a cocky smile.

Their first physical contact had been more appropriate to kids half their age. He'd yanked her ponytail and flipped up the back of her skirt.

She'd straightened his collar and run her hand daringly across the few bits of beard sprouting on his face—not enough to shave, but enough to announce to the world that he was becoming a man.

"You're someone I'd like to know better, Amelia Hazeltine," he'd said, circling her like a tomcat on the prowl, exuding sexual energy that both frightened and excited her.

"How do you know my full name?" she'd asked.

"It's on that debate trophy in the glass case on the second floor," he said. "And on the honor roll posted by the principal's office. And in the program for the fall play."

"You saw the play?"

"You were good," he said. "You're good at everything."

"Not everything," she said, embarrassed by the praise. Especially since she participated in everything at school because it gave her an excuse not to be home.

"You're talented," he said. "And smart. And pretty."

"Thank you," she said, thoroughly flustered.

"Wanta go out with me?"

She hadn't understood why a boy with Luke Creed's reputation would want to go out with a "good girl" like her.

"I don't put out," she said, staring him in the eye.

"I'm only asking you to the movies."

She saw the flush high on his cheekbones, the flicker of anger in his eyes. She'd insulted him. She would never purposely have hurt anyone's feelings. She was too sensitive to the flaws in her own family. "I'm sorry," she said. "Going to a movie sounds like fun."

She liked the smile that reappeared on his face, the twinkle that returned to his eyes.

"Great!" He hooted and hollered in a way that should have embarrassed her, because everybody on the school grounds turned to look. She found herself smiling back at him instead.

The first time he'd kissed her, they'd been sitting in the balcony of Bitter Creek's one movie theater. He'd leaned over in the dark, whispered, "Amy," and when she'd turned toward him, he'd kissed her. On the nose.

They'd both laughed self-consciously. Their eyes had caught in the flickering light from the screen, and he'd lowered his head again, and their lips had caught, and held.

Amy had forgotten to breathe. She broke the kiss when she felt like she was going to die from want of air, gasping, her chest aching. Other parts of her body ached too, which she found strange and frightening. "Luke," she whispered. "Luke."

She hadn't known how to tell him what she was feeling. Unable to ask him for what she wanted, but desperately needing . . . something.

"Let's get out of here," he said in a gruff voice.

When he took her hand to pull her out of her seat, she realized he was trembling. Her legs threatened to buckle and she sat back down. And tugged on his hand to pull him down beside her.

"I don't want to leave," she said.

"*Shut up!*" an angry voice whispered behind them.

Luke rose and tugged on her hand again. Amy glanced over her shoulder at the angry patron and rose to follow him.

He hurried her down the balcony stairs, only waiting until they were outside in the dark to press her against the side of the brick building. His hands cupped her face, and his eyes were dark and mysterious in the moonlight.

"Amy," he said. "Oh, baby."

He kissed her again, only their lips touching, and she felt something tighten deep inside her.

"I want to . . ."

"What?" she said.

"I want to put my tongue in your mouth."

"Why?"

"I heard it feels good."

"You've never done it before?"

He shook his head. "But I want to. With you."

Amy made a face. She'd been watching movie stars kiss her whole life and had wanted to be on the receiving end of one of those romantic embraces. But his *tongue*? In her *mouth*?

"If you don't like it, I can stop," Luke said. "Come on, Amy, take a chance for once. Don't be such a scaredy-cat."

It was the name-calling that made her take the risk. *Scaredy-cat.* She wasn't ever going to be afraid like her mother. "All right," she told him. "Go ahead. But if I don't like it—"

"I'll stop," he promised her.

His thumb caught on the pulse at her throat, and she knew he must have felt it racing. He grinned, then said, "Here goes nothing."

She closed her eyes and waited. She felt something wet on her lips and jerked backward.

"I haven't done anything yet," he protested. "Come back here."

She closed her eyes again and forced herself to relax. This time, she let herself enjoy the feel of his soft, wet tongue caressing her closed lips from one side to the other. To her surprise, her body quivered.

Luke slid an arm around her waist and said, "Put your hands around my neck."

She obeyed him, sliding her arms up around his neck and into his hair. That brought her small breasts into contact with his chest, which was surprisingly muscular.

He lowered his head again, his mouth closing over hers, his tongue gently seeking entrance, probing at the seam of her lips. "You have to open up for me, baby," he murmured.

Amy sighed in resignation and barely parted her lips. She felt his tongue slide into her mouth and recede. And felt another surprising quiver of excitement. Her hands tightened around his neck, and she leaned her body against his, waiting for the next intrusion. She could feel the texture of his tongue and taste him—he tasted good, like buttery popcorn and Coke.

Amy had an analytical mind, and she wanted to dissect the experience. But she was starting to feel things she'd never felt. Heat and need and desire. His tongue was moving in and out of her mouth, teasing the back of her upper lip and then receding. She sucked on it, to keep it where it was, and heard Luke gasp.

They broke the kiss and stared at one another with glazed eyes. "What's wrong?" she said.

"What did you do?"

"I don't know."

"You sucked on my tongue," he accused.

"I'm sorry."

"No, it felt good. Do it again."

Before she could protest, he was kissing her again, his tongue in her mouth, and she sucked on it, like she had before, and felt his body tense beneath her hands.

He broke the kiss again and laid his brow against hers. "Oh, God, Amy. Does this feel as good to you as it does to me?"

In response, Amy simply caught him by the ears and pulled his head down to kiss him. She found his lips closed and ran her tongue along the seam, as he'd done to her. And heard him groan.

It was almost a sound of pain, but she knew she wasn't hurting him. She pressed her tongue against his lips, seeking entrance, and he opened to her. Amy's tongue slid inside his mouth and he clasped her tight, his tongue dueling with hers, as they each sought to pleasure the other.

They were both breathing hard by the time they broke the kiss. Amy's knees were threatening to buckle again, and her breasts ached. "We better stop this," she said.

"Why?" Luke said. "You like it, don't you?"

"That's not the point."

"That's precisely the point," Luke said. "If it feels good, do it."

"Some people have to think of consequences," Amy said.

"To hell with consequences," Luke said, reaching for her.

Amy broke free. "If you want to be my boyfriend, Luke Creed, you will learn to consider consequences."

Luke had grinned at her. "Does that mean you're going to be my girlfriend?"

Amy realized what she'd done. Partnered up with someone wild and irresponsible, someone who flouted the rules at every turn. It sounded wonderful. "Yes," she said. "It does."

She'd kissed him again and used her tongue and enjoyed every long, delicious minute of it.

They'd spent the next four years as inseparable companions, but they'd never consummated the relationship.

Until prom night.

The mare had slowed, and Amy realized the animal was laboring to breathe and reined her to a stop. She felt as enervated as the mare, who stood on shaky legs, waiting for Amy to direct her where to go.

Amy slid out of the saddle and leaned against the mare, feeling the tears sting her nose and well in her eyes.

God, she was such a fool. She'd wanted someone responsible. Someone reliable. Someone she could count on to stand by her when times got tough. She'd been so sure Luke would never be that man. So she'd married Carl Nash.

And stayed with him for eleven long years, as much a captive as her mother had ever been. Her marriage had ended a year ago. She was free, back in Bitter Creek to visit her parents. Her mother, who still lived within the same four walls. And her father, who still patiently pitied her.

Amy's blond hair was too short for a ponytail these days and she pulled off her Stetson and set it on the saddle horn, then lifted the hair off her nape with both hands, so the breeze could reach the sweat and cool her. She was standing like that, eyes closed, when she heard hoofbeats.

"Hey!" a voice called out to her. "I couldn't believe my eyes. It really is you."

Amy felt her heart speed at the sight of Luke. It was as though her thoughts had conjured him. She quickly dropped her hands and self-consciously wiped her palms against the thighs of her jeans. "What a nice surprise," she said with a smile.

She felt her smile widen and didn't try to stop it. She was glad to see him. He was a piece of her past that had been mostly good. For four years, Luke had been her best friend, someone she could tell anything.

But what they'd shared had happened a lifetime ago, when they'd been kids. She couldn't expect things to be the same. She'd certainly changed. He must have, too.

He was dressed much as she was, in a worn Western shirt, jeans and cowboy boots. She hadn't spoken to him since the night of her engagement party, when he'd come to her and begged her not to marry Carl Nash.

"You look good," she said. His brown hair was too long, as usual, down over his ears and his collar. His body was still lean, but his shoulders were broader than they'd been when he was a younger man, and his forearms, where the shirt was rolled up, looked sinewy and strong. His hands were large, but they'd always been big. They just seemed to fit his body better now.

His eyes, the color of sun-ripened tobacco, looked

world-weary. That wasn't new either. But he seemed more adept at hiding his feelings than he'd been all those years ago.

"I heard you were coming for a visit," she said.

"That's funny. No one said a word to me about you being here."

She laughed at the indignation in his voice. "I didn't think our paths would cross."

"What are you doing here?"

"Your mom invited me to come riding when I had some free time." She shrugged. "I had some today."

"Where's your husband?"

"In Virginia." She had no desire to tell him about her marriage—or how ignominiously it had ended.

She could feel his eyes caressing her. He shouldn't be looking at a woman he believed was married with eyes so full of need.

"How are you?" she asked.

"Fine. You look like hell."

She laughed again. "Thanks. I see you're still incorrigibly honest when tact would serve you better."

"You look exhausted," he said. "What have you been doing with yourself?"

"I keep busy," she said evasively.

"You nearly ran that horse into the ground. Exorcising demons?" he asked.

"Could be." She retrieved her hat from the saddle horn and set it low on her forehead.

"Where are you going in such a hurry?" he asked.

"I've got a luncheon engagement. I need to get back."

"Me, too," Luke said. "Back at the homestead. We can ride together."

Amy realized suddenly that Ren had known Luke would be at lunch when she'd invited Amy to join them, but she could see no way to escape the obligation. "Fine," she said, as she stepped back into the saddle. "You talk, I'll listen."

"What do you want to hear?" Luke asked.

"I know about your divorce," she said. "How are your kids?"

"I don't get to see enough of them," Luke said. "I heard you have a daughter the same age as my eldest."

"Yes. Her name's Honor. She's the light of my life."

"How are your parents?"

"They're fine," she said. "I'd ask you about your mother, but I expect I know that better than you, since you haven't seen her yet."

"How do you know that?" Luke asked.

"I spoke with her this morning when I was saddling up at the stable at Three Oaks. She invited me back for lunch."

"I see. So we'll be having lunch together," Luke said, eyeing her speculatively. "Did you trailer your horse out here?"

"I rode the whole way."

"I've got a trailer that can take both horses," Luke said. "Your mare looks like she'd appreciate the ride."

Amy patted Lady's neck and said, "You're right about that. Sure. Why not?"

It didn't take them long to reach Luke's truck and load their horses onto the trailer. On the way back to the Homestead at Three Oaks Amy said, "Your mother is very proud of you."

"I've joined the establishment."

"I have to admit I never expected that of you."

Luke glanced at her and said, "Looks like you gave up on me too soon."

"Maybe I did," she said in a soft voice.

He hit the brakes hard and shoved the gearshift into park. The horses snorted their displeasure as they shifted to keep their balance in the trailer. "Are you happy with him?" he demanded.

Amy stared at Luke with stricken eyes.

He grabbed her arms and turned her to face him. "Because all you have to do is say the word, and I'll be standing at your door, asking for another chance. Losing you was the biggest mistake—"

She put her hand over his mouth. "Don't say things you don't mean. We're different people now, Luke. I've gone on with my life and so have you. We can't go back. It's too late."

His thumb caressed the pulse in her wrist, which was jumping crazily. She pulled her hand free and clutched it against the ache in her chest.

His fingertip caught her chin and tipped it up. "I'm only thirty-two, Amy. So are you. I'd say that gives us plenty of time for a second try. Just say the word."

It took all the strength Amy had to turn away from him. "The word is no."

She heard him swear, low and viciously, before he manhandled the truck into gear and hit the accelerator. The horses whinnied at the sudden lurch of the trailer, and Luke swore again and eased his foot off the gas. He kept his eyes straight ahead as the truck and trailer headed down the dirt road at a more reasonable pace.

Amy watched Luke from the corner of her eye and felt a surge of longing and regret. She could ride across the Texas plains all day at a gallop, but Amy knew, deep in her heart, that she'd turned out every bit as afraid to reach out and grab for life as her agoraphobic mother.

2

—◆—

Luke felt the muscles tighten in his neck and shoulders as he and Amy approached the Homestead at Three Oaks. The two-story white frame house sparkled in the sunshine, a far cry from the weathered gray look it had borne over the years his family had lived there hand-to-mouth. His heart rate accelerated, and his stomach knotted painfully as he contemplated greeting his stepfather in his dead father's home.

He'd intended to drop Amy off at the kitchen door to let his mom know they'd arrived and then run the horses over to the stable. But the instant he stopped his pickup, one of the cowhands who worked for Blackjack appeared, reached out a hand for Luke's keys and said, "I'll take care of putting up the horses, Mr. Creed, and leave your truck here when I'm done. Mr. Blackthorne is expecting you."

Luke clutched the keys, unwilling to hand them over. He'd learned growing up that it was his responsibility to water and unsaddle and groom his horse after riding him. He resented Blackjack's assumption that he would appreciate having someone else do it for him.

The appearance of the cowhand was a perfect example of the fundamental difference between Blackthornes and Creeds. Blackthornes had always been able to buy help when they needed it. Creeds had always survived by the sweat of their own brows and the labor of their own backs. It had made them strong enough to withstand every catastrophe that nature—and the hated Blackthornes—had sent their way.

The cowboy was only doing his job, and Luke knew he and Amy were already late for lunch. He dropped the keys in the outstretched hand and said, "You can unhitch the trailer and leave it by the stable."

"Yessir, Mr. Creed," the cowboy said.

Luke hated the formality. He didn't have to do everything Blackjack's way. He still had choices. As he stepped out of his truck he asked, "What's your name?"

"Slim," the cowboy said.

"I'm Luke," he said, holding out his hand.

The cowboy stared at Luke's callused hand, then looked him in the eye and reached out to shake it. "Glad to meet you, Luke."

As Amy joined them, Luke said, "This is Amy Nash."

"Hello, Slim," Amy said with a smile.

The cowboy touched two fingers to his Stetson, tipped his head and said, "Ma'am."

Some things never changed. Like the respect of Western men for Western women. In days gone by, women west of the Mississippi had been a rare, precious commodity, cared for, prized and protected. Which made Blackjack's theft of his father's wife all the more heinous in Luke's eyes.

His mother had already been pregnant with Jesse

Creed's child when Blackjack had seduced her—and she'd fallen in love with him. His mother had chosen to marry the father of her child, rather than the man she loved. Blackjack had married a woman his father picked out for him. Despite the fact that they'd married other people, Blackjack and Ren had apparently never stopped loving each other.

When Jesse had been killed, Blackjack had tried to divorce his wife, but she'd threatened to carve his beloved Bitter Creek into tiny pieces. It was a price Blackjack had refused to pay for his freedom. Their star-crossed love had remained unrequited for four long years—until Eve Blackthorne had died in a suspicious helicopter crash.

After that, they'd married lickety-split. And joined the two pieces of land that had been fought over for generations. And expected Luke to be happy about it.

Luke was never going to like seeing a Blackthorne under his father's roof. He would be courteous for his mother's sake—if Blackjack didn't provoke him. That was all.

Luke put a hand to the small of Amy's back and escorted her up the steps to the kitchen. He pulled open the screen door and held it for Amy, then let it slam behind him. He grinned as he did so, knowing full well his mother was hearing it somewhere in the house and would know he was home.

She'd admonished him all his life not to let the door slam. It had been a small, ridiculous rebellion, but now it was a defiant piece of the past he clung to, when everything else had changed beyond recognition.

"It must be hard for you coming back here," Amy said as she looked around the recently renovated stainless steel kitchen.

Luke followed her gaze, noting that everything had been modernized—again. Nothing was the same as it had been when he'd grown up, except the large, spurpitted and pockmarked trestle table that had hosted his family—his eldest sister Callie, her first husband Nolan Monroe, and their two kids Eli and Hannah, his sister Bayleigh, his crippled brother Sam, his mother Lauren, his father Jesse, and himself, the youngest.

He wondered why his mother kept the kitchen table, which seated so many, when she must sit there every morning with only Blackjack, and her memories, for company.

"Luke, you're here!"

Luke turned to find a broad smile on his mother's face and her arms opened wide for a hug, which he crossed the room to give her. He towered over her and leaned down to scoop her up in his arms. She was still slim and willowy, still wearing Wrangler jeans and a plaid Western shirt, at sixty-five. Her brown hair was salted with gray, and she wore it cut short and spiky, mussed in a way that fashionable women in the big city had to work to achieve.

Because his mother had worked in the house all the years she'd been married to his father, her skin had stayed young and unwrinkled. The past sixteen years, which she'd spent outdoors training cutting horses, had taken their toll, giving her character lines around the eyes and mouth. The sun had tanned her skin, leaving it warm and glowing. She looked healthy—and happy.

"I'm so glad you're here," she said, grasping his hands and stepping back to look him over. She frowned and said, "You're working too hard."

He laughed. She couldn't know what an understatement that was. His job demanded everything, including a few hours he should have been sleeping. "You look fine, too, Mom."

She laughed and hugged him again.

As she did, Luke saw over her shoulder that Jackson Blackthorne had appeared in the kitchen doorway. He stiffened, and his mother let him go immediately.

Luke stared at the man who'd been his father's nemesis. Blackjack was even taller than Luke, who stood over six feet, his shoulders were broad and for a man in his late sixties, his hips were still surprisingly lean.

He'd had a heart attack twelve years ago, but there was no vestige of it in his appearance. There wasn't an ounce of extra fat on his muscular frame. His gaze was sharp, his eyes flinty gray, his face craggy from years spent in the sun. His thick black hair had turned completely silver, yet he looked ten years younger than Luke knew he was.

His mother turned and reached out a hand to Blackjack.

"Come say hello to Luke," she said, taking Blackjack's hand and drawing him toward her.

Luke reached unconsciously for Amy's hand, gripping it tightly and pulling her to stand beside him.

Luke saw his mother was working hard to keep the smile on her face while she watched him worriedly for his reaction. The times he'd been to the Homestead over the past twelve years were few and far between and had usually ended with him leaving tight-lipped and angry. And upset, because he knew his rows with Blackjack made his mother miserable.

He wished he could like the man for her sake. But he didn't.

He made himself reach out a hand to Blackjack, which Blackjack took. "Sir," he said.

"So—. Luke," Blackjack replied.

Blackjack had caught himself, but Luke still bristled. He wasn't the man's son. He was never going to be his son, and Blackjack's use of the word was a surprising slip of the tongue. Did he refer to Sam that way? Luke wondered. Even the thought of it rankled.

Luke withdrew his hand, clenched his back teeth and said, "I'm not sure if you've met Amy Nash."

"Luke and Amy were high school sweethearts," his mother volunteered.

Luke felt himself flushing. His mother's statement suggested he and Amy were an item now, when in fact, it was mere coincidence that they were both here for lunch on the same day.

Or was it? Luke glanced at his mother, a crease forming between his brows. She couldn't be . . . she wouldn't dare. . . . He stared at her until he caught her eye. Her cheeks flamed and her gaze met his, as though asking him to at least consider the possibility. Luke felt a spurt of irritation. Was his mother *matchmaking*?

He'd always loved Amy, but she'd made her feelings plain during their morning ride together. She was happy with Carl Nash and wanted nothing to do with him. He wasn't going to set himself up to get rejected by her again.

Blackjack nodded his head to Amy and said, "Pleased to meet you, Miss Nash."

"It's Mrs. Nash," Amy corrected. She reached out a hand to him, since no Western man was going to shake a woman's hand unless she extended it first. "I've been looking forward to meeting you."

"Oh?" he said, raising a brow.

Amy shot Luke a quick look from beneath lowered lashes. He'd told her often enough in rude terms how he felt about the Blackthornes, and about Blackjack in particular. "You've always been a figure of mystery to me," she said.

"I'm flesh and blood, Mrs. Nash," he said with a smile meant to put everyone at ease.

"It's going to be just the four of us for lunch," his mother said. "Sam and Emma got a last-minute invitation from Emma's brother and his wife to join them for lunch at the Castle, and Sam called to see if we would mind. I told him we'd be fine."

Luke's eyes narrowed. He wondered if his mother had connived the invitation from Billy and Summer Coburn, who lived at the castle-size ranch house where Blackjack had once ruled Bitter Creek. With only the four of them at the table, he would be forced to talk with Blackjack. And Amy would be forced to talk with him. But there was nothing he could do about it now.

"What can I help with?" Amy said to break the awkward silence.

"Everything's in the oven," his mother said. "All we need to do is set the table."

"I can help with that," Luke offered. He pulled out the drawer where the silverware had always been kept, and it was still there. He took out what they would need and set it on the counter, then opened a cupboard to retrieve plates and glasses. "Where are the—"

"They're over here now," his mother said, opening a cupboard on the other side of the kitchen. She handed four plates to Amy and four iced tea glasses to Blackjack. Meanwhile, she opened a drawer and retrieved place mats and cloth napkins.

It didn't take them long working together to get the table set and the prime rib and baked potatoes and green bean casserole served. Eating gave them an excuse for the silence that settled as soon as the four of them were seated at one end of the long table.

"We didn't have much chance to catch up the other day," his mother said to Amy. "What's keeping you busy these days?"

Luke paused with the fork halfway to his mouth and met Amy's gaze, which focused on him for an instant before she turned back to his mother.

"I'm a lawyer with a small firm in Houston," she said.

Luke's fork clattered to his plate. "What?"

She smiled at him and said, "You don't have to act so surprised."

"I thought you were living in Richmond."

"Not for the past year."

"What?" Luke sputtered. "You've been in Houston for a *year* and never said a word to anyone?"

"My parents knew where I was," Amy said. *And what business was it of yours?*

Luke heard the words, even though Amy never said them. "So your husband moved his practice to Houston?" his mother asked Amy.

Luke watched the patches of red form on Amy's neck and work their way upward to her cheeks as she replied, "Carl's still in Virginia."

Another uncomfortable silence settled over the table.

Finally, Luke said, "If you're in Houston and Carl's in Richmond—"

"We're divorced," Amy said. "We have been for the past year. I moved back to Texas to practice law."

He resisted asking the question uppermost in his mind: *Why the hell didn't you tell me you were divorced?* What he said was, "I didn't even know you went to law school." He kept his voice even, but inside he was barraged by emotions—confusion, anger, excitement, frustration.

She was hiding things again. It had taken most of their four years together in high school for Amy to open up to him. Her biggest secret—her mother's agoraphobia—hadn't come out until he'd forced her to bring him home with her. Once that was out, and he hadn't run for the hills, she'd relaxed a little.

He was stung by the fact that she'd hidden her divorce, her move to Houston, her work as a lawyer. It made her rejection of his overture during their ride much worse, because it meant she knew they were living in the same town, that they were both free to pursue a relationship, and she still didn't want anything to do with him.

"I went to law school to fill the time once Honor

started school," Amy said. "Never dreaming I'd actually practice."

"Did you leave him? Or did he leave you?" Luke asked.

Amy's face blanched.

"Luke," his mother admonished. "What a thing to ask! You don't have to answer him, Amy."

"Actually, I divorced Carl," she said, staring Luke in the eye.

"So the perfect husband wasn't so perfect after all," Luke couldn't resist saying.

"No," Amy said.

"Your parents must be glad you've settled nearby," Luke's mother interjected.

Amy's eyes were locked with Luke's. She broke away, turned to his mother and said, "They enjoy spending time with Honor."

Luke noticed what she didn't say. That Honor was enjoying the time with them. It must be odd to have a grandmother who never left the house.

Silence fell on the table. Again.

"How are things at D&B?" his mother asked him with a smile that Luke could see was forced. "What's it like working for a woman boss?"

"Different." Luke could see his mother was upset by the short, curt answer and looked for something he could say to ease her discomfort.

"I've heard good things about Grayson Choate," Blackjack said. They were the first words he'd uttered since they'd started eating. Something neutral. Something guaranteed not to make waves.

Nonetheless, Luke found it irritating. "Don't believe everything you hear."

"You're having problems?" Blackjack asked.

Luke knew the comment wasn't intended to suggest he wasn't competent or capable of handling his new boss. But all the old hurts and slights and his predisposition to find anything Blackjack said denigrating caused him to say, "What goes on between me and the lawyers I work with is none of your damned business."

"Oh, Luke," his mother almost wailed in dismay. "I'm sure Jackson—"

"Don't apologize for me," Blackjack snapped at her. "I haven't said anything that needs apology. But that son of yours certainly has!"

Blackjack was holding his knife and fork so tightly Luke could imagine the stainless steel bending in his grasp. His mother's hand lay on Blackjack's muscular forearm, and Luke was sure that was the only reason his stepfather wasn't already on his feet.

Amy provided the voice of reason. "Grayson Choate's reputation as a shark is well known in the legal community," she said. "It must be challenging to work with her, Luke."

Luke tore his gaze away from Blackjack and faced Amy.

"It is." He would have left it at that, except Amy kept her eyes focused on his expectantly. "It's been an adjustment moving from the litigation section over to corporate."

"Why did they move you?" Amy asked.

"Promising associates are assigned to more than one

section of the firm, so more of the partners have a chance
to get to know them and their capabilities. I'm doing my
turn in corporate." That wasn't the whole story, but
telling the rest would have sounded like bragging.

"But you're still primarily a litigator?" Amy asked.

Luke nodded. "That's where I've focused my efforts.
I'll be representing the firm's largest client, Hyland
Pharmaceuticals. In fact, I'm working on—"

At that moment the kitchen door burst open and
Blackjack's only daughter, Summer Coburn, came
through the door, a grin on her face and a pie in her
hands. Her husband Billy followed her, with three kids
tumbling in behind him, Billy's thirteen-year-old son
Will, and Billy and Summer's eleven-year-old daughter
Katherine and eight-year-old son Jack. Behind them
came Emma and Sam and Bronc.

"We brought dessert," Summer said as she set the
pie on the kitchen counter. "Apple pie—"

"And ice cream!" Kate said as she set a half gallon of
vanilla ice cream on the counter.

Luke saw Blackjack was already out of his chair and
crossing to hug the little girl, tousle Will's black hair
and tickle Jack in the ribs. Then he shook hands with
Billy and Sam and gave Summer a big hug, followed
by a hug for Emma and the caressing graze of his hand
across Bronc's shoulder.

Luke had never felt more like an outsider in his own
home. How could they forgive Blackjack? Billy and
Sam, he meant. Billy was Blackjack's bastard son, who'd
been "Bad" Billy Coburn all his life, a dirt-poor saddle
tramp who'd befriended rich Summer Blackthorne.

It should have been impossible for Billy and Summer to marry—except it turned out Summer wasn't really Blackjack's daughter. Eve Blackthorne had informed Blackjack of the truth—that Summer's real father was Blackjack's former foreman—and threatened to tell Summer if he tried to divorce her. It had been part of the blackmail she'd used to keep Blackjack in that ill-fated marriage.

And Sam. Sam would spend his life confined to that wheelchair and had a Blackthorne to blame for it. In his youth, he'd hated the Blackthornes and had become an embittered alcoholic. Thanks to another Blackthorne, who'd forced Sam to take a hard look at himself, he'd been sober for more years than Luke could count. And now Sam was shaking hands—and smiling—at Blackjack, as though he enjoyed seeing the man.

Luke felt betrayed. It was one thing to know everyone else had been able to go on with their lives as though all those years of strife had never happened. It was another to see it played out before his eyes. He couldn't be a part of this. He refused to be a part of it.

He rose and said, "Sorry I can't stay, Mom. I've got to get back to Houston."

"Surely you can have a bite of pie," his mother said.

He felt Amy's hand on his arm, a gentle touch signaling her agreement with his mother, a silent entreaty to stay and become a part of the family whose circle remained open to him, but which he refused to join.

"Sorry," he said. "I need to get on the road."

Luke made his good-byes to Summer and Billy and

their kids, gave his nephew and sister-in-law a hug, then shook hands with Sam.

"Promise you'll bring the girls for a visit," his mother said as she followed him to the door.

"You know how busy things get," he hedged.

"Promise," his mother said, laying her palm against his cheek.

"All right," he said, knowing she was stubborn enough to keep him standing there until he agreed.

"Soon," she added.

He smiled. "As soon as I can manage it."

His mother was joined by Blackjack, who slid his arm around her waist and said, "You'll always be welcome here."

A Blackthorne offering me welcome in my father's home. It was all Luke could do to choke out to his mother, "I'll bring the girls when I can."

Then he was outside, drawing deep breaths to try and calm down.

It took him a moment to realize Amy had joined him.

"I am so disappointed in you," she said.

"What?" Luke was shocked by the unexpected attack.

"They're all trying to get along, to make a happy life for themselves, to let the past die a clean death. And you . . ."

He saw the scorn in her eyes. And felt the injustice of her accusation, the injustice of the situation. "You're asking me to forget what that man did to my father. You're asking me to forget what his family did to mine."

"No one's asking you to do anything—except be a courteous guest."

"To go along and get along," Luke snarled.

"Yes," she said. "To get on with your life. To make the best of a bad situation. We all have to do it. Life isn't a bed of roses. It's full of bloody thorns. The wounds will heal if you let them."

"They haven't," Luke said. "They won't."

"Not if you keep them open and festering. This is the only family you have, Luke. You need to make peace with the Blackthornes."

"How?" he said in an agonized voice. "I don't belong here anymore. I'm not a part of his family. I refuse to be a part of them."

"Then I pity you. Good-bye, Luke." She turned and walked back into the house and let the door slam behind her.

Luke stared after her. The last thing he wanted from Amy Hazeltine Nash was her pity.

For an instant, he was tempted to go back inside. To try and mend fences. To try and be a part of the happy family his mother was trying so hard to achieve.

But he thought of his father. And all the years his family had suffered at Blackthorne hands. And he couldn't do it.

Luke turned his back on them. And walked away.

3

Luke stared at the scruffy cat sitting at his feet, which stared right back at him. "Aw, give me a break, Snowball. Stop that yowling. You know I don't have time to pick you up. I've got to get to work."

Snowball flicked her stub of a tail. And yowled.

"I don't believe this," Luke muttered. He took one last run at his face with the razor, then rinsed it and pitched it onto the bathroom counter. He cupped his hands under the running water and splashed his face, then shut off the water and grabbed for a towel.

When he opened his eyes, Snowball was no longer sitting impatiently at his feet. She was sitting on the bathroom counter staring up at him with baleful yellow eyes.

It amazed Luke how silently the cat could move, and how nimbly, since she only had three legs. She was also missing the tip of her tail and most of one ragged ear.

"You know you're not allowed on the counter," he said to the cat.

But he made no move to dislocate her. And she ignored the disapprobation in his voice.

The only animals Luke and his family had ever owned either worked for a living or got butchered and eaten.

Snowball wouldn't have lasted long at Three Oaks. She was the most useless animal Luke had ever seen. But she'd apparently been in one hell of a fight and survived with her dignity—if not all her body parts—intact.

Snowball wasn't exactly what Luke had had in mind when he'd taken his two daughters to the local animal shelter to select a cute little kitten.

The kitten was supposed to distract Brynne and Midge from the fact that he and their mother had just gotten a divorce and be a good reason for them to come and visit him every other weekend. He hadn't been quite sure they'd want to come just to see him.

His ex-wife was allergic to fur, and a puppy or kitten had been out of the question during their marriage. Personally, Luke had thought having a "pet" was a waste of time and money. Fortunately for him, Valerie had been the villain whenever one of the girls showed up with some homeless stray and wasn't allowed to keep it.

A pet had seemed like something he could offer the girls that they wouldn't have had except for the divorce. At the time, it had seemed logical. When he thought of it now, it seemed pretty ridiculous. *Yes, your mom and I are breaking up your home, but how about a kitten to make everything better?* Hell, he'd have grasped at any kind of straw to take that godawful tragic look off their faces.

Eight-year-old Brynne had been eyeing a black cat with white boots when four-year-old Midge had spied the scruffy ball of fur hissing and spitting in a nearby cage. When Snowball jumped up and limped away from Midge's poking finger, displaying her war wounds,

Brynne had been disconsolate. She knew how it felt to go through life with a wounded body.

"We have to rescue her, Daddy," Brynne had cried.

"Snowball needs us, Daddy," Midge had agreed.

"Snowball?" he'd questioned, eyeing the ball of grayish-white fur. Snowball seemed a particularly inappropriate name for a cat living in Houston, Texas, probably the next hottest place to Hell.

Midge nodded. "Yes, Daddy. Snowball."

Luke took another look. It was possible the fluffy smudge of grayish-brownish-whitish fur reminded Midge of the only snow she'd ever seen. They'd been at the mall when a truck dumped a load of snow on the asphalt for the kids to play in, as a holiday advertising gimmick. It hadn't stayed white for long.

Snowball had come home to Luke's two-bedroom condo in downtown Houston in a cage he'd needed to buy, because Snowball hissed and spit and savagely arched her back at the two little girls who'd been her saviors.

Snowball had never become one of those sit-in-your-lap cats, but she'd suffered the indignity of being dressed in doll clothes by Brynne and Midge with a patience and indulgence that had surprised Luke. Despite Snowball's continued hissed greetings to the girls every other weekend, they swore they loved her and Luke didn't dare get rid of her.

He and Snowball had formed an uneasy truce, and since he could leave the cat alone for the long hours he spent litigating at DeWitt & Blackthorne, he'd clamped his back teeth and endured.

Being ignorant of the encroaching nature of cats, he'd let Snowball sleep at the foot of his bed—on the floor—that first night. During the night, Snowball had hopped up on the mattress, where it was more comfortable. Over the past two years since his divorce, Snowball had slowly but surely wormed her way up the bed.

These days, Luke often awoke to find the cat sleeping next to his head, and the damned animal expected him to pet her. Which he did. Even when he was running late getting out of the house to work. Like now.

Snowball yowled again. Piteously.

Luke swore under his breath, but he picked up the cat, tucked her close to his naked chest and scratched her under the chin.

Snowball closed her eyes and laid her head back in ecstasy. The feline rumble started, a distinct motor sound with a little hitch in it that reminded him of the fourth-hand Harley he'd ridden as a teenager.

Luke shook his head and grinned. If only all females were this easy to please, he'd still be a married man.

Seven hours later, Luke was damning all women, especially his new boss, Grayson Choate. He'd spent the morning reading Hyland Pharmaceutical files, wondering how he was going to represent a company whose brand-new miracle drug might be killing the very people it was meant to help.

Luke grabbed the rubbery ball Brynne had given him for his birthday and squeezed the life out of it. The ball was supposed to reduce his stress level, but every time he picked the damned thing up, he imagined his ex-wife explaining to his daughter why her father might appreciate such a gift, and the acid rose in his stomach.

He threw the ball across the room so it flattened against the wall, then opened his side desk drawer four inches and grabbed the giant economy plastic bottle of fruit-flavored Tums. They were full of calcium, and he figured he had some of the strongest bones in the firm.

He flipped off the lid and poured several into his hand, chucked the green ones into the trash can and popped the rest into his mouth. With any luck, they'd kill the acid in his stomach before he had to meet with the grieving mother who'd accused Hyland of selling an unsafe drug.

He grabbed his coffee cup, a series of uneven coiled pink pottery snakes Brynne had made for him in Girl Scouts, and took a swig of water to kill the powdery taste. He set the cup down next to the tiny handprint paperweight Midge had produced in preschool, then leaned back in his leather swivel chair, laced his hands behind his head and stretched out his long body.

He had a rough couple of hours ahead of him, and it would have been nice not to have to wear a tie today. It was Friday, and lawyers who weren't scheduled to greet the public could dress down in Izod shirts, belted khakis and docksiders without socks. Even that was a far cry from the raggedy T-shirts, worn jeans and scuffed cowboy boots Luke had worn growing up. He hadn't even been trying for that rebellious James Dean look. His family had simply been poor, and clothes got worn until they got worn out.

But dressing down had been out of the question. His

new female boss had made it clear she wanted a wrong-ful death suit against Hyland settled today—no ifs, ands or buts. Luke hadn't felt so anxious since he'd first stepped into a courtroom six years ago as a bright-eyed and bushy-tailed twenty-six-year-old UT law school grad and addressed a judge as "Your Honor."

With any luck, the plaintiff would accept Hyland's generous monetary offer of compensation for damages suffered, and the case would be closed. Slam, bam, thank you, ma'am.

But if Luke had learned anything in the years he'd been practicing law, it was "Never count your chickens before they're hatched." Things had a way of . . . going wrong.

"Mr. Creed, you're late for your appointment with Mrs. Anastasio and her lawyer."

Luke glanced at his secretary, who stood in the doorway to his office dressed like a flower bed run amuck, then back at the thick file he'd forgone lunch to read. "They weren't supposed to be here until two."

"It's 2:15."

Luke glanced at his watch. Actually, it was 2:17. "Shit. 'Scuse my French, Flo."

Flo gave him an admonishing look over the green plastic-framed glasses perched on the end of her nose and said, "How long will you be?"

"I'm coming right now." Luke shoved the documents from the contract research organization (the CRO), the clinical research coordinator (the CRC), the institutional review board (the IRB), the principal investigator (the PI) and the Food and Drug Administration (the FDA) back into the file.

It seemed everything and everybody in the clinical research process to approve a new drug for market had a set of initials. It was a whole new language Luke needed to learn, and learn fast. Especially if he wanted to prove that the most recent death attributed to Hyland's miracle drug D-Free might be the result of the patient exceeding the MTD—the maximum tolerated dose.

His phone rang, and Flo picked it up. "DeWitt and Blackthorne, Mr. Creed's office. Yes, Ms. Choate, he's here."

Flo punched the hold button and said, "She wants to see you. Now."

"Sh—"

Flo lowered her brows, and Luke bit back the epithet. "Tell her I'm on my way."

"While you're planning your afternoon, you asked me to remind you that the firm's fall picnic begins at River Oaks at 4:00."

"Sh—" Luke gave Flo a sheepish look.

"What shall I tell the attorney from Hardy, Christian and James and the grieving mother she brought with her?"

"Come back tomorrow?"

Flo was not amused. She pursed her lips and tapped a red-painted fingernail against the phone.

"Tell Mrs. Anastasio and her lawyer I'll be there shortly," Luke said. "And tell Choate I'm on my way."

The grieving mother and her attorney would have to wait. There was no putting off Grayson Choate. When the senior partner of the corporate section spoke, associates listened.

Luke listened more closely than most. When the partners met next spring to decide who would join their ranks, Luke planned to be one of the chosen. Despite—not because of—the fact his sonofabitch stepfather's great-grandfather was a founding partner of the firm.

Luke had been called to Franklin DeWitt's office six weeks ago and told by the firm's managing partner that since Hyland was the firm's largest single client, accounting for 17 percent of overall revenues, every potential partner was rotated through the corporate section in order to evaluate whether they'd be able to work with the powers that be at Hyland. Luke was to report to Grayson Choate by the middle of the following month.

Luke had been surprised to discover that he had to move his office to the corporate floor, which seemed like a lot of effort for a temporary transfer, but it was one of Choate's requirements. She wanted the attorneys she supervised to be easily accessible to her.

Choate was the first woman boss he'd had, and Luke had found her unpredictable. Which hadn't done his stomach lining any good. He'd figured the first woman to be named a partner in the firm would be tough, and she was. But she was also surprisingly feminine. Womanly. Hell, the word he wanted was *sexy*.

Choate was fifty-three but could easily pass for forty-five. She was slender and petite, with golden highlights in her chestnut hair that looked like the sun had put them there. An impossibility, as far as Luke was concerned, because she spent the entire twelve to fourteen daylight hours in the office. She dressed as though to attract a man, even though she'd never been married — or even dated — as far as Luke had been able to discover.

He shoved down the sleeves of his white Oxford cloth shirt and buttoned them, then grabbed his gray blended wool suit coat from the hanger behind the door and slid it on. As he headed into the hall, he buttoned up his shirt and shoved the knot on his red and navy rep-striped tie up until it almost choked him.

Other floors, other sections of the practice — litigation, for one — were less formal, but Choate liked her associates looking professional. Luke's job was to please his boss.

Which wasn't nearly as simple as it sounded.

Getting assigned to Choate was a mixed blessing. Being given primary responsibility for Hyland litigation was an indication of the confidence the firm had in his abilities as a litigator and a clear sign, along with the move to corporate, that he was under serious consideration for partnership. But Grayson Choate was known to eat up associates and spit out the useless remains.

The most recent associate to work for her had mixed too much alcohol with an antidepressant and then gotten behind the wheel. The fatal one-car accident had made the ten o'clock news.

Luke was his replacement.

Choate's nineteenth-floor office took up an entire corner of the solid brick building that housed the firm. Her tall, narrow windows reflected the shiny steel and glass ghetto that always made Luke feel trapped in the midst of downtown Houston. On his family's hundred-square-mile South Texas ranch, the dark nights were lit only by limitless stars, and wide-open prairies stretched as far as the eye could see. He'd never gotten used to Houston's bright lights and skyscrapers.

But this was where he needed to be to reach the pinnacle of his chosen profession. At the largest law firm in the state of Texas. The second-largest in the country. One of the largest in the world. He'd wanted to prove he could be the best. Working at D&B, he got the sorts of cases most litigators only dreamed about— millions of dollars at stake, and in this case, people's very lives.

He told himself he wasn't worried that Choate, better known behind her back as the Dragon Lady, would do to him what she'd done to all the other males who'd ventured into her domain. He was different. A survivor, like his cat. Someone who'd turned himself inside out and upside down to become what the firm expected its partners to be.

Nevertheless, his heart was pounding as he headed down the hall to the dragon's lair.

Grayson Choate had gained prestige and power in the firm over the years as the major client she represented, Hyland Pharmaceuticals, had become a behemoth. Twenty years ago, the firm had billed the fledgling company nearly a million dollars. Last year D&B had billed the multinational corporation $51,434,632.32.

Choate's office decor was the antithesis of the typical dark wood and brass-studded leather that was found in the other, primarily male, partners' offices. Luke crossed and stood behind one of the pale pink brocade-upholstered chairs in front of Choate's sculptured stone-and-glass desk.

He stood because he knew the diminishing effect of sitting in one of them, which he'd done the first time he'd met her. They were feminine objects, fragile enough to make a man feel uncomfortable, and he was a big enough man to have his knees in his chest when he sat down.

Choate wore a form-fitting, tailored white suit that emphasized her hourglass figure. The black blouse beneath it was fragile silk. It was disconcerting, when the young women in the firm tried so hard to hide their sex behind boxy clothes and bows at their necks, to find a female partner whose choice of dress was so intentionally alluring.

"What's the status of the Anastasio woman's complaint?" Choate asked.

"I'm meeting with her and her attorney this afternoon," Luke said. "In fact, they're waiting for me now."

"We've managed to make the other three complaints against Hyland over the past year since D-Free went on the market go away. I want this one to disappear as well."

"What if D-Free really is killing kids?" Luke asked. "Have we investigated—"

"The drug is perfectly safe," Choate said. "Any claim to the contrary is ridiculous, considering the strict scrutiny D-Free has received from the FDA."

She ran her fingers slowly along a thick, black-and-gold Waterman pen, and Luke struggled not to make the sexual connection that sprang to mind. He wondered if she knew what she was doing, wondered if it was subconscious behavior intended to make a man aware that she was a woman capable of raising his temperature—and other body parts.

He was too new to the section to know Choate's quirks, but he'd heard enough stories about the Dragon Lady to raise the hair on the back of his neck.

Over the past five years, ten male associates had bit the dust after going to work for her. Besides the associate who'd died, two had ended up in the hospital (one for an ulcer, the other with diverticulitis), two had quit law, one had gone to jail for beating up his wife, and four had left D&B to work for small local firms.

Maybe Choate had preyed on them sexually, Luke thought. It wasn't beyond the realm of possibility. Why else would she be dressed the way she was at the office, if it wasn't to attract male attention?

"Hyland has jumped through more FDA hoops than you can imagine getting D-Free on the market," Choate continued. "The drug has been in development for nearly twelve years, and you know what that means."

"They made a lot of mistakes before they got it right?"

The flip response was out of Luke's mouth before he could stop it. D&B wasn't likely to want a smart-ass as a partner. But he knew better than to take it back. Wimps were even worse than smart-asses.

He was relieved when he saw Choate smile.

"That, too," she said. "The point is, even with the relatively quick FDA approval after human clinical testing, Hyland only has five years of exclusivity left on its patent for D-Free in which to recoup the cost of developing the drug. As for any supposed problems with D-Free, Hyland is doing Phase IV post-marketing clinical studies as we speak."

"And there's no indication whatsoever that the drug caused the deaths of those four Type I juvenile diabetics?" Luke asked.

"None."

"Then why are these kids dying?"

Choate shrugged. "Misuse of the drug, maybe. More likely, their deaths are totally unconnected to D-Free. No link to D-Free has actually been shown in any of their complaints."

"Except that all the kids who died were taking it," Luke pointed out.

Choate waved her hand dismissively. "Coincidence," she said. "Just get rid of that woman."

"I'll do my best," Luke said. And then realized that maybe with Choate, even your best wasn't good enough. Maybe the stress of having to do miracles was what had burned out those other ten male associates.

He was waiting for some sign that their conversation was over, but Choate simply stared at him, looking him up and down as though he were a side of beef. Luke nodded his head and turned to leave.

"Luke," she said.

He paused and looked back over his shoulder. "Yes?" He didn't add the ma'am on the tip of his tongue and wondered if he should have.

"I'll expect to hear good news from you when I see you at the picnic this afternoon."

"Yes, ma'am." This time the *ma'am* slipped out. He

saw the small, satisfied smile appear and realized he should have used it the first time. He wouldn't make that mistake again.

"See you later," he said, and made his escape.

Luke wished he'd had more time to focus on Hyland before he'd moved down to the corporate floor, but he was still running himself ragged tying up ends on several litigation matters. He'd done background research on Hyland and D-Free, but he was still woefully ignorant. The FDA's drug approval process was complicated, and what he'd read about it hadn't left him feeling reassured.

The demand for AIDS drugs in the 1990s had caused the FDA to speed up its approval process, only to discover later in the decade that a number of drugs it had approved were suspected of causing more than a thousand deaths. Before they were finally withdrawn from the marketplace, the defective drugs had earned more than *five billion* dollars for the companies that produced them.

Luke had realized an important fact about the pharmaceutical industry: There was a great deal of money to be made selling dangerously flawed drugs.

He felt a special empathy for the parents of those children who'd died while using D-Free. He could understand why they'd chosen to give their children the drug because he knew the alternative treatment—taking insulin with a needle—was so grueling. And he was so well informed about the difficulties they faced, because his elder daughter Brynne had Type I diabetes.

Brynne had been diagnosed with the disease when she was five and ever since had been taking insulin shots four to six times a day simply to stay alive.

The needles were tiny, and Brynne had learned how to stick herself so the injections were almost painless. In fact, she complained that the pinprick in her finger to get a drop of blood for the test strip to determine how much insulin she needed was often more painful than the shot itself.

She gave herself shots in the stomach or the hip or even between her fingers—anywhere the needle could still be easily inserted after five years of insulin injections that had created hard, invisible, impenetrable lumps under the skin.

Luke could understand the appeal of Hyland's new drug. Three pills a day, a half hour before each meal, with the dosage based on the patient's weight, was certainly preferable to sticking a needle in your belly.

He was glad his daughter wasn't taking the drug. He and his ex-wife had discussed the possibility when D-Free came on the market and decided to wait until its side effects were better known before letting Brynne try it.

For the million or so kids with juvenile diabetes, the drug truly was a miracle. For four of them, it might have been deadly.

The cause of death in each case was diabetic coma. According to Hyland's investigative report, which Luke had found in the file, there was one significant commonality between the four deaths. In each case, death had occurred after a birthday party, where the child had overindulged in sweets, raising his or her blood sugar to dangerous levels.

But hundreds of thousands of children taking D-Free must have gone to birthday parties over the past year. And none of them had died.

Whatever other companies might be doing, Luke had a great deal of confidence that Hyland was acting responsibly. One of the reasons he'd been attracted to D&B in the first place was the integrity and skill of the lawyers who worked there. If D-Free had been liable for any of the deaths attributed to it, Choate would have made sure Hyland did something about it.

It was not only morally and ethically the right thing to do, but in the end, it was good public relations, as everyone had learned from the admissions made by corporate heads during the Tylenol scare. *Yes, there is a problem with contaminated Tylenol, but we've taken steps to provide better, tamper-proof packaging.* That forthright behavior had become a model for corporations all over America.

Luke loosened his tie as he headed down the hall toward his meeting with the lawyer from Hardy, Christian but didn't undo the top shirt button, even though he wanted to. He stopped cold in the doorway to Conference Room A.

"Amy," he blurted. "What are you doing here?"

"I told you I was a lawyer," Amy replied. But she looked as shocked as he felt.

"Why didn't you tell me you were working on a Hyland case?" he asked.

"You walked out Sunday before I had a chance to say much of anything."

Luke recalled how he'd abruptly left the table at Three Oaks. He was still having trouble wrapping his mind around the fact that he and Amy were on opposite sides of the same lawsuit.

She glanced at her watch and said, "We're waiting for Neil Ford. Are you here with a message from him?"

Luke recognized the name of the associate he'd replaced in the corporate section. "I've come in his stead."

"Then you're late," Amy said pointedly.

Luke turned to the grieving mother, who was dressed in black. "I'm sorry for my tardiness, Mrs. Anastasio. I've read the complaint, and frankly, it appears your daughter Rosa . . . "

Mrs. Anastasio stared at him with dark eyes so full of sorrow that he felt his stomach knot. He turned back to Amy and said, "The facts of this case—"

"What are you doing here?" she interrupted.

"I represent Hyland," he said, confused by the question.

"What happened to Neil Ford?"

"He died three weeks ago. Car crash."

"Oh," she said. "I didn't know."

"You must not watch the evening news."

"I don't."

She seemed upset, but he figured it wasn't so much the change in attorneys, as the fact that he was the one replacing Neil. He noticed she was chewing worriedly on her lower lip. It was a nervous habit she'd had in high school.

But sitting there in a suit, her back ramrod straight, her hair tucked behind her ears, a leather briefcase on the conference table in front of her, she looked every inch the professional.

"I should have notified you of the change in attorneys," he said. "I just came on board, and I'm still getting up to speed."

"I'd already had a few phone conversations with Neil," she said. "Did he leave notes in the file?"

"I haven't found anything," Luke said.

"That's a little odd, don't you think?"

"Maybe he didn't have a chance to transcribe them. Maybe they got pitched when his office got cleaned out."

"Maybe you should have done a little more research into the situation."

He bristled but held his tongue. As long as he'd known her, she'd seen everything in terms of black and white. Right or wrong. You were either prepared. Or you weren't. No excuses allowed or considered. It was what had caused their breakup all those years ago. She lived by the rules. He looked for ways to flout them.

He'd always thought that if she'd just hung in there with him long enough, he could have taught her the importance of *gray*.

"Shall we discuss the terms of the settlement?" he said, determined to get the meeting back on track. Flo had handed him an accordion file as he came down the hall from Choate's office, and he opened it to pull out the settlement agreement Hyland wanted Mrs. Anastasio to sign.

"Mrs. Anastasio isn't going to settle," Amy said.

"You haven't even heard the terms of the offer."

"You can't offer Mrs. Anastasio enough money to repay her for the loss of her daughter. She wants D-Free taken off the market. She won't 'settle' for anything less."

"That's absurd." Luke felt a trickle of sweat run down his back, even though he knew the firm kept the conference rooms at a chilly—and purposely uncomfortable—65 degrees.

He'd been ignoring Mrs. Anastasio, not wanting to take the chance he might empathize with her. He was surprised when she spoke.

"My daughter followed the instructions to the letter. She used that drug properly. There was something wrong with it, because she went into a coma and died."

"Hyland has done rigorous clinical testing—"

"That drug is dangerous," Mrs. Anastasio said, her voice rising. "It killed my baby! Now what am I going to do?"

Luke watched as Amy slid an arm around Mrs. Anastasio's shoulder to comfort her. He wondered why Amy had allowed her client to come to this meeting. Normally, the attorneys worked things out and presented the results of their negotiation to the client later.

"Maybe we should defer this discussion—"

"There's no need for that," Amy said. "Mrs. Anastasio is here to make it plain exactly what it is she wants from Hyland."

"You realize litigation like this could drag on—"

"We have all the time in the world," Amy said. "And plenty of money to fight you."

Luke lifted a brow. Hyland had endless resources, and Amy must know it.

She looked him in the eye and said, "When was the last time you had spaghetti, counselor?"

Luke frowned. "I don't—"

"Mrs. Anastasio is owner and CEO of Wholesome Foods."

Luke felt acid in his stomach. Wholesome Foods produced a nationally known line of tomato-based products, including spaghetti sauce. He turned to meet the grieving woman's dark, pain-filled gaze. "Hyland isn't going to take D-Free off the market, Mrs. Anastasio."

"Then you leave us no choice," Amy said. "We'll see you in court, and let a jury decide whether D-Free is killing defenseless children."

Amy was already on her way out the door with Mrs. Anastasio by the time Luke got to his feet. "We need to talk," he said to her back.

Amy paused and Mrs. Anastasio patted her arm and said, "You stay and talk. I'll wait to hear from you."

They both watched Mrs. Anastasio walk down the hall and ring for the elevator.

Amy took a deep breath and let it out before she spoke. "Considering we're on opposite sides of a lawsuit, I've got nothing personal to say to you, Luke. See you in court."

"Wait!" He caught Amy's arm as she turned to leave. "I think you owe me—"

She angled her head to stare at his grasping hand.

He let her go and watched as she straightened her polyester coat sleeve. Her suit sure as hell hadn't come from Neiman's or Lord & Taylor. Why would Amy Hazeltine Nash, who'd married and divorced a rich orthopedic surgeon, be shopping for business clothes at Target or Wal-Mart? "Why didn't you call me when you moved here, Amy?"

"Why should I have called you?" she said, her eyes meeting his. "We're a long way from the kids we used to be, Luke."

He flicked her blond hair behind her shoulder and said, "Not as far as you think."

He'd never gotten over her, and he couldn't help thinking here was a second chance. Assuming he could figure out a way to take advantage of it. The circumstances couldn't be much worse. He barely had time to jog a couple of miles in the evening, let alone date an old girlfriend. And they were on opposite sides of a lawsuit. Things could get messy if he seduced opposing counsel.

He heard himself say, "I want to see you, Amy."

She shook her head. "I don't think—"

He smiled, aware he was trying to charm her, amazed when he saw it was working. "Have dinner with me. I haven't been able to stop thinking of you since I saw you at Three Oaks."

Brynne and Midge were supposed to spend the weekend with him. He'd be seeing them for the first time since they'd headed off to camp earlier this summer. He was picking them up at Valerie's house as soon as he could sneak out of the firm's fall picnic and would be returning them by noon on Sunday.

"How about Sunday evening?" he said.

She frowned. "I'll have to see if I can get a baby-sitter. I'll call you."

Luke gave her his number but didn't trust her to call. "How can I reach you?"

"My number's unlisted. I'll call you if I'm able to find a baby-sitter."

He kept his gaze pinned on hers, willing her to give in, to give him her number. She didn't. "All right, Amy," he said. "Have it your way."

"I've worked long and hard to be able to do exactly that," she said. "So long, Luke."

Luke admired the graceful sway of her hips as she walked away, surprised by his physical response. He'd been too busy the past couple of years to even fantasize about sex. But there was no denying he wanted Amy Nash.

She was still smart, still accomplished, still extraordinarily pretty. But his need for her wasn't merely physical. He wanted his best friend back. He wanted the approval she'd withheld all those years ago. He could make her happy. He just wanted the chance to prove it.

He glanced at his watch. It was 3:15. If he hurried, he could make it to the firm picnic at River Oaks on time. Between here and there, he had to come up with some believable lie to tell Choate about his failure to settle the case.

He wasn't about to admit he'd been bucked off the bull right out of the chute.

4

Luke hated what River Oaks represented. The premier country club in Houston catered to the bluest of Texas blue bloods. Luke's stepfather was a member, but Luke felt awkward and uncomfortable every time he crossed the sumptuous threshold.

He came to River Oaks only twice a year—for the firm's fall picnic to introduce newly hired associates and the firm's Christmas party. He left his Silverado with the valet and headed inside to check in with the managing partner's secretary. Everyone was expected to participate in at least one of the activities offered—golf, tennis or swimming.

"Good afternoon, Nell," he said.

The wizened woman who'd functioned as Franklin DeWitt's right hand since he'd joined the firm in the late fifties greeted Luke with a smile. "Mr. Creed. Here's your name tag and the afternoon schedule."

Luke tucked the tag in his suit coat pocket and hefted the bag he'd brought with him that contained his swimsuit and a change of clothes.

"Mr. DeWitt asked me to remind you to meet him in the bar at six."

Luke looked at the schedule of afternoon events and saw that a meeting with the head of the firm's management committee had been penned in at the end of the sports activities and before the cocktail hour. "I'll be there," he said, saluting Nell and heading for the locker room.

Luke had discovered over the years that it wasn't as easy to keep track of associates once they'd checked in at River Oaks, and at least twice before he'd managed to skip out before supper. He'd been planning to do precisely that tonight, so he could get to Valerie's and do the kid exchange.

The meeting with DeWitt meant he wasn't going to be able to leave when he'd planned. He was going to have to get hold of Valerie and tell her he'd be late. Which was going to piss her off. She'd warned him a dozen times how inconvenient it was for him to change their arrangements at the last minute.

But he could hardly tell a managing partner that family came first. Luke had learned that lesson his first six months at D&B. God came first, the firm second and family a very distant third.

He changed in the locker room, grabbed a towel and headed for the pool area. He dove into the deep end and released a sigh of pleasure that would have been audible if he hadn't been underwater. He swam with powerful strokes to the shallow end of the pool, then did a racing turn and headed back toward the deep end.

He'd only done a couple of laps before a hand grabbed his ankle and yanked. He turned over, breaking the hold on his leg, and stood, shoving wet hair out of his eyes.

"Wanta race?" a cheerful male voice said.

"I'm gonna win, so where's the challenge?" Luke replied with a grin.

He'd been competing with Drew DeWitt since the day they'd met at the firm's fall picnic six years before. Drew was three years older—he'd spent a few years bumming around Europe and Australia before he'd headed to law school—but they were both up for partner in the coming year. Both also had something to prove, since Drew was a great-great-grandson of the other founding partner of the firm.

They'd competed for the same high-profile cases in litigation until Luke had been transferred out three weeks before. Drew had more than once saved Luke's ass during the months he fought over child custody during his divorce. He'd been sleep-deprived and distracted, and Drew had picked up the ball a couple of times when Luke had dropped it.

Luke hadn't yet had the chance to return the favor. Drew never seemed to need help. He'd never been married, but not because he couldn't attract women. In fact, Drew had a new woman on his arm every week. He was tall and lean, with shoulders that looked like he chopped wood for a living. Luke figured it was the self-deprecating smile that charmed them, along with Drew's wry wit and astonishingly blue eyes.

He was jealous of Drew's carefree attitude toward life. His friend did all the right things to make partner, but it didn't seem to matter as much to him as it did to

Luke whether or not the firm invited him into its inner sanctum. Drew was independently wealthy, the result of a trust fund.

Luke had the same sort of trust fund, a consequence of his mother's marriage to Blackjack. His daughters were welcome to it, but he didn't intend to touch one penny of Blackthorne blood money. When he made partner—and he would—he wasn't going to owe his success to anyone but himself.

"How's it going with the Dragon Lady?" Drew asked.

"Couldn't be better."

Drew lifted a skeptical brow. "Really?"

Luke wasn't about to admit the trouble he was already in. He hadn't made up his mind yet what he was going to say to Choate about the disastrous meeting with Mrs. Anastasio. He wondered if Choate knew the woman was rich and unlikely to settle. He wondered whether he was about to flunk some sort of test.

"Hey," Drew said, waving his hands. "You in there?"

Luke looked around to make sure no one was within earshot and said, "The meeting this afternoon was a bust. I'm probably not going to be able to settle this suit out of court the way Choate wants."

Drew whistled softly. "Have you told her yet?"

Luke shifted his shoulders and grimaced. "I haven't decided yet whether I'm going to lie or admit I'm stuck."

"Never let 'em see you sweat," Drew advised.

"Easy for you to say. You aren't working for the Dragon Lady."

"Is she as bad as the stories we've heard?"

"She's different. Strange. Odd." Luke was looking

for the right word, but none of the ones he'd chosen really fit.

"Strange how? Odd how?"

"She's hard to pigeonhole. Smart. Cagey. Clever." Luke made a face. "And damned sexy."

Drew laughed. "You're kidding, right?"

"I wish," Luke said. "You ever heard her name linked with anybody at the firm? Or anybody else, for that matter?"

Drew shook his head. "Nope."

"When I asked if the firm had done an independent investigation of the drug, she said it wasn't necessary. If I do one on my own, I'm liable to end up with my ass in a crack."

"Forget about what Choate wants. If you think an investigation needs to be done, do it."

Luke shook his head. "You really don't care if you make partner, do you?"

"I'm just not willing to bend myself out of shape to be what someone else expects me to be," Drew said. "It isn't worth it."

Luke wasn't about to explain why it so was important to him to make something of himself—and to do it on his own. No one had believed Luke would ever amount to anything. He'd rather have his fingernails yanked out with pliers than admit he'd spent ten years proving—to a man he hated and a woman he loved— that they should have had more faith in him.

Wonder of wonders, Amy was back. Divorced. Free to marry again. He had another chance to show her she'd been wrong. He was a nationally renowned litigator. He would soon be a partner at DeWitt & Blackthorne, which boasted 860 partners and associates. He was definitely *something*.

One of the female associates splashed Drew with the flat of her palms and said, "Hey, Drew! Want to race?"

Drew shot Luke a grin, turned to the young woman and said, "You bet!" A moment later, the two of them were splashing their way toward the other end of the pool.

Luke realized he'd better find Choate and tell her the bad news before he went to meet with Franklin DeWitt. The sooner he got all his business conducted, the sooner he could sneak out. He braced his arms on the edge of the pool and was shoving himself out, water streaming down his body and splattering against the colorful tile at his feet, when a great pair of legs appeared in front of him.

He looked up and saw it was Choate. She was wearing a thigh-length white terry cloth robe over a black racing swimsuit, but the robe was open in front and revealed a truly stunning figure.

Luke expected her to back up as he stood, but she stayed where she was—definitely in his space. He started to move sideways to give himself more room and realized his way was blocked by a young man with the whitest skin Luke had ever seen. He was narrow-chested and wore plaid bathing trunks that came all the way to his knees.

"Luke, I'd like you to meet Edward Arthur Mull the third," Choate said.

"Trip," Edward Mull said, extending his hand at the

same time as he pushed a pair of Harry Potter–like tor-
toiseshell frames up his nose.

"Nice to meet you," Luke said. The young man's
grip was surprisingly firm, and the smile he gave Luke
revealed a mouthful of very white, very even teeth.

"Trip comes to us from Harvard," Choate said. "You'll
be his supervising attorney."

Luke managed not to show his surprise as he turned
to survey Edward Arthur Mull III.

"I'll leave you two to get acquainted," Choate said.

Luke kept his gaze on Trip as the young man watched
Choate walk away. "Don't stare," he told the kid.

Trip jerked his head back around, his pale complex-
ion revealing the flush as it crept up his throat. "Sorry,"
he muttered. "She's . . ."

Luke grinned and finished, "Not what you expected?"

The kid grinned back. "Unbelievable was the word
that came to mind."

"In more ways than one," Luke agreed. "I'm going
to call you Eddie." He held up a hand to stave off
Eddie's protest. "To keep from confusing you with the
other two Trips I know at the firm."

He could see the twenty-four-year-old wasn't happy,
but that he wasn't going to complain. Good for him.
Better to learn from the outset that sacrifices had to be
made.

A very pretty, very pregnant redhead slid her arm
through Eddie's, and said, "Hi. I'm Mary Margaret
Mull."

Luke nodded. "Nice to meet you, Mrs. Mull."

"Oh, please, call me Mary Margaret." Her smile

took up most of her face. "Did I hear Ms. Choate correctly? Will you and Eddie be working together?"

"Yes, Eddie will be working for me." Luke wondered if she'd noticed the distinction.

She seemed oblivious and continued, "I'm so glad law school is done. Now we can start having a normal life."

Luke glanced from Mary Margaret to Eddie to see whether he was living in the same delusional world as his wife. He saw the troubled look in the young man's eyes as he watched Mary Margaret and realized Eddie had some inkling of the long hours he'd be expected to work, even if his wife didn't.

Luke wondered what had possessed the couple to plan a baby during Eddie's first year with D&B. The new associate wasn't going to be spending much time at home.

Luke had barely finished the thought when Mary Margaret patted her burgeoning belly and said, "We weren't planning a baby so soon, but my mom had a pool party over the summer and . . . " She grinned, sharing the humor of the situation with Luke. "Trip and I got a little carried away."

Luke saw Eddie wince at the revelation and tried to remember whether Valerie had ever been so naively candid. He had to admit he was finding the girl's bubbly honesty charming.

"Trip and I will save a seat for you at dinner," Mary Margaret said.

"I've already made other plans," Luke replied quickly. The last thing he needed was Mary Margaret Mull asking everyone where Luke was at suppertime.

"Well, it was nice meeting you," Mary Margaret said.

She turned and looked at her husband expectantly and Eddie said, "I'll see you on Monday, Mr. Creed."

Luke hesitated a second before he said, "Call me Luke." To hell with Choate's corporate section formality. He didn't have to demand the kid's respect. He was willing to earn it.

He watched the couple walk away, then searched the pool area for Choate. He found her stretched out on a lounge chair. The cover-up was gone. She'd added sunglasses and a broad-brimmed straw hat and was lathering suntan lotion on her arms.

He crossed to her, formulating what he was going to say as he watched her languid movements. "Ms. Choate," he said, to get her attention.

She handed him a bottle of Bain de Soleil and said, "I need some lotion on my shoulders, Luke. Would you mind?"

Luke managed not to jerk when their hands brushed as he took the white plastic bottle from her. His discomfort increased tenfold when he saw Drew smirking at him from the pool.

Choate had turned her back to him, and he squeezed some of the pink lotion into one hand and set the bottle beside her hip. He rubbed his hands together, then massaged the stuff onto Choate's shoulders and down her bare back. Her skin was warm from the sun and incredibly soft and smooth.

"There you go," he said, wiping his hands on his swim trunks in an attempt to rid himself of the exotic, feminine-smelling residue.

She handed him the bottle again and said, "A little more, please, lower down. Sit down, get comfortable."

Luke sat beside her, took more sunscreen, warmed it in his hands and applied it to Choate's lower spine. Her skin was supple and firm, and despite the absurdity of the situation, he found himself becoming aroused. He swiped on the last of it, then stood and said, "I wanted to give you an update on the Anastasio situation."

"There's a situation?" Choate asked as she settled back, put her feet up on the beach chair and crossed them at the ankle.

"Mrs. Anastasio owns Wholesome Foods. She has almost as much money as God. She doesn't intend to settle."

"You couldn't convince her how futile—"

"I spoke with her attorney. It was useless." Luke had already interrupted before he realized what he'd done. The head of litigation was used to his impatience. Choate was not, and it showed in the look she gave him.

"Try again," Choate said.

Luke knew better than to tell her it would be a waste of time. He'd make the second effort. But you couldn't get blood from a stone. He eyed her and thought, maybe dragons could.

"Do you know that young man?" Choate said, gesturing toward Drew DeWitt.

Luke made a face at Drew, trying to get him to swim away from the edge of the pool, but Drew remained there, grinning like a fool.

"That's Drew DeWitt," he said at last. "I worked with him in litigation."

"Tell him it's impolite to stare," she said, staring at Drew. Before Luke could turn, she rose and said, "Better yet, I'll tell him myself."

Luke stood paralyzed as Choate rose and headed toward the pool. To his amazement, Drew winked at him, then disappeared underwater. By the time Choate reached the spot where he'd been, he was at the other end of the pool. Luke didn't wait around to give Choate someone on whom to vent her spleen. He headed inside to change for his meeting with Franklin DeWitt.

Luke grimaced at his reflection as he combed his unruly brown hair. He needed a cut. His hair was hanging over his collar and curled over his ears. He could never find the time for appointments of any kind. He could barely manage the time to see his kids. Which reminded him he hadn't called Valerie yet.

He grabbed his cell phone, punched in her number and waited while it rang. And rang. "Damn it, Valerie. Pick up." She was notorious for shutting off the ringer and picking up her messages when she was damned good and ready. He heard her voice, low-pitched, southern, seductively asking him to leave a message.

"Valerie, I'm going to be a little late getting there. Go ahead and feed the kids dinner. I'll take them out for dessert."

He'd discovered he was able to communicate best with his daughters when they were busy eating. He could ask questions and they'd answer without focusing on how long it had been since they'd last seen him.

"Give me a call if there's a problem," he said, and

hung up. He realized he hadn't apologized for the inconvenience he was causing her, but he didn't want to call again just to say "I'm sorry."

He turned off his phone, because he didn't want it to ring while he was meeting with Franklin, then worried about what Valerie would do if she called and couldn't reach him. She was liable to leave for the evening and take the kids with her.

Valerie had remarried, and she and her husband Martin Hutchins, an accountant who fortunately hadn't had anything to do with Enron, lived in the modest home Luke had originally bought in The Woodlands. After the divorce, Luke had moved into the Commerce Towers downtown. If it weren't for the heat and humidity, he could have walked to work.

Housing and child support ate up the greatest part of his income, which didn't matter, because he didn't have time to spend what little remained. When he made partner, he'd earn a share of the profits of the firm, and his money worries would be over.

He headed for the bar and ordered himself a Dewar's straight up, then leaned against the polished mahogany waiting for Franklin to show up. He spied another friend of his from litigation, Nicole Maldonado, who gestured him over to her table.

"Hey, Nick," he said as he joined her. "What's up?"

She gestured with her drink, something green, gooey and girly, and said, "I'm trying to enjoy my drink in a place that reeks of testosterone."

Luke looked around and admitted the dark, heavy woods created an atmosphere that only needed cigar

smoke to make it intolerable to most women. Nicki
Maldonado had transferred in to the litigation section
three years ago from a Washington, D.C., firm, where
she'd specialized for the previous five years in antitrust
litigation. She worked even longer hours than Luke
did, both days of the weekend and most holidays.

He could see a surprising amount of cleavage above
what was supposed to be a conservative white tennis
dress trimmed in red, white and blue, which also
revealed a model-worthy pair of legs.

Nicki was very nearly beautiful but kept her auburn
hair cut boyishly short and wore Oxford cloth shirts
and pin-striped wool suits to the office, cut to conceal
her figure. He only knew she had breasts because in litigation they'd seldom worn jackets in the office, and
she was so generously endowed, there was no hiding it
in shirtsleeves. The male nickname was an attempt to
fit in, to be one of the boys.

Unfortunately, she was a woman in a firm that was
careful to keep its percentage of women who made
partner each year exactly equal to its percentage of
women in the firm—just thirty-three percent—when
the percentage of women enrolled in law schools was
well over fifty percent.

She was fighting an uphill battle. Having a male
nickname and hiding her breasts wasn't going to conceal her gender when partnership time came. He supposed that was why she worked longer and harder than
her male counterparts.

"You could have had your drink by the pool," he said
as he settled back in a captain's chair across from her.

"If I'm going to become one of the boys, I need to practice being one."

"You've got two years before—"

"Partnership is still a dream on the horizon," she admitted. "I just want to survive the cut next spring."

He took a sip of his drink and remembered what it had been like to worry and wonder each year whether the firm would inform him that he'd be better off seeking different employment. "How's your personal life?" he asked.

Nicki lifted a brow and quirked her lips into something that resembled a smile. "What personal life?"

"No boyfriend?"

"No time."

She met his gaze steadily as he perused her face. She looked tired, and she had wrinkles in her brow and bags under her eyes, even though he knew she was a year younger than he was. He also knew she'd never been married. At least he had his kids.

He glanced at his watch. It was already 6:10 and no sign of Franklin DeWitt. He'd be lucky to make it up to The Woodlands by 7:00.

"Who are you expecting?" Nicki asked.

"I'm supposed to meet Franklin DeWitt."

Nicki whistled. "Stepping up to the big boys, huh?"

"I have no idea why he wants to see me."

"Probably something to do with working for the Dragon Lady."

He shook his head. "Choate would be here if that were the case."

At that moment, Franklin DeWitt entered the bar

wearing a Western shirt cinched at the throat by a bolo tie, Wrangler jeans belted with a big silver buckle and alligator cowboy boots. It was only the young associates recruited by the firm from Eastern Ivy League schools who wore Izod shirts and docksiders. As they adopted Texas as their home, and moved up the ranks to partner, their attire became increasingly Western. Of course, DeWitt was the genuine article, born and bred in Texas.

"There you are," Franklin said as he crossed to Luke.

Luke rose and Franklin said, "Don't get up."

He joined them at the table, sitting down next to Luke. Luke glanced at Nicki and saw she was surprised, and pleased, to be included.

"You'll excuse us, won't you, Miss Maldonado?" Franklin said.

Luke saw Nicki's lips compress infinitesimally. She was a political animal. She wasn't going to make a scene. But he felt bad for her. Not only was she not being included, she was also being forced to get up and leave the table where she'd been sitting first. He stood when she did and said, "I'll catch up to you later."

Franklin DeWitt didn't even glance at her as she walked away. Luke focused his gaze on the managing partner and waited to hear why he'd been summoned.

"I wanted to ask how things are going since your transfer to corporate," Franklin said.

"Fine, sir," Luke replied.

"Choate's not working you too hard?"

Luke would have laughed if he hadn't caught himself. "Not too hard," he said with a smile.

"We need to keep Hyland happy."

"I'll do my best, sir," Luke said.

"Your best is damned good from what I hear."

Luke was astonished to hear such open praise. His annual associate review was always full of suggestions about how he could do better. "Th-thank you," he stuttered.

"We've had our eye on you for quite some time."

Luke felt gratified to hear that all the personal sacrifices he'd made had actually paid off.

"Ever since Harry Blackthorne inquired about you a couple of years ago."

Luke felt his skin prickle. "Harry Blackthorne?"

"Harry doesn't come in to the office anymore, but he's still a member of the firm. Ninety-two and still sharp as a Mexican spur."

Luke's heart was pounding in his chest. His ears felt hot and his throat was thick with fear and dread. He gripped the arms of the chair to still the sudden tremble in his hands and said, "I don't know the man. How does he know me?"

"Oh, he's Jackson's great—or maybe great-great uncle," Franklin said.

"Jackson *Blackthorne*?" Luke was feeling lightheaded. In his worst nightmares he'd never imagined anything like this.

"Yes. Your stepfather, isn't he?"

"Yes sir," Luke said. "He is." The blackguard. The bastard. The goddamned sonofabitch.

Luke fought back a wave of nausea. Had partnership always been a foregone conclusion? Had his stepfather arranged it from the beginning?

He felt rage building inside him—and an equally great despair. It dawned on him that Blackjack had never intended for him to know the truth. Franklin obviously hadn't realized Luke knew nothing of his stepfather's interference. He did his best to hide his agitation, but his whole body was quivering.

"That's it." Franklin rose and said, "You keep up the good work. See you at supper."

Luke was on his feet and shook Franklin's hand before the managing partner headed out of the bar. Luke had to sit down again, because his knees kept threatening to buckle.

How could he? How dare he? Why in God's name would he do such a thing?

A second later Choate appeared in the bar. "Did you have your meeting with Franklin?" she asked as she approached.

Luke rose on shaky legs. "Yes, ma'am." He was relieved to see she was dressed in a golf skirt and a sleeveless cotton blouse. "Although I'm not quite sure why he wanted the meeting."

"He was giving you a chance to complain about me," Choate informed him.

"I see."

Choate smiled at him. "I have a reputation as something of a dragon, in case you hadn't heard."

Luke managed to smile back. He didn't think it was politic to confirm the name she was called behind her back.

"It was a test, Luke. And you passed. If you'd complained, you'd be on your way back to litigation. And you could kiss your chances at partnership good-bye."

Luke sobered. So partnership wasn't a slam dunk? He had to *earn* it? Or was she just keeping Blackjack's dirty little secret along with everyone else?

He realized suddenly that he still wanted it. Goddamn it, he'd already earned it. He wasn't going to let a Blackthorne rob him yet again. He'd find a way to throw what his stepfather had done back in his interfering face—after he became a partner at DeWitt & Blackthorne.

Right now he had to stay calm. He had to stay cool. He had too many years invested, had made too many sacrifices. He'd been willing to pay the price, whatever it was, to become one of them. He still was.

"I'm depending on you, Luke, to handle this Hyland matter. Do we understand each other?"

Luke met her direct look with one of his own. "Yes, ma'am."

It seemed like Choate was telling him that even Blackjack's enormous influence couldn't buy her cooperation. He would have to get past her to earn a chance at the brass ring. And he would have to do it on his own.

He stared at her, wondering if his time working for this woman would end up being a blessing or a curse. Somehow, he had to find his way through the treacherous maze that ten other associates had failed to negotiate.

He remembered the feel of her skin under his hands and wondered again whether she might try to seduce him. And whether he would go along if she did.

"Time for supper," she said. "I think I'll get a drink to take with me. How about you?"

He held up the Dewar's, which he'd only sipped. "I'm fine." He wondered if he needed to wait for her, if he'd have to escort her to dinner and forgo his chance to escape.

"I'll see you in the office tomorrow," she said.

"Sunday," he corrected. "I'll be in on Sunday."

"I won't be in on Sunday," she said. "I'll see you on Monday, then."

Luke took advantage of the opportunity to get out. It was already 6:30. Damn. He hoped to hell Valerie hadn't taken the kids and gone somewhere. He hadn't seen Brynne or Midge since they'd headed to camp at the beginning of summer. He'd missed them, missed their laughter and their smiles.

He handed his ticket to the valet and stood behind a pillar where he was unlikely to be seen, but where he would still have a view of his Silverado when it appeared. Which was how he happened to see Nicki Maldonado and Justin Sterling get into the head of litigation's Mercedes together and drive away.

Luke frowned. He knew Nicki had driven herself to River Oaks, because she'd pulled in right before him. If they were going back to work to take care of some sort of emergency, why hadn't they gone in separate cars? So where were the two of them going? He was still watching when he saw Nicki lean over and kiss Justin on the cheek.

He ducked back behind the pillar and swore. Damn that bastard Sterling. He was a married man with three kids and a wife who sent brownies with him on weekends and holidays for the litigation associates who had to work. And what the hell was Nicki thinking?

Maybe she figured the bedroom was the only way to the boardroom. He didn't believe it. He wondered how long their relationship had been going on. They'd certainly hidden it well. He'd never suspected a thing.

The valet showed up with his truck, and for a moment Luke was tempted to follow them. But he had more important business. His kids were waiting for him.

As he sped along the freeway, Luke tried to imagine how much Brynne and Midge might have grown over the summer. He hoped they were looking forward to seeing him. He hoped he and Valerie didn't end up fighting. He just wanted this visit with the kids to be pleasant. That's all he wanted.

Shit. Valerie was going to be pissed. And the kids were going to feel the fallout. And he was going to be the bad guy. He just knew it.

5

There was bumper-to-bumper traffic heading north on the Hardy Toll Road caused by a minor accident in the left-hand lane, and by the time Luke reached his old house in The Woodlands, it was 7:30. He was an hour late. He hadn't called Valerie again because he knew she'd want to argue with him on the phone. He was counting on her to explain to the kids that he was working late. They'd be expecting it. He'd been late before.

But he always showed up. Always. He'd never missed picking them up once in the two years he and Valerie had been divorced. He treasured the little time he was able to spend with Brynne and Midge. He wasn't about to cheat himself out of any of it.

Luke noticed the double garage door was open and that the Volvo station wagon his wife drove was missing, while her new husband's black Porsche 911 was parked inside. He couldn't imagine Martin leaving the Porsche unattended, which meant he must be in the house. But where was Valerie? And had she taken the kids with her?

Oaks hung with silvery moss shaded the neighborhood and flowering dogwood, jack-in-the-pulpit, woodbine and ladyslippers grew in abandon. Or would have, left alone.

Every yard was manicured as often and as carefully as their owners' fingernails. Luke hadn't mowed or trimmed the vegetation in his own yard when he'd lived here and neither did anyone else. They hired someone to do it. The fathers were all too busy earning the mortgage and Porsche and private school payments, and the mothers were all too busy playing golf, tennis or bridge or volunteering for the PTA or some charity.

Between the time Luke left his air-conditioned car and the time he reached Valerie's front door, his armpits were soaked. Houston's humidity rarely got below 80 percent, and September was one of those months when folks pretty much dripped sweat all the time.

He hated the door chime Valerie's new husband had put in—it played an entire musical number—so he knocked hard on the closed door, anticipating the blast of frigid air-conditioned air when it was opened.

"Hey, Luke," Martin said through the screen door. "What's up?"

"I'm here to pick up Brynne and Midge."

"Oh. Valerie figured you forgot, since you haven't had them all summer. We had to cancel our dinner date with friends at Anthony's, since we hadn't arranged for a baby-sitter."

Luke heard the annoyance in Martin's voice. He couldn't really blame him.

"Where are the kids?" Luke asked.

"They were upset, as you might expect," Martin said. "So Valerie took them out for supper."

Luke clenched his fists in an attempt to hold onto his temper. "I left a message on her cell phone that I'd be late."

"The battery ran down. She's got it upstairs charging."

"And she didn't think to check for a message when I didn't show up?"

"Look, buddy," Martin said, "you're the one who was late. Brynne started crying, and you know how bad it is for her to get upset, and that started Midge to wailing. Valerie had to do something to distract them."

"She should have called me."

"She did," Martin said. "She got your voice mail."

Luke pulled his cell phone out of his pants pocket and realized he'd turned it off when he had his meeting with Franklin DeWitt and hadn't turned it back on. "Shit."

He pressed the buttons to pick up his voice mail and heard Valerie's angry voice saying, "Where the hell are you? I don't even have to guess. I know where you are — at the goddamned office. You don't deserve to have joint custody of these kids. You don't give a damn about them. The only thing you care about is your job. Don't bother coming over here tonight, because I've already told the girls you forgot about coming to pick them up!"

Luke pressed the end button. His heart rate was sky high and his stomach was churning. How could she be so cruel as to tell Brynne and Midge that he *forgot* about them? He was just *late*. There was a big goddamned difference!

He looked up and saw Martin leaning against the inside portal, his arms crossed. "I heard her leave the message," he said. "She was angry. What do you expect?"

"I expect—" Luke cut himself off. He wasn't going to have a conversation about his ex-wife with her new husband. What he did with his kids was between him and Valerie. He'd rather die in the heat than wait inside for them to return. "How long ago did they leave?" he asked.

"Actually, you just missed them."

"Where did they go?"

Martin shrugged. "I have no idea."

Luke made a disgusted sound, then turned and headed back down the walkway toward his car. He heard the front door click closed before he'd gone five feet.

Luke banged the hood of his truck with the flat of both hands in frustration. He could drive around The Woodlands to the places he and Valerie used to take the kids, or he could sit right here and wait. He was going to swelter unless he turned on the air, and if he was going to run the engine anyway, he might as well be driving around.

He headed straight for Chuck E. Cheese's. The girls loved pizza, and there were games there to keep them entertained. He had to wait for a mother and father to put a stroller in the trunk and belt their three kids into car seats before they could back out and make a parking space for him.

The restaurant was full on Friday night and echoed with the sound of shrieking, laughing and crying children, most of whom were racing around like wild monkeys let out of a cage. He took a quick walk around, circling the booth where they'd sat in the old days. But there was no sign of his ex-wife and kids.

Maybe Valerie had opted to have dessert first. They'd done that sometimes, going to Maggie Moo's for ice cream, making sure Brynne chose a sugar-free flavor. He had to leave his car in a no-parking zone while he ran inside. Maggie Moo's was smaller and less noisy, but no less crowded. He waded through the line of children clinging to their fathers' pants legs and babies tied in cloth carriers to their mothers' stomachs—to no avail. If Valerie had come here with the kids, they'd already gone.

He cruised around the Sonic, an old-time hamburger joint where you stayed in your car and they brought the food to you on roller skates. The upscale cars were full of teenagers who sat on each other's hoods and played loud music on their CD players and leaned out their windows and shouted at each other over Eminem and Britney.

He glanced at his watch: 8:15. Midge usually went to bed by 8:30, not that she ever fell asleep before midnight. Maybe he ought to head back to the house. But he was close to The Woodlands Mall, which was just across the street from Valerie's favorite Mexican restaurant, the Guadalajara Mexican Grille. At least he could be sure of getting a parking spot there.

By the time he got to the restaurant it was almost 9:00, and the nearby roads were congested with cars heading home from the mall. He realized he'd made a mistake not staying at Valerie's, but he was there, so he went inside.

The restaurant was Antarctically cold, and he shivered as the sweat turned to ice water on his flesh. He walked as fast as he could without running, feeling anxious, wanting his kids to be there with Valerie for more reasons than one.

If Valerie had already returned home, she could keep him out of the house when he got there, even if the kids were up. Or she could say they were already asleep, and he'd be none the wiser unless he wanted to make some noise, which he didn't.

On the other hand, if he met up with Valerie in a public place, she'd be less likely to make a scene. The kids had extra sets of clothes and toys and toothbrushes at his condo, so he could just take them and go.

He was trying not to give up hope, but when he scanned the crowd looking for Brynne and Midge's blond heads, he didn't see them.

And then he did.

Luke hurried toward a table in the back of the restaurant, hoping he wasn't mistaken. Suddenly, he realized why they were still there.

They weren't alone. They'd been joined at their table by an old friend of Valerie's from Bitter Creek.

Luke felt the breath catch in his chest as his eyes locked with Amy's. He could see it coming. He was going to end up having a fight with his ex-wife in front of his old girlfriend—the girlfriend with whom he was hoping to rekindle a relationship. He glanced at Valerie and noticed for the first time how much she and Amy looked alike, at least in superficial ways. Both blond, both blue-eyed, both beautiful.

But Valerie was wearing artfully applied makeup to disguise the fact that her eyes were a little too small and a little too close together and that her upper lip was almost nonexistent. One of the first things Luke had paid for was rhinoplasty to give her a nose she liked better, and since their divorce, she'd had her breasts enlarged.

To be honest, Amy could have used some blush. She looked like a wraith, and there were dark circles under her eyes he hadn't noticed earlier in the day. She'd eaten off the lipstick she'd worn to their meeting and was chewing on her lower lip, emphasizing the enticing bow of the upper. Her body was lithe rather than curvy, as Valerie's was. And her eyes, large and wide-spaced, look empathetic but wary.

Somehow he kept moving forward, stopping just in front of the table. By then, Brynne and Midge had seen him and came tumbling out of their chairs and ran toward him yelling, "Daddy! Daddy! Daddy!"

He went down on one knee and gathered them in, hugging them and kissing them and feeling their arms wrap tightly around his neck. They were choking him, but he didn't care. He felt the tears in his eyes and blinked them back, grinning because now all was right with his world. "Lord, you've both grown so much!" he choked out.

"Brynne! Midge! Come back here and sit down," an imperious voice commanded.

He felt his daughters' hesitation before they loosened their holds and glanced back at their mother. But he had his arms looped around their waists, and he wasn't about to let them go. He stood and took their hands in his and turned to face Valerie.

"I'm sorry I'm late," he said immediately.

"Your damned right you're—"

"Valerie," he said, his sharp tone cutting her off. He glanced at Amy, then back at Valerie. She glanced at Amy and realized that she was the one who would end up looking bad if they argued.

"Hello, Amy," Luke said. "I didn't realize you had plans to meet up with Valerie and the kids."

Amy shook her head. "Oh. No. We just happened to run into each other. It turns out Honor and Brynne go to the same school in The Woodlands. Brynne called out to Honor and I recognized Val and—" She shrugged and smiled. "It's a small world, I guess."

"A very small world," Valerie interjected. She met Luke's gaze, her blue eyes triumphant, and announced, "I've already arranged for Brynne to spend the night at Amy's."

"I don't get to go," Midge said. "'Cause I'm only six and Brynne and Honor are ten and they don't want me hanging around spoiling all their fun."

For the first time Luke noticed the pale, quiet child who sat tucked almost behind Amy.

"I haven't met your daughter," he said to Amy.

Amy slid a protective arm around the petite, blond-headed girl. "This is my daughter, Honor. Honor, this is Brynne and Midge's father, Mr. Creed."

"Hello, sir," the child said in a whispery voice.

Luke smiled, hoping to ease the girl's obvious discomfort. "I'm very glad to meet you, Honor."

"Can I go, Daddy?" Brynne said, looking up at him with eyes as dark as his own. "Please?"

"If she's going to Honor's house, can I stay with you?" Midge asked.

"No, Midge," Valerie said. "You're coming home with me."

"No, I'm not," Midge said firmly. "I'm going with Daddy."

Bless her, Luke thought. He knew better than to let his ex-wife see how glad he was his daughter wanted to be with him.

"Midge, don't argue with me," Valerie said. "I don't want to spend both Saturday and Sunday driving around Houston picking the two of you up from here, there and everywhere."

"I could drop Brynne off on my way to work tomorrow morning," Amy offered, "to save you the trip."

"Or better yet," Luke said, "Brynne and Honor could stay at my place with Midge, and I'll drop Honor off. I don't work on Saturdays when I have the kids."

"That's a good idea, Daddy," Midge said. "Then I get to play with Honor, too."

"Dad-dy," Brynne said, breaking the word into two parts so he would hear her disapproval. "Does Midge have to be around?"

"I don't think—"

Amy cut Valerie off, saying, "That's a wonderful idea, Luke. Honor will enjoy the night away from home, won't you, sweetheart?"

Luke thought Honor looked like she'd rather stand in a nest of rattlesnakes than come home with him. But

Amy leaned over and whispered in her ear, and Honor nodded solemnly and said, "Thank you, Mr. Creed. I would love to spend the night with Brynne at your house."

"Brynne and me," Midge piped up.

"Brynne and the brat," Brynne said under her breath.

"Then it's settled," Luke said. "I'll take all three girls tonight, drop Honor off at her house tomorrow morning, and bring the kids back on Sunday before I go to work, so you won't have any driving to do at all," he said to Valerie.

Valerie looked like she'd swallowed too much salt with her margarita. "You always get your way," she said. "I don't know why I bother arguing."

Luke figured the sooner he got the kids out of there, the better. "Do you want me to get the check?"

"We've already taken care of it," Amy said. "We were ready to leave when you showed up. You can follow me home to pick up an overnight bag for Honor."

Luke knew it was a big deal for Amy to trust him with her daughter. Surely if she'd taken that leap, she was going to agree to have dinner with him on Sunday. And he still had the trip to pick up Honor's overnight bag and the meeting when he dropped Honor off tomorrow morning to look forward to.

Brynne and Honor walked ahead of them while Midge followed right behind the other two girls trying to listen, trying to be a part of their conversation, as they headed across the parking lot to Amy's car.

"Midge is six going on sixteen," Luke said to Amy to break the silence that had fallen between them.

"Your daughters are lovely, Luke."

"Thanks. And thank you for what you did back there. Valerie would have kept Midge with her for spite. I haven't seen the kids since the middle of June. I've missed them. They're growing up so fast!"

"I was thinking of them when I agreed to let Honor spend the night," Amy said. "They were both pretty upset when they came into the restaurant with Valerie."

Amy's kindness and consideration of others was one of the things he'd always liked best about her. She'd always befriended the girl who was a little too odd to be a part of the crowd. Always been nice to the homely boy who couldn't get a date. He'd never been able to match her thoughtfulness, but her example had made him want to try.

In his favorite memory of Amy, she stood beside his Harley, a grin on her face and a wrench in her hand, her cheek smudged with grease. She'd spent her baby-sitting money to purchase a chain-link chrome bracket for his license tag. And she'd borrowed a wrench from the local gas station to attach it herself. He thought that was the moment he'd fallen in love with her.

Luke glanced at her now, as she trudged across the parking lot, and noticed the uncharacteristic droop of her shoulders. "You look like a horse somebody rode hard and put away wet."

She made a face and said, "Thanks a lot."

He laughed. "Most lawyers I know look tired. If they didn't work long hours, they wouldn't last long. I didn't think smaller firms ran their lawyers ragged."

"It's not work, it's . . ."

"What?" Luke prompted.

"Personal."

He wondered what was going on that she didn't think she could share with him. If she wasn't tired from work, what was it? He felt a sudden tension. Could there be another man in her life? "Is there someone else?"

"What?"

"Another man?"

"Oh, no. Nothing like that." She focused her eyes on the girls, not meeting his gaze. He didn't want to push. But he was curious. And concerned.

She wasn't talking.

They reached her car, an older Honda, and Luke wondered who her divorce attorney had been. It didn't look like she'd done too well. "Do you want to give me directions, or do I need to follow you?"

"You might want to follow me," she said. "It's not far, but it's not easy to find."

"I'll get my wheels and be right back." His pickup was only parked a short distance away.

Before he'd taken two steps, he heard Brynne and Midge arguing.

"I don't want to sit in front," Midge said. "I want to sit in back with you and Honor."

"Well, you can't," Brynne said. "We want to be by ourselves."

"You're being mean," Midge accused.

"You're being a baby," Brynne shot back.

Luke stepped in and said, "Midge, why don't you ride with me? Otherwise, I'm going to be all alone."

Midge shot her sister a smug look. "I'm going to ride with Daddy. So there."

Luke glanced at Amy and got a smile and a look of parental sympathy before he took Midge's hand and turned back toward his pickup.

He made sure Midge was buckled in, then followed Amy out of the parking lot. "How was camp?" he asked Midge.

"I wrote you a letter. Didn't you get it?"

He'd received the "letter," a postcard in Midge's bold baby printing that said, *Dear Daddy, I'm at camp. Love, Midge.* "I got it, pumpkin. Thanks. I just wondered if you liked going to camp."

This was the first year Midge had gone to Camp Tuckahoe in Georgia, the fourth year for Brynne. Midge had been begging to go for two years but hadn't been old enough until this past summer.

"I liked the plane ride to get there," Midge said. "And I liked swimming and making things. I made you a lan . . . a len . . . a thing that goes around your neck."

"A lanyard," he said. "That's great. Is it at home?"

"I don't know where it is. I thought I packed it, but I couldn't find it when I got home. I'm sorry, Daddy."

"That's okay. You can make me another one next year."

"Mommy said we're not going to camp next year."

He kept his voice measured and said, "Why not?"

"She says we're going to stay home and take tennis lessons."

"Tennis? Your mom doesn't play tennis."

"She says we have to play tennis to meet the right sorts of people."

Luke knew Midge was parroting what she'd heard. It sounded like something Valerie would say. His ex-wife had come a long way from the small town of Bitter Creek, Texas, and it seemed she wanted Brynne and Midge to take her even farther.

"What do you want to do?" he asked his daughter.

"I like camp."

"Then you'll go to camp."

"But Mommy—"

"I'll talk to your mom," he said. "And we'll work it out."

He'd been focused on Midge and had kept Amy's taillights in front of him. He noticed they'd headed into one of the neighborhoods in The Woodlands. Maybe the reason Amy didn't have a newer car or better quality clothes was because she'd taken her settlement from the divorce and put it into a nice house, Luke thought.

But they didn't stop at any of the million-dollar homes in The Woodlands. They followed the winding roads around to an apartment complex at the rear of Grogan's Landing.

Luke shook his head when Amy parked and got out of her car. She must have gotten shafted in the divorce settlement, he thought. He pulled up beside her, and Midge bounced out of the car and went running to catch up to the two older girls.

He followed Amy and waited while she unlocked the door to a small apartment. Why had she settled for so little? What had happened between her and Carl Nash, the successful orthopedic surgeon?

"Things aren't as neat as I like them," she apologized.

The girls hurried inside and down the hall to what he presumed was Honor's bedroom.

Amy grabbed at some newspapers strewn on the couch and dropped a bedroom pillow onto the floor, then picked up a blanket and folded it. He was still absorbing the fact that she must sleep on the couch when she headed into the kitchen and said, "Can I get you something to drink?"

"Iced tea would be great. Or water if you don't have any."

"I've got tea," she said.

He couldn't help seeing what was in the cupboard when she opened it to get him a glass. Not much. "What happened, Amy? How did that bastard get away without paying you enough to live on?"

She turned to face him, clutching the glass against her chest. "That subject is off-limits," she said. "Completely and totally off-limits."

"I can't think of any scenario where a judge wouldn't make him pay enough so you could afford a bedroom of your own," Luke persisted.

Amy paled. "Leave it alone, Luke."

"I'm curious how he managed it. I pay a big chunk of my salary to Valerie to support the girls."

She stared at him, her eyes stark. "The tea's in the fridge. Help yourself. I need to help Honor pack."

He stared after her as she hurried past him. He wondered if she regretted the choice she'd made all those years ago. She'd been so sure she'd be better off without him. Especially after what had happened between them the night of the senior prom.

He'd pushed too hard, she'd given in and before their labored breathing had returned to normal in the front seat of his brother's pickup, she'd regretted it.

Where seventeen-year-old Amy Hazeltine was concerned, there was right and there was wrong, and they were as different as black and white. She'd wanted some reassurance, some word of affection from him after giving him her virginity. He hadn't been able to say what she'd wanted to hear. And that had put him in the wrong.

"I need someone who can love me back, Luke. You're too busy hating the world to love anyone," she'd accused.

"I don't hate the whole world," he'd shot back. "Just Jackson Blackthorne and that bitch wife of his who got away with murdering my father and calling it an accident."

He'd figured he had good cause to be angry. Blackjack had come courting Luke's mother before his father was even cold in the ground.

"I can't do this anymore, Luke," Amy had said. "I'm going on with my life. I'm going to find someone who can make me happy. Someone who cares. Because you don't. Or won't."

He'd been hurt beyond words, seventeen and so full of himself—and mad at the world—that he'd shot back, "I sure as hell don't need you, either. Go. See if I care. Because I don't!"

He'd spent the past decade trying to prove he wasn't

the loser she'd labeled him—a rebel not only without a cause, but without the sense to know he didn't have one. In the dark, he'd dreamed of the day their paths would cross again. She'd take one look at the man he'd become—happily married, a devoted father, a partner in the largest law firm in Texas—and be damned sorry she'd let him get away.

Well, that day had arrived.

He wasn't quite the prize he'd hoped to be. A divorced husband, a part-time father and a year away from partnership—maybe. But he only had to look at her to know he'd let the love of his life get away.

Amy reappeared in the kitchen and said, "Honor's ready when you are. I see you found the tea."

He rattled the ice in the glass and drank the last of the tea he'd poured for himself. "Yes, thanks."

"Would you like some more?" she said, reaching for the refrigerator door.

"No, this is fine." He set the glass on the counter and searched for something he could ask her that would prolong his visit.

"Do you like practicing law?" he asked.

He saw the tension leave her shoulders when she realized he wasn't going to ask a more personal question.

"I love it," she said. "I think I've found my calling."

"I'm amazed a firm like Hardy, Christian would assign such an important case to a new associate. How did you end up representing Mrs. Anastasio?"

"I'm good at what I do," Amy said. "But you're right. They didn't give the case to me. I brought it to them."

"How did that happen?"

"Rosa and Honor met at school and became best friends."

"That must have been hard on Honor, losing a friend like that."

"It was," Amy said. "Honor spent the night with Rosa on her birthday. She was the one who discovered Rosa in a coma and woke up Mrs. Anastasio."

"That's tough."

"I knew Rosa, Luke. She was a responsible child. She didn't misuse that drug. There's something wrong with it."

"How much cake did Rosa eat at her birthday party? How much soda pop did she consume? How much ice cream? How much candy?"

"She might have eaten a few extra sweets. But if the drug is that unpredictable—"

"It wasn't the drug," Luke said. "The drug is safe."

"How can you be so sure?" Amy said. "Drugs have side effects that don't become known until they're in wide use."

"Four deaths isn't enough—"

"One death is too many!" Amy countered. "What if it had been your daughter who died?"

"Thank God, it wasn't." Ever since Brynne had been diagnosed with Type I diabetes, Luke had avoided thinking about all the complications from the disease that could shorten his daughter's life. Medical advances were being made every day. Promising stem-cell research was being done that might one day help Type I diabetics begin producing insulin on their own.

"Daddy, I have to go home."

Luke turned to find Brynne standing at the kitchen door with Honor on one side and Midge on the other.

"Why is that, sweetpea?" he asked.

"I don't have my D-Free."

Luke frowned. "What did you say?"

"I don't have my D-Free."

"Your mother and I agreed you weren't going to use D-Free."

"It's great, Daddy. No more shots! I've been using it all summer."

"All summer?" Amy asked in a sharp voice.

Luke turned to Amy and realized her face had paled.

"How have you been feeling, Brynne?" Amy asked. "Have you had any nausea? Any vomiting?"

"What?" Brynne asked, her brow bunched in confusion.

"I think Mrs. Nash is asking if you've been sick this summer," Luke said.

"Huh-uh," Brynne said.

"Any tingling in your fingers?" Amy reached for Brynne's hand and spread her fingers, pressing the tips to see if the blood flowed easily.

"No," Brynne said, jerking her hand free.

"Any breathlessness? Loss of balance?" Amy asked.

"No, Mrs. Nash. I feel fine."

Luke realized Amy had recited every symptom the parents of D-Free victims had listed as occurring in the days and weeks preceding their children's deaths. He'd been more upset with Valerie for putting Brynne on the drug without consulting him than concerned by the fact that Brynne was taking D-Free—until he saw how distressed Amy was.

Even so, there was more irritation than alarm in his voice as he said, "I can't believe your mother changed your medication without consulting me."

"I love D-Free, Daddy," Brynne said. "I haven't had to take a shot for three whole months. I feel . . . normal. Lots of kids have to take pills at school."

Luke hugged his daughter. He knew how she hated the shots, because they reminded her every few hours that she was a sick person. "It sounds wonderful, all right, sweetpea."

"So you see why I have to go home," Brynne said.

"I'm sorry, honey," he said. "It's too late to trek back over to your mom's house now. I've got some needles—"

"No!" Brynne said. "I'm not giving myself a shot. I don't take shots anymore. I won't do it, Daddy. And you can't make me!"

He could, of course. He had, in days gone by when she'd been younger and hadn't wanted a shot and had needed one. He focused his gaze on her, willing her to see why a trip back home wouldn't be a good idea.

"Oh, all right," Brynne said. "If I have to take shots to see you, I will. So can we go now?"

Luke noticed that Honor had a cloth bag slung over her shoulder. "You're all packed?" he asked.

"All packed," she replied in the whispery voice.

"I guess we're ready, then," Luke said, turning to Amy. "I'll drop Honor off here after breakfast. Will you still be here, or will you have a baby-sitter waiting?"

"I'll stay till you arrive," she said.

"We'll be here by nine."

Amy looked him in the eye and said, "I won't plan to leave the house before nine-thirty."

Luke gave her a lopsided grin. "I'll try to be here on time."

"I'll believe it when I see it."

"I might surprise you," he said. "By the way, how about dinner on Sunday? Are we on?"

She made a face, and he said, "Pretty please?"

She smiled and shook her head. "You know I can't refuse when you say please."

Luke met Amy's gaze and said, "It's getting late. We can work out the details about Sunday when I drop Honor off tomorrow morning."

"Sure, Luke." Amy met Honor halfway and gave her daughter a hug. "Have a good time, honey."

"I'll try, Mom."

Luke thought it seemed like a strange thing for a little girl to say. But he was too busy getting the three girls out the door, and still mulling over the disturbing fact that Valerie had been making decisions affecting his daughter's welfare without talking to him, to think much about it.

Despite Amy's alarm, he believed D-Free was safe. But Valerie shouldn't have arranged for Brynne to take it without consulting him first. He was still Brynne's father. Decisions affecting the girls were supposed to be made jointly. Tonight, after the kids were in bed, he and Valerie were going to have a very long, very serious talk.

6

"Hey, Dragon Lady, wanta fuck?"

Grayson Choate had answered the knock on her kitchen door in the dark. She was barefoot, wearing a full-length V-neck aqua silk nightgown held up by spaghetti straps, with revealing black lace across the bodice. She grabbed a knot of fabric on the young man's Izod shirt and pulled him inside, slamming the door behind him.

One of his hands caught her breast, the other crossed around her and clasped her buttocks, their bodies careening together at the hip as his mouth opened over hers.

She arched her body toward him, feeling the painful pleasure as he twisted her nipple, the rock-hard arousal pressed against her belly. His tongue was in her mouth, and she tasted the peach pie and coffee they'd served for dessert at River Oaks.

She reached for his shirt with both hands to pull it out of his khaki trousers and broke the kiss long enough to get it up over his head. His blond hair stood in spikes and his avid eyes, gleaming in the moonlight, told her he wanted her, that he could hardly wait to be inside her.

She feasted on him with her eyes, touched him with her hands, loving the feel of hard muscle beneath firm, tanned skin. She heard his indrawn breath as her fingernails crested his nipples and dug into the crisp blond curls on his chest.

His hands moved to her shoulders and caressed them. "You're a cock tease, lady," he said in a husky voice. "I thought I was going to come right there in the pool when you had Luke smear that lotion all over you."

She looked up into his eyes and laughed. "I thought you might enjoy that."

"You've got the poor guy wondering if you're going to jump his bones."

She arched a brow. "I could if I wanted to."

"But you won't," he said, his voice low and rough. "Because you're mine."

Grayson bit back the retort that she belonged to no man. She wouldn't have been able to voice it in any case, because he'd claimed her mouth again, his tongue thrusting inside, hard and wet, mimicking the sex act.

He broke the kiss this time and picked her up in his arms, heading for the upstairs bedroom, knowing his way in the dark, because he'd done it so many times before.

She laced her arms around his neck, letting her fingers enjoy the texture of the soft curls at his nape. She laid her head on his shoulder, surrendering completely, allowing him to act the part of the caveman hauling his woman off to stake his claim on her.

She'd left a small light on in her bedroom because she liked seeing the desire in his eyes, liked to watch what they did together. He let her feet drop to the plush carpet but kept his arms around her, pinning her breasts against his naked chest.

"When are you going to tell people about us?" he said.

She stiffened. They'd had this discussion occasionally over the past year, but he'd brought it up three or four times in the past two months. "You know why we have to keep what we have between us to ourselves," she said, her hand sliding down to caress him through his trousers.

He caught her wrist and moved it away, then grabbed a handful of her hair and pulled her head back, forcing her to look up at him. "Tell me again."

"Can't we discuss this later?"

"Later you'll have what you want from me and you'll tell me to leave."

She leaned her cheek against his chest, and his fingers sieved through her hair in what became a caress. She'd never admitted she cared for him. If he'd been more sure of her feelings, he would have pushed harder, pushed sooner, for some public declaration of their relationship.

She simply couldn't allow that.

She knew how the two of them would be viewed by her peers. He was eighteen years younger than she was. While that age difference was considered acceptable when the man was the elder, she'd be labeled a cradle robber. She'd become a laughingstock.

And he'd be labeled a boy toy. It was for his sake as much as hers that she wanted what happened between them to remain private. He was a good man. And a good lover. She didn't want to have to break up with him, but she would do it, if necessary, to save him from himself.

"You know what they'd say about me," she said. "And about you."

"I don't care, Gray," he said. "I love you. I want to marry you."

She jerked away, and he let her go. It hurt to know that loving him was impossible. She hadn't let herself love anyone in a very long time, and she wasn't going to start now. Especially someone so unsuitable. If only she were younger. Or if only he were older. Maybe then she'd be able to let down her guard. Maybe then she'd be able to let herself care.

Amazing how an incident in her life that had happened so long ago could come back to haunt her. It was her secret. Would remain her secret. She'd made the choice thirty years ago never to marry. She'd had good and solid reasons for her decision. Why was she questioning them now? Why had she begun to imagine herself with this young man, who was so inappropriate?

She turned to face him, her arms crossed over her chest defensively. "I don't want to fight with you."

"I don't want to fight with you, either," he said. "But I'm tired of hiding my car in your garage, coming in the back door at midnight and leaving before the sun rises. I want to wake up with you in the morning. I want to be the one rubbing sunblock on your shoulders in front of God and everybody."

"You'd have to leave the firm," she said. "And you're only a year—"

"To hell with the firm. I never needed it. I only need you."

He crossed the distance between them in two strides and grasped her arms, holding her so tight she was afraid she'd have bruises to hide. "Say you'll marry me, Gray. I need you in my life."

I need you in my life. It was an incredible thing for any man to say. More incredible to hear it from this young man, because he could have any woman he wanted. He was so wealthy, so handsome, so smart. She admired everything about him, even his ruthlessness in pursuit of what he wanted. She'd seen him in the courtroom. She'd seen him with the women he used as camouflage to hide his relationship with her.

"Why me?" she challenged. "Why someone too old to give you children? Why someone who'll sag and wrinkle long before you do?"

He smiled at her, a tender smile that made her heart clutch. She felt his hold on one arm loosen, felt his knuckles brush her cheek.

"Do you have any idea how special you are?" he said. "One in a million. One in a gazillion."

She turned her head away, then took a step back to separate them. "You haven't answered my questions."

"I don't want children," he said.

"Why not?" she pressed.

"I don't want the responsibility for molding someone else's life. It's too easy to make a mistake."

Her brow furrowed as she searched his face for clues

to what had made him so leery of becoming a parent. He'd never talked about his family. She knew from his personnel records at D&B that he'd named a sister, Samantha, as his next of kin for notification in case of an emergency. But that didn't tell her what she wanted to know.

"You seem to have turned out all right," she said. "Are you saying someone made a mistake with you?"

His mouth clamped into a thin, bitter line.

She waited him out.

At last he said, "There's nothing in my background that would give me an Oedipus complex, if that's what you're wondering. I love you because you're you, Gray. Your age only makes you more attractive to me."

"When you're my age, I'll be seventy-one," she pointed out. "It's absurd to think you'd want to be with me."

"Older men have younger wives. Nobody thinks that's absurd."

She made an irritated sound in her throat. "You're being purposely obtuse. Why not someone younger?"

"Why not you?" he countered. "You're beautiful."

She waved a hand dismissively.

He reached out and caught it, then reached for her other hand and held them to keep her from moving farther away. "You're beautiful," he repeated. "You're smart. You're respected and accomplished at what you do. You're a wonderful lover, giving and loving . . . and adventuresome."

She felt the blush heat her cheeks and lowered her eyes.

"Look at me, Gray."

He waited for her to look up at him. When she did, he said, "This age thing is just . . . it's not important. Not to me."

"Maybe not to you. It will be to everyone else."

"To hell with them," he said. "To hell with the rest of the world."

"That attitude doesn't work for me."

"We can be happy together, Gray. I know it. Please—"

She freed her right hand and put her fingertips against his lips to cut him off. "I'll think about it."

He kissed her fingertips, his eyes bright with hope and happiness.

She pulled her hand away. She was going to have to break up with him soon. He wasn't going to be put off much longer. But she'd bought some time. He wouldn't leave right away. She could enjoy him a little longer.

"Make love to me, Drew. Please."

There was another thing she liked about Drew DeWitt. He attacked everything he did with enthusiasm, including making love to her. He had the gown off her in two seconds flat, hopped on one foot as he tore the docksiders off his feet and threw them across the room, then unbuckled his belt, unsnapped and unzipped his trousers and pulled them down along with his shorts and kicked them away.

He stood before her naked, his body hard and ready. She felt her own body quiver in response. He took his time looking at her, and she felt her pulse begin to thrum. He eased the straps off her shoulders and the nightgown slid down her body and pooled at her feet.

He ran the flat of his hand down the center of her all

the way to her pubis. She spread her legs instinctively, making room for his hand as it moved between her thighs.

Her head fell back as he slid a finger inside her, then joined it with another. He kissed her ears, her throat, her breastbone, before his mouth finally latched onto her breast, suckling strongly, as his hand worked inside her.

Her hands were not idle. She touched him everywhere except where she knew he wanted her most. Teasing. Promising pleasure beyond belief. Offering glimpses of ecstasy.

Her knees were threatening to buckle, and she whispered, "I want to hold you. I want to taste you."

He made a guttural sound in his throat and let go of her, standing back to look at her, his eyes glazed with passion.

She slowly dropped to her knees before him and took him in her mouth. It was a gift. Something she'd never done before. An acknowledgment of caring that she would never voice aloud. He made a surprised sound as her hand clasped him and moved along with her mouth to bring him to climax.

"Gray," he gasped, his hands clutching her hair. "Gray, don't—Wait—"

But it was too late. She swallowed the cum, the taste salty, the joy of what she'd done sweet.

When she finally released him, he grabbed her arms and pulled her to her feet, his arms surrounding her so tightly she could hardly breathe.

"Gray, sweetheart, baby," he rasped in her ear. "God. I never . . . I can't believe . . ."

She realized he knew her too well. Knew that to put herself on her knees for any man was an admission of something she never should have admitted.

"Come to bed with me," he whispered. "I want to make love to you. I want to spend the night with you. Just tonight. Please, baby."

Baby. The word should never have been used to address a fifty-three-year-old woman, but she cherished the sound of it. Drew made the years fall away, helped ease the bite of regret for the youth she'd squandered behind a desk at D&B.

"All right," she whispered back. "Just tonight."

Tomorrow was Saturday. She would let him stay till the sun came up. They could make love in the daylight for the first time.

It would be a fitting end to their affair.

"Come to bed, Drew," she murmured in his ear.

She could feel he was aroused again. Ah, the delight of loving a younger man.

—~—

Nicki Maldonado had Stage II breast cancer. She'd found the lump while in the shower several months ago but had put off seeing a doctor. She'd been too scared to find out the truth. Her mother had died of breast cancer. Nicki had been terrified at the thought of following in her mother's footsteps. She dreaded becoming a victim of the same disease because she knew what it meant to suffer from cancer.

Nicki shuddered. Cancer wasted your body. It stole

your soul. You could fight all you wanted, rail against fate, pray to an unmerciful God. None of it did any good. In the end, you died. At least, her mother had.

The doctor wanted to do a lumpectomy to remove the 2.5-centimeter growth, followed by radiation— assuming the cancer was still confined to her breast. The chances were good, nearly 90 percent, that she'd beat the cancer if there was no lymph node involvement. But Nicki had to act now. She couldn't wait another week. She couldn't wait another day, the doctor warned. Not if she wanted to survive this disease.

Nicki had left the doctor's office today and gone straight back to work. She'd scheduled the appointment for lunchtime and hadn't told anyone where she was going. She hadn't used her firm health insurance card—and wouldn't—because she didn't want anyone at D&B to know she was sick. Sick associates didn't become partners. She wouldn't even make it past the spring cut, if the truth became known.

Oh, they wouldn't blame her release on illness. They'd merely find enough wrong with the quality of her work to indicate she wasn't going to make partner if she stayed. They'd suggest she might be happier somewhere else, where her hours wouldn't be as long, and she'd have more time to take care of herself.

Damn, damn, damn! It wasn't fair. She'd spent five years working at Bailey, Wise, Stockton, Hargraves & Kale in D.C. before she'd moved up to D&B, where she'd slaved for the past three years. She wanted a slice of the partnership pie. She'd earned it. She'd given her whole life to the law. She had no husband, no children, no interests. There was no time for any of them.

Which was why she'd let herself be persuaded into bed by Justin Sterling when he'd started sniffing around her two years ago. She knew the dangers of having an affair with someone in the workplace. But she'd been lonely and knew she'd never find the time to develop a real relationship.

Justin was tall and lean and wore a mustache that made him resemble Tom Selleck. He was smart and quick-witted and amusing. And married.

She'd figured she'd enjoy the sex without having to worry about catching a social disease. She hadn't counted on falling in love with him, hadn't counted on an affair that had gone on. And on. She was lonelier than ever, because she spent the few holidays she took off work all by herself, knowing Justin was home with his wife and family.

She'd tried, but she hadn't been able to give him up. He was all she had. And now, maybe all she ever would have.

They'd left the firm picnic for an hour yesterday to take care of an emergency at the office. She'd wanted him to take her to bed, wanted him to hold her and reassure her after the devastating news she'd received that afternoon. He'd been furious when she'd leaned over in the car and kissed his cheek.

"Goddammit, Nicki. What if someone saw that?" He'd glanced in his rearview mirror and said, "It looks like we were lucky this time. Don't ever do that again. Do you hear me?"

She'd been hurt. And angry. She could have broken up with him in that instant.

He must have realized how upset she was, because within the next couple of minutes he'd pulled his Mercedes to the side of the road beneath a live oak, taken her into his arms and said, "Saturday afternoons are all I can give you, Nicki. I'm sorry, but that's the way it is. Do you still want me to come to your apartment tomorrow afternoon?"

It would have been the perfect moment to break it off. The perfect moment to end a dead-end relationship. But she'd already committed to having part of one breast removed, and if the disease couldn't be stopped, if it followed the same course it had with her mother, she could expect to lose both breasts. No man would want to look at her, much less make love to her. She was afraid to give up what she had with Justin, for however long she might have it.

"Come tomorrow," she'd said at last. "I need you to hold me."

He'd kissed her quickly on the mouth, then started up his engine. They'd met with a distraught client, James Russo, at the office, reassured him his case was on track and arrived back at the firm picnic in time to have dessert.

That was yesterday.

Nicki had tried to tell Justin about the cancer this afternoon, after they'd made love in the bed in which she now lay staring at the ceiling. But he'd started talking about the Russo case, and how he wanted her to be sure to file a cross-complaint next week. How losing

Luke Creed to the Dragon Lady sucked. How his wife of twenty-six years was going to fat.

He'd stopped long enough at that point to kiss her flat belly, to run his hands along her long, trim legs, to cup her generous breasts—one of which would soon be pitted and scarred—in his hands. But he remained unaroused. It took longer these days for him to recover. Neither of them mentioned it.

He laid his hand across her belly and started talking again. About how his son Trey had made the Rice varsity football team as a sophomore, which meant Justin wouldn't be seeing as much of her. Because, of course, he had to be there for his son. Instead of coming to her apartment on Saturday afternoons, he would be attending his son's football games.

He hadn't said he was ending their affair. But the only time he'd been able to carve out for her when his wife wouldn't be suspicious was Saturday afternoons. So did he want a hiatus for the length of football season? Or had he been saying good-bye without saying it?

Nicki hadn't been able to share her fears with him, her utter devastation at the confirmation that she had cancer. Which had brought home to her the shallowness of their relationship. She was probably lucky his son had made the football team. She might have wasted a great deal more of her precious time—and God knew how much of it she had left on this earth—with him.

He'd walked out the door at 4:15, because he had to be home by 5:00. It was 10:30, and she hadn't yet gotten up to shower or change the sheets, which she did religiously after every Saturday encounter. It was bad enough missing Justin during the week. She didn't want the smell of him on her bed linens reminding her she was alone.

Nicki rolled over and picked up the phone from the bedside table. She stared at the numbers, which blurred as her eyes filled with tears, wondering who she could call that would give a damn.

She hit #1 on her speed dial and waited while the phone rang. "Hey, Luke," she said. "What's up?"

"Not much. What can I do for you?"

Nicki hesitated, then said, "Can I come over?"

"Now? Brynne and Midge are here."

"But they're in bed, right? So we can talk?"

"What's going on, Nick? Are you all right?"

She could hear the concern in his voice. Tears burned her nose, and a lump rose in her throat. She was tempted to blurt everything out over the phone, but she didn't think that was fair to him. She needed some advice, and he was the best friend she had. "Yes," she whispered past her constricted throat. "Now."

"Come on over," he said. "I'll be waiting."

"Be there in fifteen." Nicki hung up the phone and jumped out of bed. She threw on some Levi's and a new Texans T-shirt with the red, white and blue steer logo, then added socks and well-worn cowboy boots.

She lived in the Post Rice Lofts, the old Rice Hotel downtown that had been renovated and turned into apartments, just four city blocks from Luke. She decided to walk, even though it wasn't completely safe this late at night. Hell, when you were gambling with cancer, why not play the odds against getting mugged?

Nicki didn't wait for the streetlights to change, just watched the traffic and ran when it was clear. She felt relieved when she was inside the Commerce Towers, and gave her name to the concierge, who was expecting her.

Luke lived on the seventh floor. When she'd asked why he hadn't gotten a place higher up with a view, he'd said, "The seventh floor is as high as a fire ladder can reach. If anything happens, I want to be sure my girls can get out."

After 9/11, his choice made even more sense.

Nicki took the stairs, which was quicker than waiting for the elevator to make its way back down twenty-five floors. She was breathless by the time she reached Luke's door. She knocked and waited. Was she really going to tell him about her cancer? What if he told someone at the firm? What if—

"Hey, Nick. Come on in."

Luke stepped back as she entered and closed the door behind her. "Can I get you something to drink? Coffee? Something stronger?"

"Nothing right now," she said.

"Have a seat at the breakfast bar. I could use a cup of coffee."

She sat on one side of the bar that separated his kitchen from the living room, while he crossed into the kitchen, got a misshapen turquoise blue ceramic mug from the cupboard and poured himself a cup of coffee from a Mr. Coffee machine.

"Cheers," he said before he sipped it black. He smacked his lips, then set the mug down and leaned over the bar. "Now, what's so important that you had to come over this late at night to tell me about it."

She made a face. "I don't really know how to tell you this."

"If this is about you and Justin Sterling—"

"How on earth could you possibly—"

"I saw the two of you get into his car at River Oaks yesterday. I saw you kiss him."

"Oh," So they hadn't escaped detection.

"How long have the two of you been seeing each other?"

"Two years." His mouth was still open in shock when she said, "But I don't think he and I will be—"

"If that bastard Sterling got you pregnant—"

"I have cancer," she blurted. And then burst into tears.

She'd covered her face with her hands, so she didn't see Luke come around the bar, but she felt his arms around her, holding her, hugging her, rocking her while she cried.

She heard a child's voice say, "What's going on, Daddy? Why is Nicki crying?"

And Luke's answer, "Nicki just got some bad news, Midge. She'll be fine. Go back to bed." A pause and then, "You heard me. Go. And don't wake up your sister."

Nicki heard the sound of small, bare feet padding on the wooden floor and Luke saying, "Close your door, Miss Nosybody. We want to do some talking out here—in private."

And finally, Midge's muffled "Sheesh," and the snap of a door latch catching.

"That kid is the lightest sleeper I've ever seen," Luke said. "I think she could hear an ant walk across her pillowcase."

Nicki smiled through her tears at the image he'd conjured, then took the two Kleenex Luke handed her from a box on the end of the bar and blew her nose.

He pulled up a bar stool beside her and sat on it, put his hands on his knees and said, "Now, tell Papa all about it."

"Don't make fun of me, Luke. There's nothing remotely funny about having cancer."

He leaned back and crossed his arms. "I never said there was. I'm trying to be a friend. I just don't have much experience with this sort of thing."

"I'm sorry," she said, grabbing a couple more Kleenex and swiping at her eyes, which were leaking tears again. "This is all such a mess."

"I can see that," he said, taking the Kleenex from her and dabbing at the skin beneath her eyes.

"I must look like a raccoon." She grabbed another Kleenex and wiped at spots where she could feel her mascara running.

"You look fine," he said. "Tell me about the cancer."

"My mom died of cancer," she said. "Did I ever tell you that?"

He sobered. "No, you never did."

"I've got the same kind she had. Breast cancer. I need a lumpectomy. The doctor wants to follow that with radiation."

"What's the prognosis?"

"She says the chances are good that I'll be fine." She didn't offer him statistics, because they were meaningless until she knew whether her lymph nodes were involved. If they were, it reduced her chances of survival after five years from nearly 90 to a mere 75 percent.

"Well, then—"

"The doctors told my mother the same thing—that she'd be fine. But she ended up dying." She looked at him and said, "I'm afraid cancer is going to kill me, too." She laughed bitterly and added, "And if it doesn't, that by the time I beat it, I'll have lost any chance I have of becoming a partner at D&B."

"What is it you need from me?" Luke asked.

Nicki sighed. "I might need you to cover for me at work."

Luke shook his head. "I don't see how that's going to work with me in corporate and you in litigation. We're not even on the same floor anymore."

Tears welled in her eyes and he said, "Hell, we'll figure out something. When are you having the surgery?"

"The doctor wants to do it next week, but I've got to be in court."

"Give the case to someone else. Your life is more important—"

"I don't want anyone to know about the surgery," she said. "I don't want anyone to know about the radiation treatments. I don't want anyone to know I have cancer."

"How the hell are you going to hide it?"

"You're going to help cover for me," Nicki said.

"Couldn't you tell Justin you need me to help with something you're working on? Then, when I'm out of the office getting treated, I'll tell him I'm doing stuff for you."

Luke frowned. "Is he going to let you work for me?"

"There are some benefits to sleeping with your boss," Nicki said sardonically. "I'll tell him it's something I've been dying to work on. What are you working on, anyway?"

"I'm handling a wrongful death suit against Hyland involving a drug for juvenile diabetics called D-Free."

"I've heard of D-Free. The guy who invented it was on the cover of *Time*. Is there something wrong with the drug?"

"Might be," Luke said. "As it turns out, I really could use your help. I found out last night that Brynne is taking the drug."

Nicki sat up straight. "Is that a good idea? I mean, if there's something wrong with it?"

"There's no proof there's anything wrong with it. Except that four kids who were taking it have died."

Nicki whistled. "So, are you going to make Brynne stop using it?"

"I had a big argument over the phone with Valerie because she put Brynne on D-Free without consulting me. But she said Brynne's pediatrician swears by the stuff and pointed out how much easier it makes Brynne's life. And Brynne says she wants to keep taking it."

"Since when do kids get to decide what's best for them?" Nicki asked.

"As my ex-wife pointed out, I don't have any proof

there's anything wrong with it," Luke said. "Maybe you could research D-Free, take a look at the FDA documents, the approval process, see what you can find."

"I'd be glad to do that. I can tell Justin I'm doing it as a favor to my good friend Luke, whose daughter is taking this 'maybe dangerous' drug."

"I really would like you to take a look—when you're feeling better," Luke said. "I'll be glad to do some of your litigation scut work while you're puking up your insides after radiation treatments."

"You're thinking of chemotherapy," Nicki said.

"What happens with radiation?"

"Fatigue mostly. Loss of appetite. Some other stuff I've forgotten on purpose."

"I'm here for you Nick. You know that."

Nicki felt her throat swell with emotion as he gripped her hands. "Thanks, Luke. That means a lot to me."

"You want to stay the night on the couch?"

Nicki was tempted. It was going to be a long night. "I'll be all right," she said, freeing her hands. "Besides, what is Valerie going to say when Midge blurts out that a woman spent the night while the girls were here?"

"That would be awkward," Luke said with a laugh. "But easily explained."

"How?" Nicki said seriously. "You can't tell anybody what I've told you, Luke. No one."

He crossed his heart and said, "Your secret is safe with me. I promise."

She squinted an eye at him and said, "So, how would you explain my spending the night?"

"I'd tell her you came to my door crying because

your boyfriend is leaving you, and that I couldn't turn you away. We can count on Midge to confirm she heard you crying."

It was so close to the truth, and so far from it.

"Thanks, Luke," she said softly. "But I think I'll go home."

He rose with her and escorted her to the door. He gave her a hug and whispered in her ear, "I'm here for you, Nick. Anytime. Just call me. Or come over. You know you're always welcome."

She stepped back and reached for the doorknob before he could see the tears welling in her eyes. "Good night, Luke. See you tomorrow."

She stood in the hallway for a moment after he'd closed the door behind her and took a deep breath to calm herself. She had a friend to comfort her. She had an alibi for the lies she would need to tell. She intended to survive this bout with cancer and come out on the other side without losing a step toward partnership.

What if you're too tired to work? What if you need more radical surgery? How will you hide the truth?

Nicki headed down the hallway to the elevator. She'd seen *Gone with the Wind* twelve times. She knew how Scarlett would handle the situation. Decisively. Cleverly. Deceptively. Manipulatively. Scarlett O'Hara would do whatever was required to get her way.

When the need arose, so would Nicki.

7

Luke was still sound asleep when the phone rang on Sunday morning. He rolled over to reach for it and ran into Midge, who'd apparently crawled into bed with him sometime during the night. She made a grunting noise but didn't wake.

Snowball, on the other hand, opened one eye and stared at him reproachfully.

"You should be on the floor," he told the cat.

Snowball closed her eye and went back to sleep.

"Hello," he rasped into the phone.

"Luke? Is that you?"

He crawled out of bed with the phone and headed toward the bathroom, so he wouldn't bother Midge and Snowball, scratching his stomach through his T-shirt and yawning. "Yeah, it's me," he said quietly. "What's up, Amy?"

"I wondered if we could get together for lunch instead of dinner. My baby-sitter had something come up and she's only available early in the day."

Luke sat on the closed toilet seat and rubbed at the sleep in his eyes. "No problem. I'll pick you up at noon, right after I drop the girls off." He hesitated, then said, "Wear jeans and boots."

"Why?"

"It's a surprise. Trust me."

He heard silence on the other end of the line.

"C'mon, Amy," he said. "Take a chance."

"All right. Jeans and boots. See you at noon."

He ended the call, closed and locked the door to pee, then decided he might as well get his shower now, before Midge woke up. He'd just stepped into the shower when he heard Midge banging on the door.

"Daddy! Daddy! I can't get Brynne to wake up."

Luke felt his blood run cold. He'd dismissed Amy's apprehension about Brynne's use of D-Free, but that didn't mean it hadn't made an impression on him.

Now his daughter couldn't be woken. Was she in a diabetic coma? Was she the next D-Free victim?

He shoved open the glass shower door and leapt out. His right foot slid across the tile and he flailed his arms in a useless attempt to keep his balance. He caught the towel rack on the way down, one end of which tore loose from the wall with a crunch of plaster.

"Shit," Luke muttered, his heart racing. He was sitting buck naked and sopping wet on the tile floor. He stared at the hole in the plaster, then released his grip on the curved steel rod, one end of which remained intact in the wall.

"Daddy, please come quick." Midge was crying now, and Luke pulled himself upright on shaky legs, using the towel rack like a vine in the jungle. He grabbed the towel from the floor where it had fallen and wrapped it around his waist, tucking it in tight.

He yanked open the door, his hair dripping in his eyes and picked Midge up in his arms on the way to the girls' bedroom. Snowball trotted behind them, stubby tail held high in agitation.

"You're getting me all wet, Daddy," Midge protested, leaning back.

"Sorry, pumpkin. I thought you wanted me to come wake up Brynne."

"Why won't she wake up, Daddy?" Midge asked.

She might be in a coma. She might already be dead. Luke took a shaky breath and said, "She's probably just a little more tired than usual." When he got to the girls' bedroom doorway, he set Midge down and said, "Wait here, while I see what's going on."

The blinds were closed, blocking out the morning light, and his elder daughter lay unmoving in the gloom, rolled up in the covers in the center of the twin bed farthest from the door. Despite all the noise Midge had made, despite the noise of the towel rack being wrenched out of the wall, she was still "asleep." Luke was afraid to turn on the light. Afraid of what he'd find.

"Brynne," he said as he crossed the room. "Time to get up."

Snowball hopped up on the bed and sat down.

Luke shoved the cat out of the way. "Beat it, Snowball."

Snowball yowled in surprise at this unaccustomed treatment and disappeared under the bed.

Luke willed his daughter to move. Willed her to roll

over and yawn and stretch and groan and say she didn't want to get up yet.

But she lay where she was, face down, her arms tucked by her sides. He couldn't even tell whether she was breathing.

"Brynne," he said more loudly, almost angrily. "Get up." And then, his voice soft, tender, loving, "Get up, sweetpea. We've got to get moving."

"Is she dead, Daddy?"

He felt Midge lean against him and put a wavering hand on her head. "I don't—"

At that moment, Brynne rolled over and popped up, a superior sneer on her face. "Of course I'm not dead, stupid. I just didn't want you bothering me. Do I have to get up now, Daddy? I can't use the shower till you're done, anyway."

Luke's knees buckled with relief, and he sank onto the foot of her bed. His whole body was trembling.

"What's the matter, Daddy?" Brynne said, apparently realizing his distress.

"That was a terrible thing to do, Brynne," he said, his voice harsh with the fear that still had his adrenaline pumping.

"What did I do wrong, Daddy?"

"I thought you were really sick," he said angrily. "Or hurt." What he'd really thought was that she was dead. Or at the very least in a coma. "What were you thinking?"

Brynne's eyes glistened with tears and her chin quivered. "I was playing a joke on—"

"It wasn't funny!" he interrupted. "Don't you ever—"

Brynne broke into sobs, and he reached out and pulled her into his arms, squeezing her tight, grateful she was safe and alive. How was she supposed to know that he'd been terrified that D-Free had claimed its fifth victim? She'd only been acting like a kid—a bossy big sister, to be sure. But there was no crime in that.

"Daddy, you're squishing me," Brynne protested.

He loosened his hold but didn't let go. "I'm sorry, sweetpea. I was worried that something might have happened to you."

"What could happen to me here, Daddy?" she asked, looking up at him with tear-drenched eyes.

"Nothing, sweetpea. Nothing." He couldn't explain why he'd been so frightened. He had no proof there was anything wrong with D-Free. Honestly, he hadn't been worried about her taking it—until she'd played this scary little game.

"We'd better get going," he said, making himself release her. "I need to get you girls back to your mother on time." He was doing better. He'd only been a few minutes late getting Honor home yesterday.

"Brynne, the insulin is in the fridge, the monitor and sticks and needles are in the kitchen drawer next to it."

Brynne's face turned sullen. "I don't like having to take shots."

"You can take a pill at lunchtime," he reminded her. And realized that somehow he was going to have to find out the truth about D-Free. He decided to call his new associate, Eddie Mull, and put him on the case. If there was a problem with the drug, he wanted to know about it.

"Can I shower first, Daddy?" Brynne said.

Luke realized he was still wearing a towel. "Sure, sweetpea. Just make it fast, okay?"

"I need a shower, too," Midge said.

Luke picked her up and said, "You had a bath last night."

He helped Midge dress, which turned out to be a great deal more complicated then he'd expected.

"I want to wear my pink shorts," she said.

She'd arrived in her pink shorts Friday evening. They were spotted with taco sauce from her dinner at Guadalajara. "Your pink shorts are in the laundry," he said.

"But I want to wear them."

"They're dirty. You'll have to choose something else."

She crossed her arms, stomped her size-four foot and said, "I don't want to wear anything else."

"Don't stomp your foot at me, Mary Jane Creed," he said, using his no-nonsense voice. "Pick something else, or I'll pick it for you."

She eyed him accusingly and said, "Mommy washes my clothes when they're dirty."

"I promise I'll wash them before I see you again."

Tears brimmed in her eyes and she said, "That's not for two whole weeks! I don't want to wait two weeks to wear my pink shorts again."

What she really meant was that she didn't want to wait two whole weeks to see him again. He picked her up and rocked her and almost promised to buy her another pair of pink shorts to use at Valerie's house. But that wasn't really going to solve her problem.

"I know, Midge," he murmured as she clung to him. "I know."

Eventually, he managed to get her dressed in a sleeveless pink ruffled top and pair of cutoff denim shorts. By that time, Brynne came out of the bathroom wearing one towel wrapped around her body and another wrapped around her hair.

"You washed your hair?" he said, unable to keep the agitation out of his voice.

"It was dirty."

Brynne's curly blond hair fell almost to her waist. It would need to be dried, untangled and braided before they left, and he hadn't replaced the hair dryer that had gone on the fritz over the summer.

"You can leave now, Daddy," she said. "I need to get dressed."

The modesty was new, another sign that she was growing up. "Sure, sweetpea. I'm going across the hall to see if I can borrow a hair dryer."

"Can I come with you, Daddy?" Midge asked.

"Sure," Luke said. Then he realized he was still wearing a towel. "We'll go as soon as I take my shower and shave."

Midge hopped up on her bed to sit and watch Brynne, who said, "Make her leave, Daddy. I need some privacy."

"It isn't going to hurt to—"

Brynne cut off his protest with, "I don't want her in here while I'm dressing. Please, Daddy."

He took a look at the towel she was holding tightly around her. He could understand why she didn't want her baby sister ogling her and making comments about the two little differences on her chest.

"Sure, sweetpea. Come on, Midge. You can hang out in my room till I finish my shower and then help me shave."

He took a three-minute shower, then opened the door to let Midge and Snowball in and let out the steam.

"I want to shave, too, Daddy," Midge said.

He set her on the bathroom counter where Snowball usually perched. She sat cross-legged facing the mirror as he squirted a handful of foamy lather from a can and spread a little bit across her cheeks and chin.

Snowball jumped up on the closed toilet lid and watched the proceedings.

Luke handed Midge a razor without any blade and said, "Go to it, champ." Then he spread a handful of lather on his own face and did a quick shave, noting that Midge rinsed her razor in the sink every time he did.

They both finished at about the same time, and he wiped her face clean with a towel and then his own. She mimicked him as he lifted his chin and turned his head from side to side to make sure he'd done a good job.

He grinned at her in the mirror, and she grinned back. Brynne had never been interested in shaving with him. She'd done girl things from the start. He knew Midge would outgrow this stage soon, but he was relishing it while it lasted. He didn't have a son—or at least, the son he'd sired was never going to share mornings like this with him.

Luke felt a twinge of regret for the child he'd given up but didn't indulge the feeling. He was lucky to be able to see Bronc and know he was happy and healthy.

Luke would have liked to have a son of his own to raise, but he'd been blessed with daughters instead. They loved and trusted him, and he was devoted to them. At least, as devoted as an overworked associate at DeWitt & Blackthorne could be.

"Mommy says we're going to move away."

Luke's gaze shot to Midge. "Oh? When did she say that?"

"I don't know," Midge said. "She was talking to Martin. She said we might have to change schools. I don't want to change schools, Daddy. Do I have to?"

"Where does your mom say you're moving?"

Midge wrinkled her brow. "I don't remember. But she said we have to buy new clothes 'cause it'll be cold in the winter. I'm going to get some boots with real fur."

Luke felt chilled to the core at the thought of Valerie moving the kids away. He picked Midge up and hugged her, then set her down in the hallway. "Go see if your sister is dressed."

Snowball followed him into his bedroom, flicking her stubby tail in agitation as he dressed.

"I'm not going to let her get away with it, Snowball," he said to the cat. "She's not taking my kids away from me."

Snowball yowled to be picked up.

"Not right now," he said brusquely. He stopped in front of the mirror over the bureau long enough to shove a comb through his hair. His eyes were bleak. It wouldn't be easy to stop Valerie from moving away, especially if Martin was relocating up north for his job.

Snowball settled at his feet and stared up at him. He picked up the cat and held her close. His Adam's apple bobbed as he swallowed noisily. He couldn't lose his kids. He needed them.

He swiped a quick, caressing hand down the cat's back and said, "We'll just have to find a way to persuade her to stay right here in Houston."

Midge joined him as he stepped across the hall and knocked on his neighbor's door to borrow a hair dryer.

The young woman who answered was wearing a set of green sweats. She was a writer and worked out of her home.

"Hey, Jen," he said. "Can I borrow your hair dryer?"

"Sure." She looked from him to Midge, neither of whom had wet hair and said, "Planning to dry some flowers? It works better to press them in a book."

Midge laughed and said, "It's for Brynne."

Luke and Midge stepped inside as Jen headed into the bathroom to retrieve her hair dryer. His neighbor had let him know she found him attractive, and he'd toyed with the idea of having a fling with her, but had decided he needed a friend more.

He took the hair dryer and said, "I'll bring it back when I can."

"You'll bring it back as soon as you're done," she said. "I've got a date tonight."

"You?"

"Don't act so surprised. Some people find me charming and attractive."

He smiled and said, "I'll drop it off on my way out this morning."

Jen turned to Midge and said, "You must've grown three inches over the summer."

Midge stood up straighter and said, "I'm going to be even taller than Brynne when I grow up."

"You'll enjoy that," Jen said, sharing a look with Luke that said it would be a nice payback for Midge, who was the younger and always left behind, to end up a head taller than her older sister.

It took all Luke's patience to allow Brynne to dry her own hair. Finally, she turned to him with a woeful look and said, "I can't get all the tangles out by myself. Will you help me, Daddy?"

He was as gentle as he could be, but it was tough getting the knots out of her hair. Midge stood by offering helpful comments that inevitably made the situation worse.

"Make her go away, Daddy," Brynne pleaded.

"Midge, why don't you take the dryer back to Jen," Luke said, to give her something to do.

Midge's eyes went wide. "All by myself?"

"Sure. Why not? Be sure to say thank you."

"Okay." She picked up the dryer and left the room without looking back.

Luke heard the front door open and close and felt a qualm of unease.

When two parents lived in the same household, they usually compromised on attitudes about childrearing. When they lived separately, the children were raised one way in one home and another way in the other. Luke knew he was the more permissive parent, the parent more likely to encourage his girls to be independent and self-sufficient.

Midge's surprise when he'd sent her across the hall all by herself made him wonder if he was asking more of her than she was able to handle. He was putting the rubber band on the single braid he'd made of Brynne's hair when he heard the front door open and close again and Midge calling out, "I did it, Daddy."

She arrived in the doorway, an ebullient smile on her face, and said, "I said thank you, and Jen said you're welcome."

"Thanks, Midge. How about some oatmeal for breakfast?"

"I'd rather have Cream of Wheat," Brynne said.

Luke shrugged apologetically. "All I have is oatmeal. Or shredded wheat. Pick your poison."

"I like French toast," Midge said.

"Oatmeal or shredded wheat," Luke repeated. "We don't have time for anything else."

Brynne had shredded wheat, and he found a leftover handful of Cap'n Crunch that satisfied Midge. He didn't eat because there wasn't enough milk for a third bowl of cereal, and he didn't feel like cooking oatmeal for himself. He had to plan better for the kids' next visit. He needed to take the time to shop. He needed to get another hair dryer. He needed to do some laundry. And he needed to be on time to pick them up.

The phone rang, and it was the concierge saying

that valet parking had his truck waiting out front. They took the elevator down to the lobby and headed outside into the sweltering heat. The sky was cloudy and threatened rain. He prayed it would hold off until after his date with Amy.

He belted both girls into the backseat of the extended-cab pickup, then headed north out of town toward The Woodlands.

"How's school going?" he asked Brynne, catching her eye in the rearview mirror.

"Fine," she said.

"Do you have all the supplies you need?"

"Uh-huh," she said.

"Are there a lot of new kids in your class?"

"Some."

He wanted to have a conversation with her, but he didn't know how to do it. He had no idea what went on in her head, what she was thinking, what she was feeling. And Brynne didn't volunteer anything. He had to pry it out of her.

"How was camp this summer?" he asked her.

"Fine."

"I got to shoot a bow and arrow," Midge said.

It seemed dangerous to Luke for a bunch of six-year-olds to be playing with sharp, pointy objects. "That's nice," he said. "What sports did you play?" he asked Brynne.

"A bunch of stuff," Brynne replied.

"Like what?" he persisted.

"Oh, Daddy, do we have to talk about it?"

"No, I guess not." Luke desperately wanted to make

a connection with Brynne. What did ten-year-old girls want to talk about? She was growing up and away from him. The day would come when she wouldn't want to be with him, when she'd rather stay home and spend the weekend with her friends. He dreaded it.

"We're here," he said as he pulled up in front of Valerie and Martin's house.

"Daddy, I don't feel well," Brynne said.

Luke turned off the ignition and turned to look at his daughter. Her eyes were bright spots in a pale face, and her body was trembling. He reached for her hand and felt her skin was clammy.

"How much insulin did you take, sweetpea?"

She looked at him, her eyes stark. "Too much?"

"Yeah, I think so."

She had the classic symptoms of an insulin reaction—trembling limbs, clammy skin, lightheadedness.

"This wouldn't have happened if I'd taken my pill," Brynne said. "I don't get a reaction with D-Free."

One more miracle from the miracle drug, Luke thought.

"Let's go in and get some orange juice."

Luke had learned that insulin moved the sugar from Brynne's bloodstream into her cells to provide energy. A normal person's body produced insulin on demand. But Brynne's body had stopped producing insulin.

Without the shots she took, sugar stayed in her bloodstream and never moved into the cells, leaving her feeling tired and lethargic. Sugar would continue to build up in her bloodstream until she eventually went into a coma and died.

On the other hand, when Brynne made a mistake and injected too much insulin, it would take every single bit of sugar out of her bloodstream into her cells. She'd have nothing left to fuel her body and brain, and she'd go into a coma.

Too little insulin—bad result. Too much insulin—same bad result. The use of insulin had to be managed carefully. Mistakes were easy to make. And they had to be corrected quickly. Brynne needed a dose of something sweet immediately to replace the missing sugar in her bloodstream.

Luke picked Brynne up, because her legs were shaky. He knocked on Valerie's door and said, "Orange juice, quick."

"We drank the last of it with breakfast," Valerie said, her eyes stricken as she looked at Brynne draped over Luke's shoulder.

"You don't keep extra orange juice in the house?" Luke asked incredulously.

"We don't need it when she's taking D-Free," Valerie retorted. "D-Free keeps her sugar perfectly regulated."

"How about candy?" Luke asked.

"Candy isn't good for—"

"Forget it."

Luke heard Martin taking Midge in hand, offering her the chance to play a video game with him in the bedroom.

Luke set Brynne down on the couch and crossed to Valerie's refrigerator. He yanked it open and looked to see what he could offer his daughter that contained sugar.

"I can't believe you let her take too much insulin," Valerie accused. "Weren't you supervising her?"

"She's been taking insulin by herself for—"

"She hasn't been on insulin all summer," Valerie said. "She's been taking D-Free."

"I'm aware of that, Valerie. Right now she needs something sweet. What the hell have you got in here?"

Luke was yelling because he was frightened. He'd always been frightened when Brynne had an insulin reaction. He'd learned over the years that they could be countered with orange juice and patience. But his heart stayed in his throat until he saw his child was all right again.

"What are you looking for?" Valerie demanded.

"Something sweet, of course."

Everything in Valerie's refrigerator looked disgustingly healthy—milk, eggs, cheese, lettuce, tomato, avocado. He grabbed the bottle of chocolate sauce on the door, but it was mostly fat, just 7 grams of sugar. The boysenberry jam had 12 grams of sugar. Then he saw the lone can of Coke at the back of the fridge.

He grabbed it, popped the lid, opened cupboard doors till he found a glass, poured half the Coke into it and crossed back to Brynne.

"Coke, Luke?" Valerie said. "That's full of sugar. Brynne can't—"

"Exactly," Luke said.

Valerie shut up and crossed her arms.

"Drink this down, sweetpea," Luke said as he handed the glass to Brynne. There were 39 grams of sugar in a can of regular Coke. It was liquid, like orange juice, so the sugar in it would be absorbed quickly and bring Brynne's blood sugar back into a safe range.

Luke sat on the couch with his arm around his daughter for the seven and a half minutes it took for the sugar in the Coke to do its job, while Valerie paced worriedly back and forth behind him.

"I'm fine now, Daddy," Brynne said at last.

"You sure?"

"Yeah. I'm okay."

Luke gave a relieved sigh. Brynne had been amazingly responsible about what she ate, careful about how much insulin she took. "How did this happen, Brynne?"

She ducked her head and admitted, "I didn't check my sugar this morning. I just guessed how much insulin I'd need."

"You know better."

"I hate sticking my finger. With D-Free I don't have to. This is your fault, Daddy, for not letting me take my pills."

He didn't want to argue with her. He knew how enervating it was for her to have an episode like this. But he could see why Valerie was so determined to keep Brynne on D-Free. An insulin reaction was frightening and dangerous.

"I've got to go, sweetpea."

"Okay, Daddy."

He hugged her close and felt her hug him back. "I'll see you week after next."

"Okay, Daddy."

He was surprised to see tears in her eyes as she rose

and ran to her bedroom. He called to Midge and said, "I'm taking off, Midge."

She came racing down the hall.

For Luke, the hardest part of having his kids for the weekend was saying good-bye to them. When he picked Midge up, she clasped him around the neck and wouldn't let go.

"Don't go, Daddy," she pleaded. "Please don't go."

"I have to go, Midge."

"Take me with you. I'll be good."

"Your mom has plans for you this afternoon," he said, hoping it was true. He'd told a thousand little lies over the two years he'd been a part-time parent, in an attempt to ease this leave-taking. He left a part of himself behind every time he walked away from his children.

Whenever Midge cried, and she always cried, he died a little bit inside. Sometimes, saying good-bye was so painful he considered not seeing them anymore. Then he'd realize that if he avoided the pain, he would have to give up the joy they brought him as well. It was an impossible situation, and one that hadn't grown easier with time.

He badly wanted to confront Valerie and ask her whether she was really considering a move away from Houston. But he didn't want to upset Midge any more than she already was, so he left it for later.

"Let go, Midge," he said. "I have to go, baby."

"No, Daddy," she cried. "No, Daddy! No!"

Luke pulled her tiny hands free and said in a harsh voice to Valerie, "For God's sake, take her. I've got to go."

He turned and left the house without looking back.

He'd learned that looking back could break his heart. He heard Midge's wail and hurried to get out of her sight, so she could dry her tears and look forward to his next visit.

He sat for a moment in his pickup, his breathing patchy, his chest aching. "Goddammit," he muttered, shaking his head.

When he looked in the rearview mirror, he saw his 1985 Harley XLS Roadster tied down on the back of his pickup. He'd brought it back to Houston on impulse the last time he was home, and had worked on it late at night during the past week to feed the need he felt, after a lifetime of ranch chores, to work with his hands. He'd only gotten the thing running yesterday. It had still been tied down in the bed of his pickup this morning when Amy called to change their dinner plans.

He wondered what she would say when he showed up and asked her to go for a ride.

8

Lauren Creed was spooned against her husband in bed and had slept that way through most of the night, his strong arm securely around her. Which was how she knew he was aroused. His hand slid inside her silk nightgown to cup her breast, and she felt her nipple peak against his callused palm.

It was barely dawn, and there was only enough light in the room to see shadows, rather than shapes. She was always surprised by the extent of Jackson's desire for her, but she was glad for it. Because she felt the same physical need for him. She couldn't explain why they were always so hungry for one another, at a time in their lives when they should have been sitting in rockers on the front porch holding hands. She only knew it was so.

"What a lovely way to start the day," she said as she turned in his arms. She snuggled her face against his bristly cheek and slid her leg up over his hip.

"I have lots of lost years to make up for," he said.

It seemed amazing to Ren that they'd only been together twelve years. It seemed like a lifetime. She'd never been so happy. Or so terrified. Because she loved so deeply and had so much to lose if anything happened to Jackson.

She bit her tongue at least once every day when the urge arose to ask him to slow down, to have a care for himself, knowing his heart wasn't as strong as it once had been. She knew he would die if he had to stop working. So she sent him out the door each morning with a smile on her face, wondering if this would be the day his proud heart decided to give out.

She wove her fingers into his hair and pulled his face down to hers for a kiss. She felt him raising her nightgown, and since she hadn't put on her underwear after last night's lovemaking, he was lodged deep with one smooth thrust.

He made a guttural sound as he moved inside her, and she bit his shoulder to hold back her moans, as she moved in counterpoint with him.

It was a ballet they'd danced many times. Graceful. Fierce. Awkward. Urgent. And always, always satisfying.

She muffled her cries against his flesh and felt his body arch and stiffen as he spilled his seed within her. He held her close, his breathing ragged, his body trembling in the aftermath of their passion. She felt him ease her leg down, because he knew she'd gotten cramps in the past if she left it that way too long. But he stayed inside her and held her close until his breathing eased.

He kissed her brow and said, "Thank you for loving me, Ren."

She closed her eyes, cherishing these moments, knowing their happiness could end suddenly. Which made it all the more important for her to find a way to make peace between her husband and her youngest son.

She could understand Luke's animosity. But she was also sympathetic to the pain her son's rancor caused her husband—which was a direct result of the pain it caused her. For Luke's sake, she wanted her son to make peace with Jackson while he still could. She wanted both of them to be happy.

Which was why she'd tried her hand at matchmaking on Luke's most recent visit. She thought Amy's quiet serenity was a perfect foil for Luke's more daring behavior.

Her efforts hadn't succeeded. But that didn't mean she couldn't or shouldn't try again.

"I want to invite Luke and Amy to come visit," she said.

"You can invite all you want," Jackson said. "The question is whether they'll come."

"I'll ask Luke to bring Brynne and Midge to visit. We haven't seen them since the spring. And I'll invite Amy to come visit at the same time, and ask Luke if he can give her and her daughter a ride."

"And you think you can make this happen?"

"I can be persuasive when I want to be," she said with a coquettish flutter of her eyelashes.

Jackson chuckled and gave her a breathtaking hug. "I won't argue with that."

She reached across him for the phone and then looked at the clock. It wasn't even 6:00 yet. She set the handset back in the cradle and lay back in Jackson's arms. "I'll have to wait until a decent hour to call."

She expected Jackson to head for the shower, but to her surprise he stayed where he was. She laid a hand on his chest over his heart and felt his hand cover hers. He knew what she was doing—checking to make sure his heartbeat was strong and steady.

"There's nothing wrong with my heart, love," he murmured. "I just want to hold you a little longer."

He felt it, too. Time was running out on them. The years were moving quickly. He was pushing seventy, and she wasn't far behind. They'd both been lucky, both stayed healthy. But they both cherished every morning together, knowing it could be their last.

When Ken woke again, Jackson was singing a Faith Hill tune in the shower. She smiled and stripped off her nightgown and walked naked into the bathroom and joined him. One of the many renovations they'd done at Three Oaks had been to enlarge the shower and surround it with shower heads that sprayed them from the sides as well as from above. The water was marvelously warm and steamy and did a good job of easing the muscular aches and pains that came along with age.

Jackson grinned when he saw her and offered her the bar of soap he was using. She grabbed her washcloth from the rack in the shower and began soaping it up. She scrubbed his back while he shampooed his hair, and then he returned the favor while she washed hers.

He turned off the shower and gave her a quick kiss as he wrapped her in a warmed towel, another one of those luxuries she'd never imagined existed in the days when she and Jesse had barely managed to put food on the table, but which she'd learned to love. They brushed their teeth at dual sinks, and he combed his hair while she dried hers with a towel. While he shaved, she headed into the bedroom and dressed.

She always arrived in the kitchen first. The coffeemaker timer was set the night before so the coffee was already perked. She put two delicate china teacups and saucers on the table but always waited to pour the coffee until she heard Jackson's tread on the stairs.

She prepared oatmeal, the heart-healthy breakfast Jackson ate every morning, along with two pieces of buttered wheat toast. She usually ate one of the slices of toast with a little raspberry jam and then had a late morning snack of fruit.

She was distracted with thoughts of Luke and Amy and was surprised when she felt Jackson's arms slide around her waist from behind. She leaned back against him and said, "What do you have planned for the day?"

"Sam found those missing cows. We need to vaccinate and brand their calves."

He hadn't added that the bull calves would be castrated, but she accepted that necessity as a part of ranch life. "Where will you be?"

"South pasture."

A shiver ran through her. That was where she'd gone to picnic with Jesse the day he'd been shot. "Just . . ." *Be careful.* She bit back the warning.

All the cash-producing hunting leases she and Jesse had signed to allow big city folk to shoot turkeys and javelinas and deer on Three Oaks had expired years ago. And since her marriage to Jackson, the ranch had been financially solvent, so she hadn't needed to renew them. There would be no hunters wandering the prairies who might mistake Jackson on horseback for a javelina in the bush.

"What are you going to do today?" he asked.

"I need to work a few of the cutting horses. And I want to call Luke and invite him to visit with his girls, along with Amy Nash and her daughter."

Blackjack shook his head. "You should leave the boy alone."

"I want him to be happy."

"He has to live his own life."

"There's nothing wrong with asking to see my grandchildren."

Jackson grinned. "Uh-huh. Right."

She grinned back at him. "You can't blame me for trying."

She gave him a kiss and a hug as he headed out the door, then looked at the clock. She knew Luke would be home with the girls until just before noon, when he'd leave to take them back to Valerie's. She waited until 9:30 to call, but to her surprise, she got her son's answering machine. She called his cell and got his voice mail and left a message for him to call. And then kept herself busy until he did.

It was almost noon when the phone rang.

"Hello?"

"Hi, Mom," Luke said. "What's up? Is everything okay?"

She heard the anxiety in his voice. "I'm fine and Jackson's fine. I wanted to ask if you could bring the girls here for a visit the next time you have them for the weekend."

"I don't know, Mom. Things are pretty hectic here and—"

"I haven't seen my granddaughters for months," she said. "They grow like weeds at this age. Oh, please, bring them to see me."

"Mom, I—"

"Please," she said.

"All right," he said. "I have them again week after next."

"Wonderful." She'd already opened her mouth to ask him to bring Amy when she realized it would be better to invite Amy directly and arrange for the two of them to travel to Three Oaks together. "I can hardly wait. How are they?"

"Midge must have grown three inches. And Brynne is . . . She's taking that new drug D-Free to control her diabetes. It gives her a lot of freedom she didn't have when she was taking shots."

"Then you and Valerie have decided it's safe?"

He hesitated a beat too long before he said, "Brynne's pediatrician recommended it."

Ren heard something in his voice and asked, "Is there some problem you're not mentioning?"

"The problem is that there's nothing concrete I can point to and say there's a problem with the drug," Luke said. "Some kids who were taking it have died, but the drug has been stringently tested by the FDA, and it's been on the market for a year without any serious side effects showing up."

"So why are you worried?"

"Who said I'm worried?"

"I can hear it in your voice."

She heard Luke sigh on the other end of the line. "Amy thinks the drug is dangerous."

"Amy's a very smart woman."

"That's what worries me," he admitted. "She seems to think the drug is responsible for killing the four kids who were using it when they died."

"What do you think?"

"I'm checking it out," he said. "I'll let you know what I find when I see you."

"I love you," she said.

"Love you, too," Luke said before he hung up.

As soon as she disconnected the call, Ren dialed Amy's home number, which she'd gotten from her the previous Sunday.

Amy answered with a bright, "Good morning."

"Hello," Ren said. "How are you this morning?"

"Ren, how nice to hear from you."

"I called to invite you and Honor to come for a visit. The two of you are welcome to the horses in our stable." Amy had explained how they'd had to sell Honor's horse when they'd left Virginia, and how Amy hadn't found a good place in Houston to take Honor riding.

"Oh, you are so kind. I'm not sure when we could make it."

"How about weekend after next?" Ren said. "Luke's scheduled to bring the girls that weekend, and as we get older it's easier to have all our company at the same time."

Ren crossed her fingers at the blatant, manipulative lie and waited, hoping it had worked.

"I appreciate your invitation, but—"

"Please don't say no," Ren said. "I'm sure Honor will enjoy spending the time with Luke's girls, and to be quite honest, it would be helpful to have someone here as a buffer between Luke and Jackson."

That had been an ingenious thought and had the added benefit of being true.

"I noticed they still aren't getting along," Amy said.

"So you see, you'd be helping me out and providing Honor with a wonderful weekend of horseback riding."

"All right," Amy said. "I'll come."

"Wonderful! The best part is, you and Luke can drive down together."

"I don't think—"

"I can't imagine Luke would want you to have to make that long drive down here from Houston alone when he's making the same trip. Call him and tell him I insisted you come together."

"Actually, I'm seeing him for lunch. I'll ask, but I'm not sure he'll want to travel with—"

"My son is a reasonable man—most of the time," Ren said with a laugh. "I'm sure you two will work something out."

"Thank you for the invitation," Amy said. "I'll let you know when we'll be arriving after I speak with Luke."

"See you in two weeks," Ren said.

She hung up the phone and slumped into a chair, pressing a hand over her erratically beating heart. She'd missed her last physical because she didn't want to know if there was a problem. She didn't want to know if her time with Jackson was going to be cut short.

She felt an urgency to set things in order. To find a way to make peace between her husband and her youngest son. And to help Luke find love again. It was the best legacy she could leave them both.

—∞—

Amy's smile widened as she answered Luke's knock and saw why he'd asked her to wear jeans and cowboy boots. "You've got your Harley!"

He was wearing jeans and a black T-shirt that revealed powerful biceps. He grinned and handed her a helmet, then put his own back on.

"This is new," she said as she pulled on the protective headgear.

"We're both parents now," he said, to explain the necessity for safety over the carefree feel of the wind in their hair. "Let me help you with that," he said, adjusting the helmet strap for her.

"I can't believe this ancient thing is still running," Amy said as she hiked her leg over the back of the shiny black Roadster.

"I tied this baby on the back of my truck and brought it back to Houston with me last weekend. And then spent most of the week working late at night at a local biker garage to get it running smooth," he admitted. "But it's purring now."

He kick-started the engine and revved it.

More like a lion's roar than a cat's purr, she thought.

"Where are we going?" she asked as he headed down the drive that led to the Woodlands Parkway.

"It's a surprise," he yelled over his shoulder. "Hang on!"

Amy felt the nearly five-hundred-pound machine leap from the ground and held on tight to the man in control of the mechanical beast he'd labeled Black Beauty. It took a great deal of trust to be a passenger on a Harley. By its very nature, a motorcycle left you feeling exposed, and any mistake by the driver at eighty miles an hour was going to leave parts of you smeared across the pavement.

But there was no experience more exhilarating than being perched behind a skillful rider. And Luke was among the best. She leaned with him when he took the turns tight and close, and she hung on tight when he accelerated from zero to sixty in a matter of seconds.

The helmet didn't have a plastic face cover, and she realized why Luke hadn't provided one when she felt the wind on her face. The sun beat down on the pavement, making heat waves that shimmered in the distance, but the air whooshing past them helped keep her cool.

She noticed he'd turned south onto I-45 from the parkway, heading back toward Houston. She hung on and enjoyed the ride. Twenty minutes later, when he took the exit that led to the town of Spring, she realized where he was taking her.

When he finally brought the Roadster to a stop, he angled his head over his shoulder and said, "Thought you'd enjoy some barbecue."

She laughed. "Served on butcher paper without silverware, so you have to eat it with your fingers."

"You can't really enjoy spareribs unless you eat 'em with your fingers," he said as he helped her unfasten her helmet.

He left both helmets on the bike, testimony to the fact that this was still small-town Texas, without the need to worry about big-city thieves, and headed inside.

The barbecue—a choice of ribs or sausage—was served on two sheets of butcher paper, one up, one down, to keep the grease from getting on the red-checked plastic tablecloths.

Amy ordered ribs, while Luke ordered both, together with a bowl of pinto beans and a side of jalapeño peppers.

"Honor was a perfect guest," Luke said, once their orders had been placed. "Just a little quiet."

"Carl left some wounds, but they're healing."

He frowned. "Was he abusive? Is that what you were running from?"

"He never touched her," Amy said quickly. "He just . . . limited the things she could do."

"Like what?"

"It doesn't really matter now, does it? It was a bad situation. I just wish it hadn't taken me so long to get out of it."

"Why didn't you leave sooner?" he asked.

"Carl's parents threatened to take Honor away from me if I divorced their son."

"And you believed them?"

Amy remembered how terrified she'd been after the interview with Carl's father. "They could have done it," she said. "His family is well known and respected in Richmond. Both his father and his uncle are judges."

"So how did you end up with custody of your daughter?"

Amy took a deep breath and let it out. There was no sense trying to hide what had happened from Luke. Sooner or later it was going to come out. "The IRS came after Carl. It seems he'd been lying about his Medicare income from patient care for years. He owed millions of dollars in back taxes. They took everything we had. Then they put Carl in prison. And set me free."

"That lowdown dirty—"

"Don't, Luke."

Luke reached across the table and sought her hand, threading his fingers through hers. "I'm sorry, Amy. That must have been awful for you."

His eyes remained focused on hers, and she knew what he wanted to ask, even though he refrained from asking it: *If Carl Nash mistreated his own flesh and blood, what did he do to you?*

"Carl never hit either of us," she said. "His cruelty was more subtle than that."

He squeezed her hand, an offer of comfort that she found more profound than words.

"He says he's coming to get Honor when he gets out of prison," she said. "That's why I moved back to Texas."

"When does he get out?"

"Fortunately, not for a long time," Amy said. "But I've been saving every penny I earn to fight him when that day comes."

"I've got money, if you ever need it," he said.

"I couldn't take your money."

"Why not? We're friends, aren't we?"

She eyed him and said, "Yes. Maybe. I suppose. But we're not going to be more than that, Luke. My life is complicated enough without getting involved with you romantically. Especially with the two of us on opposite sides of the Anastasio case."

She freed her hand from his grasp, punctuating her words.

"Look," he said. "I don't want to make your life more difficult. But if plain speaking is what you want, here it is. I don't think I ever stopped—"

"Our food is here," Amy said, interrupting him.

He pursed his lips and frowned. She knew what he was going to say. It was better left unsaid. It was difficult enough avoiding his mother's matchmaking efforts. And she still hadn't told him about her invitation to Three Oaks and his mother's plan for them to travel together.

They didn't talk for the next few minutes as they dug into the barbecue. Amy grinned as she licked the grease off her fingers. "This is wonderful. I'd forgotten how good Texas barbecue can be."

"I bring the kids here sometimes," he said.

"How's Brynne doing?"

"She pulled a stunt this morning that took a few years off my life."

"What happened?"

Luke explained how Brynne had played possum, and his fear that she was in a diabetic coma. "She scared me pretty good."

"You should be scared," Amy said. "D-Free can be deadly."

"Four deaths in a year doesn't seem like very many when nearly a million people are taking the drug."

"If even *one* child had died during clinical testing the FDA would have shut down the trials until the problem was corrected."

"Really?" Luke said. "That's all it would have taken?"

"Only one," Amy said. "And there have been four deaths this year."

"The FDA approved it."

"Everyone thinks if the FDA approved it, it must be safe," Amy said. "The FDA is relying on the information provided to it by Hyland."

Luke look troubled. "You think there's something wrong with the data Hyland supplied?"

Amy nodded. "More sausage?" she asked.

"Even if I concede the approval process isn't foolproof," Luke said, leaning over to take a bite of the sausage she held, "finding where Hyland went wrong would be like looking for a needle in a haystack. Any suggestions?"

"It's hard to believe there wasn't a single 'serious adverse event'—that's what they call a death—during testing," Amy said. "Especially when there have been at least four 'serious adverse events' in the year since D-Free went on sale to the public."

"What are you saying? That the principal investigators who ran the protocols lied?"

The waitress came by with another tray of barbecue and dropped it onto their butcher paper.

"Where was I?" Luke asked when she was gone.

"You were asking whether the PIs lied about D-Free," Amy said.

"So, did they?"

"It's all a matter of interpretation."

"Explain."

"It's up to the PI on site to determine whether there's a causal relationship between a 'serious adverse event'— that is, a death—and the drug. They have a great deal of leeway to decide yea or nay. So yes, the PIs running the clinical tests could have fudged the results."

"How many people are we talking about here?" Luke asked.

"The FDA insists on a lot of different people running the clinical tests to prevent any sort of collusion. It's somewhere between 60 and 200."

"Too many," Luke said. "Someone somewhere would surely balk at lying. What happens if the PI does determine there's a relationship between the use of the drug and the patient's death?"

"A 'serious adverse event' has to be reported to the sponsor within twenty-four hours, and the sponsor has to report it to the FDA within seven days."

"How often does the FDA check up on these guys?" Luke asked.

"The FDA can come in anytime, anywhere and check out a clinical trial. And they do when they get suspicious results."

"How do they determine that results are suspicious?"

"Things like even numbers—a lot of bloodwork that

ends in zero or five," Amy said. "Or the fact that there are *no* serious adverse events."

"Are you telling me it's *normal* to have deaths during drug testing?" Luke asked, dropping a bare bone onto the butcher paper.

"There's no such thing as a perfect drug. It happens. But especially where children are involved, testing stops until the problem is resolved."

He looked at Amy and said, "So there must have been some deaths during the testing of D-Free."

"Yes, there were."

"I didn't see reports of any."

"You weren't looking in the right place. There were deaths during testing," Amy said. "Just not deaths attributable to D-Free. Every time someone taking D-Free died, the PI gave a reason why the patient expired that didn't relate to the use of D-Free."

"You think they *all* lied?"

She reached for a napkin to wipe her fingers. "Maybe not all of them. Some of them surely did."

"What about the doctors who've said D-Free wasn't responsible for the four deaths since D-Free went on the market? Are they lying, too?" Luke asked.

"I think so, yes."

"All right, I'll bite," Luke said. "How many deaths occurred during clinical trials that weren't blamed on the drug?"

"Twenty-two."

"Twenty-two!" Luke exclaimed. "When just one death would have stopped the trials?"

Amy nodded. "They were spread around, so I guess

nobody picked up on it. Especially because they didn't have to be reported to the FDA."

"Not one death was blamed on D-Free?"

"Not one," Amy replied. "The odds are astronomical that none of them was caused by the drug."

Luke reached for another rib. "I can't argue with that."

"It stands to reason that there's something wrong with D-Free. Especially in light of what's happened over the past year," Amy said.

"How do results from the clinical trials get sent to the FDA?" Luke said.

"Are you asking if it's possible to revise them somewhere along the way?"

"I guess that's what I'm asking."

"Nowadays, reports are e-mailed to the sponsor, who sends them on to the FDA," Amy said, dipping a spoon into Luke's bowl of pinto beans.

"Who's the sponsor?"

"The drug company who sponsors the clinical trials in the first place," Amy said. "In the case of D-Free, it's Hyland Pharmaceuticals."

"Hyland collects all the results?" Luke looked surprised. "Isn't that a case of the fox guarding the chicken coop?"

"The fox is on an FDA leash," Amy said. "Remember, the FDA can come in at any time and look at reports at the source. If field reports don't agree with what Hyland has turned in—they're busted."

"Who at Hyland receives all the results from the PIs?"

"The medical monitor—it's usually a doctor—signs

off on the reports, but he usually has a nurse—the clinical scientist—collate the data for him."

"So you think Hyland doctored the clinical results
and nobody noticed? That seems unbelievable considering how many people would have to be involved. It
would be impossible to keep a conspiracy like that quiet."

"Expensive, certainly," Amy said. "But Hyland is
loaded."

"Are you suggesting Hyland bought off anybody
who came up with a 'serious adverse event'? Wouldn't
the FDA find it suspicious that so many deaths turned
out *not* to be related to D-Free?"

Amy bit into a jalapeño and quickly grabbed for her
iced tea and took a swallow. "Unrelated deaths aren't
reported to the FDA. And Hyland could have hired
someone to keep track of the results of the various PIs."

"And all the contract research and site management
organizations." Luke shook his head. "It's just too many
people to control, Amy."

"Except we know the drug is causing deaths."

"Do we?" Luke said. "Maybe those twenty-two
deaths did have other causes."

Amy paused to listen to the Willie Nelson tune that
someone had played on the jukebox, then looked Luke
in the eye and said, "We'll never know unless we check."

"*We*, kemo sabe?"

Amy smiled. "I thought you wanted to find out the
truth about D-Free."

"I do."

"So do I."

Luke frowned and pushed the butcher paper away.

"What's the problem?" Amy asked.

"I'm wondering whether I'm going to end up explaining to some bar ethics committee how I ended up working for the other side. Not to mention how I'm going to explain it to the Dragon Lady."

"The Dragon Lady?"

"My boss, Grayson Choate, who told me in no uncertain terms that Hyland is innocent of any wrongdoing."

"What makes her so sure?"

"Hyland told her so."

Amy snickered. "The facts don't support that conclusion."

"You may be right. Hard to believe that not one of those twenty-two deaths during Phase III clinical trials was due to D-Free. Something stinks." He wiped his hands with a wet-wipe the restaurant had provided and said, "The problem is finding out who lied. And then finding the person at Hyland who paid them to do it."

"You think it's one person? Why not a conspiracy involving the whole corporate hierarchy? We live in the city of Enron," she reminded him. "Where corporate greed knows no bounds and has no conscience."

"If you believe there's a conspiracy," Luke said, "why haven't you uncovered it? I mean, you have a motivated client with the resources to pay for the sort of investigation that needs to be done."

"I've tried to find out how Hyland managed it, but without any success," she said. "Every PI my private investigator talked with swears D-Free is the greatest thing since Jesus turned water to wine. The FDA says they did spot checks, but couldn't find anything out of

160   JOAN JOHNSTON

kilter, so they're standing by the data supplied to them by—and routed through—Hyland."

He looked at Amy, his dark eyes filled with anxiety and said, "I hope to God I don't find anything wrong with that drug."

"Does that mean you're going to try?" Amy asked.

"You're damn right I am."

"What about the Dragon Lady?"

Luke grinned. "I've fought dragons before and won. This one just breathes a little more fire than the others."

Amy laughed.

"I like hearing you laugh," Luke said. "You should do it more often."

She smiled at Luke, realizing that despite having spent nearly their entire lunch together discussing business matters, she'd been thoroughly enjoying herself. She remembered how often he'd made her laugh when they were teenagers. And then focused on how she'd cried when they'd broken up. He wasn't reliable. He wasn't dependable. At least, he hadn't been a decade ago.

She was amazed to see a few gray hairs at his temples, noted the crow's-feet around his eyes and the laugh lines that scored his cheeks and framed his mouth. He was a father of two, who apparently took his responsibilities seriously. He was one of the best litigators in Texas.

And he'd never stopped loving her.

Amy felt an insidious yearning to be held, to be comforted, to have a shoulder to lean on. But the past ten years had taught her a great many lessons. The most important of those was how to stand on her own two feet. She couldn't rely on Luke. She had to depend on herself.

"I want to see you again," he said as they left the restaurant. "I want us to spend some time alone without the kids."

She remembered the invitation from his mother and smiled. "Funny you should mention that. Your mother's invited Honor and me to visit her the weekend after next."

It took him a moment, but he turned to her and said, "The same weekend I'm supposed to visit her."

She smiled and said, "Yep. She suggested you might be able to give us a ride."

Luke grinned. "My mother's cagey. You have to grant her that."

"Well? What do you think?"

"We'll have a built-in baby-sitter."

Amy felt a momentary qualm as she looked down the desolate highway that stretched out before them. Having their kids to chaperon was a safety net she'd welcomed. "I told her I'd come. But with everything that's going on—"

He leaned down and kissed her cheek. She stopped and stared at him. "Don't do this, Luke."

"I haven't done anything yet," he said with an unrepentant grin. "But I might as well be sheared for a sheep as a lamb."

A moment later she found herself in his arms, his mouth on hers. She kept her mouth closed, her lips pressed tight, and felt his tongue slide along the seam, seeking entrance. She shivered, her body quivering in response to the feel of his length aligned with hers.

His eyes were laughing, his lips upturned as he released her. "Well, that was fun."

She marched off ahead of him toward the Harley, her hands balled into fists so he wouldn't see they were shaking. He caught up to her quickly and said, "Don't be mad, Amy. Please."

She stopped and confronted him. "I need a friend, Luke. I'm not sure I want anything more than that. Don't you think both our lives are complicated enough?"

"You're a complication I'd welcome."

"What about what I want? Doesn't that matter?"

"There's unfinished business between us, Amy. I think we should spend some time together and see whether—"

"We can't go back, Luke."

"I can't help what I feel, Amy," he said, looking into her eyes.

She felt a warmth deep inside and fought against it. "I can't get involved with you, Luke. It would be too . . . "

"Complicated?" he said with a smile.

She lifted her chin and said, "Yes. Too damned complicated."

"All right, Amy," he said. "We'll stick to friendship. For now."

"Luke—"

He held up his hands and said, "I'll keep my distance. We'll just be two friends when we're at Three Oaks. And two lawyers working together to solve a mystery when we're in the city."

"Working together?" she said. "We're on opposite sides of the legal fence."

"We both want the same thing."

"What is that?"

"The truth about D-Free."

"What if your client's selling a dangerous drug?" Amy asked. "What are you going to do then?"

He buckled the chin strap on her helmet. "We'll deal with that problem when we come to it."

Amy got back on the Harley and gripped Luke around the waist. And enjoyed it. They were merely two old friends who were being forced to see each other because of their jobs. She didn't have to let it be any more than that.

But she liked the fact that he planned to search out the truth. And she liked the way he'd kissed her. She liked way too much about him, especially when she'd convinced herself it was too much trouble to let another man back into her life.

But Luke wasn't just any man. He was her high school sweetheart. They shared a lot of memories, some sweet, some bittersweet. And if the truth were known, she'd never gotten over him, either.

9

By the time Luke had dropped Amy off and reloaded his Harley on the back of his pickup, he was already planning how he could best research the documents on D-Free submitted by Hyland to the FDA. Nicki had volunteered to help, and he had some idea now where he wanted her to focus her inquiry. But he was going to need more help than she could give him, especially since she was going to be out of commission for a while after her surgery next week.

He retrieved his cell phone and dialed information, asking the number for Edward Arthur Mull III and then letting the operator dial it for him.

"Hello?"

"Hello, Mary Margaret. This is Luke Creed."

"Why hello, Luke. Would you like to talk to Trip?"

"Yes, please."

"Hello, Mr. Creed."

"It's Luke, Eddie. I need you to come in this afternoon."

Luke heard the hesitation, then Eddie's response, "It's Sunday."

"I know that, Eddie. Can you come in, or not?"

Luke could imagine the gears grinding as Eddie processed his request. He heard Eddie's muffled voice say, "I'm sorry about our plans, honey. I need to go in to work."

Luke heard Mary Margaret's disappointed, "Oh, Eddie, no."

And Eddie's response. "I have to go. You know I do."

Then Eddie was back on the phone. "How soon do you need me?"

"As soon as you can get to the office."

"That'll be about thirty minutes," Eddie said.

"See you there." Luke punched off the phone, waiting for the guilt to hit. He knew what it felt like to have your family plans disrupted by a call from the office. It had happened to him, and like Eddie, he'd always answered the call.

Valerie had pleaded with him to say no, begged him to give more time to her and the kids. But he'd kept his eye on the prize. He'd worked late nights and Saturdays and Sunday afternoons. And lost his family. And not even for a sure thing. He wouldn't know whether he would make partner until next spring.

Luke had drawn a line in the sand after his divorce. Every other Saturday, he skipped work to spend the day with his kids. He made up for it by working on Sunday afternoons and holidays.

Thank goodness the Dragon Lady never showed up on Sunday. Luke didn't want to have to explain to her what he had Eddie working on. Which reminded him he'd have to figure out where to have Eddie bill his time.

Associates and partners alike kept track of their day

in six minute increments, which were billed to the
client. But even brief phone calls had to be billed as a
six-minute call, so it was possible for an associate to bill
more than an eight-hour day in eight hours. However,
it was much more likely an associate would spend ten
hours in the office to end up with eight that were billable.

Firms like D&B expected associates to turn in
between 2,000 and 2,200 billable hours a year. That
often ended up requiring a sixty- to eighty-hour work
week.

Luke was tempted to bill Eddie's work researching
D-Free to Hyland. But Choate was sure to question the
hours, and she'd already told him an investigation
wasn't necessary.

"I'll have Eddie write it off as pro bono work," Luke
muttered to himself. The firm encouraged new associates to volunteer their time and legal expertise to the
community, and finding out the truth about D-Free
certainly qualified as a service to the public.

One of the things Luke liked about working on
Sunday afternoons was that very few associates or partners were in the office. The litigators might be working
and have a secretary earning overtime so they could
prepare for a Monday morning trial. But otherwise,
D&B rested on Sunday.

The fluorescent lights were off on the corporate
floor when Luke walked in. He flipped the switch and
they flickered on. He headed straight to his office and
turned on the green-shaded accountant's lamp on his
desk, noting that his answering machine had a couple

of messages. He grabbed a pen and notepad, sat down and pressed the button to listen.

"Where the hell are you? You're late and—"

He pushed the button to skip the rest of the Friday afternoon message from Valerie.

"Luke, I figure this is the best way to get hold of you before Monday. How about a game of racquetball before work? My club. Six A.M. Leave a message on my machine at home if you can make it."

Drew had a racquet club membership at the Houstonian Hotel, Club and Spa, a four-star, four-diamond resort set amid towering pines and sleek oaks only seven miles from downtown. Luke made a note to call Drew and tell him he'd be glad to play racquetball on Monday. Whacking a ball around was great for relieving stress.

"Luke, I've dictated a memo to you, but my secretary won't get it typed until Monday," Choate's voice said. "A fifth lawsuit has been filed against Hyland, another death supposedly caused by D-Free. I left the file in your in-box. Take a look, and we'll talk about it Monday morning."

Luke felt his skin crawl. Another death? *Supposedly* caused by D-Free? Did Choate not know about the twenty-two deaths in clinical testing? Or did she just not care?

He stopped the answering machine and looked in his overcrowded in-box for the file Choate had left him. He opened it and started reading.

The fifth victim was a fourteen-year-old boy. He'd been taking D-Free for almost the entire year it had been on the market. He'd shown no symptoms before he'd gone into a diabetic coma and died—two days after his fourteenth birthday.

Luke stared at the file in front of him. *No symptoms? A year on D-Free?*

One reason he hadn't been overly concerned when he learned Brynne had been taking D-Free was that she'd been taking the drug for three months without any problems. The four kids who'd died had only been taking D-Free for a matter of weeks when they'd had an adverse reaction to the drug.

In addition, all four kids who'd died had experienced some symptoms of trouble before they'd succumbed to the drug. Brynne had stayed perfectly healthy.

But here was a case where the kid had no symptoms and had been taking the drug for a year. Which meant Brynne could have a reaction to the drug this afternoon and be dead tomorrow.

Luke leaned back in his chair, unable to focus any longer on the legal document that had blurred in front of him. The kids' birthdays seemed to be a triggering event, but why? The only thing he could think of was the extra sweets they most likely would have eaten to celebrate.

Brynne's eleventh birthday was October 31, creating a horrific opportunity for her to eat too many sweets. And gave him barely two months to find out the real connection between birthday celebrations and the deaths attributed to D-Free.

Maybe combining D-Free with too much of a particular kind of sugar—something that kids ate at birthday parties?—caused a "serious adverse event." Had the company known about the problem and somehow hidden it?

But why hide it? Why not just put a warning in the literature? Drug companies seemed to get away with admitting the most godawful side effects and still convinced people to take a drug. *Mild diarrhea. Some liver damage. Kidneys may malfunction.* Hell, you could ruin half the organs in a person's body, so long as you warned them of the danger before you gave them the medication.

If there was a problem with sugar overload, it should have shown up in the Phase III clinical trials. Why hadn't the PIs noted it? Luke would have given his eyeteeth to know what reasons had been given for the twenty-two deaths that had been deemed "unrelated" to D-Free.

He wanted Brynne off the drug. Better safe than sorry. It was worth another argument with Valerie. He picked up the phone and dialed his ex-wife's number.

Midge answered and said, "Hutchins residence, Midge speaking."

"Hi, Midge," he said. "Let me talk to Mommy."

"Hi, Daddy," she said. "I miss you."

"Let me talk to Mommy," he repeated.

"In a minute, Daddy. First, I—"

"Now, Midge. This is important."

He heard her yell, "Mommy! Daddy's on the phone!"

He heard some commotion in the background and then Valerie asking, "What do you want, Luke?"

"There's been another death attributed to D-Free,"

he said. "That makes five wrongful death lawsuits. I found out this morning there were twenty-two deaths during clinical trials of the drug, although no one would admit they were caused by D-Free."

"And your point is?"

Holding tight to the phone, he said, "I want Brynne off D-Free, Valerie. I think there's at least the possibility that it's dangerous."

"You and who else?" Valerie said.

"I don't understand why you insist on taking a chance with our daughter's life."

"You don't live with your daughter anymore, Luke. Because of D-Free, scenes like the one that happened earlier today are a thing of the past. You haven't seen the difference in Brynne's life since she started taking that drug.

"She's happier, Luke. She's free of needles and test strips and constant worry about how much she eats. D-Free makes her life enjoyable. I'm not going to take that away from her because you think a drug that a million kids are using every day—without any problems whatsoever being reported in the news—might not be safe."

"Five kids—"

"Misused the drug," Valerie finished for him. "Don't question me about Brynne using D-Free again unless you have concrete evidence there's a problem."

She hung up the phone without saying good-bye or giving him a chance to argue further. Luke set the handset down carefully in the cradle, his whole body trembling with fury.

At that moment, Eddie arrived at his door and said, "I'm here. What do you need me to do?"

Luke gathered himself, then said, "I want you to research every principal investigator and clinical research coordinator in private practice or a research facility who ran a Phase III clinical study of D-Free."

"What am I looking for?" Eddie asked.

"Payoffs," Luke said. "Start with anybody who reported a 'serious adverse event' that the PIs determined was not a D-Free–related death. Got that?"

"I think so," Eddie said. "You suspect some of the PIs lied about problems so the drug would appear to be safe when it isn't."

"Exactly," Luke said.

As Eddie turned to leave, Luke said, "Bill your time as pro bono activity."

Eddie lifted a brow.

"And I'd just as soon Choate doesn't know what you're doing." Luke waited to see whether Eddie would object to either of his requests.

"Sure, Luke. Whatever you say."

"Thanks, Eddie." The kid turned to leave again, and Luke said, "This is important, Eddie. My daughter is taking D-Free."

"I'll do my best."

"Just do it fast," Luke said. "Let me know when you have a preliminary list of PIs and CRCs. I want to get some idea of how big this project is going to be."

Luke realized he hadn't finished listening to his messages. He hit the play button and heard Nicki say, "I'll be out of the office Thursday. I'll have my secretary send down the files I need you to cover. There's nothing on the docket right away, and I'm expecting to be back in the office by the following Monday. Thanks, Luke. I appreciate this."

Luke almost shut off the machine, but heard Nicki add, "I promise I'll go to work on my computer while I'm out and see what I can find in the FDA documents on D-Free."

Luke realized Nicki had never once mentioned on the answering machine why she'd be out, or what was going to happen to her. He couldn't say her caution was unfounded. The first year Luke had gone to work for D&B a male associate had learned he had multiple sclerosis. He hadn't lasted a year at D&B before he'd moved on to "greener pastures."

Luke spent the rest of the afternoon working on other Hyland corporate litigation, including a claim of patent violation in South Africa, an additional tax assessment by the IRS and a sexual harassment claim. He was typing an e-mail memo to Flo when Eddie appeared in his doorway.

"Luke?"

Luke looked up and said, "What did you find out?"

"Thought you'd like to know there were 126 PIs and CRCs involved in the Phase III clinical trials for D-Free."

Luke grimaced. "I guess it was wishful thinking to hope there were fewer than that."

"I did notice something I think might be significant," Eddie said.

"What's that?"

"D-Free was tested on Type I diabetics in every age group," he said. "But the twenty-two 'nonrelated' deaths all occurred in patients between the ages of 9 and 16."

"Meaning what?"

"I'm not sure," Eddie said. "It seems significant that no one any older or younger died."

"So you're suggesting the drug is only dangerous for kids? That once you're grown—"

"I think it has something to do with puberty," Eddie interrupted.

"Nine seems a little young for someone to be in puberty," Luke said. "If that is the triggering factor for problems with the drug."

"I thought that, too. So I looked up puberty on the Internet and guess what I found out."

"Don't keep me in suspense," Luke said dryly.

"The dictionary puts puberty at ages 12 to 14. The average age for puberty listed in current medical texts is 11 to 12. The newest study shows that the age for the onset of puberty now is even lower than that—under 9 for African-Americans and 10 to 10½ for whites."

"That still doesn't explain the death of the oldest kids. Or the youngest one," Luke said.

"Those kids could have matured sexually at a rate faster or slower than the norm," Eddie said.

Luke frowned. "The scientist who invented D-Free must have accounted for pubescent hormones interacting with the drug. That seems too obvious to be the source of the problem. Besides, if hormones interacting with the drug were the problem, why haven't more kids died?"

"I can't answer that," Eddie said. "But I think hormones are at least a part of the problem. Especially in light of this." Eddie handed Luke an article from a scientific journal that he'd printed off the Internet.

"Who is this Dr. Harold McCorkle?" Luke asked, perusing the article that had been published in the journal *Pediatrics*.

"He invented D-Free," Eddie said. "He still holds about 20 percent of the patent. He sold the rest to Hyland—where he's now Executive Vice President of Research and New Product Development."

"This article is twenty-five years old," Luke noted. "How is it relevant now?"

"McCorkle was working on a precursor to D-Free even then. His work was promising, but he had to curtail it because he had a 'serious adverse event' with a fifteen-year-old girl."

"Holy shit," Luke said.

"Apparently he solved most of the problem."

"But not all of it," Luke murmured. "I think I need to have a talk with Dr. McCorkle."

"Here's his phone number at Hyland."

Luke took the slip of paper and looked at Eddie. "How did you do in law school, Eddie?"

Eddie's flush turned his whole face pink. "Uh. I was first in my class."

Luke smiled at him, "Why doesn't that surprise me?" He handed the phone number back to Eddie and said, "Have Flo call Dr. McCorkle first thing tomorrow morning and arrange a meeting as soon as possible. Between now and then I want you to learn everything you can about D-Free and put it in an e-mail to me."

"What about the FDA approval process?" Eddie asked.

"I'll cover that myself," Luke said. "I want to know what questions to ask Dr. McCorkle when I see him."

"Right," Eddie said, grinning.

"I'll bet that sonofabitch knows exactly what's wrong with D-Free," Luke said. "And before I leave his office, I'm going to make sure he tells me everything he knows."

—∞—

Edward Arthur Mull III had been called Trip all his life—until Luke Creed had labeled him Eddie. He liked being Eddie. Nobody had too many expectations of a guy named Eddie. The nickname Trip presumed you were third in a line of egotistical—and perhaps powerful—males who thought enough of themselves and their progenitors to immortalize themselves by giving their first-born son the same name.

Eddie had so far fulfilled the expectations of his father and grandfather. He'd been groomed his whole life to go into politics. His father was a U.S. congressman from New Hampshire and, until a stroke had paralyzed his right side, his grandfather had been the senior U.S. senator from that state. Someday, Eddie was supposed to follow in their footsteps.

Mary Margaret had been chosen for him, a debutante whose family had oodles of money and no other child to will it to. Mary Margaret's family was expected to provide the campaign funds he'd need to get started in politics, which he would do after he'd distinguished himself practicing law for a few years.

He'd skipped clerking for a federal judge, the path most graduates in his position would have taken in order to add that privileged cachet to their résumés. His father and grandfather had kept their eye on the prize.

Their plan was for him to go right to work at D&B meeting influential corporate CEOs. Later, when he was a member of the U.S. Congress or Senate, he'd be able to help them with their particular interests in exchange for a significant contribution to his election war chest. Eddie had seen how the system worked. You scratch my back, and I'll scratch yours.

Eddie was glad his father and grandfather had chosen Mary Margaret to be his wife. She wasn't exactly what they'd thought she was. Oh, she'd been a debutante, and her family had money. But there was nothing remotely subdued or politically correct about Mary Margaret Kirkland Mull.

His wife had opened a lot of doors previously closed to Eddie. Not the blue-blooded, monied, aristocratic kind, but rather, the purely personal kind.

Mary Margaret expected him to think for himself. She asked him his opinion and then waited to hear his response. It had been a totally novel experience, and Eddie reveled in it. They'd met at the beginning of his last year at Harvard Law and married in June. But Eddie had undergone an earthquake of change over the past year.

He'd started wondering what he could do with his

life if he didn't go into politics. He'd started wondering what it might be like to be plain old Eddie Mull instead of Edward Arthur Mull III. Thanks to Luke, he was finding out.

Trip would never have done what Eddie had done today. Trip would have found a way to expose Luke's efforts to subvert his client's interests to someone at the firm. Or, in the alternative—because in law, there was always an alternative argument—Trip simply would not have found the information Luke had sought.

Eddie didn't give a shit whether Hyland got the shaft. Eddie didn't need Hyland's dollars to fund his campaign war chest. Because Eddie had no interest in politics.

The revelation hadn't come like a bolt from the blue. It had grown on him over the summer, as he swam and sailed and made love to his wife. He'd realized he didn't need the power his forebears had craved. He was happy just being a regular guy.

There hadn't been time before he was supposed to report for work at DeWitt & Blackthorne to change the course of his life. But he was working on it. With Mary Margaret's help.

Eddie picked up the phone and dialed his home number. Mary Margaret answered in less than a ring, as though she'd been sitting by the phone.

"Hi," he said. He didn't just love his wife. He was in love with her. Head over heels. Till death do us part. Never look at another woman the rest of his life in love.

"Hi, sweetheart," she said. "When are you coming home?"

"I've got a lot of work to do."

"Can you come home for supper and go back?" she asked. "Or even better, bring your work home with you?"

Eddie looked at the stack of files he had to go through. "I think I'd better finish up here."

"All right. If that's what you think is best." A hesitation and then, "I'll be waiting for you."

He wondered if it was just his wife, or all wives, who knew exactly the right thing to say to make a man want to chuck everything and head for home.

"Don't wait up," he made himself say. "I'll be late."

Mary Margaret didn't have to work the next morning, but she was pregnant and needed her rest.

"I love you, Trip."

"Honey, I have a favor to ask," Eddie said.

"Anything, sweetheart. What is it?"

"Call me Eddie."

He could almost feel her smile through the line, and then heard her voice, soft and tender, saying, "All right, Eddie. Don't work too late. I won't be able to fall asleep until you're home."

"I'll be home in a couple of hours," he said. "Keep the bed warm for me."

"I will."

Eddie hung up the phone and reached for a Hyland Pharmaceuticals file. He tried to imagine how he would feel if his child ended up using a drug that was purported to be safe—but wasn't. Luke must be crazy with worry. No wonder he wanted Eddie working full-time to figure out what was going on.

It stood to reason that the results of the clinical testing had been skewed. But how? The FDA did spot checks to be sure PIs weren't faking the numbers of patients involved in a study or the medicines being administered or the protocol being followed.

Eddie just needed to take a closer look at some of the clinical settings. Then he'd have a better idea of how it could be done. He picked up a document and started to read.

10

The early morning racquetball game was vicious. Luke and Drew were fierce competitors, but over the past half hour, both men had attacked the ball as though it were some vile live thing they were determined to kill.

Luke's cutoff T-shirt and white athletic shorts were soaked and both men dripped sweat onto the court, creating hazardous spots where one or the other of them slid and slammed into one of the four white walls, as they stretched out for an impossible shot. The monster could not be allowed to live.

"Watch it!" Luke shouted, as he swung his racquet with all his strength to reach a high shot bouncing off the back wall.

Drew's right sneaker landed in a puddle of sweat, and he careered into the path of Luke's swing, which caught him on the edge of the goggles he wore to protect his eyes, cracking the plastic over the left eye neatly in two and then splitting the skin across Drew's brow.

Drew swore, ripping off his goggles as blood splattered onto his gray T-shirt and the hardwood floor.

"Sonofabitch," Luke snapped. "I warned you to get out of my way!"

"You missed," Drew said with a crazy grin. "I win."

"Hinder," Luke countered. "You interfered with my shot."

"Hey," someone shouted from the glass-enclosed gallery above the court where observers could watch the game. "Shouldn't you get him to a doctor?"

Luke focused for the first time on Drew's injury and realized his racquet had flayed a two-inch cut to the bone across Drew's left brow.

Drew reached up to touch his forehead but Luke knocked his hand away. "You're gonna need stitches to close that up."

"Don't have time," Drew replied. "Gotta be in court this morning."

"I'll cover for you," Luke said. "Let's go."

Drew glanced at the steady drip of blood on the court, put his hands on his hips and sighed. "I hate hospitals."

"You in there. Here's a towel."

Drew caught the clean white towel that was thrown in through a crack in the doorway and pressed it to his face.

"I'll drop you off," Luke said, grabbing the recessed ring and pulling the door fully open to let them out of the enclosed court.

"I can drive myself." Drew took the towel from his forehead as he stooped to exit through the shortened doorway, and Luke saw it was already soaked with blood.

"I'll drive," Luke repeated. "I don't want to be responsible for you fainting and killing somebody on the way."

"Let me grab my gym bag," Drew said. "That way I don't have to come back here."

"Good idea," Luke said. He could shower at the office after he dropped Drew off at the hospital and make it to the courthouse in plenty of time to cover for Drew.

"Where's the closest hospital?" Luke asked when they were buckled into his Silverado.

"Damned if I know," Drew said. "I don't get sick."

"The Bayou City Medical Center is on the way back downtown," Luke said, as he pulled out onto Memorial Drive.

"They changed the name to Twelve Oaks."

"Just so long as they didn't move it, I can find it," Luke said.

He merged onto the West Loop Freeway and headed south. It was only a couple of miles to the Richmond Avenue exit. Neither man said anything, and Luke was glad of the quiet. His mind was still in too much turmoil to listen to the local news on the radio or some soothing jazz CD. He'd gotten a lousy night of sleep and woken at 4:00 A.M. He'd stayed in bed another hour but eventually gave up and got up, grateful for the opportunity the racquetball game gave him to vent his agitation.

He was worried that Valerie would move the kids up north, and he'd lose what little contact he had with them. He suspected that D-Free was a lot less perfect than Hyland claimed it was, and angry because he couldn't convince Valerie to take Brynne off the damned stuff.

He glanced at Drew, who still had the towel pressed hard against his wound. "You okay?"

"Yeah."

He didn't sound okay. He was staring out the window, so Luke couldn't get a good look at him. "You sure?"

Drew turned and snarled at him, "I told you I'm fine."

"What's your problem?" Luke shot back.

"That damned woman has got me so messed up I can't think straight!"

Luke stared at him. "Woman? What woman?"

"Goddammit. See what I mean?" Drew turned to stare out the window again, as though he hadn't said something cataclysmic.

"What woman?" Luke persisted.

"Forget I said anything."

"Theresa? Savannah? Carol?" Luke listed the only three women he knew that Drew had dated more than twice.

"Forget it, will you?"

"Look, it's big news when the great Drew DeWitt is dazed and confused by some woman. Fess up. Who is she?"

Drew shook his head, then grimaced and groaned.

"Your head aching?"

"Yeah, I've got a headache," Drew snapped. "And you're giving it to me."

"Tell me what I want to know, and I'll leave you alone."

"It's no one you know," Drew said.

"I don't believe you."

Drew glanced at him, tried lifting a brow and winced. "Why not?"

"Because if it was someone I didn't know you would've told me her name in the first place. Ergo, it's someone I know. So who is it? What brazen hussy has stolen the invulnerable Drew DeWitt's heart?"

"You wouldn't believe me if I told you."

"Try me," Luke said.

Drew muttered something that Luke couldn't quite make out. Or at least, he didn't think he could have heard right. "Who did you say?"

"You heard me."

"The Dragon Lady?" Luke said incredulously. "Is that what you said?"

"Yeah. Wanta make something of it?"

Luke's jaw was gaping, he was so stunned. He wasn't sure what to say. So he said nothing.

Drew finally spoke into the silence. "She dumped me over the weekend."

"How long have the two of you been seeing each other?"

"Nearly a year."

"A year! Good God almighty. How on earth— What on earth—" Luke wanted to ask how on earth Drew had gotten involved with the Dragon Lady. And what on earth had he seen in a woman so much older? Then he remembered how sexy he'd found Grayson Choate, how great she looked in a swimsuit and how soft her skin had felt under his hands.

He turned and stared at Drew, thinking of the enormous balls it must have taken to make a move on a woman like Choate. Then he thought maybe Drew hadn't made the first move. Maybe Choate had forced him into the liaison.

"Did she force—"

"It wasn't her idea," Drew said. "It was mine. I love her. And I'm not ashamed to say it."

Luke realized that the fact Drew had to say he wasn't ashamed suggested the problems inherent in such a relationship. "Apparently, the feeling isn't mutual."

Drew shot him a nasty look. "You're wrong. She does love me. She's just worried what people will say if they find out."

"You should be, too," Luke said. "She's   how many years older?"

"Her age doesn't matter to me," Drew said. "And it's nobody else's goddamn business."

"Why did she dump you?"

"Because I want to marry her."

Luke whistled. "She's that good a lay?"

Drew's hand shot out and gripped Luke's throat, and he veered through traffic as he fought the chokehold one-handed. Blaring horns followed him till he got to the edge of the freeway and shut off the ignition. He clawed at Drew's inexorable hold and fought for the breath to yell, "I was out of line, okay?"

The apology brought some spark of reason to Drew's wild eyes, and his hand loosened enough that Luke could yank it away from his throat.

"What the hell's gotten into you?" Luke demanded. "You crazy sonofabitch!"

Drew looked dazed. He'd dropped the towel and

blood dripped onto Luke's camel leather seats. Luke grabbed the towel and shoved it into Drew's hands. "Hold that against your head. You're ruining my seats."

Luke realized Drew probably had a concussion. He sure as hell wasn't thinking straight. "You gonna let me drive without trying to choke the life out of me?"

"You deserved it," Drew said. "Gray isn't like that."

Luke barely resisted blurting, *She isn't a good lay?* His sarcastic tongue would likely get him killed the next time. "If it's over between you—"

"It's not over," Drew said. "Not by a long shot. She's going to marry me."

Luke didn't argue with him. The sooner he got Drew to a doctor, the better. He had a feeling that when his friend recovered from this knock on the head, he was going to regret what he'd revealed. Luke started his pickup and carefully maneuvered back onto the road.

A few minutes later, Luke made a horn-inducing exit off the West Loop, sliding onto the exit ramp barely ahead of a car whose driver honked angrily and then shot him an emphatic finger.

Luke exchanged a grin with Drew and hit the gas as he turned left onto Richmond, right onto Drexel and left again onto Portsmouth.

Luke pulled into the Emergency entrance at Twelve Oaks Medical Center and said, "Want me to wait for you?"

Drew considered a moment, then said, "Naw. I can call a cab to take me back to the club for my car." He looked at his watch and said, "It's already seven. I need to be in court by nine. I can't be sure I'll have time to get stitched and cleaned up before then, so you're going to have to tell the judge what's happened and ask for a continuance. Harriet can give you the file. It's on my desk."

Luke and Drew had started out sharing a secretary, but as they'd gotten busier, Drew had taken Harriet and Luke had gotten Flo. "No sweat," Luke said. "I'll take care of it."

Drew was already out of the truck when he paused and leaned in to say, "Luke, I don't have to tell you—"

"Your secret's safe with me," Luke said.

"Thanks. I owe you one."

"I owed you a couple," Luke said. "Don't worry about it."

Luke was disappointed to discover, when he finally got back to the office after taking care of the continuance for Drew, that Harold McCorkle was attending a medical seminar in Brazil and wasn't expected back for two weeks.

Luke planned to use the time to ask questions and do research, in order to put McCorkle on the spot when he returned.

Luke's first call of the morning was to Hardy, Christian & James. "Amy Nash, please," he said. "This is Luke Creed."

When Amy answered the phone, the first words out of Luke's mouth were, "This is a business call."

He heard her exhale and say, "What can I do for you?"

"I need to ask, officially, if Mrs. Anastasio will agree to another settlement meeting."

"I talked with her this morning in anticipation of your call. It's not going to happen, Luke."

"I didn't think so, but I had to ask," Luke said. "Okay, our business is completed. Now, will you have dinner with me one day this week?"

Amy laughed. "You're too busy, and I'm too broke to pay a baby-sitter."

"I'll pay the baby-sitter. How about it?"

"Luke, I don't think—"

"It'll be a friendly dinner," he said. "Say yes."

She hesitated, and he imagined her twirling a length of blonde hair with her finger. "We're on opposite sides of a lawsuit," she said.

"We won't talk about work."

"What else do we have to talk about?"

"We'll think of something." He realized he hadn't read a book or seen a movie in months. What were they going to talk about? Old times, maybe. He had a lot of good memories of their time together in high school. It wouldn't hurt to remind her of a few of them.

"When?" she asked at last.

"Let's try Friday."

"*Try* Friday? What does that mean?"

He realized he was going to have to commit to a particular time and make sure work didn't interfere. He hadn't done that for anyone except his kids in a very long time. But if he wanted to develop any sort of relationship with Amy, he was going to have to rearrange his priorities. "Friday," he said. "Is eight o'clock too late?"

"No. But I can't be out past midnight," she said.

"That's when the baby-sitter I use turns into a pumpkin."

"I'll pick you up at eight and have you back before the stroke of twelve. Are we all set?"

"All set," she replied. "Good-bye, Luke."

He stared at the phone a moment before he hung up. He wondered what he was getting himself into. However much he might want a relationship with Amy, the timing sucked. He needed to spend every spare minute at work, and not just so he could make partner. He wanted to keep an eye on Eddie's progress with the D-Free research, and he'd promised to cover for Nicki this week while she had her surgery. Assuming she got permission from her boss to work for him.

Luke wasn't left to wonder long whether Nicki could rearrange her schedule. Around noon, Justin Sterling showed up in Luke's doorway and said, "Nicki tells me you need her to do some work for you."

"Yes, I do, if it's not a problem," Luke replied.

"No problem," Justin said. "How are things going?"

"Fine," Luke said. "It would have been nice if my predecessor had kept the Hyland files a little neater. Half the stuff I'm looking for seems to be missing."

"Like what?"

"I know Hyland settled three previous wrongful death lawsuits relating to D-Free, but—"

"I can tell you about those," Justin said.

"How did you get involved?"

"The guy who was doing the job before you found some stuff he didn't understand, so he brought it to me."

"You have the files?" Luke asked in surprise.

"Somewhere in my office."

Luke hid his disgust. Justin's office was stacked so high with paper it was a wonder he could ever find anything. "Want to give me a hint where to look?"

"Honestly, you'd be better off checking out the microfiche."

Luke knew that closed files were microfiched and the paper copies were stored, but the D-Free issue was ongoing. "You don't have paper copies of anything?"

Justin grimaced. "In my office. Somewhere."

"I'll check out the microfiche," Luke said. "So what was it Neil didn't understand?"

"He found data when he was doing research for the Anastasio settlement that suggested the results sent to the FDA by Hyland might not have been the same results that were submitted to Hyland by the PIs and CRCs."

"That seems pretty straightforward." And pretty damning, Luke thought. "What was it he didn't understand?"

"It looked to Neil like the names of the doctors who initially noted the 'serious adverse event' and the doctors who eventually reported it to the sponsor as an 'unrelated' death weren't always the same."

"Why was that?" Luke asked.

"That's what Neil asked me."

"What did you tell him?"

"That I had no idea, but we should sure as hell find out. Are you telling me he didn't follow up on this?"

"I don't know whether he met with anyone at

Hyland before he OD'd and crashed his car," Luke
said. "I haven't found anything that says he did."

"Then you have your work cut out for you," Justin
said.

It was hard for Luke not to jump to the conclusion
that someone had been paid off to make sure that
results that would have halted the trials didn't end up
getting reported. But he'd learned the danger of making such leaps without proof.

"Opposing counsel on the Hyland lawsuit I'm handling said she had some conversations with Neil, but
his notes weren't in the file. Any idea where they might
be?" Luke asked.

"They might be in the file he gave me," Justin said.

"Would you mind if I have one of the associates look
around your office for it?"

"I'd rather not have some kid who doesn't know
what he's looking for rummaging around in my office."

"How about your secretary? Can she take a look?"

"She's too busy."

"I need those notes, Justin. What do you suggest?"

"I'd trust you not to mess things up."

Luke grimaced. "Thanks."

Justin grinned. "Let me know if you find anything
interesting."

"Like the Leopold and Loeb trial documents?"

Justin laughed. "There might be some stuff that old
sitting around in there. Good luck."

Luke called Nicki and said, "Hey, Nick. Justin came
by, and you're all clear to work for me. Do you need a
ride to the hospital on Thursday? Or a ride home?"

"Thanks, Luke," Nicki said. "But I've arranged for a cab to take me there and pick me up."

"You sure? I'll make the time to get away." Even as Luke said it, he wondered how he was going to make good on such a promise. Nicki, of course, knew better.

"Don't kid a kidder, Luke. The offer is enough. I'll be fine."

"I could stop by your place Thursday evening," Luke said.

"I'd rather be by myself," Nicki said. "My secretary will be in touch if there's anything else you need to cover while I'm out."

"Sure thing," Luke said. "Flo is calling me," he said. "Keep in touch."

He punched the flashing button on his phone without waiting for Nicki's good-bye. "What is it, Flo?"

"Ms. Choate wants to see you in her office. Ten minutes ago."

That was Flo language for *Get your butt moving.* "I'm on my way."

Luke went through the ritual of buttoning up, snugging his tie to his throat and slipping on his suit coat as he headed down the hall. He felt apprehensive, knowing what he now knew about the Dragon Lady and his best friend. He wondered if he was going to be able to continue acting natural around her. Hell, he'd never acted natural around her.

He knocked on the open door and Choate said, "Come on in."

Luke cleared his throat as he stepped inside. Choate looked up at the sound and eyed him contemplatively.

Luke made himself stand still, his hands safely in his pockets, hiding the nerves that caused a drop of sweat to begin trickling down the center of his back.

He tried to meet Choate's eyes, but every time he looked at her he kept imagining her naked in bed. He cleared his throat again and stared at the framed Modigliani print behind Choate's head.

"What's going on with Hyland?" Choate asked.

"I called Hardy, Christian this morning to see whether Mrs. Anastasio would agree to another settlement meeting, but she's declined."

Choate's mouth twisted in displeasure. "What about the fifth lawsuit. Where are you on that?"

"I've had Eddie Mull working on it over the weekend." Which was the truth. Sort of.

"And?" Choate pressed.

"Were you aware there were twenty-two deaths during clinical trials for D-Free, but not one of them was attributed to use of the drug?"

Choate frowned. "I don't take your point."

"I think there's something hinky with the clinical trials of D-Free."

"Hinky?" Choate said. "What does that mean?"

"I have some questions about the statistics Hyland reported to the FDA."

"What kind of questions?"

Luke didn't want to make accusations against D&B's largest client without having proof. He realized he should have kept his mouth shut until he had some corroborating evidence.

"I'm still looking into the situation. I don't really

have anything I can present to you. But I'm going to be working—"

"That's why I called you in here," Choate interrupted. "I've got another Hyland matter I want you to look into."

"What about—"

"The D-Free cases will have to wait." Choate said. "We've got another problem."

"I don't think—"

"You aren't paid to argue with me," Choate said, cutting him off. "I don't want to hear another word about D-Free until I bring it up again. Is that clear?"

"Yes, ma'am," Luke bit out.

"How's that South African patent case coming?"

"I'm working on it." Considering he'd known nothing about patent law when he'd started, he was making remarkable progress.

"Get back to me with your thoughts tomorrow morning."

Luke stared at Choate, not quite believing what he was hearing. There were attorneys at the firm who specialized in patent law, in tax law, in international business, who would have been much better qualified to tackle the file he'd been given. He wondered if the ten previous associates who'd worked for Choate had brought that fact to her attention. He decided that somewhere along the line one of them must have. Yet, she'd sent a patent matter to his desk to be reviewed— by tomorrow morning.

"Any issue in particular you'd like me to address?" he said.

"I want to know on what grounds you'd pursue the case against the patent violator," she said. "You don't need to report in person. You can e-mail me a memo."

"I'm on it." Luke was out the door and on the way back to his office when it dawned on him that Choate might very well have given him "busy work" to keep him occupied and away from the D-Free issue. Why was that? What was he missing? Was this another test he was supposed to pass to prove his worthiness to become a D&B partner?

If he couldn't do the D-Free research himself, he'd have to find another way to pursue the matter. He knew he was taking a chance that Choate might discover what he was up to. But considering what was at stake— his daughter's life—he figured it was worth the risk.

He stopped by Eddie's office and said, "What are you doing tonight?"

"I'm taking Mary Margaret out for dinner, to make up for the interruption of our plans—"

"Cancel your reservations. I need you."

Luke could tell Eddie wanted to protest. But he picked up the phone and started dialing. Luke didn't wait to hear how Eddie explained to his wife that not only were their plans canceled, but he likely wouldn't be home until after bedtime.

Luke needed to know the truth about D-Free. If he wasn't going to be allowed to discover it during the normal course of investigating the pending lawsuits, then he'd do it on the sly. The Dragon Lady could breathe all the fire she wanted. Truth and right would be his armor and buckler.

He just hoped to hell he got the proof he needed before his shield melted in the heat.

—⁂—

Amy had no close girlfriend with whom to share the excitement of being invited to dinner by Luke Creed. She'd learned it was better not to make a pal of her secretary, and she needed to get home to Honor every day, so she hadn't established friendships at work.

But there was someone she could call who knew Luke and would appreciate the significance of the invitation. Her mother.

During her marriage to Carl, Amy had spent every holiday in Richmond. Since her mother never left the house, and her father refused to leave her mother alone, she'd seen little of them over the past dozen years. But she'd kept in touch over the phone. She'd seen her parents frequently during the year since she'd returned to Texas, but she'd discovered it was easier to talk with her mother over the phone than when she was sitting across from her, in the house that had become her mother's prison.

She dialed the number and waited for the answering machine to come on before she said, "Mom, this is Amy. Will you please pick up?"

Her mother used the answering machine to screen out telemarketers. There was no question of whether she was there, only how long it would take her to get to the phone.

"Hello," her mother said. "I'm here."

And would be until she died, Amy thought. "How are you?"

"Your father brought me a new book of crossword puzzles. I'm learning lots of new words."

Her mother could have spent her days sleeping or watching TV, Amy knew, and no one would have been the wiser, but she was surprisingly functional. She did projects for the poor and puzzles to keep her mind active and had learned to shop on the Internet and have everything delivered to her door.

"Have you thought about what we talked about?" Amy asked.

"We can't afford a counselor," her mother said. "And I don't want to take drugs."

"I want Honor to get to know you, Mom. We can't get there as often as you could get here for a visit. Please, won't you try?"

"I don't know why you have to work in Houston."

"I need the money I can earn in the city," she said.

"How are you?" her mother asked.

"Luke Creed asked me out for a date Friday night," she said as casually as she could.

"Oh, Amy. Do you think that's wise?"

"We're just friends, Mom."

"I would think you would have learned your lesson with Carl."

"What lesson is that, Mom?"

"To be careful. To guard your heart."

She knew her mother only wanted to spare her pain. But Amy didn't want to spend the rest of her life without love. Life was full of risks. And sometimes you got hurt. But the alternative was to spend the rest of your life alone.

"I'll be careful, Mom," she said. "I've got to get back to work."

"Take care of yourself, Amy."

"I will, Mom." Amy carefully hung up the phone and leaned back in her chair.

Talking to her mother had made her realize that by insisting that she and Luke could only be friends, she was putting up walls to protect herself. How long before she'd be afraid to have friends? Or interact with others? Or leave the house at all?

She liked Luke. And she was attracted to him. Why was she so afraid to let him get closer? Why was she so afraid to let a relationship develop between them?

She didn't want to be hurt, of course, if things didn't work out between them. But if she didn't take that gamble, she would never find someone with whom to share her life.

She wasn't going to end up like her mother. She was going to keep taking risks. She was going to reach out to Luke on Friday night. And see what happened.

11

—⁘—

Grayson Choate rolled over in bed toward her lover and ran her hand across his chest, marveling at the cut muscles in his abdomen. Drew was lying with his hands clasped behind his head, staring at the ceiling. He was angry with her and too stubborn to give up and leave. She'd decided she might as well take advantage of his presence.

"Don't," he said tersely.

She stopped her hand where it was, grazing the ridge of muscle that ran along the side of his flat stomach and down toward his groin. She didn't know what it was called, only that it was a male part of him that she found particularly fascinating. "I told you I didn't want to see you again, but you showed up at my door anyway," she said. "You can leave at any time."

He sat up abruptly and leaned over her, one hand braced near her head, the other across her body, so there was no chance of escape. "You didn't have to let me in. You wouldn't have if you didn't want me here."

He was right about that. She'd wanted him. Here. In her bed. What she didn't want—or need—were the complications he was creating in her life. "I won't deny I enjoy you in bed," she said. "I've always been honest about that. But you've become . . ." She stopped short of saying *annoying*. That would hurt him. Besides, it wasn't true. "I do appreciate the heads-up where Luke is concerned."

He swung away from her, his legs dropping over the edge of the bed, his hands on his knees, his shoulders slumped. "I'm not proud of myself for that," he said. "Luke is my best friend."

She sat up and edged closer behind him on the bed, so her naked breasts brushed his bare back. "And I'm your lover," she murmured in his ear. "I appreciate your loyalty, Drew."

He glanced at her over his shoulder, his eyes troubled. "He told me this morning you've got him working on everything but the D-Free cases. If you know the truth, why don't you level with him?"

"What is the truth?" Gray said. "There's a problem with every drug out there."

"Luke's daughter is taking D-Free."

Gray eyed Drew sharply. "He didn't tell me that."

"He didn't know it when he started working for you. But you can see why he's so interested in finding out whether the drug is safe. I haven't forgotten what you told me about it."

Gray grimaced. That was another problem with lovers who came from the workplace. You had to watch every word out of your mouth. "There's just no proof," she said. "Any warning about the drug would be premature."

That wasn't precisely true. At least, not since her last discussion with Harold McCorkle. But that information

wasn't for dissemination to the public. Considering
Drew's relationship with Luke, it wouldn't be safe to
share it with him, either.

"I've changed my mind about us," she said. "I was
wrong to send you away."

He turned to face her, his eyes searching, mistrustful.

She was sorry she'd ended their relationship the way
she had. But she'd been frightened by how much she'd
enjoyed waking up with him in her bed on Saturday
morning. Worried by how dear his face had looked to
her in the pink light of dawn. Panicked when he'd
taken her in his arms and held her close and murmured, "I love you," as the first harsh rays of sunlight
brightened the bedroom and revealed the stark difference between his youth and her . . . maturity.

She'd kicked him out. And then regretted it. So
when he'd shown up tonight wanting to talk, she'd let
him in. And let him love her.

She couldn't even say she'd seduced him. Although
one of her fondest memories was of Drew's first tenta-
tive forays in her direction, and the fun she'd had enticing him, and finally accepting him into her bed.
Tonight he'd been hungry for her, taking what he
wanted, slaking his need and appeasing hers, leaving her
breathless and panting on the cool, sapphire-colored
tiles on the kitchen floor.

Then he'd picked her up and carried her upstairs and
made love to her again. Slowly, joyously, with love and
with tender care, leaving her confused and distraught.

It was only supposed to be a sexual relationship.
That's what young men wanted from older women–

their experience in bed. Their willingness to have fun and let go. Their lack of interest in the word *commitment*. She knew how the game was played.

Somewhere along the way, Drew had changed the rules.

For her part, Gray had started noticing all the female celebrities who'd married men more than a decade younger than themselves—Madonna, Elizabeth Taylor, Joan Collins, Mary Tyler Moore. And all the virile male celebrities who'd found much older women attractive— John Travolta, Burt Reynolds, Randy Travis and Pierce Brosnan. They'd loved, and many had even married, their older lovers.

Gray found no comfort in those anomalies. Celebrities lived in a different world than she did. The male partners in D&B would be outraged at—and threatened by—her choice of a younger husband. How dare she not choose one of them? They were already jealous of the power she wielded because she had her hand firmly wedged in Hyland's very deep pocket. She was convinced they would find a way to get rid of her if she married a much younger man.

Was she considering it?

She couldn't believe she was thinking about marriage with this young man. After her father had beaten her mother to death—and then shot himself—when she was sixteen, she'd vowed never to marry. Ever.

Over time, she'd realized it wasn't the institution of marriage that had caused the problems between her parents. It was her mother's passive response to her father's violence. Gray had fallen in love twice as a young woman. But when it came time for marriage, there had been . . . glitches.

Her first love had wanted her to quit work and raise a family. She hadn't been willing to give up her independence. Her second love had opted out when he realized he couldn't keep up with her financially.

Those lessons had been brutal, but effective. She hadn't needed a third. Since then, she'd kept her liaisons private, short and sweet.

Until Drew.

He was happy to let her pursue her career. And he had far more money than she'd ever earn in her lifetime. This time the problem was hers. She wished the age difference didn't bother her. But it did. It might not matter to him now, but it would. She didn't want to let him all the way in, because she feared the agony she would suffer when he left her, which he inevitably would.

"I wish you'd let me tell Luke what I know," Drew said.

Gray was startled from the fantasy she'd been pursuing. "What?"

"I want to tell Luke about Dr. McCorkle's concerns."

"No," Gray said. "That information is confidential."

"His daughter—"

"I know," Gray interrupted. "A lot of kids are taking D-Free. That doesn't change my responsibility to my client."

"What about your responsibility to all those kids?" Drew questioned.

"We're waiting for the results of Phase IV studies,"

she replied. "I'll be standing right beside Dr. McCorkle when he has something substantive to tell the public. Until then, Luke has to stay in the dark. Can you imagine the repercussions if he took his daughter off D-Free and later something was discovered to be wrong with the drug? Everyone would think he had information that hadn't been available to the public."

"We do know something the public doesn't know. And Luke isn't just anyone. He's—"

"I know," Gray said. "Your best friend. But honestly, what are the chances his daughter will become a victim? Infinitesimal."

Drew raised his brow skeptically.

"Look at the numbers," Gray insisted. "Nearly a million people have been taking D-Free for the past year with no—" She corrected herself, "Virtually no—adverse results."

"It would be a tragedy if—"

"I don't want to argue with you about this," Gray said impatiently. "If you're going to stay, we have to change the subject."

"All right," Drew said. "I want you to come home with me at Thanksgiving and meet my family."

"That wouldn't be wise." His family were DeWitts. Word of her visit was sure to get back to the powers that be at the firm.

"I want my mother to meet you."

Gray lifted a brow. "That isn't a meeting I'd welcome."

"She'll love you."

"She'll give me a speech about leaving you alone,

about how I'm ruining your life and keeping you from marrying and having a family."

"She wouldn't do that," Drew said. "She knows I don't want a family."

"How does she know that?" Gray asked.

"I've told her so."

"Mothers don't believe their sons when they say things like that," Gray said.

"Believe me, mine did. You're going to find out if you come, so I might as well tell you now."

Drew hesitated and Gray waited patiently for him to speak, as she'd learned to do, rather than prompting him to say what was on his mind.

Drew took a deep breath and said, "My brother Dusty committed suicide when he was twenty-three."

She suspected the details of his brother's death had something to do with his attitude toward becoming a parent, but she didn't ask him to explain. She didn't want to know any more about the things that made Drew DeWitt tick than she already did. "I'm sorry," she said.

"Will you come?"

"That's a couple of months off. Ask me again in November," she said, buying time, forgoing a commitment.

He turned and pushed her flat on the bed and laid his body over hers, his legs insinuating themselves between hers, his weight borne on his elbows. His hands threaded into her hair and he held her head so she was forced to look into his piercing blue eyes. "I recognize a sidestep when I see one," he growled low. "I'm not going anywhere, Gray. I'm here to stay. Get used to it."

"If you're asking if you can stay the night, the answer is no," she said. "I have to get up early tomorrow and—"

His mouth covered hers, his ravaging tongue darting between her lips. He shoved her legs apart with his knees and thrust himself inside her. She realized she was insidiously wet and ready for him. He made a grunting sound as he settled himself to the hilt, then lifted his head to look once more into her eyes.

"All right," she said breathlessly. "Just tonight. But you're not to make a habit of—"

He shut her mouth with his own and took her deep again. As her arms circled his body and pulled him close, she realized she wanted him to stay. Wished he could stay always. Wanted the story to have a happy ending. Of course, she knew that wasn't going to happen. But she didn't have to give him up yet. Not quite yet.

She had at least until Thanksgiving, when she would make it very clear that their relationship was over. She would not be going home with him to meet his mother.

—∾—

Nicki had to spend the night before surgery in the hospital. The surgery she was having Thursday morning wasn't quite as simple as she'd told Luke. She was having a lumpectomy, all right. But she might be having a great deal more.

Her doctor planned to do a biopsy while Nicki was under anesthesia and wait for results from the lab. Considering her family history, if the cancer had spread,

Dr. Fredericks was going to remove the entire breast, as well as the lymph nodes.

Nicki didn't take the sleeping pills the nurse had given her. She didn't want to be drugged in the morning. Around 2:00 A.M., when she was still staring at the ceiling—and listening to the snores of the woman in the bed on the other side of the curtain in her room—she realized she'd made a mistake.

Fear was keeping her awake. And the dire nature of what she faced on the morrow was making her remember something she'd tried very hard over the past year to forget.

She saw herself the day ten months ago when she'd shown up at Dr. Fredericks's office after taking a home pregnancy test—which had turned out positive. The nurse had smiled at her as she stepped onto the scale to be weighed and said, "Congratulations, Mrs. Maldonado."

"I'm not keeping this baby," she'd snapped back. "And it's *Ms.* Maldonado."

The nurse's smile had disappeared and she'd bustled away. Nicki had been appalled at how angry she'd sounded, but still felt resentful of the look of pity the nurse had given her. She felt trapped and unhappy with the only option she felt was open to her. *I'm not keeping this baby.* And she hadn't meant she was giving it up for adoption.

Dr. Fredericks's expression had been somber, her lips a flat line of disapproval in the examining room, as she listened to Nicki's request for a D&C to terminate the pregnancy.

"I don't like to see abortion used for birth control," the doctor said.

Nicki felt the blood drain from her face and clenched her hands together to control their trembling at the use of the word she'd avoided even thinking, a word she wasn't willing to say aloud. "I . . . It . . . We . . . "

"What about adoption?"

"I want to terminate the pregnancy," Nicki said, hearing the defensive anger back in her voice. No one was going to change her mind. Especially not some judgmental female doctor. "I will be more careful," she heard herself saying. Meaning, *This won't happen again.* As though that made up for the fact that she'd gotten pregnant and needed to escape the consequences of her carelessness.

She'd been taking the pill during her relationship with Justin, taking responsibility for birth control because it would be disastrous for both of them if she got pregnant. Then she'd gone on a business trip and forgotten to bring her pills. It had only been two days. She'd figured it wouldn't matter, but she'd suggested condoms to Justin. He hadn't wanted to use them. And she hadn't insisted.

This had been the result.

She hadn't told Justin she was pregnant. She didn't want to hear him say he didn't want the baby. And yet, what else could he say? He already had a wife and children. He'd never said he loved her. They'd just had a convenient . . . sexual relationship.

Nicki had considered having the baby, considered leaving DeWitt & Blackthorne and going to work for a smaller firm and becoming a working mother. But she'd

realized that the demands of her job would keep her
from spending much time with the child. It would be
raised by baby-sitters and child care centers and become
a latchkey kid. What kind of life was that for a child? It
would be better for everyone if she just . . . got rid of it.

The brutality of that thought had made her cry.
She'd done a lot of crying in the week or two she'd
given herself to think about what she was doing before
she'd gone to Dr. Fredericks and asked for a D&C.
"Scraping out the womb" didn't sound as bad as the
word for what she was really doing.

Dr. Fredericks had given her a stern lecture, but
she'd also agreed to do the D&C. An afternoon off from
work, a medical expense that Nicki hadn't claimed on
her insurance . . . and a lifetime to think about what
she'd done.

Now Nicki lay in the hospital bed, staring at the rec-
tangular fluorescent light fixture overhead, letting the
tears drip down her cheeks without wiping them off.
She'd never let herself grieve for that lost child, never
let herself even think about what she'd done, let alone
feel the shame of it. Or the sadness of it.

It had all caught up to her tonight, and she felt a terrible, agonizing grief for the unborn life that had been
lost.

She heard the woman in the next bed snuffle, heard
the sheets rustle as she turned over. She felt an ache in
her chest, a tightness in her throat. She didn't dare cry
aloud. Not with someone else in the room.

Over the past year, Nicki had gone on with her life,
which had kept her too busy to contemplate what she'd

done, or to think about the future in any terms except as a partner at D&B. She was thinking now. And feeling. And hurting. And regretting.

She should have taken the damned sleeping pill.

Nicki turned her face into the pillow to stifle the sob that erupted. Her body heaved, and another strangled sob broke free. She pressed the pillow more tightly against her mouth and howled with pain.

My baby, my baby, my baby.

She hugged the pillow close, the way she would have clung to her child in a dangerous gale.

Nicki was still rational—and cynical—enough to wonder if she would be regretting her actions so much if she weren't in the situation she was in now. If she didn't believe she'd given up the chance to be a mother forever and ever.

Maybe not. But she did regret what she'd done. She wished she'd made a different choice. It was too late to change the past, but she could alter the path she was on. She could turn her life in a new direction.

Nicki made lists for everything. When she had to make a decision, she drew a line down the center of a piece of paper and listed PRO on one side and CON on the other. She did it now in her head.

REASONS TO STAY AT D&B	REASONS TO LEAVE D&B
	No time for a personal life
	No time for a romantic life
	No time for a family life
	No time for a life

She tried to remember why it had been so important to become a partner at D&B, why she'd been so willing to give up so much for the sake of becoming "one of the guys."

There was only one reason she could think of. It seemed silly in light of everything she'd given up. Quite simply, Nicki had never failed at anything she'd attempted. Giving up on partnership at D&B would have been admitting not just to failure, but to failure on an enormous scale.

She took the next logical step and asked herself why it was so important not to fail. She smiled to herself, feeling her mouth curve against the pillow she still held there to suffocate sound.

She'd wanted to succeed in order to please her father—and earn his love.

Oh, God. What a fool she was. She was never going to earn her father's approval by making partner at D&B. All her straight-A report cards, all her tennis trophies, becoming valedictorian of her high school class, being selected for Phi Beta Kappa, being on the law review, getting hired by DeWitt & Blackthorne, none of it had made a difference in the attention he paid to her. Why had she believed her acceptance into the male world her father so cherished would make him look at her any differently?

You never loved me, Daddy. You just wanted to show me off to your friends. I performed right on cue. But not anymore, Daddy. I'm through. I'm done. I can't win your

love. I've failed, all right? I admit it. I quit. I don't care
anymore. I . . .

She stuffed the pillow against her face and wailed at
the loss she felt. She was giving up on something she'd
never really had a chance of winning in the first place.
Her father couldn't love her because she wasn't the son
he'd always wanted. She was a daughter.

Nicki's eyes were gritty when she awoke at the sound
of a nurse bustling around her.

"Take this pill, dearie. It'll help relax you before
your surgery."

Nicki grabbed at the pill and swallowed it. She
wasn't going to make that mistake again.

As she lay there, watching the sun rise, she thought
of the things she would need to do when she left the
hospital.

She made another list.

TO DO:

1. Break up with Justin—before the football season
   is over.

2. Quit job (After finding better job—one that
   doesn't consume so much of my life).

3. ~~Seek a significant other.~~ Find a husband who
   wants children.

4. Have three kids, two girls and a boy.

Nicki smiled as she wrote the last item on her list. As
long as she was making a wish list, she might as well

make it precise. It no longer mattered if things didn't turn out as she'd planned. She'd conceded failure once, when she'd admitted she could never win her father's love. She could do it again.

Her eyes suddenly filled with tears. How could she possibly pursue the goals she'd just listed while living under the cloud of cancer? Nicki had watched women who survived surgery that left them maimed and chemotherapy that left them bald and coughing up their guts. Their initial elation at having survived turned to wariness when they realized, *It could come back*.

They lived the next five years one year at a time, waiting for the anniversary of their surgery to see if they remained free of the disease. It was humbling to celebrate one year of life at a time, as though it were a gift, knowing that until you'd remained cancer-free for at least four or five years, the disease might come back and claim your life.

Nicki realized she must have dozed again, because the next thing she knew, Dr. Fredericks was there, brisk, brusque and efficient.

"Do you have any second thoughts on what we've discussed? Is there anything else you'd like to know before we go in to surgery?" the doctor asked.

Nicki shook her head. "I've signed the release. Do what you have to do."

"Take it easy, Nicki."

Nicki gave her doctor a hard-won smile. "Do I look that bad?"

"You didn't sleep, did you?"

Nicki made a face. "Not much."

"It'll all be over soon."

Nicki thought it was a particularly poor choice of words. Even if she ended up with a lumpectomy and radiation treatment, she still had the specter of cancer hanging over her head for a very long time to come. To the contrary, this was not going to be over anytime soon. "See you when I see you," Nicki said.

It was the best she could do.

Nicki had been through something very similar to the surgical procedure that followed when she'd had the D&C the previous year. It felt like she'd barely been wheeled into the operating room when she awoke to a distant voice saying, "It's all over, Nicki. We just took out the lump. The cancer hadn't spread. You're going to be fine."

Nicki was disoriented, afraid she was dreaming, afraid she was hearing what she wanted to hear, and that the truth was far worse. "What?" she said. "Are you sure?"

Then she saw Dr. Fredericks's smiling face. It was the smile that convinced her she was all right. She'd never seen Dr. Fredericks smile.

"The statistics are on your side, Nicki. As soon as you've recovered from the anesthesia, you can go home."

Nicki felt the lump in her throat. Felt the tears welling again and was too weak to blink them back. "Thank you," she managed to croak.

Dr. Fredericks patted her shoulder and said, "I'll see you before you check out."

Nicki spent the rest of the morning waiting for the anesthesia to work its way through her system and got an okay after lunch to leave the hospital. She wished she had a girlfriend who could have come to get her, but she didn't have time for girlfriends. It was awful not having a shoulder to lean on. She could have called Luke, and she thought he would have come to get her, but that wouldn't be fair to him. So she called a cab.

She realized it had never once crossed her mind to call Justin. He simply wasn't there for her. She reminded herself that whatever happened, she was going to end her affair with him. She'd been given a second chance, another lease on life—for however long it lasted. It was time to move on, time to rethink what was important in her life.

Nicki was at home dozing fitfully when she heard a loud knock on her door. She sat upright too quickly and realized the painkiller she'd taken had worn off. She looked at the clock and saw it was 9:00 P.M.

"I'm coming," she shouted. She started to put on a robe but realized she couldn't move her right arm well enough to wriggle into it. "To hell with it," she muttered as she shuffled toward the front door wearing a football shirt and sweatpants.

She opened the front door to her loft and found Luke standing there with several batches of paper-wrapped flowers that looked like they might have come from the grocery store.

"I was shopping for dinner when I realized today was your surgery and that I hadn't heard from you," he said.

Then she realized he had a bag of groceries that had

been hidden by the colorful bouquets of cut flowers.

Tears filled her eyes for the third time that day. She lifted her hand to wipe them away and cried out as she realized she'd pulled the stitches in her breast.

"Hey," Luke said, stepping inside and closing the door behind her. "Why don't you go over there and have a seat at the bar while I make us a late supper? You haven't eaten, have you?"

She hadn't been hungry. "No. But you don't need to—"

"I've gotta eat," Luke said with a grin. "I might as well cook for two."

"Thanks, Luke." Nicki crossed into the kitchen area and sat on a barstool and watched as Luke pulled two steaks from the bag along with two potatoes. He stuck the steaks in the oven to broil and made a pincushion of the potatoes with toothpicks and stood them on their stilted legs in the microwave.

"I got asparagus instead of a salad," he said. "I know you like that."

"Thanks, Luke." Amazing that he remembered such a thing. She'd mentioned it once when they were out for a business dinner. She doubted Justin had a clue what she liked and didn't like in the vegetable department.

With little ado, Luke put the food in front of her and laid a place for himself next to her. He sat down on the barstool beside her, then jumped up and said, "I forgot the drinks. What do you want?"

"I'd better stick to water."

He poured them each a glass of ice water and sat down again to eat. During the meal, he filled her in on what had happened during the day. "So you see," he finished, "the firm didn't come to a stop because you took a day off."

"I'm okay," she said, telling him what he hadn't asked. "Dr. Fredericks got the cancer—without doing a mastectomy or cutting out any lymph nodes."

Luke lifted his brows in surprise but didn't point out the obvious—that she hadn't told him her entire breast and lymph nodes were at risk.

"Radiation starts next week," she said.

"How are you feeling?"

"Better than I thought I would," she told him. "By the way, remind me what is it you want me to look up for you on the computer."

"Are you sure you're well enough to work?"

"If I get tired, I'll quit."

He eyed her assessingly, then said, "All right, if you promise to take it easy, there is something I'd like you to research for me."

"I'm listening."

"I want you to look at any principal investigators or clinical research coordinators who reported a 'serious adverse event'—that is, a death—during the clinical trials of D-Free, and decided it *was not* caused by the drug. Got that?"

"Got it," Nicki said. "How many guys are we talking about?"

"There were twenty-two deaths during clinical trials," Luke said. "I want you to take a look at each investigator's finances, see if they might have been paid to make a false report. I've asked Eddie to look into this, too. But you might have more time to work on it than he does right now."

"You want it, you got it."

Luke put a hand on her knee and said, "I don't want you to do this if you're feeling bad. If you need to rest—"

Nicki put her hand on top of his. What a shame he'd been as committed to his career as she'd been to hers. Luke was a man who knew how to care, even if he didn't allow himself the time to do it. "Thanks, Luke. I'll take it easy. And I'll get the answers you need."

"It's important, Nick, or I wouldn't ask."

"I know," Nicki said. "It's all important. That's why we've given up our lives to do it."

Luke looked at her quizzically.

She released his hand and turned back to the last of her steak. "Don't mind me," she said. "I've had an epiphany today."

"Want to share it?"

She smiled, felt the tears well in her eyes, and said, "No. I don't think so. This is something I'm going to have to work out for myself."

"I'm here, Nick. Just call if you need me."

"Thanks, Luke. I can handle it." She was very good at being self-sufficient. Very good at being detached. It was going to be a challenge sharing herself and her life with a husband. She could hardly wait to get started.

12

‿m‿

Amy was both excited and anxious about her Friday night date with Luke. He'd called later in the week and offered to cook dinner for her at his condo, which meant she'd be staying in town after work, rather than driving home to The Woodlands. That left her with the problem of what to wear to work that could also double as an outfit for their date.

Amy hadn't read *Good Housekeeping* for more years than she could count, let alone *InStyle*, *Glamour* or *Cosmopolitan*, any of which magazines, she was sure, would have a fabulous spread on how her business suit could be transformed from "the office to night life" by unbuttoning buttons on her cotton blouse—or wearing something silk in the first place—and exchanging her sensible black pumps for three-inch red heels.

She arrived at the door to Luke's condo wearing exactly what she'd worn to work that morning. The A-line navy linen skirt and collarless V-neck jacket that she'd worn over a wide-collared white cotton blouse looked a great deal the worse for wear.

She'd brought a pair of three-inch heels and a camisole top to work with her in a small bag, but at the last minute she'd chickened out and hadn't changed into them. Luke would think she wanted to be attractive for him. Amy wasn't sure she wanted to send that message.

She knocked on Luke's door and heard metal clanging as though a pot had fallen on the floor. A moment later Luke opened the door, grabbed her hand and pulled her inside.

"I'm having a little trouble in the kitchen. Come on in."

He didn't let go of her hand, just tugged her along behind him. She was surprised to feel calluses on his fingertips and wondered what kind of physical labor he was doing—and when—that built up calluses.

She barely had time to focus on the decor in his living room as he hurried her through it. Or rather, the lack of decor. There were pictures of the kids on the walls, a saddle brown leather couch, an overstuffed green chair and ottoman and a glass coffee table. An oriental rug lay in the center of the room. Four padded wooden stools ranged along the bar that separated the living room from the kitchen.

Spartan. Spare. Bare. Those were the words that came to mind as he dragged her into the kitchen.

"Would you mind chopping up the vegetables for the salad?"

Before her on the kitchen counter sat enough vegetables to make a salad for twelve, along with an aluminum bowl that might have been what she'd heard landing on the floor. She smiled and asked, "Are we having salad for supper?"

"Hell, no," Luke said, pointing at a package wrapped

in freezer paper lying beside a broiler pan. "Steak. I wanted to make my mom's mashed potato recipe, but I got a late start. Guess I'll have to settle for microwaving them."

"I don't mind," she said, taking off her suit jacket and crossing around to place it on the back of one of the barstools.

She was glad to see Luke was still wearing what he'd apparently worn to work—although the tie was gone. He'd opened a few buttons on his wrinkled blue cotton shirt and rolled up his sleeves, but he was still wearing a pair of sharply creased navy suit pants and shiny cordovan shoes. She noticed the striated muscles on his forearms, where veins stood out the way they did on a man's arms. She wondered again how he stayed in such good physical shape.

Not that his looks were important to her.

She unbuttoned her own cotton blouse and was rolling up one sleeve when Luke came around the bar and helped her.

"I wanted this evening to be perfect," he said, as he briskly rolled up her sleeve. There was nothing lover-like in his actions. She might have been one of his little girls.

Except when he was done, his gaze met hers. And lingered too long.

He backed up and ran an agitated hand through his hair. "I wanted to have all the cooking done and dinner on the table for you. I even bought some candles." He waved at a pair of ivory tapers on the kitchen counter still in their cellophane wrappers. "When I started looking for something to put them in, I realized Valerie got the candlesticks in the divorce." He made a face. "We're going to have to make do with plain old electrical light."

Amy smiled, relaxing as she realized Luke was every bit as nervous as she was. "Don't worry. We'll manage fine." She reached out to give him a friendly pat on the shoulder, but he took a step closer and enclosed her in his arms.

"I'm glad you're here, Amy."

She felt her breasts crushed against the hardness of his chest and realized how tall he was in comparison to Carl. Her head nestled beneath his chin, and she felt the slimness of his waist as her arms naturally circled him.

As with the glance, the hug went on too long, until she was aware of the way their bodies fit together, aware of his heartbeat, aware of the sudden tension between them.

One of his hands slid down her back until it rested above her buttocks. The other slid up into her hair and cupped her head. He gave a slight tug, and her head fell back so she was looking up into his brown eyes. Her breathing was suddenly unsteady, and her heart began to pump a little harder.

"What are you doing, Luke?" she asked quietly.

"This feels right."

"This feels dangerous."

His lips tilted in the beginning of a smile. "You always were the careful one."

"Someone has to be prudent."

His hand caressed her head, and he pressed a very

"safe" kiss to her forehead. "It's nice to know my conscience is back in town."

She jerked free, not liking the mocking tone in his voice and stung by the nonsexual gesture of affection that conceded she was trouble he didn't need.

"I can leave right now if you want."

He shook his head and said, "Don't go. I knew this was going to be awkward. But—"

She grabbed her suit coat and was halfway to the door by the time he managed to get in front of her.

"I can take a hint," she said, the hurt coming through in her voice.

"Aw, Amy," he said as he gathered her up in his arms.

She struggled against his hold. "I want to leave, Luke."

"If you're going to bolt anyway, I might as well do what I didn't do because I didn't want you to bolt."

His mouth settled on hers.

She kept her lips pressed together, but his tongue slid along the seam of her mouth, seeking entrance. She pushed against his chest with the heels of her hands, but his hold was inexorable. She was angry, and afraid, because she realized how much she'd wanted exactly what was happening to happen. She opened her mouth to protest, and his tongue slid inside, warm and wet and oh, so familiar.

At the same moment, his hand slid down to her rear end and lifted her up against his unmistakable arousal.

Amy felt a quiver of feeling arc through her all the way to her toes and rose up to fit their bodies more closely together. Her tongue slid into his mouth, seeking the taste of him, and she made a humming sound as their tongues dueled. His arms tightened around her as he responded with a growling sound deep in his throat.

Amy acknowledged what she'd known ever since she'd accepted Luke's invitation to dinner at his home. She hadn't come here for food. She'd come for another kind of sustenance entirely. She needed to feel Luke's arms around her, wanted to taste him, to touch him, to recapture, if only for a moment, the passion that had been lost so very long ago.

He walked her backward toward the bedroom, never letting go of her, kissing her until she could hardly think, until all she wanted was her naked body pressed against his and him inside her.

She heard the bedroom door slam against the wall, felt the give of carpet under her feet. The room was dim, the dark, masculine shutters closing out the last light of the day. The bed was enormous, and Luke yanked at the spread with one hand, tearing it and the sheet and blanket away before he bore her down beneath him.

A ball of dirty white fur streaked past Amy's head with a yowl.

"Ohmigod!" she cried. "What was that?"

"That was Snowball. My cat."

"You have a cat? You don't believe in pets. What are you doing with a cat?" she said, shivering as he planted kisses beneath her ear.

"I picked her up at the animal shelter after the divorce—for the girls."

"Honor never said a word about playing with a cat when she spent the night."

Luke kissed his way down her throat. "That's because Snowball hid under the bed. She's kind of a lone wolf. Like me."

Amy was breathless from what Luke was doing or she might have pointed out his use of a dog family metaphor to describe his cat. She rejected his application of the metaphor to himself. Luke might have been a lone wolf once upon a time, but the description wasn't appropriate for someone so attached to his daughters. She wondered if he realized how far he'd come from the angry, rebellious kid he'd been in Bitter Creek.

"Amy, Amy," he murmured against her mouth. "It's been so long. I need you. I want you."

Amy needed him, too. Wanted him, too. His hand slid across her belly and down her thigh.

His clothes were in the way and she tore at his buttons. Their mouths were meshed, their breathing harsh, as their clothes were shoved aside.

"Have you got something?" she asked.

"What?" He lifted his head from her throat to look at her with eyes that glittered with passion. "What?"

"Some protection," she rasped. "Have you got a . . . " She was a grown-up. She could talk like one. "Have you got a condom?"

Luke froze. "Oh, shit."

Amy felt her heart sink. "You don't." She said it as a statement, not a question.

"No. I wasn't planning . . . That is, I haven't . . . "

One part of her was glad Luke hadn't believed they'd end up in bed. She wondered if he'd just run out of condoms, or if he hadn't needed any since his divorce. She wasn't about to ask.

Luke rolled off her onto his back and lay stretched across the bed with his arm over his eyes. "Damn it all to hell."

Amy wasn't sure whether she felt glad or sad that he hadn't offered to run out to a convenience store to get some. She sat up shakily and rebuttoned her blouse, which was open to the waist. She wasn't sure how he'd managed that, but a quick glance in his direction revealed that she'd not only unbuttoned his shirt, but pulled it out of his trousers.

He wasn't wearing a T-shirt, and she noticed the whorl of hair that surrounded his navel above the button of his slacks. She blushed when she realized she'd unbuckled his belt, as well.

She stood with her back to him and tucked her blouse into her skirt. She turned, managed a gamine smile and said, "Well, at least we won't go hungry."

Luke removed his hand from his eyes, stared at her incredulously and then grinned. "And they say the way to a *man's* heart is through his stomach."

Amy laughed. "Touché."

He stood up, pulled off his shirt, stripped his belt out of the loops and sought out a light blue wool V-neck sweater in the chest of drawers. He pulled it over his head and said, "All right, baby. Let's go make us some grub."

He'd called her "baby" all through high school. It was a loving endearment, one she hadn't heard since then. It reminded her how much history they had together.

Under the bright kitchen lights, Amy realized how narrow an escape she'd had. What if she'd slept with Luke? What if the sex had been as good as the kisses had been? Was there really any hope of a long-term relationship with Luke? He spent all his time at the office, just as she did. And what little time he had left, he gave to his girls. What if he'd only wanted a sexual fling?

Amy began pulling open kitchen drawers till she found the paring knife she wanted, then started to work on the tomatoes, cucumbers and mushrooms. Luke unwrapped the steaks and seasoned them, then turned the oven broiler on to let it preheat.

The silence was oppressive, and Amy sought a safe subject they could discuss. "How are your sisters doing?" she asked.

"They're both happily married to Blackthornes," he said. "Like my mom."

Amy heard the bitterness in his voice. "It sounds like you think they all betrayed your father."

Luke grimaced. "Dad is dead. And they all seem happy."

"Too bad you didn't have another sister," Amy said in an attempt to lighten his mood. "She could have married Owen's twin brother Clay and made it a full sweep."

She was relieved to hear Luke chuckle.

"Clay's single," he said, "if you're interested in snagging a Blackthorne."

"No thanks. I've had my fill of wealthy men." Amy began tearing lettuce leaves. "To be more precise, I've had my fill of marriage."

"Yours was that bad?" Luke asked as he stuck toothpicks in the potatoes, creating something that looked like a pincushion.

"Yeah. It was. What are you doing?" Amy asked curiously.

"I can stand them up in the microwave so they cook more evenly," Luke said, as he did just that.

"Good idea," Amy said. "I've always thought potatoes—"

"Are you still in love with him?"

Amy was caught off guard by the question. "What?"

"I want to know," Luke said. "Especially since I get the feeling you're using what happened with Carl Nash as an excuse not to get involved with me."

"I got burned, Luke. Can we leave it at that?"

He leaned back against the counter and said, "I suppose we could. But I hope you won't."

Amy felt flustered with Luke's gaze focused so intently on her. She kept her eyes on the lettuce, tearing it into tiny, bite-size pieces to keep her hands busy. She reminded herself she'd promised not to put up walls between herself and Luke. But when she spoke, she found herself answering in short, factual sentences that didn't reveal any of the pain she'd endured.

"There isn't much to tell," she said. "I married Carl. He went to jail for cheating the government. I divorced him."

Luke grunted. "I thought his family was loaded. Why would he take that kind of chance?"

"His father and uncle have money, which Carl will inherit someday. He made a good living as a doctor. But he was spoiled. He wanted more."

"And you never saw it coming?"

Amy sighed and turned to face him. She had to share, she realized. She had to let him into her life and see where it led.

"My marriage to Carl started out like a fairy tale," she said. "He owned a wonderful redbrick colonial home in the historic Fan district of Richmond. His family was well known and respected, and we were feted by everyone as new Virginia royalty. It was quite a heady experience for a girl from tiny Bitter Creek, Texas. But it didn't last long."

"What went wrong?"

Amy met his gaze with bleak eyes and admitted, "He wasn't faithful. And he didn't care that I knew about his infidelities."

"Why the hell didn't you walk out on him?"

Amy was caught off guard by Luke's anger. It took her a moment to realize he was angry with Carl, not her.

"That bastard didn't deserve you."

"No," Amy said. "He didn't."

"So why did you stay?"

"I was already pregnant by the time I knew his true character." She laughed bitterly. "Actually I didn't know the true depth of his weakness—that he was also a liar and a thief—until much later. By then his father had made threats that I found very convincing."

"You should have come home, Amy. You should have asked me for help."

"What could you have done against all that wealth and power?"

"I would have used my stepfather's influence, if that's what it took to set you free."

She stared at him, surprised. "You would have asked a man you hate to help me?"

"I'd have gone to the devil himself."

She believed him. Tears welled in her eyes.

His arms closed around her, and he gently rocked her. "Don't cry, baby. You're free now. It's over. I'm here. And I'm not going anywhere."

Amy looked up at Luke and said, "I wish you wouldn't say things like that."

"I wish I hadn't let you go."

"You didn't 'let me go,'" Amy said, pushing against his shoulders to free herself from his embrace. "I dumped you."

Luke grinned. "I stand corrected. I wish I hadn't done what I did to get dumped."

Amy tried to remember what it was he'd done that had been the last straw. "What was it you did?" she asked, her brow furrowed.

"You mean besides that fiasco in the front seat of my brother's truck on prom night?"

Amy felt two hot spots on her cheeks. "That was more my fault that yours," she said. "I thought I knew what I was doing. I didn't."

"Obviously I didn't, either, or we wouldn't have been done so fast," Luke said with a rueful smile.

Amy was surprised to hear herself laughing. "It was pretty quick, wasn't it?"

Luke laughed with her. "Don't remind me!"

Their laughter stopped as their eyes caught. It

would take longer if they tried again, his eyes promised. It would be everything they'd both wanted it to be the first time, when they were too young to know the import of the step they were taking together.

Amy took a deep breath and held it as she let herself get caught up in the fantasy.

Which was the moment Snowball chose to jump up onto the kitchen counter, arch her back like a cardboard Halloween cutout and hiss at her.

Amy cried out in fright and threw herself into Luke's arms. She hid her face against his chest, so she could feel his chest heaving with laughter. She tried to back up, but his arms tightened around her.

"Thank you, Snowball," he said to the cat. He stroked the cat's back, which flattened as his hand ran along the length of it. "I think she was jealous," Luke said.

The animal actually began to purr.

"You let your cat walk on the kitchen counter?" Amy asked.

"I don't allow it. Snowball's not too good at following rules."

"Reminds me of someone else I know. You realize you've spoiled that cat rotten."

"Yeah. I have," Luke conceded. "But she pays me back by keeping me company when I'm alone at night, so we're even."

Amy met his gaze and realized, when she saw the look in his eyes, that when Luke had said both he and the cat were lone wolves, he might more honestly have said *lonely* wolves.

The microwave pinged.

"Potatoes are done," Amy said, backing out of his embrace. "You can turn our steaks while I finish up the salad. I don't know about you, but I'm hungry."

She could see he didn't want to let her go, but the steak was spitting and smoking in the oven, so he turned to take care of it.

"Shoo!" Amy said to Snowball.

The cat gave her a disdainful look, then made a graceful three-legged leap to the floor.

When Amy had finished up the salad, she asked, "Would you rather eat at the bar?"

"I eat alone at the bar every night. I was looking forward to dinner at the table with you."

"Do you have place mats?"

He shook his head.

"We don't need them," she said quickly. "I'll put the silverware on the table while you get us something to drink."

"I would have gotten a bottle of wine, but I know you don't drink."

She'd learned to drink wine during the years she'd lived with Carl, but she said, "Iced tea would be great."

"It's in the fridge," he said. "I'll get the butter and sour cream for the potatoes, if you'll pour the tea."

It didn't take long, with both of them pitching in, before they were sitting at the table with their dinners before them.

"This looks great," Amy said.

"Is your steak well done enough?" Luke asked. "I know you don't like it as rare as I do."

Amy cut into the blood red steak. It was too rare, but she wasn't about to send Luke back to the kitchen to cook it any more. She cut a slice and chewed vigorously. "It's perfect."

Luke shot her a relieved smile.

"I have to admit I was a little anxious about coming here for dinner," she said.

"Why is that?" Luke asked as he mashed butter and sour cream into his baked potato.

She grinned. "I thought we'd end up in bed."

Luke laughed. "I know I'm going to hate myself in the morning for not making a stop at the drugstore on the way home."

"I'm glad you didn't," Amy said. "It feels like I've known you forever, but—"

"I feel the same way."

"But we don't know each other," Amy continued. "We were kids twelve years ago. Now we're adults and parents and—"

"And I'm still attracted to you."

"I'm attracted to you, too," Amy admitted. "But we have to be sensible about this, Luke. There are other people in our lives whose feelings have to be considered."

"Our children?"

Amy nodded. "Honor is . . . She's just learning how to assert herself. I don't want to upset that balance. And your girls—"

"Brynne and Midge already love you."

"Brynne and Midge will resent anyone who steps into their mother's shoes," Amy said. "And we've both been ignoring the fact that we're on opposite sides of a significant lawsuit."

"Choate has taken me off the Anastasio case."

"Why did she do that?" Amy asked.

"Maybe because I've been asking a lot of questions about D-Free."

"Who's replacing you?" Amy asked.

"A friend of mine, Drew DeWitt. You can count on him inundating you with paper when you send over your next set of interrogatories."

"What are you going to do?"

"I intend to go straight to the horse's mouth to find out the truth about D-Free."

"The horse being?"

"Dr. Harold McCorkle. The guy who came up with the idea for D-Free. I'm meeting him at Hyland headquarters when he gets back from a medical conference in Brazil week after next."

"Even though you're no longer assigned to the case? Won't that get you into trouble with the Dragon Lady?"

"I don't have much choice. My daughter's taking that drug, and I need answers she isn't giving me."

"Do you really think McCorkle will tell you anything you don't already know?"

"I'm pretty good at questioning witnesses," Luke said. "We'll have to see."

They reminisced about the kids they'd known in high school during the rest of the meal.

"I've got ice cream in the freezer," Luke said when they were both done. "But I thought we could have that a little later."

"Sounds good to me," Amy agreed as she helped Luke stack the dishes in the sink.

"Are you sure I can't help you wash—"

Amy was interrupted by the ringing of the phone. Luke picked it up, listened, then handed it to her. "It's your baby-sitter."

Amy's heart was in her throat, as she imagined all the things that could have happened to Honor. Amy listened to the baby-sitter, then said, "Put her on the phone." The sound of Honor's tearful, whispery voice made Amy's heart thud heavily in her chest. "Honey? Uh-huh. Uh-huh. Go back to bed, honey. I'll be home soon."

She saw the resigned look on Luke's face even before she hung up the phone. "I'm sorry to cut our evening short, but I have to go home."

"Is Honor all right?"

"She's too anxious to go to sleep by herself. And it's getting too late for her to be up."

Luke glanced at his watch. "It's barely ten."

"I know it's early. But I have to go." She was already reaching for the suit coat she'd put on the back of the bar stool.

Luke took it from her and helped her put it on. "I've enjoyed this evening. Will you have dinner with me again sometime soon?"

"It's not easy for me to get away during the week," Amy hedged. "Besides, we have the weekend at Three Oaks to look forward to." She wasn't going to come here again. Tonight had proved it wasn't safe for them to be alone with each other until she was sure she wanted Luke back in her life. At Three Oaks they'd be well chaperoned by both children and parents.

"Thanks for tonight," he said as he leaned down to give her a short but sweet kiss.

His tenderness was almost more seductive than the passion she'd experienced earlier in the evening. She slid her hand around his nape and drew his head down to kiss him back. And just as quickly released him.

"Good night, Luke," she said, backing away toward the door. Somehow she stepped on Snowball's stub of a tail. The cat screeched bloody murder, and sheer terror propelled Amy back into Luke's arms.

She was trembling with fear and surprise and made the mistake of looking up into Luke's laughing eyes. Her lips curved into a smile, and soon she was laughing with him.

As he lowered his head, she raised her mouth to his and let him give her the kiss she'd denied herself when she'd been in such a hurry to get out the door. It was so easy to give herself up to passion. And so dangerous.

She broke the kiss at last, breathless, trembling with need, her knees rubbery again, but this time because nature wanted her prone so she could mate.

"I've got to go," she gasped. She was out the door before Luke could say anything that might make her want to stay.

13

—∽—

"Dr. McCorkle isn't seeing anyone today."

Luke stared in disbelief at the secretary who stood between him and the man who had the answers he sought. "I have an appointment."

"Dr. McCorkle isn't taking any appointments," the secretary said without apology. She went back to typing on her computer keyboard as though he weren't still standing there.

McCorkle's secretary was a middle-aged woman wearing a form-fitting dress Luke figured was a half size too small, her hair up in a ratted twist high on her head, with too-red lipstick and black eyeliner that gave her a hard edge. But judging from the size of her desk, and its placement directly outside the door to McCorkle's office, she wielded a great deal of power.

It seemed worth a try to charm her, so Luke smiled. "I'm sure if you give him a quick call, he'll—"

"Dr. McCorkle specifically told me this morning he needed peace and quiet to review some materials."

The office behind her had enticing walls of frosted glass through which Luke could see movement. "I need to speak with Dr. McCorkle—"

"Nothing you have to say to Dr. McCorkle could be important enough to disturb him."

"What's your name?" Luke asked, fighting to keep his voice neutral.

"I'm Ms. Walters, Dr. McCorkle's executive assistant."

Luke processed this new information. An executive assistant. Who acted toward her boss like an overprotective secretary. Luke glanced at his watch. It was 9:15 on Monday morning. McCorkle had arrived back in the States on Friday night. Luke was only fifteen minutes late for his appointment. "Look, Miss—"

The woman stopped typing and said, "It's Ms. Walters."

"Ms. Walters," Luke persisted. "I'm representing Hyland in its D-Free litigation—"

"I know exactly who you are, Mr. Creed. I'm sure Dr. McCorkle will be able to see you later this week."

Luke stared at McCorkle's executive assistant in exasperation. "I've already waited two weeks for Dr. McCorkle to return from Brazil. I need to speak with him now. Not later this week, not next week, not next month," he said. "Now."

Ms. Walters stared him down. He had to give her points for bulldoggedness.

At that moment, the elevator behind Luke chimed pleasantly and opened to reveal a uniformed delivery-man with a package and a clipboard. He hurried to Ms. Walters's desk and set a package down, then held out a clipboard to be signed.

As Ms. Walters was signing for the package, Luke walked around her, opened the door to McCorkle's office and stepped inside. She was out of her chair an instant later, but it was an instant too late. Luke was already inside.

"Hello, Dr. McCorkle. I'm Luke Creed. I need to talk with you about D-Free."

Ms. Walters stepped into the doorway and said, "I told him you were busy reviewing reports and couldn't be disturbed."

McCorkle gave her a confused look. "I meant I didn't want to be disturbed by anyone except Mr. Creed. Of course I want to speak with him."

Luke saw Ms. Walters was flustered when she turned to face him.

"I'm sorry, Mr. Creed," she said. "Apparently, I was mistaken. Please make yourself comfortable. May I get you some coffee or something else to drink?"

"I'm fine," Luke said.

"Thank you, Ms. Walters," McCorkle said.

McCorkle's executive assistant shot Luke a narrow-eyed look before she closed the door behind her. Luke was suddenly grateful that Flo had never shown signs of becoming the sort of powerhungry martinet that guarded McCorkle's door.

On the other hand, Luke was sure Ms. Walters had saved McCorkle from many an unwanted interview.

"Have a seat," McCorkle said, gesturing to the sitting area in one corner of his enormous, patent holder-size corporate office.

Luke glanced longingly at the functional chairs in front of McCorkle's desk, then headed for the over-stuffed seating arrangement in the corner.

McCorkle was already seating himself in the lone chair, leaving the L-shaped couch to Luke.

McCorkle looked nothing like the stereotypical research scientist—the nerd in a lab coat. He was wearing glasses, but they had small, trendy metal frames, and he obviously had an expensive barber and an even more expensive tailor. He was of medium height with a wiry build. His receding gray hair was closely cropped, and his gray eyes were direct.

"How can I help you?" McCorkle asked.

"I want to know about D-Free."

"So you said," McCorkle replied. "What is it you think I can tell you?"

"Whether the drug is killing kids."

McCorkle pulled a pack of cigarettes from his suit coat pocket and, without asking whether it would bother Luke, lit one with a silver lighter he took from a small pocket in his vest. He took a deep drag and exhaled without turning his head, so a cloud of smoke hit Luke in the face.

The smoke reminded him of home. Most of the cowboys who worked at Three Oaks smoked. Luke had smoked himself until he'd become a parent. It wasn't until he'd come to the big city that he'd run into restrictions on smoking indoors, mostly in state, federal and other public buildings. Apparently, there was no such rule in the corporate offices of Hyland Pharmaceuticals. Or McCorkle was exempt from it.

"I've already had this discussion with Grayson Choate," McCorkle said. "I don't understand why it's necessary to repeat everything to you."

Luke didn't want McCorkle complaining to Choate, especially when he wasn't supposed to be here in the first place. But he needed to know what Choate knew about the drug.

"I've been representing Hyland in the most recent D-Free wrongful death suits," Luke said. "In doing background research, I discovered the twenty-two 'unrelated' deaths during clinical trials. I know all those deaths occurred in patients between the ages of nine and sixteen—as have the five deaths since D-Free went on the market."

Luke met McCorkle's gaze and said, "I know about the problem you had with hormones causing a death when you were first developing the drug."

"Then you know I solved that problem," McCorkle said, exhaling another plume of smoke.

"Did you?"

"Of course. Otherwise, the drug would never have mustered FDA approval."

"What about all those 'serious adverse events' during clinical trials?" Luke asked.

McCorkle shrugged. "You've read the reports. None of them were deemed by the PIs and CRCs on site to be related to the use of D-Free."

"Have you looked at the incidents yourself?" Luke asked.

"To be honest, I have. In fact, that's what I discussed with Choate."

Luke held his breath. This was what he'd come to hear.

"There are a couple of them that I found . . . suspicious," McCorkle admitted.

"Just suspicious?"

McCorkle stubbed out his cigarette in an ashtray on the coffee table. "What is it you expect me to say, Mr. Creed?"

"I want the truth."

McCorkle fished in his pocket for his cigarettes. "There's nothing wrong with D-Free. It works. The FDA says it's safe."

"Do you personally think it's safe?"

"We have found nothing in any of the Phase IV clinical studies that suggests—"

"Have there been any more deaths?" Luke persisted.

McCorkle hesitated a beat too long before he said, "One. But—"

"It was not related to the drug," Luke finished for him.

McCorkle's pointed chin came up. "I've let this go on long enough." He stuck the pack of cigarettes back in his pocket, clearly agitated. "I called Ms. Choate when I learned you wanted to meet with me," he said. "She told me to find out what you wanted and send you back to her."

Luke felt his heart speed up. He should have known. He should have let it go. But how could he? It wasn't just his own daughter at risk. It was every kid taking D-Free.

"Get out, Mr. Creed. Your questions aren't welcome. And neither are you."

"If you believe some of the deaths during clinical trials are suspicious—" Luke began.

"Watch your step," McCorkle warned. "Don't be making statements about D-Free that affect its marketability. Give me an excuse, and I'll sue you personally and every partner in DeWitt & Blackthorne."

Luke didn't see the point in trading threats. But the fact that McCorkle felt compelled to threaten him made Luke even more worried about the safety of the drug.

McCorkle crossed to the door, opened it and said, "Ms. Walters, my visitor is leaving."

McCorkle's assistant appeared at the door, a false smile on her face, and said, "I'll show you out."

"One last question," Luke said, pausing at the door. "I don't—"

"If you were the parent of a daughter with juvenile diabetes, would you keep her on the drug?"

"I'm not in that situation, so I couldn't say."

"I am," Luke said. "My ten-year-old daughter is taking your miracle drug. I need to know the truth. Is it lethal? Is D-Free killing kids?"

McCorkle's face paled, and his lips flattened to a blade.

"How dare you accuse Dr. McCorkle of anything so heinous!" Ms. Walters hissed.

Luke hadn't seen Walters moving up behind him.

"Dr. McCorkle is a man without peer, a genius, a—"

"Man who may be keeping lethal secrets," Luke said through tight jaws.

Red splotches appeared on Ms. Walters's throat. "You

can't say slanderous things like that about Dr. McCorkle and get away with it."

"Ms. Walters." McCorkle's voice was low and calm. "That will be enough."

"He has no idea who he's speaking to," Ms. Walters said to her boss. "He has no idea."

"Will you please show my visitor to the elevator," he said.

Ms. Walters eyed Luke malevolently. "It will be my very great pleasure."

Luke kept his eyes straight ahead as he walked to the elevator. The instant the doors closed him inside he heaved a sigh of despair. He'd let his mouth get away from him this time. *Is it lethal? Is D-Free killing kids?* He was sure that would get back to Choate.

It was bad enough throwing six years of sacrifice down the drain. But he hadn't gotten anything definitive out of the scientist. Just the awful gut feeling that his daughter was engaged in a deadly game of Russian roulette.

As he stepped out of the elevator on the ground floor of Hyland headquarters, he pulled out his cell phone and called Amy. When she answered he said, "My meeting with McCorkle wasn't as productive as I'd hoped."

"You didn't find out anything useful?"

"McCorkle admitted to being suspicious of the clinical trial results."

"Which means he may be worried about his responsibility for the deaths that have occurred."

"I think he's probably realized that kids are dying,"

Luke said. "I'm not so sure he's convinced that he's the one responsible for killing them."

"He's the one who reported those faulty statistics to the FDA. In my book that makes him responsible," Amy said.

"With any luck, Choate will give me the rest of the story. I'll be seeing her right away, because McCorkle called and told her I was coming to meet with him. And she told him to send me back to her when I was done talking with him."

"Oh, no! What's going to happen to you?"

"I guess I'll find that out when I report to Choate." Trust Amy to think about consequences. Luke thought of the ten associates who'd preceded him with Choate and decided that getting the boot was a distinct possibility. Seeing McCorkle had been a calculated risk. The worst part was, he still had no facts with which to confront Choate, and it would be professional suicide to go over her head to the management committee without something more than unfounded suspicions.

He saw now that he'd been foolish to hope McCorkle would admit anything to him when confronted. At least the meeting had served one purpose. McCorkle's behavior had convinced Luke the man was hiding something. Which meant there was very likely a problem with the drug.

It wasn't much, but it was all the ammunition he had to fight back with, if Choate threatened to fire him.

"Any chance at all Dr. McCorkle will admit his suspicions about D-Free to the public?" Amy asked.

"I doubt it."

"What makes you so sure?"

"You'd have to be pretty greedy and ambitious—and downright heartless—to face a father asking whether the drug is safe for his child and refuse to give him an answer."

"Is that what happened?"

"Pretty much."

"Are you going to get fired over this?"

Luke heard the concern in her voice. "I don't know, Amy. But it was something I had to do."

"You did the right thing, Luke."

His throat tightened with emotion. "Thanks."

"I've got another call," she said. "Let me know what happens with Choate."

"I will." He stared at the phone, then disconnected the call.

Luke had never let himself think what the future might hold if D&B let him go. He'd been totally focused on one thing: becoming one of them. He'd thought he would be willing to make any sacrifice, but he was beginning to think they wanted too much. Did he really want partnership if it meant overlooking corporate malfeasance? If he had to give up his self-respect and the respect of those he loved?

Flo greeted Luke the instant he got back to his office with, "Ms. Choate wants to see you. Yesterday."

"Tell her I'm on my way."

Luke was surprised at his reaction to the summons. A few weeks ago, it would have struck terror in his heart, because Choate held his career in the palm of her hand. But Amy's return had caused him to take a hard look at his life. He hadn't given up hope of becoming a partner, but he'd reassessed the price he was willing to pay for the privilege.

Luke stuck his head in Choate's doorway and said, "Harold McCorkle said you wanted to see me."

"Come in." The Dragon Lady was wearing funereal black, which seemed appropriate to Luke, who figured the chances were good he was about to get buried. He crossed and stood behind one of the ridiculous chairs in front of her desk.

"What am I going to do with you?" Choate said.

The comment sounded like something a worried parent would say to a wayward child. She was stroking her pen again, as though it were the butt of a whip she was thinking of using on him.

Luke figured he had nothing to lose, so he said, "Dr. McCorkle told me he spoke to you about his problems with D-Free. I want to know what he had to say."

"I don't see what purpose that would serve," Choate said. "There's nothing you can do with the information."

"My daughter is taking D-Free."

Choate leaned back in her chair but said nothing.

"You can see why it's important for me to know whether the drug is dangerous."

Choate remained mute.

Luke resisted the very strong urge to yank her out of the chair by her black lapels and shake the information he wanted out of her. He merely gripped the back of the chair until his knuckles were white and said, "If you know something, I'd like to hear it."

"What McCorkle told me is privileged information. I can't share it with you," Choate said at last.

"Goddammit! Stop playing games with me. My daughter's life is at stake."

Choate observed him with unblinking eyes. "Get control of yourself. If you think there's something wrong with the drug, you're free to have your daughter discontinue its use. I'm not going to give you information that might later compromise D&B."

"So it *is* dangerous."

"You haven't been listening to me. I've said no such thing."

Luke made a disgusted sound. "Are we done here?"

"Not quite." Choate dropped her pen, leaned forward in her chair and said, "How am I supposed to trust your judgment? You've ignored my directives on this case, insulted a major client, delivered work I requested in an untimely manner—that patent memo was a day late, and you know how important timeliness is to our clients—and you have the junior associate under your supervision billing hours to some pro bono project I've been told nothing about."

Luke didn't try to defend himself.

"But it's your unethical behavior that concerns me most."

"*My* unethical behavior?"

"You should have informed me—and Hyland—that opposing counsel on the Anastasio case is an old girl-friend of yours."

Luke froze. How could Choate possibly know about

his previous relationship with Amy? He suddenly realized Drew must have said something to her.

His silence gave Choate time to realize the mistake she'd made. But instead of making up some explanation of how she'd discovered his previous relationship with Amy, she went on the attack again.

"I will not have associates who work for me haring off on their own. You are not authorized to speak with anyone at Hyland without first coming through me. If I hear that you've done so again, you're fired. Is that clear?"

"Yes, ma'am." The sneer Luke managed not to show on his face was there in his tone of voice.

"Get out of here," Choate said, her body vibrating with angry tension.

Luke felt a tremendous sense of relief that she hadn't fired him, and immediately wondered why she hadn't.

He suddenly realized it was because she didn't have cause. A tardy memo and a low-level associate billing unexplained pro bono time weren't sufficient grievances to bring before the management committee. Keeping his former relationship with Amy from Hyland might be an ethical breach, but it could be easily corrected by informing both clients of the fact that he and Amy had known each other twelve years ago and getting a waiver.

No, the only serious misstep he'd taken was to confront McCorkle—and threaten the firm's enormous revenues from Hyland. All Choate would have to do was disclose his behavior at Hyland to the management committee. Considering what was at stake, they would likely have booted him right out the door.

Only, Choate hadn't done that. *Why not?*

Because if she'd brought that kind of accusation against him, he would have had the opportunity to explain *why* he'd confronted McCorkle.

Luke suddenly realized that the management committee might not know that Choate was helping McCorkle hide the truth—or at least had no inkling that she had suspicions about D-Free that she was concealing from them.

Which meant she was vulnerable. He just needed proof that McCorkle had tampered with the results he'd sent to the FDA. He needed something he could take to the management committee, who might see the wisdom of advising McCorkle to tell the public the truth about D-Free.

Luke turned at Choate's door and said, "Does the general partnership know what you're doing? Do they know the risk you're taking with innocent lives?"

Choate came out of her chair. "You're walking a fine line, Luke. A dangerous line. Don't think you can go over my head or behind my back without serious damage to your position here at D&B. The partners won't thank you. They won't want any part of you."

Luke heard what she was saying. His partnership was on the line. Hell, he'd probably already crossed that line. He knew he should keep his mouth shut and get out, but there was something else bothering him, and some vestige of his reckless youth prompted him to say, "What I don't understand is why? What do you get out of keeping the problems with D-Free a secret?"

"I'm representing my client's interests," she said in an icy voice. "A concept you can't seem to grasp."

Luke bit his lip on the retort that sprang to mind. He wasn't willing to get off his carousel pony and concede his chance at the brass ring was at an end. Not yet. He might yet be able to expose Hyland's illegal behavior and become a D&B partner next spring.

Choate was a powerful adversary, and she wasn't going anywhere. If he hoped to survive at D&B, he had to figure out a way to get what he wanted without burning any bridges with her.

"I'm worried about my daughter," he said.

It was the absolute truth. And a reasonable excuse for his insolent behavior.

"Of course you are," Choate said, lowering herself back into her chair. She obviously knew an olive branch when she saw one. "Do your job, Luke. That's all I ask."

"Yes, ma'am," he said. "Is that all?"

"That's all."

Luke turned and left without another word. And headed straight for Eddie Mull's office. He stepped inside and closed the door behind him.

Eddie looked up, surprised at Luke's abrupt intrusion.

"What's up?" he asked.

"I want you to find out everything you can about Harold McCorkle's personal life," Luke said without preamble.

"His personal life?"

"I want to know how many times he pees in a day," Luke said. "I want to know if he's got a girlfriend. I want to know if he goes to gay bars. I want—"

"You think he might be gay?"

Luke shook his head. "I just want to make it clear to you that nothing is off-limits," he said. "I want to see if there's anything in McCorkle's life that will give me some leverage to get the truth about D-Free out of him."

"So he didn't divulge anything in your meeting today," Eddie concluded.

"He admitted to being suspicious of some of the clinical results," Luke said. "The kicker was, he called Choate and told her about our meeting. Choate just called me on the carpet and told me to butt out. Which means I have to keep a low profile long enough to smooth her hackles."

"So I get to be your eyes and ears where Dr. McCorkle is concerned," Eddie said.

"I hate putting you in this position."

Eddie grinned. "I'm enjoying it. Don't worry, Luke. I'm pretty good at keeping a low profile myself."

"Thanks, Eddie."

Luke had already exited Eddie's office when he leaned back through the doorway and said, "Oh, yeah. It might be a good idea to expand your search by one more person. See what you can find out about Dr. McCorkle's executive assistant, Ms. Walters."

"You want it, you got it," Eddie said.

"Thanks, Eddie. I appreciate it."

Luke wondered if Eddie was going to have to cancel

more plans with his wife. Even a week ago, the thought wouldn't have occurred to him. Now it bothered him to think of pregnant Mary Margaret Mull sitting home alone.

What if he'd taken more time off to spend with Valerie and the kids? Would the world have come to an end? Probably not. Would he still be married? Probably not.

The latter answer surprised Luke, but since he'd reconnected with Amy, he'd realized that the problems in his marriage hadn't all been about the small amount of time he'd spent at home. If he'd loved Valerie more, maybe he would have made a greater effort to spend time with her. But once the physical attraction had worn thin, there hadn't been much substance between them.

Would he have made different choices if he'd been married to Amy? Luke wasn't sure he would have. He would still have wanted to prove to her that he was someone worthy of her love. To him, that meant providing his wife with the financial security that had been just beyond the grasp of his family the whole time he'd been growing up at Three Oaks. And since he refused to make use of the trust fund Jackson Blackthorne had set up for him, and had something to prove to his stepfather, as well, he probably would have been just as driven to succeed.

So what made him think he could carve out some sort of life with Amy now? Especially since both of them had demanding careers and children that had a claim on their time?

For the first time since he'd been hired to work at DeWitt & Blackthorne, Luke found himself considering an alternate universe. What if he went to work for a law firm that didn't demand his blood and guts every day? Would he still feel like a success if his job became merely a way of making a living, rather than consuming his entire life?

Could he really give up a dream he'd harbored—and nurtured—for the past six years? If he walked away from D&B, if he took a less prestigious position with a smaller firm, would he feel like a loser the rest of his life?

Luke hadn't realized where he was headed until he found himself at Drew DeWitt's office on the litigation floor. He stepped inside and closed the door.

Drew looked up in surprise.

"Choate knows Amy Nash used to be my girlfriend. If she finds out anything else personal about me, we're no longer friends."

Luke opened the door again and left without saying another word, or allowing Drew to answer him.

He was striding past Justin Sterling's office on his way back to the elevator when he remembered the Hyland file that Neil Ford had handed over to the head of litigation. Justin's office was empty, and Luke decided it was worth a quick look to see if he could find the missing file.

For the third time, he closed a door behind him. The only person who had the right to complain about him being there had already given him permission to look around, but Luke didn't want word to get back to Choate about what he was doing.

As he eyed the enormous piles of paper that littered the room, Luke realized that searching Justin's office for one particular file was going to be a great deal harder than finding a needle in a haystack. At least a needle was sharp and shiny and had a different texture from hay. One file looked pretty much like another.

Still, Luke welcomed the opportunity to be alone, doing a job that didn't require any mental exertion, as a chance to calm down after his confrontation with Choate. A half hour later, he was starting to feel frustrated and impatient. He was ready to give up when he spied a tab on a file that looked familiar. It was halfway down a five-foot-high pile of paper.

Luke carefully worked his way down the pile, creating a new pile on the floor blocking the narrow walkway Justin had created that led from his door to his desk. Too damn bad, Luke thought. This was important. And it was Justin's fault there was no other place to put the files he needed to move to get to the one he wanted.

Luke actually smiled when he reached the file, opened it and found handwritten notes from Neil about his phone discussions with Amy.

He left Justin's office and headed for his own, anxious to see what Neil might have discovered about Hyland and D-Free that had remained hidden since his death.

14

It was a sign of how much Luke's priorities had changed that he kept his promise to bring Amy and Honor and his kids to visit his mother the following weekend. His professional life could not have been in a bigger shambles, but he dropped everything at six o'clock on Friday and headed to The Woodlands to pick up Amy and Honor. Then he swung by and picked up his daughters before heading south to Three Oaks.

Once they were out of the bumper-to-bumper traffic in metropolitan Houston, it was a straight shot down U.S. 59 to Bitter Creek, a distance of a little over 200 miles.

He'd brought pillows and blankets for the girls, who were buckled into the backseat of his extended-cab pickup. Brynne and Honor kept themselves busy listening to radio-edited versions of Eminem on what had turned out to be matching Hello Kitty portable disc players.

Midge made a nuisance of herself when it became clear the two older girls weren't going to include her.

"Dad-dy," Brynne complained. "Midge is bothering us."

"I want to listen," Midge protested, grabbing for Brynne's earphones.

"Ouch!" Brynne cried. "Daddy, Midge pulled my hair!"

"Mary Jane Creed, behave yourself," Luke said in his sternest voice.

Midge burst into tears, which caused Brynne to complain again about the noise she was making.

Amy said under her breath, "Would it be all right if Midge comes up here?"

"I want her wearing a seat belt."

"I can belt her in with me."

"Anything to get some peace and quiet," Luke muttered.

"Come on up here, Midge," Amy said. She helped the little girl climb over the seat, buckled her in and put an arm around her, then kept her entertained until the drone of the wheels on the road and the dark coolness of the cab eventually wooed her to sleep.

"Thanks for taking care of Midge," Luke said. "I should have realized there would be problems with the three of them cooped up in such a small space for so long."

"She's a charmer," Amy said.

"A noisy one," Luke agreed. "One of the things I never realized when I became a parent was how precious silence would become."

Amy chuckled.

"I always expected Midge to be quiet like Brynne. But they have totally different personalities."

"I only have Honor, so I wouldn't know."

"Why didn't you have more children?" Luke asked. "You're good with kids."

"I wanted more," she admitted. "Carl didn't."

"Would you like to have more?"

"Hypothetically? Yes," she admitted. "But the circumstances would have to be right."

"Meaning?"

"I'd want to have a supportive spouse who loved kids as much as I do," she said.

"I'd like to have more kids, but that doesn't seem fair with the demands of my job."

"You can always change jobs," Amy said.

Luke smiled wryly. "I may end up doing that whether I want to or not."

"I thought the situation with the Dragon Lady had been resolved."

"She didn't fire me. But it's a good bet she isn't going to recommend me for partnership. I'm looking for that piece of information that will give me the leverage I need to go over her head to the management committee."

"But you haven't found it?"

"Not yet." To his disappointment, he hadn't found anything pertinent in Neil's Hyland file.

"I've got a couple of the best minds in the firm working on it," Luke said.

Amy lifted an inquisitive brow.

"Nicole Maldonado and Eddie Mull. They're friends, as well as fellow associates," he said. "I actually felt guilty leaving the office tonight, knowing I've asked Nick and Eddie to keep reviewing the D-Free clinical trial documentation."

"But you did leave the office," Amy pointed out.

"Yes, I did." Luke brushed a hand over Midge's blond curls. "It's taken me a while to wake up to what's important in life. I may be a slow learner, but once I figure something out, it sticks."

"Any regrets?"

"Who doesn't have them?" Luke said. "It would be nice to rewind my life and play it again knowing what I know now. For a start, I wouldn't have messed things up with you."

"I wouldn't have loved you if you'd been anyone other than who you were," she said quietly. "I loved that you were undisciplined and unfettered and defied authority. You did what I never had the courage to do."

His mouth twisted ruefully. "If you liked me then, it's no wonder you're not interested in the man I've become."

"Who said I'm not interested?" Amy said. "The truth is, I wouldn't be interested in you now if you were still the person you were then."

"Now you're confusing me," Luke said with a laugh.

"I've changed, too," she explained. "I don't need to live my life vicariously anymore. I've stepped away from the sidelines. I'm having adventures of my own."

"Which means you don't need someone like—"

"You're missing the point," she interrupted. "I don't want to have those adventures by myself. I want to share them with someone special who can appreciate me for who I am, with all my flaws and foibles."

"You have flaws and foibles?" Luke said, pretending to be shocked. "I had no idea."

Amy laughed. "I'm not going to name them for you," she said. "But nobody's perfect."

"Once upon a time, I thought you were," Luke said. "You seemed so sure of what you wanted out of life. You knew what was right and what was wrong, and you always did what you believed was right."

"You make me sound like a prig. Was I?"

He grinned. "A bit of one, yes. In those days I found prigs appealing."

Amy laughed again. "Thank goodness. I wouldn't have made it through high school without you."

"I don't think I can make it through the rest of my life without you."

Amy had been enjoying their banter, and the bald statement of need caught her off guard. Her mind was racing, trying to come up with a response that didn't make light of his feelings. Especially because she'd begun to let herself imagine the two of them ending up together.

"I can't say it hasn't crossed my mind to wonder what it would be like to be married to you," she said. "The possibility has its appeal."

He snorted. "That's comforting."

"Don't be angry," she said, laying a hand on his forearm. He couldn't jerk away, because he was holding the wheel, but she felt the muscles tense beneath her touch. She removed her hand from his arm and caressed Midge's blond curls.

"We have three children whose needs have to be considered," she said softly.

"Are you saying you don't think I'd make a good father for Honor?"

Now he sounded hurt. "Of course not," she said. "But it's been barely a year since Carl—"

"How long are you planning to wait? Till she's grown?"

"That's not fair," Amy said. "Your girls have had two years to adjust to the fact that their dad—"

"I've stayed a part of their lives. From what you've told me, Carl Nash isn't going to be a part of Honor's for a long, long time. When is he supposed to get out of prison, anyway?"

"In a couple of years," Amy said. "Maybe less. He gets time off for good behavior."

"I'm willing to be there for Honor right now," Luke said. "She and Brynne get along great. And having a baby sister or brother to play with would go a long way toward keeping Midge from feeling left out."

"You seem to have everything all planned out."

Amy couldn't keep the sharpness out of her voice. It sounded wonderful. She was just afraid to believe in the fairy tale—again. She didn't want to wake up and discover that Luke Creed wasn't Prince Charming after all.

"We've been apart for twelve years," she said. "And we've only seen each other a couple of times over the past month. What makes you think we'd be at all compatible as a married couple?"

"I don't believe people fundamentally change," he said. "I'm still physically attracted to you. I've always liked you and admired you. And from everything you've said, your experience with Carl Nash only made you a better, stronger, more self-reliant person. I think we have as good a chance as most couples of making it together."

"I don't want to make another mistake."

"I don't, either."

"So what's your hurry?"

"I suppose that's a result of 9/11," he said.

"How so?"

"Life is uncertain. You have to live every day as though it were your last. Because it might be."

"So we should rush into marriage?" She smiled at him and said, "We might very well live to regret it."

"I'd be willing to take the chance."

"I need more time," she said. "I need—"

"To weigh the pros and cons. To figure out where the lines of black and white fall, and make sure you don't end up making any choices that might have shades of gray."

He seemed to be making fun of her, but Amy refused to defend her decision-making process.

"I'm sorry," he said after a moment of silence. "I know what I want, and I guess I was hoping to talk you into wanting the same thing. I'll back off and let you enjoy the weekend. Just promise me you'll think about it."

She doubted she would think of anything else. "All right. I will."

Luke slowed the truck as they left the pavement and turned onto a dirt road. When they bounced through a deep pothole, Midge stirred and asked groggily, "Are we there yet?"

"Just about," Luke replied.

Midge sat up and scrubbed at her eyes with fisted hands. "When will it be morning?"

"We've still got a whole night to get through," Luke told her.

"Will Nana and Pap-Pap be waiting for us when we get there?"

As Luke pulled up behind the house at Three Oaks, his headlights revealed his mother sitting next to Blackjack on a wooden porch swing, his stepfather's arm securely around her. "There they are now," he said.

"Brynne, Honor, wake up," he said. "We're here."

Brynne was slow to respond, and Amy saw Luke look worriedly over his shoulder.

"She's stretching," Amy said, to reassure him his daughter was all right. It must be awful for him knowing she was still taking D-Free. She'd heard part of the violent argument he'd had with Valerie at the door when he picked up the girls, and her adamant refusal to give in to his "ridiculous paranoia."

By the time Luke braked his Silverado, Ren and Blackjack had turned on the porch lights and were heading down the back steps. They reached Luke's truck in time to embrace Brynne and Midge as they tumbled out the doors.

"You must be Honor," Ren said as she greeted Amy's daughter.

Honor was standing half-hidden behind Amy, and Amy put a hand on her shoulder to urge her daughter forward. She was glad when Honor reached out to take the hand Ren offered her and shook it.

"Yes, ma'am," she said in her whispery voice. "I am."

"Welcome to Three Oaks," Blackjack said to Honor. "Your mother tells me you're quite a horsewoman. We've found a spirited gelding for you to ride this weekend."

There was no mistaking the lift of Honor's chin. "Thank you, sir."

Amy could have kissed Blackjack for acknowledging Honor's skill on horseback. After that, Honor seemed much more at ease. When Ren took Midge's hand and said, "Time to get the three of you settled in your room," Honor seemed happy to follow her inside, her head bent next to Brynne's as the two girls exchanged confidences.

That left Amy and Luke with Blackjack. Amy could tell Luke was uncomfortable being alone with his step-father, but she wasn't willing to run off without greet-ing him.

"Thank you for inviting us to visit," she said. "Honor hardly slept last night, she was so excited about the opportunity to do some riding."

"I'm glad you could come," Blackjack said to Amy. His welcome seemed to include Luke, but Amy couldn't be sure.

"Sir," Luke said with an acknowledging nod of his head.

"I'm glad you came," Blackjack said. "Your mother was afraid you would end up canceling at the last minute."

Amy heard the implied criticism and was sure Luke must have, too. She was pleased when he merely replied, "I'm glad I didn't have to disappoint her."

She could see the measured answer had surprised Blackjack, who said, "Do you need any help with the bags?"

"You can help Amy with her things, if you don't mind," Luke said. "I can take care of the rest."

Amy showed Blackjack which bags in the pickup bed were hers and Honor's, and let him carry them into the house and up the stairs, even though she could easily have managed them herself. She stayed behind to talk with Luke, who had overnight bags clutched in both hands.

"Can I help you with anything?" she asked.

"Got it," he said, as he put a plastic grocery bag filled with healthy snacks in his teeth and kicked the truck door closed with his boot.

She reached for the plastic grocery bag he held with his mouth and said, "I've got it."

He let her have it and headed inside.

"I'm glad to see you don't intend to lock swords with your stepfather all weekend."

"I'm not going to be the first one to draw a weapon," he said. "The rest is up to him." He stopped by his sister Callie's former bedroom, where Amy could hear the girls chattering excitedly, and dropped off Brynne and Midge's overnight bags. "Do you need anything from me, Mom?" he asked.

"We have everything under control." She turned to Amy and said, "Jackson brought up Honor's things. I'll make sure she gets settled, if you'd like to get settled yourself."

Amy realized that Honor hadn't even noticed her arrival and said, "If Honor asks, will you tell her where I am?"

"Certainly," Ren said.

Luke led Amy down the hall to his sister Bay's bedroom. "You're in here."

"Where will you be?"

He grinned and said, "Across the hall. Unless I get a better offer."

She smiled and shook her head. "I've had a long day. I'm going to bed. Alone."

"Want to take an early ride tomorrow morning?" he said.

"How early?"

"Dawn. It's beautiful here. It'll probably be the only time we have alone all day."

"I don't know. Honor might wake up when I'm gone and—"

"She might not," Luke said. "Come with me, Amy. Please."

"Well, when you put it like that," she said, "how can I resist?"

He gave her a quick kiss on the mouth, then backed up a step before she could object. "Set your alarm for five. I'll knock on your door. Be ready."

She closed the door and leaned back against it. She knew she was flirting with danger.

It felt absolutely wonderful.

—⟆⟆—

Luke was surprised to see Amy when he peeked into the girls' room later that evening to make sure they were all right.

"Oh, it's you!" Amy whispered, holding a hand to her heart. She was sitting beside Honor, who appeared to be drifting off to sleep.

"Sorry to scare you," he whispered back. "I wanted to check on the girls before I go downstairs to see my mom."

He crossed around the double bed, avoiding the spots where he knew the wooden floor creaked. He tucked the covers under Brynne's arms and leaned down to kiss her forehead. Then he crossed to the child's bed that had been set up along the wall for Midge, tucked her foot back under the covers and brushed a sweat-dampened curl from her cheek.

"Luke," Amy said quietly.

He turned and waited for her to speak.

"You'd make a good father for Honor."

"Thanks, Amy. I'll see you in the morning."

He left quickly, because he was tempted to drag Amy down the hall to his bedroom and make love to her till they were both too exhausted to go riding in the morning.

He headed for the kitchen, where he'd agreed to meet up with his mother. He wasn't pleased to see that his stepfather was sitting at the kitchen table with her.

"Join us," his mother said, patting a chair beside her.

It would have been rude to take a chair at the other end of the table, which was where he'd rather have sat. He pulled out the chair and turned it around and straddled it with his arms crossed over the back of it, facing the two of them.

He searched his mind for some subject to discuss, but it was completely blank.

"How are things at work?" his mother said.

"Fine."

"That's not what I hear," Blackjack said.

Luke sat up and dropped his hands to his knees. He eyed Blackjack and said, "What have you heard?"

"It's not what you think," his mother interjected.

He turned on her and said tersely, "What do I think it is, Mom?"

"Oh, Jackson, I knew we shouldn't get involved."

"Involved in what?" Luke said, looking from one to the other like a baited bear. "What the hell is going on here?"

"Watch your tone of voice, young man," Blackjack said.

Luke rose from his chair. "Who the hell are you to—"

His mother stood, putting herself bodily between him and his stepfather, who'd risen to match Luke's aggressive stance. "Sit down, Luke," his mother said. "Please. Sit down and listen. We only want to help."

Luke heard the distress in her voice. He hated the helpless feeling he always got in Jackson Blackthorne's presence. He hated even more his knee-jerk contrary response to anything Blackjack said. He was a grown man, not a helpless boy of sixteen whose father had just been shot, ripping the foundations of his life asunder. All that had happened sixteen years ago. He had to let it go.

He sat back down and crossed his arms over his chest. He immediately wished he hadn't assumed such a defiant—and defensive—posture. But it was too late to undo it now.

He waited until his mother and Blackjack were also seated and said, "I'm listening."

"I'm aware of the problems you're having with Grayson Choate," Blackjack said. "More specifically, the difficulties you've encountered investigating the D-Free clinical trials."

Luke felt the back of his neck and his ears heating. "What business is that of yours?"

"Your mother is worried about Brynne."

"I'm investigating D-Free," Luke said. "I'm trying to find out whether it's safe."

"I'm aware of that," Blackjack said. "So is Franklin DeWitt."

Luke's eyes rounded. "DeWitt knows about the problems with D-Free?"

"He has his concerns," Blackjack said. "Especially since that fifth wrongful death lawsuit was logged in against Hyland."

"Why hasn't he said something? Done something?"

"Apparently, he's waiting to see how Choate will handle the situation."

Luke's brow furrowed. "Why would he wait for—" And then Luke realized what must be going on. It was plain even to him that Choate must have rubbed a lot of the male partners the wrong way. She was untouchable so long as she was Hyland's connection to the firm. But what if she took a misstep? What if she made a wrong choice? What if she misadvised Hyland and the company got a public relations black eye?

"It's politics," Luke muttered in disbelief. "God-damned firm politics!"

Blackjack nodded. "According to Franklin, the rest of the management committee, of which she is one, doesn't approve of a lot of the things she's done—and is doing—but they haven't been able to oust her, since she controls Hyland, which provides so much of the firm's revenues. But—"

"This time she's stepped over the line," Luke concluded.

"If they can prove she's involved in the illegal and unethical tactics Hyland used to get D-Free approved by the FDA, they can force her out."

"I have needles and insulin for Brynne while she's here," his mother said. "If you want to take her pills away."

"I do," Luke said. "What would be even better is if you could keep her here a while, so I don't have to fight with both Brynne and Valerie to keep her off the drug."

"We'd be happy to keep the girls," his mother said.

"The question is, what excuse can I use with Valerie—"

"Brynne can come down with chicken pox," his mother said. "She hasn't had it yet."

"I don't think Valerie has, either," Luke said, "so she'd probably be glad to have the girls stay here."

"Which gives you maybe a week to ten days—the

course of the disease—to flush out the truth about Choate and Hyland," Blackjack said.

Luke swallowed hard. What if he couldn't do it? What if Choate and McCorkle had hidden the truth too well for him to discover it? "I feel like I ought to get back in my truck and head for Houston right now."

"Tomorrow morning is soon enough," Blackjack said.

"How long ago did you speak with Harry Blackthorne?" Luke said.

He saw that Blackjack knew what he was asking. *How much of what I've accomplished at D&B can I take credit for myself?*

"I wanted to talk with him the day you started work at D&B," Blackjack admitted. "Your mother wouldn't let me. She said you could make it on your own. And you did."

"When?" Luke insisted.

"The day after your associate review last year. I wanted to find out how you were doing. I wanted to see whether you were going to make it on your own." He smiled ruefully and admitted, "I didn't want your mother to be disappointed in you."

"So you fixed it—"

"I didn't have to fix a goddamn thing," Blackjack said, overriding him. "Harry told me the word was you would likely be invited to join the partnership. Unless you got caught having a wild fling with some partner's wife or ended up in jail for something they couldn't get you out of."

Luke felt a thrill of elation. He'd made it on his own! That bubble quickly burst. He might have made it, if he hadn't run head-on into an immovable object named Grayson Choate. It seemed he was going to be number eleven in the long line of male associates the Dragon Lady had decimated.

Blackjack rose and said, "Good luck, Luke."

Luke rose and shook his hand. "Thank you, sir." He met Blackjack's gaze and said, "For everything."

He thought he saw a tick in the older man's cheek.

Blackjack turned to Luke's mother and said, "We'd better get to bed. We're going to need all our strength to keep up with those three girls for the next week."

"Three girls?" Luke said.

"Jackson's right," his mother said. "If you want the chicken pox story to work with Valerie, Honor's going to have to stay, too."

"I'm not sure Amy's going to be willing to go along with that," Luke said.

"Why don't you check with her tonight and see," his mother said. "If she'd rather take Honor home, we'll come up with something to tell Valerie that will make sense."

Luke took the stairs two at a time and hurried down the hall to Amy's bedroom. He was fighting a sense of euphoria that didn't make sense, considering the fact that even if the managing partners managed to oust Choate, there was no guarantee he'd still be made a partner.

They might very well not want someone around who knew they'd kept their mouths shut—even if it had only been for a brief time—about a dangerous drug, in the hope that Choate would cross the line far enough that they could force her out.

Luke knocked on Amy's door, and when she opened it a crack to see who was there, he slid through and closed it behind him. She was wearing a plain white V-necked men's cotton T-shirt that covered her rear end but left her thighs and legs bare.

"What are you doing in here?" she whispered.

"We have to leave tomorrow morning."

"What's happened? Is Brynne all right?"

"Brynne is fine. Well, she has chicken pox," Luke said with an enigmatic smile.

Amy frowned. "What? She was fine an hour ago. Oh, dear. I guess that means Honor is infected, too."

Luke took her by the shoulders and said, "Brynne doesn't have chicken pox. That's just what we're going to tell Valerie so Brynne can stay here and take insulin shots instead of D-Free."

"Oh, Luke. You can't—"

"It wasn't my idea. My mom came up with it. But it's a good idea, Amy. How would you feel about leaving Honor here with my girls for the next week and coming to Houston with me tomorrow morning?"

"Tomorrow morning? We just got here."

"Uh-huh. And I'm leaving in the morning. You're welcome to stay, but I've got to get back to town."

"Whoa, whoa," Amy said. "Slow down. Tell me what's going on."

Luke sat Amy down on the bed and joined her while he explained his conversation with Blackjack. "So you see why I need to get back. Are you coming with me?"

"I don't know—"

"We could be together at my place next week—without the kids."

Amy eyed him sideways. "Assuming you bother to come home from the office next week. I've seen the kind of hours you work."

"We'd have the nights to ourselves," Luke said. "We'd have a chance to spend time with each other. Say yes, Amy."

"In the middle of a train wreck, he wants me to think about romance."

"Life doesn't stop for a train wreck," he said. "It moves on around it."

"I'll go home with you—assuming Honor is okay with the idea of staying here alone."

He eased back on the bed and laced his hands behind his head. "She's going to be fine. You'll see."

Amy crawled up to lay her head on the pillow beside him. "You're crazy, you know, to let yourself get sucked into firm politics."

"I don't have to like the situation to take advantage of it." He unlaced his hands and turned on his side to face her. "I'm going to miss riding with you tomorrow morning."

"You were going to try and seduce me on the prairie, weren't you?" she said with a soft smile.

"I was going to try."

"You've got me alone right now. Give it your best shot," she said, gazing at him from beneath seductively lowered lids.

He grinned. "Uh-uh. You're not going to tease me again and leave me high and dry. I don't have—"

"I put some condoms in the bedside table," she said. "Just in case."

"Well, well," he said. "There are hidden depths to you, Mrs. Nash, that I can see need to be plumbed."

He didn't wait for her to respond, just took her in his arms and kissed her, thrusting his tongue deep, the way he wanted to thrust himself deep inside her.

"I don't want to hurry," he murmured in her ear when they both came up for air. "I want to take my time. I want this to be good for you."

"For both of us," she said. "We have all night. I'm not going anywhere."

Luke made love to her the way he wished he could have the first time, when he'd been so inexperienced and uncertain and excited that when he'd broached her, it had been over almost before it had begun.

He pulled her shirt off and took his time admiring her small breasts and slightly rounded stomach. He smiled at the simple cotton underwear before he pulled that off, too, leaving her bare to his admiring gaze.

"It's not fair to keep your clothes on when mine are off," she said.

It seemed Amy had a few moments she wanted to relive, as well, because she took her time undressing him, pausing long enough to feel the shape and the hardness of him through the layers of cotton and denim before she unbuckled his belt and unsnapped and unzipped his jeans.

He sat up long enough to pull off his boots and socks,

then let her help him shove down his jeans and shorts before he joined her on the bed. He couldn't get his fill of looking at her. "You're beautiful."

"Let me return the compliment," she said, running her hand across his shoulders and down across his abdomen.

"Men aren't—"

She put her fingertips on his mouth. "You are. To me." She finished her declaration with a kiss that made his toes curl.

He took his time. And she took hers. He prolonged the moment when their bodies would be joined as long as he could, but at last their need for each other was too great to be denied. He seated himself deep as she arched her body up to meet his thrust.

"It feels good," Amy said in a ragged voice.

"Yeah." It was all he could manage to say. His throat was raw with emotion. He worked in her a long time, until he felt her body begin to spasm and arch and she made a savage, animal sound in her throat.

There was nothing gentle about their mating. It was desperate, feral. He didn't know why he wanted this particular woman, why he needed her. He only knew he did.

He muffled his cry of satisfaction at her throat as he spilled himself inside her.

It was much later, after she'd fallen asleep, that he glanced at the night table and saw the condom still sitting there in its foil packet.

15

—∽∽—

Luke shuddered every time he recalled his last fifteen minutes at Three Oaks before heading back to Houston.

He'd gotten up before dawn and slipped into his own bedroom to shower and dress, then headed down the hall to wake up his daughters to tell them he and Amy were leaving.

He found Brynne already awake and hunting through her overnight bag for her D-Free.

"I can't find my pills, Daddy," she said anxiously. "They're gone!"

"That's because I took them last night," he said as he sat on her side of the double bed. "Come here, Brynne, and sit beside me."

Brynne crossed and sat beside him.

"I don't want you taking D-Free, sweetpea. It isn't safe."

Brynne jumped off the bed and turned to face him, her eyes wide with disbelief and horror, as though he'd announced he was canceling Christmas. "You can't do that!"

"What's going on?" Midge said as she sat up in bed.

"Brynne and I are having a talk. Go back to sleep."

"What are you talking about?" Midge asked, shoving her covers aside and padding barefoot over to him.

Luke gave up and pulled her into his lap. He felt her lean back trustingly against him as he focused his gaze once more on Brynne. She had her hands on her hips, and she was staring at him with wary, worried eyes.

"Mrs. Nash and I have to go back to town this morning, but I've arranged for you two girls and Honor to stay here with Nana and Pap-Pap for the rest of the week."

Midge clapped her hands and said, "Yippee!"

Brynne looked at him aghast and said, "The whole week?"

Either Midge's clapping or Brynne's dismayed cry or both woke Honor, who sat up and said, "A whole week of what?"

"My dad says we're stuck here for a week," Brynne said.

"Can we go riding every day?" Honor asked him.

"Sure," Luke said. It was easy to make promises someone else would have to keep. "Why don't you go say good morning to your mom?"

Honor took one look at Brynne's flushed face and said, "Okay." A moment later she was gone.

"I'm supposed to go to Jeanie Wilson's birthday party on Wednesday," Brynne said angrily. "She's going to think I don't like her."

"You can explain when you get back," Luke said.

"How are we supposed to get home?" Brynne demanded.

Luke hadn't really considered that problem, but he quickly said, "I'll come back to get you."

"When?"

Luke didn't know when he'd have the answers he'd need to confront the management committee, so he said, "I'll give you a call when I can come."

"I don't want to stay here if you're leaving," Brynne said. "I only came here to spend time with you."

"I have to go, Brynne. And I need you to stay here."

"I didn't bring enough pills with me to last all week."

"Your grandmother has a glaucometer to check your blood sugar levels and insulin and needles."

"I don't want to take shots!" Brynne shrieked. "I won't do it. I want to go home to Mommy. Take me home!"

"Sheesh," Midge said. "She's really mad."

Luke realized—too late—that he should have taken Brynne someplace where they wouldn't wake up the rest of the house to explain why he'd taken her pills away. It was too late for that now.

"Settle down, Brynne." This sort of agitation wasn't good for her. It spiked her blood sugar levels.

Brynne looked him in the eye and held out her hand and said, "Give me back my pills, Daddy."

"I'm not going to do that, Brynne."

She stomped her foot and squeezed her hands into fists and screamed in rage, "You can't do this, Daddy. It's not fair."

"Life isn't fair," he said. "You know that."

She was crying in earnest now. He set Midge aside and took a step toward Brynne to comfort her.

She put her hands out to ward him off and said,

"Stay away from me. I hate you! I want Mommy. I want Mommy."

"What's going on in here?"

"Nana, Daddy won't give me my pills!" Brynne cried as she raced past him and hugged her grand-mother around the waist.

"Brynne's being bad," Midge said to her grand-mother. "I'm being good."

"Go see Pap-Pap," his mother said to Midge. "He's in the kitchen. Tell him I said he has to share his Krispy Kremes with you."

"Krispy Kremes!" Midge shouted as she hurried out the door. Luke heard her pounding down the stairs as he turned his attention back to Brynne.

She was clutching her grandmother, who was smoothing her hair and murmuring to her.

He met his mother's gaze and saw the sympathy there. He was glad she didn't offer him advice on how to handle his daughter. But honestly, he had no idea how he was going to calm Brynne.

"I'm doing this for your own good, Brynne," he said.

"I want my pills," she sobbed. She turned to face him, her nose runny, her eyes wet with tears and said, "I don't want to take shots, Daddy. Please don't make me take shots."

Luke's viscera clenched. His child was begging him to spare her pain. He would have given anything for her not to be sick. But she was. And the only safe treat-ment was for her to take a shot of insulin.

He met his mother's gaze, unable to hide his distress.

"Don't worry about her," she said. "We'll be fine."

He didn't want to leave while Brynne was so upset, but he wasn't willing to give her the only thing that was sure to calm her. "Take care of her," he told his mother.

"I'm leaving," he said to Brynne. "I'll call you, sweet-pea."

She turned her face away from him and hid it against his mother's robe. Luke felt sick.

He met Amy coming toward him as he headed back down the hall.

"Is Brynne all right?" she asked.

"My mom's taking care of her. She'll be fine once she realizes no amount of crying is going to get her back her D-Free. How's Honor?" he asked.

"A little shaken by Brynne's outburst. But she's looking forward to the week here. She can't believe she's getting to miss school. And spend a week horseback riding."

Luke wished his own daughter was as happy with the arrangements he'd made. "I'm ready when you are," he said.

"I just need to get my overnight bag. Do we have time for a cup of coffee?"

"We can get one in town on the way." The sooner he was out of the house, the sooner Brynne would calm down.

He stopped in the kitchen long enough to say good morning to Blackjack. He shouldn't have been surprised to see Midge sitting in Blackjack's lap chattering away. She was a friendly kid. But he was surprised at Blackjack's indulgent manner toward a little girl who was no relation to him, except by marriage.

"Amy and I are leaving now," he said.

Blackjack looked up and said, "Don't worry about the kids. We'll take good care of them."

"Thanks," Luke made himself say. It was the first time he could remember being less than curt with his stepfather.

"Good luck," Blackjack said.

Luke realized he was going to need it.

The drive back to Houston was quiet. Amy slept, because he'd kept her up half the night making love to her. He mulled over what tack he ought to take with the D-Free investigation he was running with Eddie and Nicki, especially in light of the information Blackjack had given him.

It seemed he might have an ally in Franklin DeWitt. That was good news, considering how tenuous his situation with Choate was. It seemed to him she'd been building a case against him that she could use to have him fired.

He dropped Amy off at her apartment after making arrangements to meet her for dinner at his place, then headed straight to the office.

Once he got there, he called Valerie and explained that both girls had come down with chicken pox and that his mother had offered to keep them at Three Oaks until they were no longer contagious.

"I didn't think you'd had chicken pox," he said.

"No, I haven't," she confirmed. "Thank you, Luke. That was very considerate. But I didn't send enough D-Free with Brynne for more than a day or so beyond the weekend."

"She can take insulin until she gets home," Luke said casually. He waited for Valerie to object, but she didn't.

That had been easier than he'd expected. He hesitated, then said, "Valerie, Midge said there was a chance you might be moving up north."

"I've been meaning to talk with you about that, Luke. There just hasn't been a convenient time."

"When were you planning to bring it up, Valerie? The day you left?"

"Don't yell at me, Luke."

"I'm not yelling," he said, controlling his anger with difficulty. "You'd know if I were yelling."

"I don't like you when you're like this."

Luke took a deep breath and let it out. "Where is it you're planning to move?"

"Martin's family is all in Vermont. He's been offered a position with his father's firm."

"When am I supposed to see the kids if you move that far away?"

"School holidays. And over the summer, of course."

Luke didn't point out that the girls enjoyed going to camp over the summer. He made himself ask, "When is this move supposed to take place?"

"Martin's father would like us to come as soon as we can tie things up here."

"Brynne's birthday is coming up at the end of the month. I want to be there to celebrate it with her." And to make sure, if she was still taking D-Free—since birthdays seemed to be a triggering factor for problems with the drug—that she didn't overindulge in sweets.

"I'm afraid that isn't going to be possible, Luke."

"It's the least you can do, Valerie, considering you're taking my children away from me."

"That's not at all my intention."

"Whether you intend to or not, that will be the result if you move up north."

"I don't want to argue with you about this, Luke."

"Should I roll over and play dead and pretend it doesn't matter?"

"I have a nail appointment, Luke. Can we discuss this later?"

"I want to discuss it now."

"I'm hanging up the phone, Luke."

"Goddammit, Valerie. I—" But she'd already hung up the phone. Luke felt helpless and frustrated. If Martin was relocating because of his job, there wasn't much chance Luke could legally block Valerie's move out of state with the kids. But unless he could be certain Brynne wasn't taking D-Free, he wanted her close when her birthday rolled around. He would just have to talk Valerie into letting him take the girls trick-or-treating before they moved away.

He felt a growing sense of urgency. And a growing frustration that he couldn't find the answers he needed to prove whether—and under what circumstances— D-Free was dangerous.

He called Nicki's office, but got no answer, so he tried her home.

"Hey, how are you?" he said when she picked up the phone.

"Still a little sore."

"I'm glad to see you're at home taking it easy."

"My priorities have changed," Nicki admitted. "I'm opting to have a personal life. You might want to try it."

"Believe it or not, I'm working on it," Luke said. "I thought I'd check and see if you've had a chance to do any computer research on Hyland."

"Not Hyland per se," Nicki said. "I have some good stuff on the Dragon Lady."

"Really?" Luke said "Go for it."

"Would you believe she and Harold McCorkle used to be an item?"

"You've got to be kidding. When was this?"

"Twenty years ago, at least. When he was still a fledgling research scientist trying to invent a wonder drug for juvenile diabetes."

"How on earth did you discover something like that?"

"I found a picture of them together in the newspaper society pages at a fund-raiser for cancer research."

"No wonder McCorkle called her when I contacted him behind her back," Luke said.

"I'd like to know whether the romance is ongoing."

"Huh-uh," Luke said. "She's got another boyfriend."

There was silence on the other end of the line, and Luke swore under his breath. "Forget I said that. I promised to keep what I know to myself."

"Which means the Dragon Lady's paramour is a good friend of yours, someone willing to confide in you." A pause, and then Nicki gasped. "Drew DeWitt. Ohmigod."

Luke swore again. Lawyers were just too damned

good at deduction. "If you say a word to anyone, I'll have your tongue cut out and stapled to your door."

Nicki laughed. "Gotcha. Oh, but that's rare. Whose idea was it for the two of them to hook up?"

"You're not getting another word out of me," Luke said. "And don't you dare say anything to Drew."

"How he can have anything to do with that woman is beyond me."

"What do you mean?"

"I'm willing to bet she's part of this D-Free cover-up."

"Proof, Nick. We need proof."

"I'll find it," Nicki said. "Just give me time."

"We're running out of time."

"I hear you, Luke. I'm on it."

Luke hung up and headed down the hall to Eddie's office. He wasn't surprised to see Eddie was there working. "Any new information on D-Free?"

"Choate has me working on something else."

Luke hit the door frame with both hands. "Figures."

"I'll get back to it as soon as I can," Eddie said. "Thanks."

Luke usually didn't work on Saturdays when he had the girls, but he was behind on his work for Choate. He spent most of the afternoon finishing up a memo to her. He called Drew's office and got no answer but knew Drew might very well be in the law library on the litigation floor doing research, so he took the elevator upstairs.

But Drew was nowhere to be found, and he decided to call it a day and head home for his evening run.

Luke preferred to run after work because it gave him

a way to release all the tension that had built up during the day. He stopped off at his condo to change into running shorts, a sleeveless T-shirt and his Nikes before he headed back out, waving at the concierge as he exited.

Luke usually took the same route, heading down Walker toward Sam Houston Park. He jogged in place while he waited for the light, then took off again. Luke used the time to clear his mind and always felt refreshed after his run.

The sky threatened rain. He was grateful for the clouds, which cut the reflected heat off the pavement. He had just crossed the street at the Hyatt Regency and was making his turn for home when he heard the sound of screeching rubber as a car accelerated in traffic.

Luke had a second to realize the speeding car was white before it bucked up over the curb. He leapt away too late, and the automobile sideswiped him.

He flew through the air with his arms and legs akimbo, then felt excruciating pain as he skidded along the hot asphalt. He heard a woman screaming.

Then everything went black.

———ᐧᐧᐧ———

When Amy let herself into Luke's condo with the key he'd given her that morning, she found a note that said he'd gone jogging, and that if she arrived early, to make herself at home. Amy looked at her watch. Actually, she was thirty minutes late. She'd timed her arrival to accommodate Luke's usual tardiness.

She presumed he'd decided to take a longer run and made herself useful by starting the spaghetti and meatballs he'd suggested they have for supper. She found everything she needed in the kitchen. When she looked up again, she discovered an hour had passed.

She petted the cat, which had leapt up on the counter and said, "Where is he, Snowball?"

She called Luke's office, thinking he might have stopped by there and forgotten the time, but she got no answer. Where was he? If he was going to be late, he should have given her a call.

Amy felt warm and realized she was flushed. She was flushed because she was angry. She'd brought an overnight bag with her, because Luke had asked her to spend the week with him, and she'd decided it would be a good opportunity for them to get to know each other better. But this was not a very auspicious beginning.

She'd asked Luke once why he was never on time.

"I always intend to make it on time," he'd said. "I just . . . get distracted."

Amy believed Luke's perpetual lateness constituted his own private rebellion against following the rules. It was a harmless enough way of defying authority. Maybe, someday, he would no longer feel he needed to fight the rest of the world, and he'd allow himself to be on time.

What had happened tonight? Amy wondered. What could possibly have distracted Luke so completely that he'd forgotten about their plans for dinner?

Amy froze. Maybe something had happened to one

of his daughters—an accident while out riding horse-back, or one of a myriad of accidents that occurred on a ranch. Or what if Brynne had found the D-Free Luke had discarded in the trash and had had an adverse reaction to the drug?

Amy knew that last scenario was far-fetched, but she'd scared herself enough to pull out her cell phone and call Luke's mother.

"Hello, Ren," she said. "How are the girls?"

"Everyone's fine here. Valerie called. Luckily Brynne and Midge were taking a nap, so I didn't have to lie to her. I hope Luke can get everything resolved soon. I never realized how uncomfortable I'd be lying to Valerie. I don't want to if it can be avoided."

"He's working on the problem," Amy assured her.

"The girls are playing a game of Scrabble with Jackson. Do you want to speak with Honor?"

"Yes, if you don't mind," Amy said. When Honor came on the line, she said, "Hi, honey. Are you having a good time?"

"The greatest, Mom. I have to go. It's my turn."

Amy thought Honor's unwillingness to remain on the phone was proof positive that she was enjoying herself. Amy found herself talking again to Ren. "Have you heard from Luke today?"

"He usually calls closer to bedtime," Ren said. "Why? Is there a problem?"

"No," Amy said. "Everything's fine." Luke had just "forgotten" about their dinner together. "Thanks again for showing Honor such a good time."

"It's our pleasure, Amy."

After Amy disconnected the call, she began to imagine all the horrible things that could have happened to keep Luke from showing up. It wasn't difficult. She had a vivid imagination.

Maybe she ought to find a phone book and start calling hospitals to ask whether he'd been admitted. Or she could call Valerie to see if she had any idea what might have happened to him. On the other hand, if Luke had merely "forgotten" about their date, or was just seriously, unforgivably late, a phone call to Luke's ex-wife would be humiliating.

Why hadn't Luke called her? He must have known she would be worried. How could he be so inconsiderate?

Amy heard her cell phone ringing and grappled for it. She'd dropped it back in her purse after the last call, and it had fallen to the bottom. She shoved aside her compact and her wallet and punched the button to take the call at the same time as her cell phone came tumbling out of her purse.

"Hello?" she said breathlessly. There was a moment of silence on the other end of the line.

"Amy?"

"Luke! Where are you?"

"In the hospital. I'm all right," he hurried to reassure her.

Amy felt her knees turn to jelly and sank onto the couch. "What happened?"

"I got tagged by a hit-and-run driver."

"Oh, my God. Oh, Luke. Where are you hurt? Are you really okay?"

"I've got a dislocated shoulder and a bad bruise on my knee and some scratches on my face, but otherwise, I'm fine."

Amy's throat had knotted, and she had to clear it twice before she could say, "Where are you? I mean, what hospital?"

"St. Joseph's. You don't have to come—"

"I'm on my way," she said and disconnected the call.

She was trembling too badly to get up at first. Her first few steps were wobbly, but as the blood flowed back into her extremities, she began to move faster. Soon she was running for the door in her three-inch heels. The heels she'd worn to look sexy for Luke. Who'd been late for their dinner date because he was in a hospital emergency room.

It almost took longer to get her car from the valet than to drive the few blocks to St. Joseph's. Finding a parking place took longer than the drive had.

Amy sat in her car for a moment with the ignition off and contemplated her behavior since she'd learned that Luke had been hurt. She'd reacted as though Luke were someone special in her life. Someone important to her. Someone who was a great deal more than simply an old friend.

At one point during the past evening, when it seemed Luke had forgotten about her, she'd considered walking out his front door and never coming back. It was frightening to contemplate why she'd stayed and waited and worried.

The hospital smelled like hospitals always did, of antiseptic and medicines and fear and death. Amy got the number of Luke's room from the receptionist, who informed her that visiting hours were over and she'd have to come back tomorrow.

Amy said, "Thank you. I'll do that." Then she marched down the hall to the elevator and headed upstairs. The nurse's station was empty and the hall was quiet. Amy didn't question her luck, just scooted down the hall until she found Luke's room, pushed open the door and slid inside.

A small light was on above his bed, and she could see the enormous white bandage on his cheek. He was lying on his back with his right arm bound across his chest.

She crossed the room on tiptoe and stared down at him, her eyes welling with tears. She reached out and brushed a lock of hair from his forehead—and nearly jumped out of her skin when he opened his eyes.

"I thought you were asleep," she said.

"I'm a little groggy from the painkiller they gave me," he admitted. "What are you doing here? What time is it?"

"Past suppertime," she said with a smile. "How are you?"

"Alive," he said. "Which I wouldn't have been if my reflexes had been any slower."

Amy sank onto the bed beside Luke and clutched the hand he held out to her. "Thank God for your reflexes."

"It was no accident, Amy."

She stared at Luke. "What do you mean?"

"Whoever ran me down meant to kill me. He had to

jump the curb to get to me. I'm lucky I'm still in one piece."

"Why would anyone want to run you down?"

"I've been asking myself all evening who would benefit if I were dead." He shot her a crooked smile. "You'd be amazed at all the people who might be glad to see me gone from the face of the earth."

"Do you really think someone tried to *murder* you?"

"It might have been an accident. The driver might have lost control of the car or been distracted so the car swerved into me." He met her worried gaze and said, "But I'd swear the driver was looking right at me when he headed his car in my direction."

"The driver was a man?"

"I'm not certain of that," Luke said. "I think so. He was wearing a baseball cap and sunglasses and had the visor down—and I was busy jumping out of the way."

"Were you able to give the police a description of the car? Were there any witnesses?"

Luke smiled. "You're starting to sound like a lawyer, counselor. By the way, I'm sorry I missed dinner tonight." He squeezed her hand.

Amy realized her feelings for Luke seemed out of proportion to the little time they'd spent with each other since they'd met again. Was it possible she'd never stopped loving him? She pulled her hand free and said, "You were going to explain who might want you dead."

"For a start, Valerie would be able to move to Vermont without me raising a ruckus."

"Is she really moving your girls to Vermont?"

"As soon as they can get packed," Luke said grimly.

"We had an argument on the phone before I headed out for my run. If I didn't know she was in The Woodlands, I might have suspected her of slamming into me."

"What are you going to do?" Amy asked.

"About what?"

"About your girls moving away." Amy couldn't imagine only seeing Honor during the summer and on holidays. It would be unbearable.

Luke moved restlessly, apparently trying to get more comfortable.

Amy reached over and rearranged the pillows behind his injured shoulder. "Is that better?"

"Yeah. Thanks."

She realized he hadn't answered her question. Probably because he hadn't yet figured out what to do about his kids moving away. "Who else do you think might want you dead?"

"McCorkle maybe," Luke said. "Or that bulldog assistant of his."

"If McCorkle went around killing everyone who thought D-Free was dangerous, there would be dead bodies all over the place," Amy said. "Surely he's not to blame."

"I can only think of one other person who might want to harm me. And you're going to think I'm crazy if I mention her."

"A woman?" Amy scrunched up her brow in thought. "I give up. Who is it?"

"The Dragon Lady."

Amy shook her head. "That doesn't make sense. What does she gain?"

"I can't help thinking about Neil Ford's 'accident.' I took a look at Neil's notes. There's nothing substantive there, but it's pretty clear from at least one passage I found that he was excited about something he'd found out."

"Nothing more?"

"Whatever he wrote was missing from the file," Luke said. "I wonder if he told Choate what he knew. Maybe she didn't want the bad word about D-Free getting out."

"Why does your Dragon Lady care so much about keeping D-Free on the market? She's acting like the lost profits are coming out of her own pocket."

Luke shot her a stunned look. "Holy shit. I think you might have hit on something, counselor. I have no idea whether Choate owns a piece of D-Free. It wouldn't be kosher if she did—since she's counsel for the company.

"But she's represented Hyland for twenty years—which is about how long McCorkle's been working on the drug. And Nick told me earlier today that Choate and McCorkle were a couple twenty years ago. Maybe she does have her own money invested in it."

"Maybe she owns a piece of the patent," Amy suggested. "That would certainly give her a motive to want to shut up anyone like Neil—or you—who was suspicious of the drug."

"You're brilliant! Of course. It's got to be something like that."

Amy was pleased by the compliment, but if she was right, Luke was in a great deal of danger. "Let's presume for a moment that the person who ran you down, or arranged to have you run down, is any one of the people you've mentioned. How are you going to protect yourself in the future?"

"The best defense is a good offense," Luke said. "Once I get some proof that Choate is in collusion to keep D-Free on the market when she knows it isn't safe, I can go to the management committee. They'll do what Choate's refused to do—advise Hyland to take D-Free off the market."

"You realize that once you go over Choate's head you'll be ending any hope you have of becoming a partner at D&B. It's political suicide."

"What choice do I have? Choate isn't going to disappear quietly into the night. Meanwhile, kids are dying."

"How likely is it you can find proof that Choate is involved in any of this?"

"Remember those twenty-two deaths during clinical trials you told me about?" Luke said. "Both Nick and Eddie have been looking at Hyland's records, investigating the PIs. It turns out that in twenty of those twenty-two deaths, the doctors who eventually signed off on the 'serious adverse event' saying D-Free was not responsible were *not* the doctors running things at the time the death occurred."

"The PIs all quit before the reports were filed?" Amy asked incredulously.

"Quit, got fired, died, crashed their car, went on vacation, took maternity leave, broke a leg. The list of reasons why the PIs didn't submit the required documentation are endless. And they're nearly all different."

"Isn't it possible those reasons are all legitimate? That the PIs just . . . weren't available?"

"Twenty of them?" Luke said. "Out of twenty-two reported deaths? Doesn't that strike you as odd?

"How can there be any sort of collusion when there are so many different reasons why they didn't submit the report?" Amy asked.

"The point is, someone else—another doctor, listed on the report as a sub-investigator—filed the report," Luke said. "I think someone made that happen. I think Neil Ford found out who it was. And got killed for it."

"That's quite a stretch."

"It's true Neil was taking an antidepressant," Luke said. "But he didn't drink and drive. Not according to his girlfriend. She was adamant about it. I think the reason that car hit me today was because I'm getting too close to the truth about what really went on during the D-Free clinical trials. Someone wanted to make sure I didn't blab about what I've found out.

"My death wouldn't have been suspicious, either," Luke said. "Just an 'accident while out jogging.'"

"So how do you keep whoever went after you from succeeding the next time?"

"I won't be jogging again anytime soon," Luke said with a wry smile, as he nodded toward his bound-up arm and swollen knee.

"The fact that you're not out jogging isn't going to stop someone who's determined to see you dead," Amy said with asperity. "You've pointed out how inventive whoever it is has been in accomplishing his—or her—aims. Are you going to the police?"

"With what?" Luke said. "Speculation?"

"What about siccing the FDA on Hyland?" Amy suggested. "Why not point out what's happened to the D-Free investigators? Surely the FDA—"

"The FDA doesn't like to be told they've made a mistake. It's a political organization, with people who have reputations at stake."

"D-Free is clearly not as safe as the FDA was led to believe," Amy said. "Anyone can see—"

"There have been a lot of coincidental vacancies in the position of investigator," Luke finished for her. "That's all they are. Coincidences. I haven't been able to find anything to connect all those leaves of absences and accidents and maternity leaves. Nothing, Amy. Until I do, I have no proof of any wrongdoing."

"Just a trail of dead people," Amy said bitterly. "Which might someday include you."

"I can take care of myself."

"Oh, really?" Amy said. "Look at you. You're in the hospital with a dislocated shoulder and cuts and bruises."

"I'm alive," Luke said. "And more suspicious than ever. There are answers, Amy. I just have to find them— before Halloween."

"Halloween?" Amy said. "What happens on Halloween?"

"It's Brynne's eleventh birthday. Birthdays seem to be a triggering event for the D-Free deaths. And Halloween is a diabetic's nightmare. I want to make damned sure Brynne is off the drug for good before then."

"Didn't you say Valerie wants to take the kids to Vermont right away?"

"That's what she told me."

"What are you going to do if you haven't discovered the answers you need before she leaves?"

"I don't know," Luke said. "I only know I'm not going to take a chance with Brynne's life. I'll do whatever I have to do to keep her safe. Even if it means keeping her here in Texas when Valerie moves away."

"Are you talking about kidnapping your daughter?"

"Valerie and I have joint custody. It isn't as though I'm not entitled to see my daughters."

"You aren't entitled to steal them away in the night."

Luke winced as he sat up straighter in bed. "It's my job to safeguard my family."

"So prove there's something wrong with D-Free!"

"Don't you think I'm trying?" Luke said. "Dammit, I can't find any proof!"

"What about the associates you have doing research for you? Surely they—"

"They're both already giving me as much time as they can spare. Eddie has been up to his eyeballs in assignments from Choate. And Nick has been busy catching up from the two days of work she missed—Just busy as hell," Luke amended.

"Meanwhile," he continued, "Choate has given me impossible deadlines for Hyland legal work that has nothing to do with D-Free. So I haven't been able to do any research either."

"I could carve out some time to help," Amy said. "In fact, since I don't have Honor at home, I've got some extra time I could give you in the evenings this week. When are you coming home?"

"Tomorrow, if I have anything to say about it."

Amy realized Luke had taken her hand again. She squeezed his hand, then freed her own and said, "Let me know if you want a ride home."

"Thanks for coming, Amy."

"I was . . ." She didn't say *concerned*. That implied too much caring. "Worried about you."

"I'm sorry I missed our dinner. You're welcome to stay at my place tonight."

"I wouldn't feel comfortable doing that without you there," she said. "I'd better get going. I've got a long drive ahead of me to get home. I'll see you tomorrow."

"Good night, Amy."

"Good night, Luke." She hurried out of the room and down the hall and didn't stop hurrying until she reached her car. She told herself she was running from the smell of the hospital, which reminded her of the years she'd spent married to Carl, the surgeon, that she was merely anxious to get back to the home she'd created for herself and her daughter.

But as she sat in her car, her chest heaving, her eyes filling with tears, she admitted she'd been running for a different reason entirely. Not running toward home. Running away from Luke.

Amy was afraid to put her life in another man's hands. She certainly didn't want to love a man so much she could be hurt again. She'd barely gotten her life back under control after her divorce. Her feelings for Luke were threatening the status quo, and she'd just agreed to get even more involved in his life than she already was.

She wished Luke's daughter weren't taking D-Free. Then she could make some excuse to get out of doing the research she'd promised to do. She could quickly and quietly back out of Luke Creed's life.

But Brynne was taking D-Free.

Amy sighed. She had no choice but to help. She would just have to heed her mother's warning, and guard her heart as best she could.

16

—⚬⚬⚬—

Luke checked out of the hospital late Saturday night AMA—against medical advice. The doctor had wanted to keep him under observation for twenty-four hours. Luke figured if he could walk, he was fine. He'd taken a cab home and gone to bed.

And woken up Sunday morning feeling like a Mack truck had hit him, even though it had only been a compact car. His cheek was scabbed and sore beneath the bandage, and his dislocated shoulder ached like a sonofabitch. His knee was so bruised and swollen he couldn't bend it, and he realized as he hobbled to the john to pee that there was no way he was going to make it in to work.

He'd been able to wiggle the fingers of his right hand the previous evening, but even that little movement hurt this morning. He couldn't walk to work, and there was no way he'd be able to lift his leg on and off the gas and brake to drive.

He called his mom because he'd said he would and because, he realized, he missed his daughters.

"Hi, Mom."

"Luke, we've been so worried ever since you called from the hospital. How are you?"

"I'm home. I'm fine."

"Can you tell me any more about what happened?"

"It was just an accident, Mom. I was jogging and a car jumped the curb and hit me." It was the absolute truth and made it sound like an accident unlikely to happen again in a million years.

He reassured her he was fine and explained where he'd been standing when he was hit and how odd it had felt flying through the air and how glad he was that he hadn't suffered more than just minor bumps and bruises.

He listened while she explained how worried they all had been, the girls, too, because Midge had answered the phone and refused to get anyone else until the nurse Luke had asked to dial the call for him identified herself and explained why she was calling.

"I've been racking my brain for a way to distract them so they don't worry about what's happened to you. A friend of mine who runs a beauty parlor has agreed to open up this afternoon so all of the girls can have a manicure."

"I'll bet they went crazy when you suggested that."

He heard his mother chuckle. "Especially Midge."

"Would you call Brynne to the phone?" he said at last.

"Hi, Daddy," Brynne said.

"Hi, sweetpea. How are you doing?" He waited, expecting—fearing—another tirade about D-Free that would end with *I hate you*.

"I was scared when Nana told me you were hurt."

Luke felt an ache in the back of his throat. "I'm going to be fine, sweetpea."

"I miss you, Daddy."

"Nana says you're going to the beauty parlor with her this afternoon." Luke was expecting Brynne to say she wished she could be with him.

Instead, she said excitedly, "I'm going to get a real manicure, Daddy. With pink fingernail polish."

"That sounds great," Luke said, accepting the inevitable with as much grace as he could muster. "Can you call Midge to the phone?"

"Midge!" Brynne shouted at the top of her lungs. "It's Daddy," he heard Brynne explain as she handed over the phone.

"Hi, Daddy," Midge said. "I'm going to the beauty parlor with Nana and Brynne and Honor. I'm getting a manicure. With red fingernail polish."

"Red?" Luke said. "Don't you think red is . . . a little . . . bright?"

"Red is my favorite color, Daddy."

Perfect for a six-year-old, he thought with a wry smile. "I'm sorry I didn't call you last night like I promised." Before he'd left, he'd run back upstairs and promised the girls he'd call every night at suppertime.

"That's okay," Midge said. "Nana got Domino's for supper, and I got to drink some Coke."

It was hard for Luke to hear that he'd been happily replaced by pizza and Coke. "I'll call you when I can," he said.

"Don't be sad, Daddy," Midge said.

How had she known? Luke wondered. "I'm okay, baby. I—"

"I'm not a baby, Daddy," Midge corrected him. "I'm six. I gotta go, Daddy. Nana's calling me."

Midge hung up the phone without giving him a chance to say good-bye.

Luke dropped the phone and slumped back onto the bed. He had an empty feeling in the pit of his stomach. This was what it might be like if Valerie took the kids and moved up north. He might be reduced to unsatisfying phone calls, where whatever the girls were doing in their real day-to-day lives was infinitely more interesting to them than a phone conversation with their absent father.

He wouldn't be a part of their lives, not like he was now. Even now, sometimes he felt like he didn't see enough of them. They were growing up so fast. Brynne was turning into a young woman before his eyes. And as Midge had firmly told him, she was no longer a baby.

Luke had never realized before how important his children were to him. Never realized how much he looked forward to their visits. Never realized how having those two little girls in his life gave it value and substance. He was a father, with the responsibility for molding and guiding two unique individuals into happy, healthy, productive adults.

His girls anchored his existence. How was he going to survive without them? What would give his life the same meaning they gave to it? What else was really important to him?

Partnership at D&B paled in comparison to the human relationships that might be lost to him.

Which made him think of Amy. He hadn't realized how important she was to him, either, until he'd lost her. He didn't want to make that mistake again.

He picked up the phone from the bed and dialed Amy's number. "Hi," he said when she answered.

"Hi, yourself." Her voice was low, throaty, sleepy. It sounded sexy as hell. He could hear the rustle of sheets and wished he'd woken up in bed with her this morning. But for the accident, he very well might have.

"How are you feeling this morning?" she asked.

"Sore all over," he admitted. "My shoulder aches and my knee is stiff."

"When are you being released from the hospital?"

"I checked myself out last night."

"You're home?"

"Yeah. I'd come see you, but I can't drive. Can you come here?"

He held the phone, waiting for her to decide whether she was going to come over.

"How about if I bring something for lunch?"

"That would be great," he said. "I'll see you around noon."

Luke stared at the phone for a moment after he hung up. Amy was coming for lunch. He wasn't going to spend the day alone after all.

He tried lying back down, but he was too restless to sleep. The sooner he found out how the twenty suspicious deaths reported by sub-investigators in clinical trials had been concealed from the FDA, the better chance he had of living a long life.

McCorkle was the one who'd submitted the supporting documentation to the FDA on behalf of Hyland. But it was doubtful he'd done the paperwork himself. So what nurse had filled everything out for his signature? Was Ms. Walters—the executive assistant— also a nurse? Had she been the one who collated all the clinical trial documents and submitted them for McCorkle's signature?

He made a note to ask Eddie whether Ms. Walters was a nurse and stepped into the shower.

He skipped the shave, since his right arm was still bound against his body, but managed to brush his teeth and comb his hair. He had a problem figuring out how to dress himself and eventually shimmied into some jeans and pulled a T-shirt over his head, sticking his good arm out the armhole. His bound arm was no use anyway.

Then he called Eddie Mull.

"Hi, Eddie."

"Hi, Luke. You don't have to say it."

"Say what, Eddie?"

"You need me at the office."

"I need you at the office, Eddie."

"Oh, Eddie," he heard Mary Margaret moan in the background.

"I'm sorry, Eddie," he said. "But someone tried to run me down last night. I think it might be someone connected with this case."

"What? Really?"

"Honest to God. The situation has gotten serious. I want you to find me some answers. And I wanted to warn you to be careful. I can't say for sure, but there's a chance you might be in danger."

"Are you kidding?"

"I think somebody got rid of Neil Ford. Somebody definitely came after me. I have to believe whoever it is knows you're researching D-Free, too."

"What's wrong, Eddie?" Luke heard Mary Margaret ask.

He heard a muffled, "Nothing, honey. I have to go to work, that's all." Eddie came back on the line and said, "What is it you need me to do?"

"The key to this whole mess is the twenty suspicious deaths signed off on by sub-investigators that weren't reported to the FDA," Luke said. "I don't care how you do it, just find out how Hyland managed to keep those deaths quiet."

"Actually, I already have an answer to that," Eddie said.

"You do? Why didn't you call me?"

"I tried last night. I couldn't reach you."

Luke looked and saw his message light was blinking. "I was in the hospital last night, and I haven't checked my messages this morning. Don't keep me in suspense."

"I'd rather show you. Can you meet me at the office?"

"I'm in no shape to go anywhere. Why don't you come here and bring what you've got?"

"How soon—"

"The sooner the better. I'll be waiting. Have you got

my address?" Luke gave it to him, then said, "Would you mind stopping for doughnuts on the way? I don't have anything in the house to offer you for breakfast."

"I'll bring some Krispy Kremes. How about some Starbucks coffee? Mocha latte no foam?"

Luke laughed. "Get yourself a Starbucks if you want one. I'll have some Maxwell House perking here."

Luke felt excited when he hung up the phone. Eddie had found something. Luke wondered if it would be enough to get Hyland to voluntarily take D-Free off the market. He realized he hadn't asked Eddie whether Grayson Choate was implicated. He'd know soon enough.

While he was waiting for Eddie to arrive, Luke called Nicki at work. When he got no answer at her office, he tried her home.

"Hey, it's me," he said when she picked up the phone. "Glad to see you're taking it easy."

She snorted. "I've been checking out whether Choate has any financial interest in D-Free, like you asked. Luke, she owns three percent of the patent."

"What did you say?"

"You heard me. She owns three percent of the patent on D-Free."

"It's unethical for her to own an interest in a client's business. She could get into serious trouble with the bar for something like that."

"Yeah, she sure could."

"How was she able to hide that?" Luke asked. "How come nobody knows about it?"

"Her interest in D-Free is owned by a subsidiary of a

subsidiary of a subsidiary, which is owned by Grayson Enterprises, which is owned by Grayson Choate."

"You're amazing," Luke said. "Now, what do we do with that information?"

"It certainly gives her a motive to help McCorkle hide a defect in the drug."

"It gives her a reason to want the D-Free wrongful death suits settled quickly and quietly," Luke said. "And a reason to keep me from investigating the deaths during clinical trials."

"Luke," Nicki said, when he didn't speak for a moment. "You need to get your daughter off that drug."

"Believe me, I'm working on it, Nick. Eddie's on his way over. Do you want to join us?"

"No thanks. But I'll look forward to hearing what he's found out."

"Thanks, Nick. I owe you one."

"You're welcome, Luke."

Luke figured it was going to take Eddie about forty-five minutes to an hour to get to his place if he stopped at Starbucks for coffee and at a grocery for some Krispy Kremes.

An hour and a half later, when there was no sign of Eddie, Luke started to worry. He called Eddie's house, but got no answer. He chafed at the restrictions his injuries placed on him. He wanted to go somewhere. Do something. But he had to sit and wait.

Luke wondered whether Choate knew he had Eddie researching D-Free. He was pretty sure McCorkle had no idea Eddie was involved, nor did his assistant. Had Eddie talked to someone on the phone who'd informed

Choate or McCorkle? Had Eddie been intercepted somewhere along the way?

Luke phoned Eddie's house again. Again there was no answer. Mary Margaret was nowhere near her due date. He wouldn't have gone to the hospital with her.

Unless something had gone wrong. Unless—

Luke stumbled in his hurry to get to the door to answer the knock and swore at the pain in his knee. "I'm coming," he yelled.

He felt an enormous sense of relief at finding Eddie at the door. And anger. "What the hell kept you? You're an hour late."

Eddie looked embarrassed. "I . . . My wife. It's Sunday morning and . . . "

Luke realized suddenly what had kept Eddie from jumping out of bed. He smiled, then grinned, and finally laughed. "I'd have stayed in bed, too."

Eddie turned pink to the roots of his hair. "I've got all the information here in this file," he said, lifting a heavy file he had tucked under his arm. His other hand held both a cup of Starbucks coffee and a bag of Krispy Kremes.

"I'll take those," Luke said, relieving Eddie of the doughnuts. "Let's sit at the kitchen table."

Once they were both settled with coffee and doughnuts in front of them, Eddie shoved his out of the way and opened the file.

"Here's how they did it," he said as he laid a series of files in a row in front of Luke. "Remember, a 'serious adverse event' has to be reported to the sponsor within twenty-four hours. However, the sponsor then has a window of time—not long, but enough for their purposes here—to report a 'serious adverse event' to the FDA."

"I knew that much," Luke said.

"It's the responsibility of the principal investigator, a doctor at the site of the clinical trial, to determine whether the death or serious illness or whatever—the 'serious adverse event'—is related or nonrelated to use of the drug."

"Uh-huh," Luke said.

"I think the sub-investigators were contacted at each of the clinical trial sites where there was a drug-related death and paid to intercede and make sure the site provided a report that cleared D-Free of responsibility in the incident," Eddie said.

"You're telling me someone had, what—126 doctors on their payroll? They'd have to have that many, wouldn't they, to cover all their bases, since there were 126 sites for the trial? That would cost a fortune."

Eddie shook his head. "The sub-investigators were paid for their work by the PI at the site. The twenty sub-Is who had to file 'fixed' reports were paid a significant bonus."

"You can prove that? You have evidence of that?"

"There was money going into their bank accounts that didn't come from their paychecks," Eddie said.

"Anybody ever suggest you make a living as a private investigator?" Luke said with a grin.

"Actually, I've been considering it."

For a moment, Luke thought he was joking. Then he realized he was serious. "Really?"

"I've been enjoying this work a lot more than the legal research I've been handed," Eddie said. "I'm not done, by the way. There's more."

"More? I'm all ears."

"The money to pay the sub-investigators came from Harold McCorkle's Bank of America personal money market account."

Luke frowned. "Surely he wouldn't be that stupid. It's too easy to trace that sort of thing."

"Stupid or not, that's where it came from."

"Can you find out who the nurse was that prepared the documentation for McCorkle's signature?"

"Ms. Walters is a nurse. She did all the paperwork at Hyland's end that went to the FDA."

"Which means she's probably every bit as guilty as McCorkle," Luke said. "Did you see Grayson Choate's name connected to any of this? Is there anything to tie her to any of these illegal reports?"

Eddie shook his head. "Nothing. You know she owns three percent of the patent."

Luke smiled. "Nothing gets by you, does it?"

Eddie smiled back. "I'd make a good private investigator."

"Now I just have to figure out what to do with this information," Luke mused.

"The FDA would have a field day," Eddie said.

"I'm not sure we can ethically give it to them, not when D&B represents Hyland Pharmaceuticals."

"Hyland broke the law. They continued trials on a drug that was killing people—still is killing people. That's murder," Eddie said.

"Not to mention what happened to Neil Ford," Luke said. "Any ideas who might be responsible for his death?"

"I can take a look at it, if you want."

"Let it go for now. Somebody already tried to run me down. I don't want them coming after you, too. Maybe the person I need to confront with all of this is Choate."

"I don't envy you that meeting."

"I'm not looking forward to it myself," Luke said. "But it has to be done. Thanks, Eddie. Go ahead and leave the file here. I'll take it with me when I finally go in to the office."

"You're not going in tomorrow?" Eddie asked, surprised.

Luke gestured at his bound arm. "I've got an excuse not to be there. I'm recuperating from an accident."

"From what I've heard, that wouldn't have stopped you in the past."

Eddie was right. Luke had gotten thrown from a horse over Christmas once and come back with a broken arm. That hadn't kept him home. Getting in to the office didn't seem as important as it once had.

"I'm going to use tomorrow to plan my strategy—here at home," Luke said.

"Maybe you can go over Choate's head to the management committee," Eddie suggested.

"I thought about that. I'm not sure it would work."

"Why not?"

"Choate's on the management committee. Besides, if she is a part of this mess, the D&B partnership might be held legally—and financially—liable. There wouldn't just be the five deaths after FDA approval to pay for, there'd be the twenty others during the clinical trials. That could end up bankrupting the D&B partners."

"So it's to their advantage to protect Choate," Eddie said.

"Yep. It sure is."

"If you can't go to the partnership and you can't go to the FDA, where are you going to go?"

"That, my young friend, is what I'm going to spend the rest of the day figuring out. Go home. Spend some time with your lovely wife."

"I'm already gone." He stopped at the door and said, "Call me if you need anything. I want to help."

"Thanks, Eddie. Have a nice day with Mary Margaret."

Eddie grinned. "I will."

Luke could hardly wait for Amy to arrive, so he could share what he'd learned. There was some flaw in the drug that had been covered up in clinical testing. Which was a shame, Luke realized, because D-Free really was a miracle drug for so many of those who used it.

Why hadn't McCorkle just kept experimenting until he solved the problem? Why had he lied and covered up the deaths from the drug?

The only answer Luke could come up with was greed. One of the first things Choate had pointed out was the fact D-Free only had five years to go on their exclusive patent for the drug. Maybe McCorkle figured it would take him the whole five years to figure out the problem. Or maybe he'd been trying to figure out the problem for twenty years and had finally decided it had no solution.

Something triggered a reaction that caused diabetic coma and death. Now that Luke knew what he knew, he had to get his daughter off D-Free. And he had to do it before her birthday. And if Valerie wouldn't agree? If Valerie remained stubbornly convinced that D-Free was just fine?

Luke clenched his teeth in frustration.

What if he wasn't allowed to reveal to the FDA what he'd discovered about D-Free? What if he couldn't get Hyland to admit the drug was dangerous? Was he going to go to the newspapers? Was he going to throw away everything he'd worked for over the past six years?

He watched the clock, willing it to move. He wanted to talk with Amy about what he'd discovered. He wanted to hear what she would suggest. He wanted to see if she would think he was so crazy now if he suggested kidnapping Brynne.

17

—m—

"Come in," Luke said to Amy. He wrapped his one good arm around her, catching the fast-food bags between them, and kissed her on the mouth. He felt her surrender to the moment and wished both arms worked, so he could do more than just hold her. He backed her up against the door, because his knee was killing him, so he could keep on kissing her.

He ignored Snowball's yowls until the cat bit his ankle. "Ow!" he said, jerking away. That wrenched his bad knee and he moaned.

"Are you all right?" Amy said.

"Damn cat," he muttered, glaring at Snowball.

Stubby tail flicking in agitation, Snowball glared back.

"Your cat wants some attention," Amy said with a grin, as she set the bags of KFC on the breakfast bar that separated the living room and kitchen.

"I got original recipe. That's what I remember you liked in high school."

"That's still my favorite," Luke said. "I've got some Coke in the fridge."

"I got myself a Diet Coke," Amy said. "I was pretty

sure you wouldn't have 'diet' anything in the house."

"You're right about that."

He followed her into the kitchen, backed her up against the refrigerator and kissed her again. Deeply. Thoroughly. Satisfyingly.

When he came up for air, he realized Amy's hands were entwined in his hair, and her hips were pressed close and caught between his widespread legs. He leaned back against the kitchen counter to take the weight off his bad knee.

"I needed that," he murmured against her ear. He inhaled and said, "Your hair smells good."

"Mmm?"

He saw her eyes were dazed, dreamy. He brushed a strand of hair behind her ear and said, "It smells the same as it did in high school."

"It's strawberry shampoo."

"I like it."

"I know."

She leaned her cheek against his chest and her arms circled his waist. "This feels good."

He rocked her gently, enjoying the feel of her in his arms. "We need to do this more often."

"I'm willing if you are."

He stopped rocking. "You are?" He wanted to see her eyes, but she kept her face pressed against him. "What are you thinking?"

"I was wondering whether people are fated to be together. I mean, I thought you were out of my life forever. But here you are."

"I always thought we should be together," Luke said.

"I know."

Left unsaid was the fact she hadn't always felt that way, that she'd walked away without looking back.

"Stay here tonight," Luke said. "Be with me."

She leaned back and looked up at him. "You're crazy."

"I'm hungry for you."

She barely caressed his wounded cheek with her fingertips, and he winced. "You're in no shape for a roll in the hay."

"No rolling. I promise," he said with a teasing smile. "No rocking, either."

"You were always best at slow dancing."

He realized she was flirting with him, something she'd never had to do all those years ago, because he'd swept her off her feet and they'd become a couple and there was no question of her needing to attract him. He dipped his head and kissed her again, wanting the closer connection with her. They were both breathing hard by the time she broke the kiss, and his hand was up under her shirt, inside her bra, caressing her naked breast.

She put her hand over his outside her shirt to hold it still. "Luke," she whispered. "We have to stop this or we're going to end up in bed."

"What's wrong with that?"

She glanced pointedly at his arm held by the sling, and his cocked knee and the bandage on his face.

He smiled and said, "All right. Let's eat."

She stepped back and went to the sink. He was surprised to see her hands were trembling as she washed them. But when he tried to walk, his legs were unsteady, and it dawned on him that whatever drew them together was powerful enough to leave them both rattled.

The chicken was greasy as hell and about as good as fried chicken could get. As they ate, Luke explained what he'd learned from Eddie and Nicki that morning.

"You can't keep this a secret," Amy said. "D-Free is dangerous. People need to be warned."

"I have to confront Choate first," Luke said. "She deserves a chance to explain herself."

"What is it you're hoping Choate will do?"

"She can't ignore what I've discovered. I'm hoping that if I confront her, she'll tell McCorkle the gig is up, and Hyland will make a public announcement concerning the danger to kids between the ages of nine and sixteen of using D-Free."

"And if she doesn't? Then what?"

"I can always go to the management committee."

"Who will give her a slap on the wrist—because she controls such a huge portion of the firm's revenues—and send her on her way. She's going to escape this mess scot-free," Amy predicted as she wiped her hands on a paper napkin. "Watch and see if she doesn't."

They threw away the leftovers, wiped down the table and then headed back to the living room. Amy settled on the sofa, displacing Snowball, who arched her back, hissed at Amy and then retreated. "I would have been glad to share the couch with her," Amy said, as the cat crouched under the dining room table.

"Get used to it," Luke said to the cat as he eased into

his overstuffed chair and carefully arranged his knee
on the ottoman. "She's going to be around a lot."

"You sound pretty sure of that."

"Just hopeful," Luke said. "I wish there were some
way to hold Choate accountable," he said, continuing
their previous discussion. "But I don't have proof of any
wrongdoing on her part. There's nothing to link her to
the doctored reports sent to the FDA. And she
wouldn't be the first lawyer to secretly own a little piece
of a company she represents."

"What if Choate refuses to do anything?" Amy
asked. "What will you do then? How are you going to
get the word out to parents about the potential harm to
their kids if they're taking D-Free?"

Luke pursed his lips. "I haven't figured that out."

"You have to tell someone with the authority to
make that information public."

"Who would you suggest?"

"The FDA."

Luke shook his head. "Can't do that. Hyland is a
D&B client."

"I can tell them."

Luke stared hard at Amy. "You can't say a word
about this to anyone."

"Why not?"

"Because the only reason you know is because I've
told you. You'll get me disbarred."

"I can—"

"Lie?" Luke interjected. "That's what you'd have to
do to explain where you got the information about
D-Free."

"If Eddie and Nick found out about mistakes in the clinical trials through Internet research, I could have, too."

"Eddie and Nicki had access to Hyland files because of our representation of the company—files not available to you."

Amy crossed her arms. "I'm not going to sit by and do nothing while more kids have a deadly reaction to D-Free."

"You have to trust me. I'm going to take care of this."

"When? How?"

Luke wanted to be out of the chair, wanted to be moving, but the deep cushion held him prisoner. He pushed, one-armed, wrenching his dislocated shoulder and grimacing with pain, as he struggled to get out of it. Once he was on his feet, he limped toward the kitchen.

"I want something to drink." He also wanted to escape Amy's demanding questions.

Amy followed him. "I don't understand the problem."

He whirled on her, biting his lip to keep from crying out as he twisted his bad knee. "The problem is, I've spent six years working my way up in the firm. In the spring, D&B is going to be selecting partners. How I handle this matter can make the difference in whether I'm in or out."

Amy stared at him, disbelieving. "You'd choose partnership in a law firm over the lives of innocent children?"

"I'm trying to come up with a way not to have to make that choice."

"Because you'd choose partnership in the firm."

"I've given up everything to get where I am—my family, my free time, my personal life. I don't want to throw all that time and effort down the toilet."

"Saving lives is more important—"

"There have only been five deaths in a year, Amy. D-Free has been used by nearly a million people. That's a minuscule risk when you consider—"

"I don't believe what I'm hearing!" Amy said. "Those five lives were very important to the people who lost them—and their families. How would you feel—"

"I'm only saying—"

"How would you feel if one of those children was Brynne? You're making excuses so you don't have to make a choice."

Amy turned abruptly and left the kitchen.

Luke limped after Amy and grabbed her arm, "I never said I wasn't going to make sure the truth gets out. I just want to do it in a way—"

"That doesn't require any sacrifice from you."

"What's wrong with that?" Luke demanded. "Why does everything have to be black and white with you? There's not just one way to do a thing. Goddammit, there are shades of gray."

He watched her nostrils flare. Saw her lips press flat and her hands ball into fists. Her voice, when she spoke again, was carefully measured. "Have you told Valerie what you've told me about the problems with D-Free?"

"Not yet. At least, not all of it. But I will."

"It must be nice to know that your child will be safe," Amy said. "Even if others aren't."

"That's a low blow, Amy."

"It's the truth."

"I'm not going to argue any more with you about this."

"If you don't do something, Luke, I will."

"You don't trust me at all, do you?" It was a bitter pill to swallow. She hadn't thought much of him when he was a teenager, and things hadn't changed much in the years since. She wanted him physically now—as she had then. But the fundamental differences in the way they looked at life hadn't changed.

Luke felt a sinking feeling in his stomach. He wanted to live up to her expectations of him. He just wasn't sure he could.

"I told you I'm taking care of the situation," he said. "And I am. Don't do anything you'll regret."

"Is that a threat?"

"I'm not the one making threats," Luke said. "You are."

"I don't understand your reluctance to tell what you know."

Luke met Amy's gaze and held it, unwilling to explain himself. She wasn't a man—who was judged by his peers according to his status at work, his income, the size of his house and his car and the diamonds in his wife's pierced ears. It was easy for her to say "chuck it all." Not so easy for him to throw away everything he'd worked for over the past six years.

"I'm glad you came by today," he said.

"Are you?"

He felt the knot in his gut tighten. "I want to be with you, Amy. I'd like it if you'd stay."

"I have things I have to do this afternoon."

"Will you come back tonight?" When she didn't answer right away he said, "Think about it. I'll be here."

He wished he could be the knight in shining armor she expected him to be. There were no kisses when she left. She was very careful not to touch him at all.

After Luke closed the door behind Amy, he limped to the bedroom and sat on the bed with his shoulder supported by a pillow. He wasn't happy about the way their lunch together had ended. But what had he expected?

To be honest, he'd hoped that she'd support him. Her response wasn't out of line, however. Why should she trust him? She only knew the Luke Creed who'd roared through town on his Harley, who'd gotten suspended for defacing school property, who'd bought beer with a fake ID. And who'd gone off to Somalia with his National Guard unit and come home to find his paraplegic brother Sam engaged to Emma Coburn, the woman Luke had gotten pregnant the night of Amy Hazeltine's engagement party.

He was going to need more than luck to mesh his life and Amy Nash's. Luke wondered what it was about her that made him want to be a better man, to live up to the standards she expected from him. He would have to wait and see how the Dragon Lady responded to the information he'd discovered. That was soon enough to decide whether he was going to throw away his chances at partnership to blow the whistle on D-Free.

Luke hadn't realized he'd dozed until someone pounding on the front door woke him. He yelled, "I'm coming," scaring Snowball off the pillow beside his head, then painfully dragged himself out of bed, limping to the door. "I'm coming," he growled again as he reached the door.

He opened it and said, "What the hell do you want?"

"I came by to see if you're okay. Since you're obviously fine, I'm outta here."

Drew had already turned to leave when Luke said, "Come in. Take a load off."

Drew turned back around, and when he passed by, Luke saw he had a package under his arm.

"What have you got there?" Luke asked.

"Beer, peanuts and popcorn."

"What for?"

"Football, of course." Drew crossed and turned on the TV, switching channels until he found the Dallas Cowboys football game.

Luke didn't argue, simply lowered himself into his chair, eased his knee up onto the ottoman, caught the beer bottle Drew threw at him, opened it and took a swallow. He fumbled the package of cheddar popcorn Drew pitched at him, then picked it up off the floor and opened it, as Drew popped open a can of beer nuts.

Neither man said anything as they watched the game. Luke's mother hadn't allowed him to play football in high school, not after Sam's accident on the football field had put him in a wheelchair. It was a blessing in disguise, because Luke probably would have been thrown off the team. He hadn't wanted to follow rules of any kind, and the coach had been strict about all sorts of things—like not smoking, not drinking and making practice on time.

Nevertheless, Luke had grown up loving football. In most small Texas towns—Bitter Creek was no exception—the entire population turned out for the high school football game on Friday nights.

"Who's winning?" Luke asked.

"Who cares?" Drew said. "I only came by to find out how you are."

"How did you know about my accident?"

"That new guy gave me a call, the one who's been doing all the research on D-Free. Said he thought I might like to know what happened to you, in case you hadn't contacted me. Which you hadn't. How did you end up walking in front of a moving car?"

"It swerved into me on purpose."

Drew turned to face him. "No shit?"

"Somebody made a serious effort to wipe Mrs. Creed's little boy off the map."

"Why?"

"Guess I was getting too close to the truth about D-Free."

Drew's lips flattened to a slash across his face. His eyes narrowed. "You going to tell me what the truth is?"

"Not before I tell Choate," Luke said. "It's not that I don't trust you—"

"Hell and damnation," Drew muttered. "I was afraid of something like this."

Luke sat up straight in his chair. "Afraid of what, Drew?"

"Gray made an obscure comment about Neil Ford's 'accidental' death, but I didn't think much about it. Until now."

"I'm listening," Luke said.

"She didn't think Neil would've drunk anything if he was taking an antidepressant."

"Why not?"

"She said he was anal about everything. Precise. Said he probably took the pills the minute he should."

"Why couldn't he have O.D.'d? Why not crash his car into a wall to get away from her?"

Drew arched one brow. "I won't take offense on Gray's behalf, because I know you're in a lot of pain right now. Gray had just spoken with Neil on the phone. He seemed excited, not depressed."

"Did she tell all this to the police?" Luke asked.

"Yes."

"Do you know if they investigated other possible causes of Neil's death?"

"He didn't have any family to push them into doing more than what they did, which was to look at the results of the autopsy, which revealed the combination of prescribed drugs and alcohol."

"Why didn't Choate pursue it?" Luke asked.

"I don't think she wanted the police looking too closely at what Neil was working on."

"Because she's known all along there's something wrong with D-Free?"

Drew hesitated. "She's never said so in as many

words. Nothing definite enough that I could say to you 'Take Brynne off the drug.'"

"So what makes you think she knows it's dangerous?"

Drew shrugged one shoulder. "I suppose it's more a case of what she hasn't said. She's never denied it's dangerous. And she's never confirmed it's safe."

"Not A, not B, therefore C," Luke muttered.

"What?"

"Never mind," Luke said. "Why aren't you spending the day with the Dragon Lady?"

"She's at work."

"Why aren't you at work, too?"

"I'm here with you."

"How would you like to drive me in to the office?" Luke said.

"Now?"

"I need to talk to Choate," Luke said. "And there's no time like the present."

18

Luke could hear Choate talking on the phone in her office. He stopped outside the door and scrubbed a hand across the day-old beard that shadowed his face. He looked down and realized he was still wearing the jeans and T-shirt—with one arm hanging out—that he'd put on that morning. Choate could like it or lump it.

He hadn't given up on the possibility of making partner at D&B, but somewhere between home and the office he'd realized he was going to have to reach his goal despite Choate, not because of her.

He limped into the doorway where she could see him and waited for her to get off the phone.

"I'll have to call you back," Choate said as she spied him. "I have something that needs attention here."

As she hung up the phone, Luke crossed to her desk and stood behind one of the pink brocade chairs.

She eyed him assessingly and said, "You look like you need to sit down."

"I'm fine right here."

"Eddie told me about your accident," Choate said.

"If he did, then you know it was no accident."

"You really believe someone tried to kill you?"

Luke looked her in the eye and said, "Not just someone. Someone at Hyland."

"That's absurd."

"Is it? What really happened to Neil Ford?"

"What do you mean? He was killed in a car accident," Choate said.

"I think he found out the same thing I've found out. That twenty deaths during the D-Free clinical trials were caused by the drug. And that doctors were paid off by McCorkle to lie in their reports to Hyland."

The frown of confusion on Choate's face looked genuine. "McCorkle paid them off? That's impossible."

"I can prove money came out of his personal bank account to pay off the doctors."

"Please, sit down so we can talk about this," Choate said.

Luke didn't want to sit in one of those pink chairs, but his knee was killing him. He sank into a chair and managed not to groan in relief. "You need to confront Harold McCorkle and get him to make a public announcement about the dangers of D-Free to kids between the ages of nine and sixteen."

"What's wrong with D-Free?" Choate asked.

"Are you telling me you really don't know?"

Choate hesitated long enough before replying that Luke realized she knew something and was deciding how to answer him. At last she said, "When we had the first D-Free lawsuit after the drug went on the market, Harold went back to look at the reports during clinical research. He'd taken the doctors' word for it that the deaths during clinical testing were unrelated, so he didn't report them to the FDA."

"Surely that many deaths should have sent up a red flag, even if they were unrelated," Luke said.

"I suppose it would have—if he'd seen the reports as they came in."

This time it was Luke who looked confused. "He's the guy in charge. If he didn't see the reports, who did?"

"Ms. Walters, of course. Harold is a busy man. She's been with him for twenty years. He trusts her implicitly."

"Trusts—present tense? I suppose Walters pays all his bills and has access to his bank accounts," Luke said.

"As a matter of fact, she does."

"So 'the secretary'—no, make that 'the executive assistant'—did it? She intercepted the 'serious adverse event' reports, paid off the doctors and hid the truth from her boss?"

"It appears that way."

"Why would she do it?" Luke asked. "What does she get out of it?"

"Harold asked her that very question," Choate said.

"I'm all ears."

"She did it for love."

Luke couldn't believe he'd heard her right. "*Love?*"

"She's apparently been in love with Harold for years. She's watched him struggle—and fail—to solve the problems with D-Free. She decided to make sure this version of the drug would be approved. So she figured out a way to hide any serious adverse events."

"Why isn't she in jail right now?" Luke asked. "And D-Free off the market?"

"There's a problem."

"You're damned right there's a problem," Luke said. "My daughter—and a lot of other kids—are taking a drug that can kill them, and nobody's done a damned thing to get it off the shelves."

"Ms. Walters wasn't acting under orders from anyone in the company, or with their knowledge or consent, but she is an employee of Hyland. If her part in this conspiracy is revealed, both Harold and Hyland could be found additionally culpable."

"And the problem is?"

"We represent Hyland."

"We don't represent McCorkle. How about letting him take the heat?"

"It all goes back to Hyland," Choate said.

"Get to the point," Luke said.

"The point is, Hyland wants to avoid the appearance of irregularity—"

Luke snorted at the euphemism.

Choate continued, "And it's not to their advantage to take the drug off the market right now because—"

Luke could feel the blood begin to pound in his temples. "They only have five years left on the patent," he finished for her. "You've got to be kidding me."

"I'm dead serious."

Luke stared at her, wondering what his next move should be. "I want to talk to McCorkle," he said.

"What purpose would that serve?"

"I want to hear from him that he's willing to leave D-Free on the market."

"The decision isn't Harold's," Choate said.

"Why not? He was the monitor for the flawed clinical testing. Now that he knows there's a problem—"

"Hyland would rather pay off the victims than recall the drug."

"They can't do that."

"It's done all the time," Choate replied. "With all sorts of products. Like tires the manufacturer knows might be defective, but which are too expensive to recall. Or gas tanks that explode on impact."

"As I recall, in both those cases, the company ended up admitting fault and paying for their mistake."

"Ah, but not as much as it would have cost them to admit their mistake in the first place."

"Then let me make myself clear. I'm not going to let Hyland get away with doing it," Luke said.

"You're not going to say a word. Or you'll find yourself out of a job."

"I can find another job."

"Not if you've been disbarred."

"There's no one who'd condemn me for exposing Hyland's—"

"For betraying your client's trust? Everyone in the legal community will condemn you. No one wants a lawyer who can't keep his mouth shut."

"Someone has to say something," Luke said. "For the sake of the kids who are dying."

"Before you go to anyone outside the firm, I'd like you to meet with the management committee."

"Why?"

"To discuss the matter."

Luke was disturbed that Choate seemed to welcome

a meeting between him and the management committee. Why wasn't she worried? What did she have up her sleeve? What exculpatory information did she have that he didn't yet know?

Luke realized meeting with the management committee might be a trap. But he really didn't see where he had any other choice, if he hoped to convince the firm's power brokers of the need to disclose the problems with D-Free to the public.

He met Choate's gaze directly and said, "How soon can you set it up?"

"I should be able to arrange for you to meet with everyone tomorrow morning around nine."

"I'll be there."

"Good. Now, why don't you go home and rest."

"One more thing," Luke said.

Choate lifted an inquiring brow.

"Was it also Walters who did whatever she did to Neil Ford that caused him to have that accident? Was it Walters who tried to run me down?"

"I'm not sure either of those events occurred as you've depicted them," Choate said.

"I didn't jump in front of that car," Luke said, holding onto his temper with effort.

"Perhaps the driver was distracted. That happens."

"Yeah, shit happens," Luke said bitterly. "I'll see you tomorrow morning."

She gestured to his gimpy leg and said, "How are you getting around?"

"I've got a ride." He was halfway out the door when Choate's voice stopped him.

"Luke?"

Luke turned and waited for her to speak.

"I hope your daughter is all right."

He bit his lip on what he wanted to say. *If she is, it's no thanks to you.* If Choate had cared at all, she'd have told him the truth the first time he asked about D-Free. He didn't respect her. He didn't like her. But he still had to work with her. At least until he gave up on his dream of partnership at D&B.

"I'm on my way to find out how she is right now." Luke turned and limped down the hall to his office. He hadn't told her he knew about her three percent interest in Hyland. He was saving that for the management committee meeting. He wanted to see how she would wriggle out of that.

When Luke got to his office, he found Drew whirling himself in circles in Luke's swivel chair. Drew caught the desk with his hands, took one look at Luke and said, "No good, huh?"

"She's known everything all along."

Drew frowned. "Everything? Are you sure?"

"She admitted that Hyland is choosing to pay off any wrongful death suits rather than make a public announcement about the problems with adolescents using D-Free."

"She's only Hyland's corporate counsel, Luke. She doesn't make company policy. She only advises the company about what makes legal sense."

"What about what makes moral sense? What about a company conscience? Who supplies that?"

"The guys who own the company, I guess," Drew said.

"Bingo! Did you know Choate owns three percent of the D-Free patent?"

Luke saw Drew's hands tighten on the desk but otherwise, he didn't react. "Did you hear what I said?"

"What do you expect me to say?" Drew said as he shoved himself out of the chair. "So she owns three percent of the patent. So what?"

"You don't give a damn, do you?"

"I don't want to talk about this," Drew said as he headed for the door.

Luke stepped forward to block his way. "She doesn't care, Drew. She doesn't give a shit if kids are dying."

"I don't believe that."

"You've got blinders on where she's concerned," Luke said. "Wake up and smell the garbage, Drew. Grayson Choate is a manipulative, deceitful bitch."

Drew's body tautened. "Watch what you say, Luke. Friendship doesn't excuse—"

"She doesn't care about anyone or anything but herself."

"That's enough, Luke."

"She's a cold-hearted, mean-spirited—"

Drew had drawn his fist back to punch Luke but hit the wall instead. When he pulled his hand back, there was a hole in the plaster and his knuckles were bleeding.

Luke saw the pain in his eyes. "I'm sorry, Drew. Not sorry for telling you what I think of her. Just sorry for your sake that she isn't a better person."

"I'm sure Gray has her reasons—"

"Greed," Luke interrupted harshly. "Money. *Dinero.* Cold, hard cash."

Drew's nostrils flared and a muscle ticked in his cheek. His hands clenched into powerful fists, and Luke braced himself for the blow he was sure was coming. Once again, Drew managed to bring himself back from the brink of violence.

"Get yourself another ride," he said. "I can't stand to look at you anymore."

A moment later he was gone.

Luke called one of the limousine services that the firm used and had the driver take him to Valerie's house. He asked the driver to wait as he limped up the walkway. He rang the doorbell and gritted his teeth while it played the Aggie fight song.

Valerie opened the door, took one look at him and said, "What happened to you?"

"I had a little accident. I'm fine."

"Why are you here?"

"I need to talk to you. Alone."

"What could you possibly—"

"It's important, Valerie." He heard the sharpness in his voice, knew that she would know that it meant he was on the brittle edge of self-control. She'd pushed him there often enough in the last days of their marriage.

"Well, don't stand there. Come in. You're letting out the air-conditioning. Martin and I are barbecuing out back," she said, as she led him through the house.

Luke suppressed the groan as both his knee and shoulder protested the trip down her steep back steps to the Mexican-tiled patio.

"Will you leave us alone, Martin?" Valerie said.

Martin handed Luke a spatula, hitched a thumb over his shoulder in the direction of the grill and said, "Keep an eye on the burgers. They need to be turned in another minute or so." As he passed Valerie, he patted her behind and said, "Make it quick, honey. I'm hungry."

Luke set the spatula down on the redwood picnic table and turned to his ex-wife. "You need to—"

"I'm glad you've come, Luke," she interrupted. "Martin's father had a heart attack and wants Martin to come right away and take over the business. I've been putting off telling you because I knew you weren't going to be happy about it, but we're leaving as soon as the girls get back here. And by the way, what the hell is going on at Three Oaks? Every time I call, your mother gives me some lame excuse why the girls can't come to the phone."

"The kids don't have chicken pox, Valerie. I made that up so I could take Brynne off D-Free."

"Well," she said. "I feel a lot less guilty now about telling you that I have a company coming tomorrow to pack up the house."

Luke felt his heart lodge in the back of his throat. "You can't take the girls away from me, Valerie."

"Of course I can. I'm the primary custodial parent. Where I go, the girls go."

"I hardly get to see them now. Phone calls won't be enough."

"You can have them every other Christmas and Thanksgiving, and they can come stay with you during school breaks and summer vacation."

"The girls go to camp for six weeks in the summer."

"I suppose that will be up to you, since you'll have them over the summer," Valerie said.

"I don't—"

"There's something else," Valerie said.

"What?" Luke said, his fear coming out as irritation.

"I'm pregnant."

"You told me you didn't want any more kids," he blurted. He'd have been more than happy to have more.

"Not with you, no," she said. "I know that sounds awful," she hurried to say. "But you know yourself we weren't getting along, and I didn't see how having more kids was going to help anything."

She was right. But that didn't prevent his stomach from turning over.

"The hamburgers need to be flipped," she said.

"To hell with the hamburgers."

Valerie glared at him, then retrieved the spatula and crossed to the grill to turn the hamburgers.

"Leave the girls here with me, Val," he said, using the shortened form of her name for the first time since their divorce.

She dropped the spatula back on the table and put her hands on her hips. "You couldn't take care of them. You know what your schedule is like, Luke. They'd spend all their time with a babysitter. That wouldn't be fair to them." She hesitated, met his gaze and said, "Or you."

The awful thing was, she was right. He'd struggled over the past two years to carve out one Saturday every other weekend. With Valerie, the girls had a mother waiting for them when they got home from school.

Luke swallowed over the painful lump that had risen in his throat. He was going to lose his daughters. They would grow up and away from him and he would meet them as strangers over the Christmas holidays every other year. And there wasn't a damned thing he could do about it.

"There's one more thing we need to get settled before you move away," he said.

She waited, her mouth twisted in a moué of displeasure.

"I want Brynne off D-Free."

"We've had this discussion—"

"It's dangerous, Val. It's killed five kids over the past year and twenty during clinical trials."

"Luke, you know how—"

"I mean it, Val. She has to get off that stuff. How much more proof do you need than what I've already given you?"

"Why hasn't there been some public announcement, if the drug is so dangerous?"

Luke hesitated. Ethically, he couldn't tell her what he knew. But if there was ever a gray area, this was it. "The company has decided it's more profitable to let a few kids die and pay off their parents to keep quiet than to take the drug off the market."

She stared at him, stunned. "That can't be true."

"Believe me, it is," he said. "You should also know that birthdays are a 'triggering event' for a deadly reaction to the drug. I'm especially worried about Brynne because she has a birthday coming up."

Valerie looked shaken. "I'll have her take insulin until her birthday is past."

"I want her off the drug period," Luke said. "Listen to me, Val. I mean it. Brynne's life is at stake."

"I'm not going to argue with you, Luke. I told you I'm willing to take her off the drug temporarily. That should satisfy you."

"Val, I'm begging you—"

"Don't bother," Valerie said. "We'll be gone soon and Brynne's day-to-day struggle to manage her disease will no longer be your problem."

"She's still my daughter," Luke said angrily.

"And my responsibility except for the time she's with you. If you want to take her off D-Free during the summer, go ahead. You'll have a fight on your hands, because she's not going to want to prick her finger to test her blood and take shots five or six times a day. But, hey, if that's what you want your daughter to have to endure—when she could be taking three pills a day instead—go right ahead."

"Don't you get it?" Luke said. "She could die."

"That's been a danger ever since Brynne was diagnosed with this disease," Valerie said. "D-Free makes life a lot easier for her. And I don't intend to take that away from her."

Luke could see he was banging his head against the wall. He might end up having to kidnap his daughter after all.

"How long before and after her birthday should Brynne be taken off the drug?" Valerie asked.

Luke stared at her. He had no idea. If that had been

easy to figure out, McCorkle would have solved the problem by now. As far as Luke knew, the best scientific minds at Hyland hadn't been able to figure it out.

He shoved a hand roughly through his hair. "I don't know."

"A week, two weeks, a month? You realize Brynne's birthday is is only a few weeks away."

Martin appeared at the back door and said, "Valerie, I smell something burning."

"Oh, damn." As Valerie expertly flipped the charred hamburgers onto a plate, she called to Martin, "The burgers are done, Martin. Come on and let's eat."

"Val—"

"You're welcome to stay for dinner, Luke," she said. "So long as you don't say another word about D-Free."

"I've got a car waiting for me," Luke said.

As the limo drove out of Valerie's neighborhood, Luke realized it wouldn't be much of a detour to stop by Amy's apartment. He debated whether to call her first on his cell, but decided he didn't want to give her the chance to tell him not to come.

When the limo pulled up in front of Amy's apartment, the driver asked, "Do you want me to wait?"

It was nearly dark, and Luke could see lights on inside, but that didn't mean Amy was home. Or that she would let him in. "Just until I get inside."

When he knocked, Amy opened the door and urged him inside. "How did you get here?" She peered out, saw the limo and said, "What are you doing here? Has something happened to Brynne?"

He waved the limo away as Amy closed the door

behind him. "Brynne's fine. But I don't know for how long."

Amy gestured him to the couch and helped him lift his injured leg up onto the cushions and put a pillow behind his back. Then she retrieved a chair from the kitchen table and sat down across from him.

"Now," she said. "Tell me what's wrong."

"Martin's father had a heart attack. He's agreed to run his father's business for him while he recuperates. Valerie told me they'll be leaving for Vermont as soon as Brynne and Midge get home from Three Oaks."

"Oh, Luke. I'm so sorry."

"Valerie says I can have the girls every other Christmas and summer vacations. She agreed to take Brynne off D-Free temporarily—at least through her birthday—but she won't agree to take her off it permanently."

"Oh, God. Doesn't she realize what could happen?"

"I've told her," Luke said. "She thinks I'm exaggerating the risk."

"What are you going to do?"

"Kidnapping sounds pretty good right now. I met with Choate today, but she won't do anything."

"So Hyland isn't going to make any announcements."

Luke shook his head. He waited for Amy to urge him to action, but she said nothing. Maybe she figured she'd already said everything there was to say.

"I'm meeting with the D&B management committee tomorrow morning," he said. "Choate set it up."

"Oh?"

"I have to find a way to persuade them it's to the firm's advantage to have Hyland confess and repent now, before someone else exposes the problem."

"That makes good sense," Amy said.

A silence fell between them.

"Come here," he said, patting the sliver of couch beside him and scooting over to make room for her. She lay down beside him, her face pressed against his throat.

Luke was surprised to realize all he wanted was to hold her, and to be held. He felt a tickle in his throat and swallowed over the growing thickness.

He tightened his good arm around her. "I'm afraid, Amy."

"Of what?" she said softly.

"That Brynne and Midge will go on with their lives and forget about me. Brynne is old enough to have memories. But Midge is so young . . . I don't . . . "

He fought back the sob, refusing to let it out. He swallowed noisily. Swallowed again.

He felt Amy's hand smoothing his hair. Heard her voice murmuring comfort. "It's all right, Luke. Everything will be all right."

She kissed his cheeks, his eyes, his nose. "Please don't cry," she said. "I can't bear it."

He felt the tear slide down his cheek, but his hand was bound, so he couldn't scrub it away.

She barely touched her mouth to his, but the kiss was electric, filled with passion and emotion—and oblivion. He didn't want to think anymore. He didn't want to hurt anymore.

He felt a quiver go through her as she slid on top of him and pressed herself against the length of his body. He tested the seam of her mouth with his tongue and tasted her as she opened to him. The kiss was fierce with need, powerful with longing.

She shoved her shorts and panties off as she straddled him, then freed him from his trousers and impaled herself with a groan of pleasure. He clutched her waist as she rose and fell on him, driving them both toward climax. She voiced a harsh, guttural sound as he emptied himself into her.

She fell forward onto his chest, at the very last second adjusting her body so she didn't put any pressure on his injured shoulder. He lay with her, holding her close, letting the languor steal over him.

"I'm here, Luke," Amy murmured as she settled beside him. "I'm not going anywhere."

Luke gave up the struggle and slid down the black hole that promised surcease from pain.

19

Gray was sitting at her desk at home when she sensed, more than heard, someone behind her. She tensed for a moment, wondering if it was an intruder. She felt a hand caress her nape and knew who it was.

"I was hoping you'd come by tonight," she said, dropping her pen and turning in her chair to look up at Drew. "It's late. Where have you been?"

"I was chauffeuring Luke around."

"All night?"

He bent and kissed her, and she tasted bourbon. So he'd gone to a bar somewhere. Or been home drinking alone.

"Come to bed," she said, rising and reaching for his hand.

He pulled free and said, "I want to talk, Gray."

She heard the slight slur in his voice caused by too much alcohol. She eyed him warily and saw the sullen droop of his mouth, the slight narrowing of his blue eyes. She crossed past him and headed for the kitchen, where there was coffee to sober him up—and a door for escape. He followed uncomfortably close on her heels.

"How about a cup of coffee?" she said, rummaging

around in the kitchen cabinets, keeping a safe space between them.

Drew came up behind her with surprising quickness, levering his hands on the kitchen counter on either side of her, trapping her. "I told myself it didn't matter to me," he said in a whiskey-rough voice, his lips against her ear. "But it does."

"What are you talking about?" She tried to turn around, but he pressed his body harder against hers, keeping her captive.

"I was willing to give you the benefit of the doubt," he continued without answering her. "I told myself you were just doing your job, that your allegiance was to the client."

"Drew, let's sit down and—"

His hand covered her mouth and nose. For a second she panicked, thinking he meant to suffocate her. But his hand slid down clumsily so it only covered her mouth, and she realized the alcohol had caused him to misjudge.

Her eyes darted around the kitchen, looking for some weapon she could use to protect herself. The counter was completely empty. Bare of anything that would tell anyone whether she liked toasted bagels, or made banana milkshakes or carved up oranges for herself at night. She eyed the drawer where she kept an assortment of large kitchen tools but realized Drew would intercept her long before she'd located something that could be used to stab or maim him.

She tried talking behind his hand, but he clamped it tighter. She froze, afraid Drew might accidentally cover her nose again. She realized her body was stiff, her muscles tightened to strike out, and she forced herself to relax. She could still use her fingernails, and she was wearing a pair of high-heeled bedroom slippers, which she might be able to use on his instep, if he backed up a little to give her the space to move.

She had known there was a dark side to Drew DeWitt. It was part of what had drawn her to him. The bright, boyish smile, the all-American good looks on the outside—and a tortured soul on the inside. She was glad he'd never shared his inner torment with her. It meant she could keep her secrets from him in return.

She'd enjoyed flirting with danger. But there was something deadly about Drew now that raised the hairs on her flesh, something dark and sinister that she'd never suspected. She was certain that how she responded, what she did and what she said—when she could speak again—might mean the difference between living and dying.

"Your name fits. The Dragon Lady. Breathing fire and destruction without a care for the innocents who might get burned," he said, his lips caressing her ear.

She reached up a hand and laid it on his wrist, applying light pressure in an attempt to get him to free her mouth.

"Oh, no you don't," he said, pressing her hard enough against the counter to hurt her, and using his other hand to pull her hand free. She laid both her hands flat on the counter in front of her, so he could see she was no threat to him, and waited, breath caught in her throat, until he eased off the pressure.

"Stand there and listen," he growled. "That's all I want from you. No tricks to make me want you."

She suddenly realized he was aroused, and that it would be easy for him to take what he wanted violently.

How drunk was he? Certainly enough to blur good judgment. Enough to do something he might regret when sober?

"I know about women like you," he said in a low, harsh voice. "I have intimate experience with them. My aunt Eve, for one. There was a piece of work. Got away with murder. Literally. And my grandmother. Killed herself. But not before she'd done her dirty work on her grandsons."

Gray forced her body to relax back against him.

"My brother Dusty—" His voice caught, and she heard him swallow hard. "Dusty didn't deserve what happened to him. I tried to talk him out of it. I talked and talked until I was hoarse. I thought he might put the gun down. But he looked right at me and . . ." A low, animal sound of pain issued from his throat. "I don't want to remember. But I do."

She realized he'd loosened his hold on her mouth, and she reached up carefully and pulled his fingers free.

As suddenly as he'd captured her, he released her completely and took a step back. "Christ. What the hell am I doing?"

When she turned, he'd backed up another two steps and was scrubbing his eye sockets with his fists.

"What are you doing, Drew?" she asked. "What is this all about?"

His eyes looked anguished. "I loved you."

She noticed he'd phrased it in the past tense.

"I wasn't ever going to love a woman, but I fell in love with you. I wonder now if it was because I was drawn to the darkness in you, because it's what I know best." His lip curled in a sneer. "Women who hate the world and everything in it—especially themselves."

Gray gasped. She hadn't believed mere words could hurt so much. She felt as though she'd been slashed with a knife. "Get out, Drew. Go."

He shook his head. "Not yet. Not before I say what I've come here to say."

She put her hands to her ears. "I'm not listening to any more of this. You're drunk. Get out of my house before I call the police."

He moved faster than she'd believed possible, faster than she could escape. Once more she was held captive. Only this time, he held her in a savage lover's embrace, one arm around her waist, the other snatching at her hair, pulling her head back so far she thought her neck might snap.

"Drew, you're hurting me," she said, trying—and failing—to keep the panic from her voice.

"Wouldn't want to do that," he said bitterly.

But the strain on her neck eased immediately.

His eyes bored into hers, his lips thinned to a blade and his nostrils flared as he breathed heavily, as though there wasn't enough oxygen in the room. "You'll have to go on killing kids without me in the picture."

"What?"

"I hope the blood money you make from that damned, deadly drug keeps you warm in bed at night."

"I have no idea—"

"Don't lie to me!" His voice was thunderous, his features feral. "I know what you've done, Gray. And I know you did it for the money." He looked at her, his brow furrowed, and asked, "Why? You have everything. Why do this?"

For an instant she was tempted to tell him. But that would leave her too vulnerable. He was forsaking her. Making the split easier by doing it in anger and disgust and disillusionment. Unless she wanted to keep him forever, she was better off letting him go.

For a moment she was tempted to tell him everything. She felt a powerful surge of longing to be connected to him. To explain why the money was important. To reveal the secrets she'd kept for so very long. But the moment passed.

She looked him in the eye and said, "A woman can never be too thin or too rich."

He made a disgusted sound, and she was sure he realized the quip for what it was. A dismissal. A willingness to let go. A final rejection of his plea for honesty.

His hand circled her throat, and she felt one last flare of panic. She knew he could easily strangle her. The malice was there in his eyes. The strength was there in his hand.

But his fingers never tightened. His fingertips caressed her flesh as they circled to grip her nape and pull her toward him.

She came, because she wanted this last kiss. Even though she knew it would be bittersweet. Even though she knew it meant good-bye.

"I was angry enough to do murder when I came here tonight," he murmured against her lips. "There's a very thin line between love and hate. I'm not sure which I'm feeling now."

"Perhaps it's both," she whispered. She was suddenly afraid he wouldn't kiss her, that he'd go away without giving her this last offering of love. She thrust her hands into his hair and urged his head down to hers.

The kiss was fierce. She felt his anger and his need. His disappointment. And his love. She felt hunger rise inside her and forced it back.

She broke the kiss, because she knew that if she didn't, he would carry her upstairs and this would all start over again. It wouldn't last. His intellect would overcome his emotional attachment to her, and he would leave. And when he did, it would be ugly.

"Good-bye, Drew," she said. "I do love you."

"Do you?"

Could he doubt it? She saw in his eyes that he did. Perhaps that wasn't so surprising. She'd been very careful to hide what she felt. "It doesn't really matter now, does it?"

She saw the sadness in his eyes and lowered her own to avoid looking at him as he said, "I suppose not."

She didn't move as he crossed to the kitchen door, opened it and closed it quietly behind him.

The sob took Gray unawares. "This is ridiculous. Why am I crying? He was just a good fuck." She swallowed over the ache in her throat and whispered, "A great fuck."

A tear slipped onto her cheek. She reached up and swiped it away, as though to deny its existence. It was quickly replaced by another. She pressed a fist against the knot in her chest, but it didn't relieve the terrible ache she felt inside. Hard to believe a broken heart could cause such actual, physical pain.

"To hell with it," she muttered.

Gray slid down the side of the cabinets onto the kitchen floor, pulled her knees up to her aching chest and cried.

―∽―

"It's over, Justin," Nicki said. "Done. Finished. Ended."

"There was no need to have me drive all the way over here to tell me that, Nicki," Justin said.

He looked almost bored, Nicki thought. Certainly irritated. Inconvenienced. She'd called him on his cell phone when he was supposedly watching the Cowboys football game. She hadn't heard the TV in the background. She'd asked him to come over, even though it was Sunday, and he was home with his family.

"It's important," she'd said. "I need to talk to you."

"Can't it wait till tomorrow at work?" he'd said.

"This is personal. I'd prefer not to discuss it at the office."

The threat was there, that if he wasn't willing to discuss it with her at home, she would discuss it at the office.

"All right," he said at last. "Let me have dinner with my family. Then I'll tell my wife I have to go back to the office. I should be there sometime around eight."

He hadn't come until after nine. And he hadn't called to say why he was going to be more than an hour late.

It was appalling to think she'd wasted two years on such a deplorable specimen of manhood. She was glad to finally be getting out of a bad situation. She could have told him good-bye over the phone tonight. But Nicki had wanted the satisfaction of seeing his face when she dumped him.

She'd imagined his surprise. Heard his protestations against ending their affair. His pleas for her to continue seeing him. And the pleasure of denying him her company.

It hadn't turned out even a little bit like she'd imagined it.

Justin had been surprised. But so far he hadn't evidenced a shred of disappointment. It was as though she'd told him his golf partner was being changed. He wasn't going to grieve over it, let alone give up golf. He would simply find a new partner.

Which was when it struck her why he wasn't sorry to be losing her. *He's simply going to replace me.*

Nicki quivered as her body was overtaken by a firestorm of jealousy. She felt enraged. Outraged. Who was he planning to sleep with next? There were a number of new female associates in litigation. Which one would he choose?

Then she had another, even more devastating thought. Maybe Justin hadn't been home watching a Cowboys football game. Maybe the loathsome man had started spending his Sunday afternoons with a different woman, keeping Nicki in reserve until he was sure the other "other woman" would work out.

Nicki was having trouble catching her breath, having trouble seeing past the red spots in her eyes. Her body seemed to respond in slow motion as she turned to confront Justin.

"Who are you fucking? Who is she?"

To her horror, the despicable man didn't even bother denying her accusation. He looked her in the eye and said, "Penelope Herter."

Penelope Herter was a brand new associate who'd started with the firm in September. She was ten years younger than Nicki, and possessed enormous—certainly uncancerous—breasts.

"You—You—" Nicki was gasping, so furious she couldn't think of a word contemptuous enough to call Justin. "Yellow-bellied coward," she said. "You didn't even have the courage to confront me and tell me it's over. You just laid down with some other bitch!"

"*Bitch* being the operative word," Justin shot back. "You've been a pain in the butt to be around lately, in case you hadn't noticed."

"I've got *cancer*, you fool! I've had a hunk of my breast cut out. Not that you've noticed. You haven't been near me in almost a month."

Justin gaped. "What?"

Nicki wailed in distress. She'd ruined everything. Justin would inform the management committee— Justin was *on* the management committee—that she was sick. Her career at D&B was over.

"Why didn't you say something to me?" he said.

"It was none of your business. *Is* none of your business," she corrected.

"I have a responsibility to the firm—"

"Shut up!" she screamed. Not a word of comfort. No offer to hold her. Not a single gesture of sympathy. Nothing but talk about what he owed the firm. "The firm? You don't give a damn about the firm," she said. "Or its associates," she added. "Except to figure out ways to screw them." She knew she should keep her mouth shut, but she was too angry, too hurt. "And to kill them."

His eyes narrowed. "What the hell are you talking about, Nicki?"

"I've been in Neil Ford's computer files, Justin. The ones you tried to erase."

"I don't know what you're talking about."

"It was all there in black and white, Justin. Everything Neil found out about you. The threats you made. His fears about what you might do. He didn't die accidentally, did he? I'm going to make sure everyone knows what you did to Neil. And why."

"Neil Ford had a car accident."

"After you forced a bunch of pills and alcohol down his throat."

Justin's eyes narrowed. "I suppose you've already blurted all this to Luke Creed."

"You can kiss your ass good-bye, Justin, because it belongs to me. I'm going to do my best to see that it lands in jail. Better yet, six feet under. I'm sure there's a judge out there somewhere who'd get a kick out of sentencing a dirty lawyer to death by lethal injection."

"It was pretty stupid of you to admit all this."

Nicki eyed Justin with sudden alarm. The hot flush of humiliation and anger and jealousy was beginning to recede, replaced by icy fear. "You wouldn't dare—"

"I've got nothing to lose," he said. "I even have an explanation for what's about to happen. I'll admit to the affair, since I imagine my fingerprints are all over this place. I'll explain that I was feeling remorseful and wanted to return to my wife. You threatened to kill yourself if I left you, but I insisted our affair couldn't continue."

"That sounds like you, all right."

"I'll be so sad," he continued. "Tears will flow, and I'll express tremendous regret at your loss. Because you must have followed through on your threat after I left."

"No one will believe I would do such a thing."

"You've just told me you have breast cancer. Maybe the combination of the two—having cancer and losing your lover—put you over the edge. I'd believe it."

"It won't be so easy to make my death look like an accident," Nicki said, truly frightened now. "I'll fight you. Without a suicide note, it will look exactly like the murder it would be."

Justin crossed to the window, fiddled with the latch, then shoved it open as far as it would go. "Not if you jump out the window."

Nicki stared at her eighth story window and saw the opening was easily large enough for an adult to fall through. The former owner had been an artist, and part of what she'd loved about the loft was the feeling of light and space created by the enormous windows. She fought a rush of paralyzing fear.

She had to keep moving. She had to keep thinking. She ran for the door, but Justin was there ahead of her.

"I'll scream," she said.

"If you were going to scream, you already would have," he said calmly.

Nicki opened her mouth to scream but discovered she was too frightened to draw enough breath to make a sound. She knew there were scissors and a letter opener on her desk, either or both of which would make formidable weapons. She bolted in that direction.

Justin was there before her.

She'd always liked the fact that he was a big man, big in the way Texas men are—tall and sturdy as an oak and broad-shouldered enough to block out the sunlight. Justin had added a few pounds over the years, but they apparently hadn't slowed him down. He was blocking the desk long before she got there, grinning, enjoying the deadly game, daring her to try to get past him.

She was frozen in place, her breathing patchy, when he suddenly backed up, crossed his arms and smiled. Then he laughed. "I don't have to kill you."

"Why not?" she said warily, wondering if his insouciance was intended to put her off guard so he could launch a sneak attack.

"I have a better way to keep you quiet."

"I guarantee you nothing is going to keep me from revealing what I know," she said.

"I can discredit you."

She snorted in disgust. "How, exactly, are you going to do that?"

"I don't think I'll make the mistake that you have of putting all my cards on the table."

"The instant you walk out that door, I'm calling the police," Nicki said.

"And telling them what? A managing partner of one of the largest law firms in the nation tried to kill you? Who would believe it? What was my motive?"

"We were lovers. You—"

"My wife knows about my infidelity. She'd have to be a fool not to know. She chooses to look the other way. It would be distasteful to both of us if you confronted her, but it wouldn't end our marriage."

"I'd tell them how I'm not the first person you've threatened. I'll tell them how Neil intended to blow the whistle on D-Free. How he intended to get the drug taken off the market."

"Aside from the fact that Neil was acting outside the interests of one of our largest clients, why should that matter to me?"

"Because . . . " Nicki bit her lip, realizing it would be dangerous to tell him everything she knew.

"Just *because*?" Justin said. "I'm afraid that's not going to be enough, Nicki. You're going to need a better reason than *because*."

It was the snide expression, along with the obnoxious, supercilious grin on his face, that loosened her tongue. "Because you own twelve percent of the patent for D-Free, Justin. That's why you killed Neil. He found out what I found out. He discovered you were interfering with the investigation of D-Free because if the truth about the drug ever came out, you would lose millions of dollars in patent royalties. You killed him to protect your profit. Money is a great motive, Justin. The police will eat it up."

Justin's face turned a mottled red, and his mouth screwed into an ugly frown. "You're as stupid as Neil was. The crazy bastard wouldn't listen to reason."

"So you murdered him."

He charged without warning, and Nicki hesitated, unsure for an instant whether she should run for the door and try to get all the locks unlocked or race for the kitchen and a weapon.

Justin reached out a large hand and said, "Gotcha."

He had hold of her T-shirt and she lowered her head and backed right out of it, leaving her naked above the waist and wearing only a pair of fringed cutoffs.

Justin stood with the shirt in his hand, gawking at the stitches on her breast. "Christ. What did they do to you?"

While he was held in thrall, revolted by the damage left after her surgery, she tried to bolt past him into the kitchen. But his reflexes were too quick. He grabbed her around the waist and headed for the open window.

"They'll never believe I jumped out the window," she shrieked.

"We'll have to see, won't we?"

Not without a shirt on! she wanted to yell. But that might be the only clue she could leave that she hadn't done this voluntarily. She wondered if she could stop him by admitting she wasn't the only one who knew about his financial interest in D-Free. She'd e-mailed Luke everything she'd learned. But Justin might go after Luke right away, before Luke knew to be wary of his former boss. She knew that if he had the time, Luke would figure out the truth.

And avenge her death.

"You're making a mistake," she said as she writhed in Justin's inescapable grip. "Turn yourself in. A good lawyer could get you off. Look at O.J. He's a free man."

"Shut up," he said.

Nicki had always heard a person's life flashed before his eyes in the moments before death. She was staring death in the face, and all she could think was how pissed off she was that she'd wasted the last two years of her life with this man. If she had another chance, she would find someone who loved her and love him back. She would—

"Out you go!" Justin said.

Nicki grabbed hold of the window frame and refused to let go. She felt the blood streaming from her breast, where the strain of hanging on for dear life had torn open the wound. More evidence of a struggle—if there was enough of her left when she hit the ground for someone to notice.

When he tore one of her hands away, she put her bare feet up on the window frame, to keep Justin from shoving her out. She could feel herself losing the battle, feel the inevitability of what was coming.

"Luke knows!" she screamed in desperation. "He knows! I called and told him everything. This isn't going to solve anything!"

But Justin kept pushing.

"Help!" she screamed. "Somebody. Anybody. I don't want to die!"

Justin put his hand over her mouth to shut her up.

She grappled with his hand, scratching futilely at it. She wanted the wounds she left to give evidence of her struggle. She kept one hand braced against the window, and with the other she reached upward toward his face, her fingers curved into claws.

He caught her wrist before her hand ever reached his flesh. "Huh-uh," he grunted. "None of that."

Nicki kept waiting for someone to come to the rescue. This was where Luke should show up at the door and save the day. She listened hard for the sound of anyone at the door, strained her eyes in that direction, looking for someone, anyone, to save her life.

But no one came.

20

Luke awoke with a start. For a moment, he wasn't sure where he was. Then he heard Amy breathing evenly beside him on the couch. He angled his head and surveyed her shadowed features in the light that seeped through the curtains from the parking lot. He felt a swell of emotion, a surge of protectiveness. He wanted to lift her burdens and carry them. He wanted to hold her in his arms and keep her safe.

He watched her stir and stretch, and his gaze caught on the curve of her hip. He reached out a hand and followed the line of her body from waist to thigh.

"Feels good," she said in a sleepy, gravelly voice.

"Looks fantastic."

She smiled as she opened her eyes. "Hi."

"Hi, yourself."

"I fell asleep. What time is it?"

He checked the luminous dial of his watch. "A few minutes after ten."

"How about an early midnight snack?" she said, sitting sideways on the edge of the couch and stretching, her hands going up and wide and drawing her breasts up along with them.

He leaned over and took her nipple in his mouth and suckled gently.

Her hands twined in his hair, and she arched her body toward him and groaned. "Oh, God," she said. "You have to stop that . . . in about a million years."

He let go and leaned back to observe the ecstasy in her expression.

She gazed at him from lowered lids. "How do you do that?"

"Do what?"

"Turn me on so fast. Make me want you again. I . . . " She leaned forward and kissed his lips, her mouth moist, her lips pliant.

Luke was already breathing hard when the jarring sound of the phone made him jerk away. He stared at the portable phone lying on the coffee table, then glanced at Amy.

"One of the kids," he said, his heart pounding in sudden fear.

"Honor," she said.

He saw his own anxiety reflected in her eyes as she grabbed for the phone, gripping it hard and holding it against her ear as she asked, "Is she all right?" And then, "Oh. Yes. How did you . . . "

She handed the phone to Luke. "It's for you."

He felt a spurt of panic, terror that something dire had happened to Brynne. "Is Brynne all right?"

"I have no idea," a male voice replied. "Turn on your TV."

"Eddie?" Luke said, recognizing the voice at last. "How the hell did you know where to find me?"

"I called your house and got no answer. Then I called Drew DeWitt and got no answer. So I called your ex-wife. She suggested I might find you here. Turn on the TV, Luke."

Luke was distracted for a moment when Amy stood and then bent over to retrieve her clothes from the floor beside the couch. He watched as she stepped into a pair of bikini panties, then pulled on her khaki shorts.

He rose, his jeans open and hanging low on his hips, and limped the couple of feet to the TV on a stand near the couch and switched it on. "What channel?" he asked as he zipped and buttoned his jeans.

"I'm watching the local affiliate of NBC," Eddie said.

Luke listened to the news anchor explain that police were investigating an apparent suicide in downtown Houston, a jumper, who was causing traffic to snarl. Anyone heading into downtown was advised to avoid Texas Avenue between Travis and Main streets.

"I give up," Luke said. "What is it I'm supposed to be seeing?"

"It's Nicki, Luke," Eddie said.

Luke's heart skipped a beat. "Nick? How do you know that?"

"They've described everything about her except her name, including the fact that it's someone from the eighth floor of the Lofts. It's her, all right."

"It can't be Nick," Luke said. He felt Amy's comforting hand on his back and shook it off. "She wouldn't commit suicide."

"Have you checked your e-mail lately?"

"Cut to the chase, Eddie," Luke said. "What's going on?"

"Nicki sent you an e-mail earlier today, with a cc: to me. She found out Justin Sterling owns twelve percent of D-Free. She reconfigured Neil Ford's computer files from the office—the ones that somehow got erased after his death."

"How did she do that?"

"A recovery program, I suppose. Anyway, it turns out Justin offered Neil money to keep what he found out about D-Free to himself."

"Did Neil take the bribe?"

"What do you think? And Luke, Justin is there. At the scene. I saw him on TV."

Luke felt a chill run down his spine. What he thought was that all this time, he might have been barking up the wrong tree. He'd been right that Neil's "accident" had most likely been no accident. But the villain wasn't the Dragon Lady or anyone from Hyland. It was someone who hadn't even been on Luke's radar screen.

Luke could see it now. Justin asking Neil to keep quiet. And Neil refusing. And then Nicki confronting him with what she knew. He could understand Justin's desperation. He owned an enormous share of the patent—and why was that?—and he'd lose the goose that laid the golden egg if the FDA yanked the drug off the market.

But had Justin been desperate enough to commit murder—twice?

Maybe Justin was on the scene at Nicki's because he

and Nicki had been lovers, and he cared about her. Maybe Neil's accident had been an accident after all, and he was barking up another wrong tree.

And how could he be so sure Nicki wouldn't commit suicide? She had breast cancer. Maybe she'd lied to him about the extent of her cancer. Maybe they'd discovered during her operation that she was too sick to recover from the disease. Maybe . . .

Luke needed to see the circumstances of her death for himself.

"I'm going over there," he said to Eddie.

"I'll meet you," Eddie replied.

"You stay the hell away. This is getting too damned dangerous."

"But—"

"That's an order." Luke disconnected the call as he stuck his feet back in his docksiders.

"What's going on?" Amy said.

"That jumper in downtown Houston was Nicki Maldonado. I need to go."

"I just realized I don't have wheels," he said. "I need to call a limo to pick me up."

"I'll give you a ride," Amy said, sliding into her open-backed tennis shoes.

"My former boss Justin Sterling is at the scene. Eddie thinks he might be responsible for Nick's death. I'd rather not let him know you and I have any sort of personal relationship. I don't want to give him an excuse to come after you, too."

"He's not going to bother me."

Luke lifted a brow. "Why is that?"

"Because if he attacks one of us, he's going to have to get both of us. Double murders are way too complicated to pull off without a hitch."

"That's a comfort," Luke said sarcastically.

She grabbed her keys and headed out the door without replying, and Luke limped out behind her.

When they got downtown, they found the street around Nicki's building roped off by yellow police tape. Amy dropped Luke off as close as she could get.

"You can valet park at my condo," Luke said, as he handed her the keys to his apartment. "Wait for me there. I promise I'll fill you in on whatever I find out."

"Be careful."

"I will." Luke was trying to figure out how to talk his way past the police barrier when he spied Justin talking to a plainclothes cop. Luke called out to Justin, who said something to the detective, who waved Luke inside the yellow plastic that cordoned off the area.

"What are you doing here?" Luke said to Justin.

"I was with Nicki when she . . . She just . . . went out the window."

Luke felt the hairs stand up on his neck. "How did it happen?" He was surprised to see what looked like tear tracks on Justin's face.

He held up a briefcase and said, "I stopped by to drop off some work—and to break up with her. She threatened to do something desperate unless I stayed with her but . . . I couldn't do that," Justin said in a choked voice.

"That doesn't sound like Nick," Luke said to the detective. "She wasn't suicidal."

"I think it was the cancer," Justin said.

Luke let his shock show. Of course he'd known Nicki had breast cancer. But he'd been pretty sure she wouldn't have told Justin, since he was one of the managing partners. And yet, Justin knew.

"Cancer?" Luke said.

"She had breast cancer. She was despondent about that. And when I told her things would have to end between us . . . I just wish there was something I could have done. I grabbed her. I tried to stop her. She backed right out of her shirt and right out the window."

"Are you saying it was an accident?" Luke could see Nicki's bare, bloodied arm hanging out beyond a sheet that had been used to cover her.

"She threatened to kill herself," Justin said, "but I'm not sure she meant to go out the window."

"What was the window doing open?" Luke asked.

"Hey, who's asking the questions here?" the detective interjected.

"Well?" Luke said, his hands on his hips.

"That's a good question," the detective said. "Why was the window open?"

"I have no idea," Justin said. "It was open when I got there."

"Nick always kept the windows closed and the air-conditioning on," Luke said. "She hated the heat and the humidity."

"Do you know the deceased?" the cop said.

The deceased. Hearing Nicki described that way made her death real. Had it been a simple accident? Had Nicki been depressed about her cancer? He knew she'd been in love with Justin, so maybe she'd been upset when he'd broken up with her. But suicidal?

It seemed too coincidental that Nicki should send that e-mail this afternoon and end up dead tonight.

Luke stared at the man who'd been his boss and his friend for the past six years. It was impossible to imagine Justin as a murderer. A multiple murderer. Why would he do it? Sure, he'd lose some money if D-Free was taken off the market. But as a managing partner, Justin's share of the profits of D&B must be enormous. How much money could one man spend?

"I'd like to go home," Justin said.

"I'm done with you for now," the cop said. "I'll be in touch tomorrow. Don't leave town."

"My home and my work are here, detective," Justin said.

"Yeah. That's what they all say."

Luke took one last look at Nicki's covered body. He would find out the truth. And if Justin was responsible, he would pay.

"I'll see you tomorrow," he said to Justin, and limped off in the direction of his condo.

"I'm not sure I'll be at work tomorrow," Justin said.

Luke stopped and turned to him. "There's a management committee meeting tomorrow morning at nine. I don't think you'll want to miss it."

Justin's eyes narrowed. "I'd forgotten about that. Can I give you a lift home?"

"No thanks," Luke said. "I don't think it's safe to get into a car with you right now."

When Justin frowned, Luke said, "You look pretty

shaken up. Nick dying like that right in front of your eyes, and all."

Luke knew he was a fool for baiting the man, taunting him. But he felt angry—and guilty—over what had happened to Nicki.

"I could use a drink," Justin said. "Your place is just a couple of blocks from here, isn't it?"

The last thing Luke wanted was Justin coming up to his condo when Amy was there. "There's an Irish pub on Main that's even closer."

"Fine." Justin gestured to Luke's gimpy knee and said, "Can you make it?"

Luke's knee was killing him, but he wasn't about to get into a car with Justin. "I'm fine."

Justin shrugged "Let's go."

"You won't be able to keep your involvement in Nick's death out of the papers," Luke said as they headed down the street.

"Probably not," Justin said.

Luke had spent many a Sunday night at the Irish pub, when he returned from a visit to Three Oaks and wanted to forget he was Jackson Blackthorne's stepson. The pub was dark and had wooden booths perfect for the sort of private conversation he wanted to have with Justin.

Luke ordered Guinness. Justin set his briefcase on the table and ordered Chivas straight up.

"This is going to be devastating for my wife," he said, as he fiddled with the combination lock.

"You should have thought of that before you started shacking up with Nick."

Justin's eyes widened. "You knew?"

"I saw you together at River Oaks."

"I see." The Chivas arrived and Justin swallowed it in one gulp.

Luke played with his beer. He wasn't the least bit thirsty. He worried what Amy would think when he didn't show up immediately. He wondered if she'd come hunting for him. He hoped she'd stay where she was safe. He stared at the briefcase on the table, wondering why Justin would bring work with him on a visit to his lover.

"I'm listening," he said to Justin.

"Nicki told me she called and told you about . . ." Justin looked around, saw the booths on either side of them were filled with people and lowered his voice. "About my ownership of D-Free."

Called? Nicki had e-mailed, she hadn't phoned. So why had she lied to Justin? Unless she hadn't wanted him to know just how much information she'd passed on to Luke.

Luke was glad he'd gotten the heads-up from Eddie. "Yeah," he said. "What's going on with that?"

Justin shrugged one shoulder. "I bought into it so long ago, sometimes I'd forget I had it. Then, last year, D-Free went on the market and pow, I'm making money hand over fist."

"Must have been nice."

"It was. Is," Justin corrected.

"Except, there's something wrong with D-Free."

"Yeah. Maybe."

"You know better," Luke said. "Neil Ford told you so."

"Ah," Justin said. "I wondered if Nicki had passed that bit of information along as well."

"She did."

"Who all knows about this?"

"So far? Just you and me." Luke wasn't about to put Eddie's head on the chopping block, so Justin could cut it off.

Justin gripped his briefcase with one hand and lifted his glass with the other. The waitress nodded and headed back to the bar to get him another drink. "What happened to Neil was an accident," he said.

"And I suppose Nick just fell out of her window," Luke said, unable to keep the sarcasm from his voice.

Justin met his gaze and said, "You can't prove otherwise. In either case."

Justin had as much as admitted that he was responsible for both deaths. Luke wished he'd thought to bring a tape recorder. But only people in the movies thought of things like that.

"Between the press and the police, I could make your life damned uncomfortable," Luke said.

"But you won't do that."

"Why not?"

"Because you want to become a partner at D&B. Even if I were guilty as sin, the partners wouldn't appreciate you attacking one of their own."

"We'll see about that tomorrow," Luke said.

"Yes, tomorrow. The meeting of the management committee Choate asked for. That's for you?"

"That's for me," Luke confirmed.

"What is it you hope to accomplish?" Justin asked.

"We can discuss that tomorrow morning," Luke said as he rose. "Right now I'm going home."

"You might want to do some thinking tonight."

"About what?"

"For one thing, Franklin DeWitt won't be there tomorrow. He's out of town. As the senior partner remaining on the committee, I'll be chairing the meeting."

Luke wondered if Choate had arranged it that way, and if she had, whether she knew of Justin's guilt and was protecting him.

"I'm not the only one with something to lose," Justin said. "Remember that."

Luke wondered if Justin was referring to Choate's three percent interest in the D-Free patent. Or maybe there were more partners who owned a piece of D-Free. Maybe all of them?

The thought was alarming. There weren't a lot of hours between now and the meeting at nine o'clock tomorrow morning in which to find out how deep into the D&B partnership the D-Free conspiracy ran.

"I'm going to bring you down, Justin," Luke said. "I owe that to Nick." Then he turned and limped away.

21

—m—

Luke debated with himself long and hard after he arrived back at his condo, then picked up the phone and called Jackson Blackthorne. His heart was thudding in his chest as he listened to it ring. He heard a clatter as the phone was apparently dropped and then Blackjack's voice saying, "Who the hell is calling at this ungodly hour?"

"It's me," Luke said.

"Luke? Are you all right? What time is it?"

"It's past midnight, sir." Luke gripped the phone harder and said, "I need your help."

He heard the astonished silence on the other end of the line, then his mother's anxious voice in the distance saying, "Is he all right? What's wrong?"

Followed by his stepfather's muffled reply, "He called for me, Ren."

And then a silence, during which he knew his mother was absorbing the significance of that statement.

"What can I do to help?" Blackjack said.

"I need to find Franklin DeWitt. I thought you might have some idea where I could start looking."

"You'll know exactly where he is in the next couple

of hours or I'll know the reason why," Blackjack replied.

He sounded exactly like the powerful adversary Luke remembered from his childhood. He had to remind himself that this time Jackson Blackthorne's not inconsiderable resources were being martialed to help him, not to hurt him.

"Thank you, sir," Luke said.

"Luke," Blackjack said softly. "My name is Jackson."

Luke had to appreciate the wily bastard's timing. He'd have to be a sorry sonofabitch to deny his stepfather the courtesy of calling him by his name after what Blackjack had just agreed to do for him. "Thanks, Jackson."

"You're welcome," the old man said. And then hung up.

"I take it he's going to help us find Franklin," Amy said as he returned the phone handset to its cradle.

"He's going to do his best," Luke said. "Which means we'll be hearing back from him in the next couple of hours."

Luke believed it was imperative for Franklin to helm the management committee. That way, Justin couldn't take advantage of the situation to have Luke dismissed from the firm for some imaginary malfeasance and escorted off the premises by uniformed D&B security personnel.

Luke heard a knock on the door and opened it to find not only Eddie but Mary Margaret. "This is a surprise."

"Justin knows I've been working with you," Eddie said. "I feel safer having her here with me."

"Welcome, Mary Margaret," Luke said.

"I brought some herbal tea," she said, heading for the kitchen.

"I'll make some strong coffee," Amy offered.

Luke turned to Eddie, pointed to the computer on a desk in the corner of his living room and said, "It's all yours."

"What am I looking for, exactly?" Eddie asked.

Luke explained what he wanted, and where he thought Eddie might find it, then spent the next two hours alternately hovering over Eddie's shoulder and limping back and forth across the living room, as he argued his strategy with Amy for the coming confrontation.

He frowned when there was another knock at the door. He opened it to find Drew.

"I couldn't sleep and was watching a rerun of the news and heard what happened to Nick. I didn't call because I figured you'd hang up on me. I want to help," Drew said. "What can I do?"

Luke handed Drew half of the stack of papers Eddie had printed off the Internet and said, "Start reading." He explained to Drew what they were looking for as he shut the door behind him.

It was a long night.

Mary Margaret had long since gone to bed in Luke's room. Eddie was slumped down in a chair in front of the computer, his eyeballs jumping as he scrolled through materials on the screen. Drew was in the kitchen making another batch of coffee. Amy was sitting on the couch, hunkered over some medical reports. Luke's knee had finally given out, and he'd taken a seat in his chair near the phone, his leg up on the ottoman, a stack of printouts in his lap.

Blackjack's call came as the sun was rising.

Luke grabbed for the phone, and Amy and Eddie converged at his shoulder. Drew came on the run from the kitchen, and Mary Margaret appeared in his bedroom doorway as he put the phone to his ear and listened.

"Yes, sir," Luke said, grinning in relief and exultation and giving the gathered crowd an emphatic thumbs-up. "That's great. So he'll be there. That's good news."

He looked around at the expert team of lawyers—Amy, Drew and Eddie—who'd helped him marshal his plan to defeat the forces of the Evil Empire, and said, "I'm as ready as I'll ever be."

He felt Amy caress his shoulder as she settled beside him on the arm of his chair, watched Eddie hug his wife, saw Drew drop onto the couch and stretch out with his hands laced behind his head.

"Thank you . . . Jackson." Luke had managed not to say the reflexive *sir* this time, but *Jackson* hadn't tripped easily off his tongue either. He knew it would, over time.

"I'll be there on Friday with Amy to pick up the girls," he said. "We'll be glad to wait and have dinner with you." He glanced at Amy for her agreement, and she nodded. He lowered his gaze, eased open his balled fist and said, "The feeling is mutual."

He hung up the phone feeling both triumphant and sad. Thanks to Blackjack, Luke would get the chance to have his say at the management committee meeting. But by going to Blackjack for help, Luke had conceded defeat in the war he'd waged virtually alone since his mother's remarriage.

If his father were alive, Luke would have kept on brawling with Blackthornes, as his father and grandfather and great-grandfather had before him.

But his father was dead. And his mother loved a Blackthorne, who'd welcomed her children with open arms. Luke had only needed to ask, and Blackjack had willingly used his power and political influence to help a stepson who'd done nothing but torment him for the past twelve years.

It was past time for the feud to end. Luke had been the last holdout, the last survivor standing, more willing to die than to surrender his hate. It had been terrifying to finally let go of his animosity. He knew, suddenly, why his father had never been able to do it.

It took a lot more courage to forgive a lifetime of transgressions than to continue fighting.

He felt Amy's kiss at his temple and heard her whisper, "I love you, Luke."

He felt joy surge through him and couldn't stop the smile that flashed onto his face. He tugged her into his lap and held her close, letting the knowledge that he was loved flow over him and through him, a soothing balm and an energizing force.

She lifted her face and he kissed her, hoping that she would know without the words that he felt the same. But when he met her gaze again, he made a gift of them. "I love you, too, Amy."

She smiled and said, "I figured you might. But it's nice to hear that you do."

"Hey, you two lovebirds," Drew said. "We've got a lot more work to do before the management committee meeting this morning."

Luke kissed Amy one more time, said to her, "Hold that thought," then pushed her out of his lap.

Luke took a quick shower and dressed while his crack team of lawyers assembled the materials he needed to take with him. He carefully slid his arms into a starched white Oxford cloth shirt, then put the white duck medical sling back around his neck, arranging his right arm in it so his injured shoulder wouldn't be jostled. He donned a pair of sharply creased dark gray wool-blend trousers and black wingtip shoes. He tucked his shirt in and zipped his trousers and added a black leather belt with a plain silver buckle.

He couldn't tie his tie, so he didn't bother wearing one. Shaving was too much effort, so he didn't do that either, leaving his face with two-days' growth of dark beard. He didn't have another bandage for his cheek, so he left it bare, brandishing the bruises and scrapes like a medal of valor.

He tried draping his suit coat over his shoulders but couldn't manage it, and finally decided it would just get in his way. So he left it on the bed.

When Luke entered the living room, everyone turned to stare at him.

"I'll be damned," Drew said.

"Sharp," Eddie said.

"I'm impressed," Mary Margaret said.

"You look . . . " Amy never did fill in the adjective.

He knew it wasn't the shirt and trousers that had elicited their admiration and approbation. It was his bearing and posture, the steely look in his eyes and the stubborn lift of his chin, which announced just how determined he was to win the battle he was about to fight.

"Why aren't the rest of you ready for work?" Luke asked.

"We're not moving until we hear what happens," Drew said, crossing his arms.

"None of you?" Luke said.

Amy and Eddie and Mary Margaret shook their heads.

"We're staying put until we hear you've succeeded," Eddie said.

He noticed that none of them expected him to fail. He felt lucky they couldn't see how his knees were quaking beneath his trousers.

Amy handed him his briefcase as though she were a medieval lady fastening the buckle of his sword before sending him into battle. She gave him a soft, sweet kiss for luck, then stood back and said, "We're all counting on you."

Luke knew there was a great deal more at stake than losing face with his friends. He truly was engaged in a battle—a fight for justice and right—and if he failed, innocent lives would be lost.

He squared his shoulders, then shot them a cocky smile and said, "Bring on the Dragon Lady."

Everyone laughed, and that eased the tension. Which

enabled Luke to get out the door without any of them noting his clammy hands or the terrified battering of his heart.

Luke was armed with all the evidence the five of them had been able to gather. And he had one more trick up his sleeve. A jack-in-the-box Drew had planted that morning, ready to spring open and wreak havoc. But he wasn't at all sure he would prevail against the powerful forces that he knew would be arrayed against him.

Flo was apparently watching for him, because the instant he came within view of her cubicle outside his office she said, "Ms. Choate called. You're late. The committee has been waiting for you since eight this morning."

Luke glanced at his watch. It was 8:23. He wondered if Choate had moved up the meeting from nine o'clock as some sort of mind game to rattle him. Or maybe he hadn't remembered the time correctly. All that mattered now was getting to the meeting as quickly as possible.

"Where are they?" he asked Flo.

"Conference Room A." She surprised him when she said, "Good luck, Luke."

He wondered how much she knew about what was going to happen in Conference Room A. A great deal, he decided. The secretaries always knew everything, because the lawyers depended on them to type it up on the computer. He wondered if a secretary somewhere in the firm was right this moment producing his termination papers.

"Thanks, Flo," he said. "I'm going to need all the luck I can get."

He took a better grip on his briefcase and headed down the hall.

Luke stopped in the doorway to Conference Room A and observed the five managing partners. Franklin DeWitt headed the management committee, and he knew Grayson Choate and Justin Sterling. He wasn't as familiar with Riley Burgess, a pipe-smoking Yale man who supervised the tax section, or Waverly Morris, a rabid vegetarian who ran the firm's environmental law practice.

"Glad you could finally make it, Creed," Franklin said, spying him in the doorway.

Luke didn't apologize or explain. He didn't wait to hear their accusations. He stepped into the room with sword slashing.

"I've come here to tell you why Grayson Choate should be fired and Justin Sterling arrested for murder."

He saw Choate's head snap up. Watched Justin's eyes narrow. And felt a rush of satisfaction at the utter astonishment on the faces of the other three men.

He set his briefcase at the opposite end of the table from where the five partners had arranged themselves as an intimidating force to be reckoned with. He knew they'd planned his isolated placement at the other end of the long mahogany table to point out that he was only one against many.

But Luke never sat down. He stood, taking the role of the wise and learned elder dictating to the uniniti- ated and the uninformed.

He saw that Choate, at least, realized what he was doing. He held his breath to see whether she would

stand and take the floor from him. He watched her
gaze flick from partner to partner, but it must have
been plain to her, as it was to Luke, that the rest of
them were waiting with bated breath to see what he
would do next.

Her gaze returned to him, and he noted her mocking
smile and the nod of concession to his superior tactics.

"This should be interesting," she said.

Luke opened his briefcase, pulled out the documentation Eddie had managed to retrieve from the
Internet—thanks to information Drew had provided—
and slid it down the full length of the table, so it came
to rest in front of Franklin DeWitt.

"You have in front of you confirmation of Grayson
Choate's and Justin Sterling's collective ownership of
51 percent of the patent of the drug D-Free, currently
being marketed by DeWitt and Blackthorne's major
client Hyland Pharmaceuticals for treatment of Type I
diabetes."

Waverly Morris muttered, "Good God."

"Ms. Choate received a 51 percent interest in the
patent of D-Free from Hyland in the days when it was
doubtful D-Free would ever receive FDA approval, in
lieu of moneys that would have been due to the firm
for legal services rendered. She took the interest in the
patent as her portion of her partnership profits.

"She then traded 12 percent of her interest to Justin
Sterling in return for his assistance in helping her to
intercept complaints about D-Free Hyland referred to
the firm for action. He then arranged discreet financial
settlements with distraught parents of children who'd

died using the drug, so they didn't bring lawsuits against Hyland for the wrongful death of their children."

All of the men began talking at once.

"How can you possibly know—" Riley Burgess said.

"I've never seen any—" Waverly Morris said.

"You can't prove—" Justin Sterling said.

"All of you shut up," Franklin said in a firm, quiet voice. When the room was silent he said, "Are you saying, Luke, that there have been more deaths of children taking D-Free than the five whose parents have filed lawsuits?"

"That's exactly what I'm saying." Luke sent another batch of papers sliding down the shiny conference room table. "Forty-three, that I could confirm."

"There's no way you could know something like that," Choate said. "There would be no public records if no lawsuits were filed."

He looked her in the eye and said, "We—my associates and I—did it by correlating the dates of large withdrawals from bank accounts held by you and Justin Sterling with computerized hospital records confirming deaths of children from diabetic coma."

The three partners whom he hadn't accused stared at Choate and Sterling, and then at him.

"Go on, Mr. Creed," Franklin said, removing his wire-framed bifocals from behind his ears with both hands and laying them on the polished surface in front of him. "We're listening."

"I'm not interested in bringing down the firm or ruining lives—except for yours, Justin," he said.

"Why you—"

"Sit down, Justin," Franklin said without taking his eyes off Luke.

"What is it you want from us?" Waverly asked.

Luke looked from one partner to the next as he stated his demands. "First," he said, "Choate and Sterling will divest themselves of their interests in the D-Free patent."

"You mean, just sell it?" Justin asked.

Luke shook his head. "It goes into a trust fund."

"With your name on it?" Justin said with a sneer.

"To be used for research to find a cure for diabetes," Luke said.

"That's ridiculous!" Choate said. "My ownership of the patent for D-Free was the result of money legitimately owed to me."

"But paid in an illegal manner," Luke retorted. "You can put it in trust, or I can expose it to public scrutiny."

"I could understand how you might report us to the bar for an ethics violation," Justin said.

"Where you'd likely get away with a slap on the hand," Luke interjected in a harsh voice.

"But why should the public care whether a couple of lawyers own an interest in D-Free?" Justin finished.

"Justin is right," Choate said. "My interest and Hyland's interests aren't even in conflict. We both stand to profit from the sale of D-Free."

"But you and Justin together own a controlling interest in the patent, and you knew D-Free wasn't safe. You could have made sure the drug was taken off the market. Instead, you not only concealed the fact that D-Free was dangerous from the public, you manipulated files referred to you by Hyland and concealed a serious problem from the very people—Hyland Pharmaceuticals—who depended upon you to give them wise counsel.

"You've singlehandedly jeopardized Hyland's hard-won reputation as a company that deals honestly with its customers in favor of a rapacious grab for profits."

"That's a goddamned lie!" Justin said.

Luke turned to Choate and said, "Is it, Ms. Choate?"

There was no give in her. No remorse. No defeat. "You'll have to do better than make unsubstantiated accusations," she said.

"Very well." Luke stepped to the phone on the credenza along the wall, dialed an interoffice number and said, "You can send him in, Flo."

"Send who in?" Choate said with the first sign of concern. "No one outside the firm is allowed in management committee meetings."

"I'll decide who's welcome here," Franklin said, staring down Choate. He turned to Luke and said, "The floor is yours, Mr. Creed."

Luke opened the conference room door and Harold McCorkle walked in. Luke noticed McCorkle was careful not to look at Choate. Jurors usually turned away from a defendant they'd found guilty of wrongdoing.

"Be seated, Dr. McCorkle," Franklin said. "For those of you who may not know, this gentleman is Harold McCorkle, Executive Vice President of Research and New Product Development at Hyland and the man who invented D-Free."

McCorkle addressed his comments to Franklin

DeWitt. "I came here to tell you I was deceived by this woman."

Since Choate was the only female in the room, there was no need to gesture to her and McCorkle didn't. Luke watched Choate's face pale, but she never lost her composure.

"And I believe she deceived the board of directors of Hyland as well," McCorkle continued. "I told the board precisely that at a meeting earlier this morning. Later today, Hyland will announce to the public the withdrawal of D-Free from the marketplace, pending further FDA tests and approval."

"What the hell's going on, Grayson?" Justin said angrily. "Hyland can't do that, can they? We own 51 percent of the patent. We're the ones—"

"This young man," McCorkle said, interrupting Justin's tirade and gesturing toward Luke, "has saved Hyland from a devastating, I might even say catastrophic, public relations nightmare by showing me why Ms. Choate advised Hyland to pay off wrongful death claims rather than to do the right thing, which is to take the drug off the market."

"Your time has certainly changed, Harold," Choate said.

For the first time, he looked at her. Luke saw his fists were knotted so tightly his knuckles were white.

"I thought it was only five deaths. *Five.* Because that's how many lawsuits were filed. I thought they might not be a result of the drug, there were so few and they've been spread out over a year, and the clinical tests had proved the drug was safe."

McCorkle took a shuddering breath and continued, "Then I discovered, when my executive assistant was forced to confess, that she'd lied and doctored the results, that there were *twenty* deaths during clinical testing. And now I find out there were *forty-three*—" McCorkle was so furious there was spittle spewing onto the conference table. "*Forty-three* more that you purposefully concealed from me. That's *sixty-eight* deaths from a drug I invented to save lives!"

"I can add, Harold," Choate said.

"Can you subtract?" he said. "Because I've conferred with the board of directors, and as of today, DeWitt and Blackthorne no longer represents Hyland Pharmaceuticals. For any purpose. Anywhere. Anytime. Ever again."

A collective gasp of disbelief, of dismay, of utter horror rose from the other end of the table.

Luke saw Choate's folded hands tremble before she slid them under the table. He watched her chin slide up a notch, watched her shoulders straighten. He decided she was one of those people who would choose to face a firing squad without a blindfold.

"Well, Ms. Choate," Franklin said. "What do you have to say for yourself?"

"I will, of course resign from—"

"No," Franklin said. "You will not."

Choate looked confused.

"You're fired, Grayson," Franklin said. "We will announce your departure from the firm for unethical—and perhaps even illegal—behavior as publicly as we possibly can, and offer our services to help anyone who believes they've suffered harm at your hands to recover as much money as they can in damages from you."

Choate's face was so pale, Luke thought she might faint.

She rose with an amazing amount of dignity. But she didn't respond to Franklin's threats. She turned on Luke.

"This is all your fault!"

"Oh, God, I hope so," Luke said fervently.

She looked around the room and this time her eyes came to rest on Franklin DeWitt. "You've wanted to get rid of me since the day I got here. If I can ever do you harm, know that I will."

"You're not going to be hurting anyone," Franklin said. "Get out, Grayson. You're through. You've lost the bludgeon you've held over our heads for years. Hyland is no longer your client. And without Hyland, you're nothing."

Luke saw the two D&B security men appear in the doorway the same time Choate did.

She had brought nothing with her into the conference room. And she was leaving with less than that.

McCorkle rose and said, "If you gentlemen will excuse me, I have work to do."

All of the lawyers rose when McCorkle did, and Franklin walked him to the door.

"I know you're angry right now, Harold," Franklin said. "But I don't think you should throw out the baby with the bathwater. Think of how much it would cost Hyland to bring another firm up to speed on all your legal matters. I'm sure we can come to some accommodation, now that the one bad apple is gone from the barrel."

Luke had to admire DeWitt. It was what lawyers did. Negotiated and compromised and looked for solutions.

Luke realized Justin was edging his way toward the conference room door. He stepped into his path, making it clear if Justin hoped to leave, he was going to have a fight on his hands.

As the door closed behind McCorkle, Franklin turned back to Luke, then eyed Justin and said, "I believe you had one more matter you wanted to address, Mr. Creed. Sit down, Justin," Franklin said. "The meeting's not done."

"I'm through with all of you," Justin said, trying to bluff his way out of the room.

"Sit down," Luke said in a hard voice. "Or I'll sit you down."

"With one arm?"

"Tied behind my back," Luke confirmed.

Luke could see Justin sizing him up, trying to decide whether Luke could really take him with the use of only one arm. Luke widened his stance, balled his left fist and focused his gaze on Justin, daring him to try.

Justin proved he was a coward and a bully by sitting down.

Luke returned to the head of the table and said, "Would you like to tell them how you murdered Neil Ford and Nicole Maldonado, Justin? Or shall I?"

Riley turned to Justin, eyes widened in horror and said, "What have you done, Justin?"

Justin said, "Fuck you, Riley. I didn't do anything any of you wouldn't have done."

"I doubt whether they'd resort to murder," Luke said.

"Those were both accidents," Justin said with a defiant smirk. "You can't prove otherwise."

"Unfortunately for you, Justin, I can."

"You're lying!" Justin said, bolting out of his seat.

"Sit down, Justin," Franklin admonished. "Mr. Creed has the floor."

As Justin sank back into his seat with a sullen look, Luke focused his gaze on him and said, "Neil discovered that you and Ms. Choate owned 51 percent of the patent for D-Free. You tried to bribe him, but he wasn't interested in the blood money you offered him. So you arranged for him to have an accident."

"Just exactly how did I do that?" Justin said.

"You took him to a bar near your home and made sure he got drunk," Luke said implacably. "Then you put his own prescription drugs in his drink and once they'd taken effect, you sent him out the door to drive home by himself."

"Prove it!" Justin challenged.

"You tried to erase Neil's computer files, where he'd kept a diary about everything—including your attempt to bribe him, and his fear that his life might be in danger. But you didn't do a very good job of it," Luke said.

"Ms. Maldonado recovered those files. She confronted you with what she'd found. And you threw her out an eighth-floor window to her death!"

Luke had expected another uproar at his accusation, but he saw only shocked, pale and shaken faces.

Luke watched Justin's features change from defiant to defensive as he realized the other partners had begun to believe Luke.

"He can make accusations all day," Justin said righteously. "But there isn't a shred of proof."

"Oh, but there is," Franklin said.

Luke watched Justin's face and saw the flash of fear when Franklin spoke. "What proof?"

This time Franklin picked up the phone on the credenza and dialed an interoffice number. "Nell, please send those gentlemen waiting in my office to Conference Room A."

"I'm leaving," Justin said.

"Sit down," Riley said, grabbing his sleeve to keep him from rising.

"You're not going anywhere," Waverly said, gripping Justin's other arm.

"We really don't condone murder, Justin," Franklin said in a ruthless voice. "It isn't good for business."

"I never—I didn't—"

"Ah, there you are, gentlemen," Franklin said, rising to greet the two men in suits. "Detective Washington. Detective Morales. Did you find what you were looking for?"

The black detective, Washington, said, "We did."

"Then he's all yours," Franklin said, gesturing toward Justin.

"What is this?" Justin said. "What's going on?"

"Are you Justin Sterling?" Detective Morales asked.

"Yes," Justin said reluctantly.

"You're under arrest for the murders of Neil Ford and Nicole Maldonado."

Justin was dumbfounded. "I have the right—"

"You have the right to remain silent. You have the right to an attorney. If you cannot—"

Justin interrupted several times, but Morales finally finished the Miranda warning and said, "Do you understand these rights as I have stated them to you?"

"I'm a lawyer. Of course I understand them."

"Put your hands behind your back, please."

Justin resisted, and the two men, both burly, both experienced at their jobs, caught him from either side and cuffed his hands tightly behind his back.

Justin looked helplessly at Luke. "Luke, help me."

Luke thought of Nicki falling to her death. And Neil Ford dying in a fiery car crash. And said nothing.

"You can't—I have—I'm not—" Justin was hyperventilating.

"Take it easy," Morales said. "Anybody got a paper bag?" the detective asked.

Riley saw a paper takeout bag one of the secretaries must have discarded. "Here," he said.

Detective Morales held the empty paper bag over Justin's mouth and said, "Here. You just need to breathe a little carbon dioxide. That's it. Nice slow breaths."

Justin's eyes were panicky over the top of the brown paper bag, and Luke could see him jerking against the plastic cuffs on his wrists.

"I'm okay now," he said a minute later. "You can take the bag away."

The detectives tugged on his arms to lead him away,

but he stood his ground and stared at Luke and said, "How?"

It was Franklin who said, "I got an anonymous call very early this morning suggesting that Nicole Maldonado and Neil Ford were murdered, and that proof could be found on a laptop computer hidden within the stacks of files in Justin Sterling's office."

Sterling shook his head in shocked disbelief. "But her computer was—" He bit his tongue and looked guiltily around the room.

"Missing after her death," Luke said.

"Of course," Franklin said, "as a law-abiding citizen, I immediately called the police and told them what the caller had said. And the fact that you'd actually been at Ms. Maldonado's apartment at the time of her death and might have removed her computer before the police arrived, and the fact you worked with Neil, and the fact I'd received that call, combined to give the police probable cause to get a warrant to search your office."

"Which we did this morning," Detective Washington said.

"And found Ms. Maldonado's laptop—with some very incriminating evidence—exactly where the caller said it would be," Detective Morales said.

"But don't you see?" Justin said. "Whoever called must be the murderer. Whoever called would have had to put it there to know exactly where it was."

"Or saw you hide it there," the detective said.

"I didn't hide it *there*, I—" Justin caught himself again and looked with wild, panicky eyes around the room.

But there was no mercy for him in anyone's eyes. Least of all Luke's.

He was still protesting his innocence as the detectives led him from the room.

When Justin was gone, Franklin walked over to Luke and said, "However did you find the damned thing wherever it was he hid it?"

Luke looked him in the eye and said, "I have no idea what you're talking about."

He'd just followed a hunch, responding to the way Justin had been gripping his briefcase last night. He'd waited out of sight and followed Justin and watched him drop something into a dumpster behind the bar. He'd retrieved Nicki's laptop, and Drew had planted it in Justin's office before dawn this morning and made the call.

He'd expected Amy to dissent, because when it came to black and white, planting evidence was definitely in the gray area.

But she'd looked him in the eye and said, "Do it. Sometimes you have to break the rules."

Franklin pursed his lips thoughtfully. "Very well, young man. Keep your secrets."

Luke realized he was trembling with the aftershocks of everything that had happened. It was over. He'd done it. Choate was gone. Justin was on his way to jail. Within hours, D-Free would be off the market.

"Gentlemen," Franklin said, turning to Waverly and Riley, "We have the power to offer this young man something I believe he's earned today. What do you say? Shall we?"

"I vote aye," Waverly said.

"The same," Riley said.

"Then it's unanimous. I'm sure the partnership will concur with our recommendations. You are hereby invited to become an equal partner in DeWitt and Blackthorne, Mr. Creed. I think you've shown you're more than up to the challenge."

Luke could hardly believe what he was hearing. He'd done nothing else for six years but dream of this moment. The power. The prestige. The wealth. The respect of the man he hated and the woman he loved. He'd worked so hard, he'd sacrificed so much. He couldn't believe he was going to do what he'd just realized he was going to do.

Somehow, now that he had the brass ring in his hand, Luke realized it wasn't at all what he wanted. There was something golden within his reach.

"No thank you, sir."

"What?"

Luke saw the shock on Franklin's face. The consternation on the faces of the other two partners.

"For six years, all I could think about was becoming a partner here," Luke admitted. "But I think I'd rather lead a different sort of life, one that gives me time for the really important things."

"What could be more important than the kind of work we do here at D&B, where fortunes are made and broken and lives are at stake?" Franklin asked.

"The woman I love. And my two daughters, Brynne and Midge."

Franklin shook his head. "I don't know what your stepfather is going to say about this."

Luke met Franklin's gaze and said, "I don't really give a damn."

Franklin laughed. "I see why he's so fond of you."

Luke was startled by the revelation.

"The door is always open," Franklin said. "It's been a pleasure, Luke," he added, extending his hand.

The handshake made it all final. Luke was finished. The dream was over. Then he realized Amy was waiting for him at home, along with Drew and Eddie and Mary Margaret.

And suddenly, he couldn't wait a moment longer to see them, to laugh and shout, and share this victory with them.

"Thank you. Good-bye, sir," Luke said, pumping Franklin's hand and grinning like an idiot. Because he knew, as he hastened out the door, that he wouldn't be back.

22

Luke stopped only long enough on his way out of the building to thank Flo for keeping Harold McCorkle hidden. "You were a lifesaver," he said, kissing her cheek.

Flushed and flustered, Flo handed him a note and said, "You got a call from your ex-wife. She sounded excited. She wants you to call her back. Now."

He'd learned to respect Flo's intuition about what was important, and it was unusual for Valerie to call him at the office, but he was too excited and anxious to get home to stop for anything.

"I'll call her on my cell," he told Flo, and limped as fast as his knee would allow toward the elevator and freedom.

Downtown traffic was crawling, and Luke caught every light. At one of them, he grabbed his cell phone, punched in Valerie's number and said, "What is it?"

When he hung up, he stared straight ahead, seeing nothing, stunned.

A horn blaring behind him woke him up, and he moved through the light, drove a block, made another turn and reached the Commerce Towers. He struggled out of the pickup at valet parking, gave some quick instructions to the valet and ignored the pain in his knee as he stumbled into the Towers.

He hit the elevator button four times, urging it to hurry, then burst from the opening doors onto his floor and hobbled quickly down the hall to his apartment.

The door wasn't locked, and he threw it open hard enough that it banged against the wall. He stood there, disheveled and panting.

Amy took one look at his face and said, "You won!"

"We won!" He caught her one-armed as she hurled herself against him, grinning as he absorbed the sound of her joyful laughter.

He felt Drew thumping him on the back and watched as Eddie swung pregnant Mary Margaret in an exuberant circle. Then they were all gathered round, asking questions and demanding to know what had happened.

"Choate got fired. Justin went to jail. And D-Free is off the market," he said.

There was more cheering and high fives.

"I've got to call Mrs. Anastasio," Amy said, grabbing for the phone.

"I don't know how to thank all of you," Luke said, looking around his circle of friends. "I just want to remember this moment."

"I've got a bottle of champagne in the fridge," Eddie said.

When Luke raised a brow, Eddie confessed, "It was Mary Margaret's idea."

Luke grinned at her and said, "Good thinking, Mary Margaret."

While Amy gave Mrs. Anastasio the news that D-Free was no longer on the market, Eddie poured the Moët & Chandon into Mickey Mouse juice glasses Luke had on hand for Brynne and Midge.

When at last they all had a glass of champagne in hand, Luke held his up and said, "To good friends."

They smiled at each other, clinked glasses and drank.

"It would be fun to be invisible and follow you around tomorrow to see the look on everyone's face when you walk the halls of D & B," Drew said.

"I'm not going back," Luke said.

The laughter stopped abruptly. The faces around Luke sobered.

"You mean tomorrow?" Eddie said.

"I mean ever."

"Shit," Drew said, slamming his glass down on the dining-room table. "I knew those bastards would fire you!"

"Those idiots don't know a good thing when they see it," Eddie said.

"I'm so sorry, Luke" Amy said. "You can't let—"

"They offered me a partnership."

His revelation was met by shocked silence. Then everybody started talking at once.

"Oh, Luke, that's wonderful!" Amy said. "You must be ecstatic."

He grinned and said, "I turned it down."

He laughed at the look of astonished disbelief on the faces around him and said, "I don't want it. Honestly. I have other plans."

"Like what?" Drew said.

"I wish I could stay and explain how I plan to spend the rest of my life." Luke grabbed Amy's hand and said, "But Amy and I have someplace to go. You guys can lock up when you leave."

"Where do you—"

"Don't ask questions, Amy. Just come with me," Luke urged.

She looked at him, trust in her eyes, and said, "All right."

"So long, you guys," Luke said. "Thanks again for everything."

A moment later he was in the hall with Amy.

"What's going on, Luke?" she asked.

He threaded his fingers with hers and said enigmatically, "You'll see."

The valet had his truck waiting, with his Harley XLS Roadster now strapped securely into the bed.

Amy eyed his gimpy knee and his arm in the sling, then eyed the motorcycle dubiously.

"Trust me," he said with a grin. "Get in."

He was surprised how long she lasted before she asked, "Where are we going?"

"First, we're going to pick up our kids." He'd taken his arm out of the sling to drive, and he held his hand out to her, needing the warmth of her touch. When she reached toward him, he twined their fingers together. He took a breath and said, "Then, I think we should get married."

He felt a momentary qualm when she didn't answer. He took his eyes off the traffic to glance at her and saw that tears had brimmed in her eyes.

"I'm willing to wait—for a little while," he said. "So you can be sure this is the right thing to do. But—"

"I will."

"What?"

"I will marry you," she said, smiling at him through her tears. "Right now. As soon as you want."

"Hot damn!" he said and grinned. "You haven't even heard what I'm going to do, now that I'm not going to be a big-city lawyer anymore."

"What are you going to do?" she asked with a laugh that told him she really didn't care, that anything he did was all right with her.

He felt his heart thudding. He knew it was the right thing, even if the idea was still a little scary. "I'm going to see if my mother and stepfather will give me a job working for the Bitter Creek Cattle Company."

"Oh, Luke, really?"

"Would you mind practicing law in a small town like Bitter Creek?" he asked. "I'm not sure whether I'll end up representing my family's corporation or herding cattle. But I miss the ranch. I want to live there again."

"I miss Bitter Creek, too. I miss seeing my mom. I know Honor will love it, because she'll be able to have a horse again."

"My girls will—" He stopped in midsentence and gripped her hand harder and said, "I haven't told you the best part!"

"Better than what you've already told me?"

"The best thing that's happened since I can remember," he said. "Valerie called. She and Martin aren't moving to Vermont."

"Oh, Luke, that's fantastic! What happened? Why aren't they leaving?"

"Martin got a better job offer working for a big company in Houston—more money and better hours than he'd have working for his dad. So he and Valerie decided to stay here."

"Now you'll be able to see the girls on weekends," Amy said.

Luke shook his head. "That's the only time I *won't* be seeing them."

"What? I don't understand."

"Valerie said that back when they were planning the move to Vermont, she and Martin talked about how hard it was going to be on me not to see the girls. Since she's expecting another baby, they considered the idea of letting me keep the kids during the year, and she and Martin taking them on holidays and over the summer."

"Oh, Luke," Amy said. "Oh, my God. Are you saying she's . . . She's giving you back your kids."

"Yeah," he said. "She is."

"When?"

He swallowed back the ache in his throat and said, "Valerie and I decided they should stay in the same school until Christmas. They'll be spending Christmas with Valerie, then come to live with me in Bitter Creek."

"Honor is going to love having Brynne as a stepsister."

"We'll see how long that lasts once they're sharing a bedroom," Luke said. "You realize, of course, that we're going to have to come up with a playmate for Midge."

"I can't wait for us to make a baby. He'll be beautiful."

"You already know it's a boy?"

Amy shrugged and laughed. "I'm putting in my order, anyway. We'll have to wait and see what we get."

He shot her a yearning, hungry look, "How soon can we start?"

"Stop the truck."

Luke laughed and yanked the wheel and hit the brakes. As soon as the truck was parked on the berm, he had Amy in his arms. He kissed her thoroughly, and she kissed him back.

"Oh, Luke," she said, when they both came up for air, "I want us to be happy."

"We will be," he promised.

"How can you be so sure?"

How could he know the future? Nothing in life was certain. But they loved each other and had three great kids and, he realized with a start, now that he'd made his peace with Blackjack, a million dollars in the bank!

"You haven't answered me," she said. "How can you be so sure we'll be happy?"

He grinned, "Ask me that again in fifty or sixty years. I'm sure I'll have all the answers by then."

She laughed, and he joined her, filled with the joy of loving her and the promise of the future.

He waited until she was buckled back in, then started the engine and checked the rearview mirror. Behind him stood the tall skyscrapers of Houston, glistening in the noonday sun. He merged onto the endless highway.

Ahead of him lay home.

ACKNOWLEDGMENTS

The idea for this book originated with an article in *The Miami Herald* titled, "FDA Speeds New Drugs, Invites Risks." The article caught my attention because I'd been taking an FDA-approved drug that was suddenly suspected of causing serious, life-threatening side effects. I wondered, What if . . .

As soon as I began to do research, it seemed everyone I met was involved in the pharmaceutical industry. On a plane on the way to a national writer's conference in New Orleans, I met Candice Scheiner, RN, a clinical research monitor. On a Windjammer cruise in the Grenadines I met Paul Beighley, MD, whose offices provided a site for clinical testing. When I joined the Sierra Club Singles in Boulder, Colorado, I met Lee Bryant, who works in the pharmaceutical industry. And when I bought a second home, it turned out my nearest neighbor, Caroline Knight, was a study coordinator for clinical trials.

To all of them, I want to say thanks for sharing their knowledge of the clinical research process. Any mistakes in the use of material they provided to me are mine.

I also want to thank Jeanie Merka and Caroline Knight, who read the manuscript for me, and Robert Dean Pope, a partner in Hunton & Williams in Richmond, Virginia, a colleague in days gone by, for taking time from his busy schedule to answer questions for me.

As always, I want to thank my writing friends for their encouragement during the journey of writing this book. And a special thank-you to my editor, Maggie Crawford, for her unwavering support.

Dear Readers,

I found Drew DeWitt too intriguing to leave behind. The Bitter Creek saga continues in Jackson Hole, Wyoming, where Drew will meet his match—and another Blackthorne enemy—in *The Rivals*. For those of you who've waited so patiently for Clay Blackthorne's story, he'll also be there to confront the daring, daunting Grayhawks of Wyoming. I hope you enjoy the excerpt from *The Rivals* which follows.

The Bitter Creek saga also includes *The Cowboy*, *The Texan* and *The Loner*. You should be able to order them on the Internet or find them in your local bookstore.

If you'd like to read more about the Blackthorne family, look for my Captive Hearts series set in Regency England, including *Captive*, *After the Kiss*, *The Bodyguard*, and *The Bridegroom*. For those of you intrigued by the Creeds and the Coburns, check out the Sisters of the Lone Star trilogy, *Frontier Woman*, *Comanche Woman*, and *Texas Woman*.

I love hearing from you! You can contact me directly through my web site, www.joanjohnston.com. I answer e-mail as I receive it. You can write to me at P.O. Box 7834, St. Petersburg, FL 33734-7834. If you'd like a reply, please enclose a self-addressed stamped envelope.

Take care and happy reading,
Joan Johnston

Pocket Books
Proudly Presents

The Rivals

Joan Johnston

Available in paperback
from
Pocket Books

**Turn the page for a preview of
The Rivals. . . .**

Sarah was making oatmeal raisin cookies when she got the call from her sister-in-law that Sarah's brother Mike was drunk again and had run the tow truck off the road on his way back from a job. Theresa couldn't leave the kids alone and wanted Sarah to please rescue Tom and then go tow some idiot out of the Hoback River.

"No problem, Theresa," Sarah said. "I'm leaving now."

She drove her Teton County Sheriff's vehicle, a white Chevy Tahoe, to pick up her brother and returned him to his home above the Teton Valley Garage. She picked up a pair of waders, since she was going to find herself in cold water before the night was out.

As she headed south out of Jackson in the tow truck, she could see how the cowboy's pickup might have ended up in the river. The roads were icy and fog hindered visibility. She slowed when she neared the mile marker she'd been given and looked for signs of a vehicle off the road. A pair of headlights came on in the middle of the river, and she pulled to the side of the road, angling the tow truck so its headlights lit the vehicle far below.

As Sarah stepped out, the driver rolled down his window. She shouted to him over the rush of water, "Are you all right?"

"I'm fine," he said. "I'm waiting for a tow."

"I'm your tow," she called back, as she began unwinding the cable she would need to pull the pickup out of the river. She stumbled down the steep embankment, sliding in the shale, a flashlight in one hand and the frame hooks attached to the winch cable in the other.

As she headed into the river, the driver's side door opened and the passenger started to get out.

"Stay in your truck until I get you to the edge of the river," she said.

"You're going to need help," he said.

"Stay in your truck," she said more firmly, flashing the light in his eyes. "You'll only be in my way."

She picked her way carefully across the shallow river to the front of the pickup and bent to locate the openings in the frame and attach the mini-j-hooks. She swore when her leather gloves got sloshed by icy water, but finished the job as quickly as she could, before pulling her leather gloves off and substituting a pair of woolen ones she'd brought along. Then she tramped back through the water to the driver's door.

When she flashed the light at the driver a second time, she realized his head was bleeding. "You're hurt! Why didn't you call the paramedics? An accident with injuries needs to be reported to the police."

He dabbed at his head with a bloody kerchief and said, "It's just a bump. I'm fine."

She eyed him dubiously, then said, "I think I can get your truck out of here in one piece. Be sure the brake is off and the transmission is in neutral. You can help by steering till I get you closer to the riverbank. Then you're going to have to get out. There's always a chance this rig will tip and roll when it comes out of the water and heads up that incline."

Sarah climbed up the hill and began winching the pickup toward the edge of the river. The tires bumped over the stones in the river bottom, then came up against some sort of obstacle that held the truck fast. She eased the slack on the cable and headed back down the slope. When she checked the right rear tire she found it hooked on a submerged log. She kicked at the log a couple of times with her booted foot, but it wouldn't budge.

She came around to the driver's window and said, "It's stuck on a log. Try starting it up. Maybe you can back it off."

"The engine won't turn over," the man said. "I've already tried it." He took a look down at the water. "Damn. Guess I'm going to get my feet wet after all."

"I can attach the winch to—"

Before Sarah could explain the man had stepped down into the frigid river.

He almost fell face first into the water. Sarah caught him with an arm around his waist and felt him sag against her. "You *are* hurt," she said.

"I'm fine," he said, straightening. "I was a little dizzy there for a moment. Water's freezing."

Sarah lifted his arm around her shoulder, slid her arm more snugly around his waist and said, "Next time the roads are icy and it's foggy, maybe you'll take your time around the curves."

"It wasn't my fault."

Sarah sighed. "It never is."

She couldn't help noticing how tall he was. She was 5'10" in her bare feet, and he was several inches taller, lean and lithe and muscular, like most cowboys she knew, who spent their days doing physical labor from the back of a horse.

"I'm fine. Really," he said straightening and freeing himself from her supporting grasp. "Let's take a look at that log."

"I can winch it—"

He was already slogging through the frigid water toward the rear of the pickup. "Mmm. I see," he said as Sarah focused her flashlight on a branch of the log that stuck out above the water line.

He gave the submerged log a couple of hard kicks with the heel of his boot, and it broke in half. He reached down and yanked the log from under the wheel. "That should do it," he said.

Sarah caught him as he swayed and almost fell. He tried shrugging her away, but she slid her arm firmly around his waist and said, "All right, big man. You've proved you have the muscle. Now let's see if you have brains enough to let me help you."

The flashlight was in the hand she had supporting him, with the light aimed up at his face, and she saw a grin flash as he sagged against her.

"Yes, ma'am," he said. "Whatever you say, ma'am."

Sarah helped him up the hill and into the cab of the tow truck, where the heater was running full blast. In the light that had come on when she'd opened the door, she saw his face was pale, and his teeth were clenched to keep them from chattering.

"Those boots need to come off," she said, suiting word to deed. It wasn't easy getting wet cowboy boots off his feet, but she knew he'd warm up faster with them off. She peeled his socks off, revealing feet that were long and narrow and ice cold. She rubbed each of them briskly and realized his wet Wranglers were dripping ice water onto her hands.

She tugged at his soggy jeans and said, "Those better come off, too."

He lifted a brow suggestively, then reached under his anorak for his belt buckle and undid it, before unsnapping and unzipping his jeans. He lifted his hips and she pulled on the hems of both legs until they came off. He was wearing some kind of snug black underwear that hit him mid-thigh.

She handed him a gray wool blanket and said, "Wrap yourself in this. I'll be back in no time."

Within fifteen minutes she was back in the cab expecting to find the cowboy warmed up. She was troubled to see that his eyes were closed. "Hey, are you all right?"

His eyes blinked open and he scooted upright.

"Sorry to fall asleep like that. I had a late night last night."

"You shouldn't be driving when you're tired. That's what causes accidents."

"It wasn't my—"

"I know," she interrupted. "It wasn't your fault. At least you were wearing your seat belt. You might have been killed, taking a flying leap off the road like that." She reached over to peer into his eyes, her flashlight angled slightly away to keep from blinding him. She could see they were blue. An astonishing blue. The sort of blue that made you want to keep on looking.

He looked right back at her. And grinned. "Last time a woman looked that intently into my eyes, she—"

Sarah flushed and backed away, shutting off the flashlight, buckling herself in and putting the tow truck in gear. "Spare me the details. Where do you want me to drop you and your pickup off?"

"You can leave the pickup at the Jackson Hole Garage. I could use a ride to my ranch, if you don't mind."

Sarah didn't usually provide cab service, but it was late and he was wet, half-naked and hurt. She didn't want to have to report the accident, because she was going to get in trouble with her boss for taking the tow if she did. And she wouldn't have felt right about making him take a cab from the garage. He might not make it home.

"Where's your ranch?" she said, eyeing him curiously. She knew most of the ranchers around town, and she didn't know this man. The way he'd been dressed, in a plaid wool shirt, worn jeans, and boots, she'd figured him more for a cowhand than an owner. "Is there someone who can take care of you overnight? You shouldn't be alone. You might have a concussion."

He cocked another brow at her. "There's nobody there right now except me."

"Where is there?" Sarah asked.

"Forgotten Valley."

Sarah turned to stare at him. "Forgotten Valley is owned by a couple of guys from Texas."

"Drew DeWitt, at your service, ma'am."

Sarah frowned. "I didn't think the owners lived there."

"I moved back in December."

"Moved back?" Sarah said skeptically. "I didn't realize you'd ever—"

"Moved in," Drew corrected. "Quit my job in Houston and moved here to . . ." He paused and said, "But that's another story."

"I've got time. It's a long ride back to Jackson."

Drew shrugged. "I needed a change of scenery."

"And you could afford to quit your job?"

He shrugged again. "It was just a job."

"Your work wasn't important? What did you do?"

"I was a litigator with DeWitt & Blackthorne."

"A lawyer? I can see why you wanted to get away," Sarah said. "What is it you plan to do now that you're here in Jackson?"

"I haven't decided."

"I suppose if I'd quit my profession and moved a couple thousand miles away, I'd need more than six weeks to figure out what to do with the rest of my life, too. Just don't do your thinking on the highway," she said. "That way you're more likely to stay among the living long enough to come up with another life plan."

"I was forced off the road," he said.

Sarah frowned. "Where's the other vehicle? Did the driver run? Do I need to be looking for another reckless driver out there somewhere?"

"It was a friend a mine—and no, I'm not going to tell you who it was," Drew said. "It was an accident. No one was hurt—"

"That bump on your head really should be looked at by a doctor," Sarah interrupted.

"I'm not going to a doctor," Drew said firmly.

"Have you got someone to stay with you overnight—just in case?" Sarah asked. "A girlfriend? A wife? A friend? You shouldn't be alone."

"I'm not married. And I don't have a girlfriend . . . anymore," he said bitterly.

"Ah," Sarah said, eyeing him speculatively. "So you came here to nurse a broken heart."

He didn't say anything, which Sarah took as a confirmation of her guess. She figured he must really have loved the woman to have quit his job and moved away when the relationship ended. "She dumped you?" Sarah asked.

"I don't want to talk about it."

"She dumped you," Sarah concluded. "What did you do to her?"

"I didn't do anything. She—Look," he said, "this is none of your business."

"It became my business when you let yourself get distracted and drove off the road."

"I told you—"

"I know. It wasn't your fault. A mystery woman drove you off the road. That woman wouldn't have been the one you broke up with in Houston, would it? You let yourself get distracted by thoughts of her and—"

"I wasn't thinking of her. She never crosses my mind. I'm over her," Drew insisted. "Your job is to drive, not to interrogate me."

"Well, actually . . ." Sarah hesitated, then said, "I'm a Deputy Sheriff. I'm only driving this truck because . . . I'm helping someone out."

From the corner of her eye, she saw Drew slowly run his eyes down her body. She shivered, as though he'd touched her with his hands.

"Well, well, well," he said. "So you're the law in Teton County."

"Just one of many deputy sheriffs," she said.

He turned to face her and said, "Are you going to write me a ticket?"

"For what? Being in the wrong place at the wrong time?"

His gaze stayed on her as he said, "Or maybe being in the right place at the right time. I met you, didn't I?"

Sarah frowned. No one had flirted with her in so long, she wasn't quite sure Drew DeWitt was actually showing that sort of interest in her. But if he was, she had to nip it in the bud. The DeWitts and Blackthornes were rich folks. All he could possibly want from her was a quick roll in the hay.

Sarah sucked in a silent breath at the thought that crossed her mind. *Why not? He's not going to be in town long. The rich folks never do stay. It's been so long since a man touched me. A man this handsome has likely bedded a great many women and knows his way around the sheets. So why the hell not?*

It wasn't possible for her to have a casual affair with someone local, because the gossip would be devastating. And until she knew for certain that Tom, her husband who'd abandoned her, was dead, she wasn't willing to get emotionally involved with anyone. And she missed being kissed and touched . . . and held in a man's strong arms.

She returned Drew's gaze as long as she dared, then turned her eyes back onto the road.

The tension in the truck was palpable, like static electricity that was going to spark the instant Sarah dared to touch him. Drew didn't say anything, just kept looking at her, caressing her with his eyes.

Sarah was remembering his long, muscular legs and long, narrow feet, and the bulge in his fitted briefs when she'd stripped off his jeans.

She felt a growing tautness in her breasts and belly, as though he were already touching her. She took a hitching breath and let it out, and loosened her iron grip on the steering wheel.

She wanted to take him up on his unspoken offer. She wanted to go to bed with him and have incredible, mindless sex. She needed a man. And he seemed willing.

Sarah pulled up at the Jackson Hole Garage and lowered the pickup and unhitched it. Drew could call the garageman tomorrow with instructions. When she stepped back into the truck, she noticed Drew had pulled on his still-wet jeans and his boots.

"You look uncomfortable," she said.

"My place isn't far from here. They'll be off soon enough."

There was enough sexual innuendo in his voice to cut with a knife, but Sarah neither acknowledged nor deflected it. "I think I know the way, but why don't you go ahead and give me directions."

Sarah followed Drew's instructions, heading down Spring Gulch Road, which quickly turned to dirt as she left the main highway. The ranch was located in a valley thirty miles wide and eighty miles long that lay between the east and west Gros Ventre Buttes. Forgotten Valley

Ranch was bordered beyond the butte on the west by tributaries of the Snake River, which was marked by the growth of aspens and cottonwoods.

It was an idyllic spot, with a one-story, split pine ranch house that had been added onto for the better part of century, surrounded by cottonwoods that had been planted by pioneers. It was a working ranch that even in this modern day ran black baldies and herefords and the occasional longhorn steer, where cowhands grew hay in the summer that was baled in rolls to feed stock from a sleigh in the winter.

Sarah pulled up in front of the main house, which was dark. The foreman's house, which was set across an open yard, was also dark. She looked at her watch. It was only nine o'clock, and the foreman was apparently already in bed. That wasn't unusual, since his day probably started around 4:30 A.M.

"I appreciate you coming to the rescue," Drew said.

Which reminded Sarah she hadn't charged him yet for the tow. "I'll be sending you a bill."

"I'd better get inside and get warmed up," Drew said.

He opened the door and Sarah squinted her eyes against the excruciatingly bright dome light. He hesitated, then pulled the door closed again, and leaned over and touched his mouth to hers in the darkness.

Sarah was too shocked to resist.

His lips were soft. His touch gentle.

Sarah's throat ached with longing. Her lips pushed back against his and opened to his probing tongue. She gasped at the warm wetness. And drew back with a shudder, staring into his glittering eyes.

"Come inside with me," he said.

FINALLY
A WEBSITE
YOU CAN GET
PASSIONATE
ABOUT...

Visit
www.SimonSaysLove.com
for the latest information
about Romance from Pocket Books!

READING SUGGESTIONS

LATEST RELEASES

AUTHOR APPEARANCES

ONLINE CHATS WITH YOUR
FAVORITE WRITERS

SPECIAL OFFERS

ORDER BOOKS ONLINE

AND MUCH, MUCH MORE!

Love is in the air

with these bestselling romances
from Pocket Books.